Death Cut

A BETH GETTY MYSTERY
BOOK 3

KAREN NEARY SMITHSON

DEATH CUT (A Beth Getty Mystery, Book 3)
By Karen Neary Smithson

Published by TouchPoint Press
www.touchpointpress.com

Paperback ISBN: 978-1-956851-63-2

Editor: Stephanie Marrie
Cover Design: Sheri Williams
Cover Photo Credit: Karen Neary
Author Photo Credit: Pierre Parker

Connect with the author
https://www.karennearysmithsonbooks.com/

First Edition

Printed in the United States of America.

PRAISE FOR
THE BETH GETTY MYSTERY SERIES

"*Death Cut* proves, yet again, Karen Neary Smithson's absolute mastery of the murder mystery genre. Vivid characters, cinematic prose, and thrills around every turn! The suspense had me riveted. I couldn't put it down! This book is an extremely satisfying conclusion to an epic series. I loved it!"
—Candice Jarrett, Award Winning Author of *Mortal Tether*

"*Death Unmasked* is definitely un-put-downable! Unquestionably, an unpredictable story, my favorite kind."
—Amy's Book Review

"From its evocative opening to its breathtaking finish, Karen Neary Smithson blends a bit of Irish culture with a dead-on description of Venice, Italy in *Death Unmasked*, while telling an engrossing thriller about a woman seeking justice for a murdered friend. Sibèal "Beth" Getty's 'sixth sense' gives her a unique quality in the world of female sleuths."
—Debbi Mack, *New York Times* bestselling author of the Sam McRae Mysteries and *Damaged Goods*

"Smithson weaves murder, intrigue, and Venetian history into her latest novel, *Death Unmasked*. Everyone's hiding secrets. Love affairs turn into obsessions. Hidden identities reveal past mistakes. The novel is ripe with description and double-dealing, and a mystery full of so many twists and turns it will have readers guessing until the very end."
—R. Lanier Clemons, author of the Jonelle Sweet Mystery Series

"*Death in Disguise* is a brilliantly written mystery that pulls the reader head-first into the pages with an eclectic array of well-drawn characters. The story unfolds at a rapid pace and builds intrigue and suspense. The ending will blow you away!"
—Kim Hamilton, author of *Accidental Lawyer* and the Accidental Lawyer Short Read Series

"*Death in Disguise* had me hooked from the first page. With a varied cast of characters, and one twist after another, fasten your seat belts for a thrilling ride!"
—Shawn Reilly Simmons, author of the Red Carpet Catering Mysteries

"*Death in Disguise* is everything I could ever want in a mind-boggling mystery. I was pulled in from the beginning and amazed by the ending, which I never saw coming. Murder, romance, deception, infidelity [and] celebrity characters fill the pages of a very exciting book. I really loved *Death in Disguise*. Please, do not pass this one up but put it at the top of your reading list."

—Trudy LoPreto for *Readers' Favorite*

"*Death in Disguise* is a gripping mystery that had me addicted from the first page."

—Laura M. Snider, author of *Witches' Quarters*

"*Death in Disguise* is full of action and suspense, with a great twisty ending that will take you for a loop."

—Jennifer Haskin, author of the Freedom Flight Trilogy

"Sweet and well-meaning Betty Getty is an unlikely hero in *Death in Disguise*, a Hollywood 'whodunnit' that has all the ingredients for a great mystery: fame, money, murder, intrigue, and a touch of the Irish."

—m. m. burke, author of *Gymrat*

"Smithson has a unique writing style that turns up the volume with over-the-top characters, detailed descriptions, and lots of emotional ups and downs. *Death in Disguise* will hook readers and brings them along on a wild ride into the private back rooms of Hollywood glitterati, the backstretch of the horse racing biz, and the secret rooms of some very dark characters."

—L.R. Trovillion, author of the Maryland Equestrian Series

"An exciting and thrilling murder mystery, *Death in Disguise* is sure to send chills of fear down the spine of the stoutest reader, and often uses the reader's momentum to steer them to a place where anyone can kill."

—*InD'tale Magazine*

"*Death is Disguise* is definitely well worth the read even if you're not a mystery reader. My favorite part was the protagonist's intuitive nature. If you enjoy mysteries, you'll love this book."

—Kathryn Ramsperger, author of *The Shores of Our Souls*

For my dear friend Shirley Pratt

Other books in the Beth Getty Mystery series

Cast of Characters

Sibèal "Beth" Getty: An Irish born fashion model who believes her sixth sense, *fey*, guides her in solving crimes

Shane Dalton: Art Theft Detail investigator and Beth's husband

Skye Andrews: Film actress and Beth's friend, married to Zach Greyson

Zach Greyson: Oscar-winning actor, art collector, herpetologist, and a lover of fine things

Emma Andrews: Skye's seven-year-old daughter, junior equestrian, and cat fancier

Alma Perez: Zach's personal chef

Gavin Collins: Shane's former partner with the Los Angeles Sheriff Department

Thompson "Thom" Boyle: Director of the movie *Dark Grace*

Cody Evans: Personal assistant and romantic partner of Thom Boyle

Antonia "Toni" Wright: Actor turned academic looking for a comeback. Former lover of Zach Greyson

Jane Reid: Ambitious mother of Isabella Reid

Isabella Reid: Ingénue with a teenage crush on director Thom Boyle

Louise "Willie" Wilson: Thom's former lover, has-been A-lister, bit-player, and props assistant

Jeremy Fox: Baltimore City homicide investigator

Tamera Stevens: Divorced mother of three and Jeremy's partner in the homicide unit

Darnell Stevens: Tamera's ex-husband and narcotics investigator

1922 Characters

William Desmond Taylor: Hollywood director murdered in 1922

Mable Norman: Silent screen actress active from 1910 to 1927 addicted to cocaine

Mary Minter Miles: Child star dominated by her mother and supposedly in love with W. D. Taylor and murder suspect

Charlotte Shelby: Broadway actress and mother of Mary Minter Miles. Long time suspect in the murder of W. D. Taylor

Margaret "Gibby" Gibson: Stage and silent screen actress, she confessed to the murder of W. D. Taylor before her death in 1967

Author Note

The Art Theft Detail is no longer an investigative specialty in the Los Angeles Police Department. Since its inception in 1993, the two-detective unit recovered nearly 123 million dollars in cultural property.

In *Death Cut*, I've used artistic license to resurrect the defunct art crime unit so that Shane could continue doing what he loves best—being a detective—but without facing the tragedy and emotional stress involved with the investigation of homicides.

Please follow Karen Neary Smithson on Twitter, Facebook, and Instagram.

Chapter One

"Cut! Print!" Thom Boyle stepped away from the digital viewfinder. "We'll wrap this baby up in the studio. See you all in LA." The movie director flashed two thumbs up at the actors beyond him and then in the direction of the crew. When he caught Toni's eye, he blew her a kiss.

He'd put together a crackerjack team, and with their know-how and a bit of movie-magic luck, they'd have a winner on their hands. He saw himself walking the red carpet but squashed the presumptuous thought, not wanting to jinx the project. With a long sweep of his eyes, he took in the activity surrounding him. The carpenters had already jumped into action, dismantling the street façade to be reused in another movie or TV show. Just another way to cut costs and benefit the environment. Wires, extension cords, mics, lights, cameras, all the necessary equipment needed to make a film would be packed and transported to the studio in Century City. In a few hours, no trace would be left behind that they'd even been there.

But, he thought, shaking his head, the location shoots had been fraught with problems, from a major cast change to running over the allotted time frame. Instead of bitching, the crew rolled with the punches. If only the actors had taken a page from their book, it would've made life a helluva lot easier.

Thom checked his watch. He had plenty of time before a late afternoon meeting with the director of photography, his pal, and longtime associate, Frank Daniels. But right now, he had to take care of the problem, making him crazy. Skye Andrews' attitude. He'd had it with her complaints and demands. *I'll make it crystal clear that if she doesn't straighten up and fly right, she'll kiss her star billing goodbye.*

Thom grabbed his cap emblazoned with the movie's title, *Dark Grace,* from where he'd dropped it on his canvas back chair. He pulled it on and hurried toward his leading lady. "Look, Skye—"

"I'm still angry at you." She turned and stepped away.

He grabbed her arm.

"Let go," Skye said, raising her voice.

Thom felt the eyes of those on the set bore into him. He released her.

"Meet me in my trailer," he said, tempering his voice. "We need to talk. Smooth over a few issues we've been having." Thom swallowed hard as her eyes flashed with anger. He'd have to take a different approach. *Appeal to her ego.* "After our little chat, we can watch the dailies. I'd like your input." He knew the offer of viewing the initial prints of the day's scenes would pique her interest. Unlike most actors, who refused to watch dailies, fearing it would hamper their acting process, Skye Andrews couldn't get enough of seeing herself on screen.

Her lips pressed into a tight line.

"I swear, Skye, you were phenomenal." As he suspected, her eyes softened, as well as the tightness along her jaw. "Come on." He flashed a wide smile hoping they'd be able to end the divisiveness brewing between them during the location shoots in Baltimore. He valued their longtime friendship. He also didn't want to burn any bridges that might keep her Oscar-winning husband, Zach Greyson, from declining to work with him because of any hard feelings Skye might be harboring.

"Alright." Skye took a few steps in the direction of her trailer. "I'll meet you in about fifteen minutes," she said without a backward glance.

He'd accepted the fact she'd been stressed out during the filming and made allowances for her unbefitting behavior. During their other collaborations, she'd embodied the essence of professionalism. He pulled the cap off and raked his fingers through his thinning hair. *Must be PTSD. The after-effects of being stalked by a psychopathic killer determined to break Skye before ending her life.* He studied the white embroidered words stitched on the cap's front panel. *I should've released Skye from her contract. This wasn't the right time for her to make this kind of movie. She should be starring in a chick flick. A comedy. A soppy romance. Not a dark drama, dealing with the occult and the ritual murder of a nun. I should've closed my ears to her pleas. And Skye's reassuring words that the horrifying nightmare was behind her.*

Thom plunked the cap back on his head. He believed Skye's unbridled ambition hinged on the hope that this role would launch her to the stardom she craved. She'd be awarded her rightful place among the crème de la crème of Hollywood elites. *But enough is enough. She's a damn good actress. One day she'd find that place but perhaps not now. But, who knows.* He shrugged. Maybe *Dark Grace* will be the ticket that brings Skye Andrews the recognition she pines after.

He blew out a stream of air. *Actresses. They're all prima donnas.* As quickly as the denouncement entered his mind, it fled as he visualized Toni. Known to millions of moviegoers as Antonia Wright. Working with her seemed like day and night from other actors he'd directed during his long career. Prompt. Prepared. Professional. Not to mention a gem of a talent. He believed she would've been a survivor in this cutthroat business if she hadn't opted out years ago. At the height of her career, Toni turned to academia. Earned a Ph.D. in electrical engineering.

I guess she wanted the world to know she's more than a pretty face with a killer body who could convincingly spurt out other people's words.

Even so, she kept her hand in acting by accepting guest roles on TV shows and bit parts in blockbusters. Basically, she'd eased into a quiet life as an adjunct professor at UCLA. Things changed a few years ago when Toni decided conquering Broadway would be a challenge. One she accomplished the night she won a Tony.

Toni won a Tony. He smiled. *She wants to reclaim bragging rights for the five-pointed terrazzo and brass star that bears her name on Hollywood's Walk of Fame.* He sucked in a mouthful of air. *A comeback.*

3

She wants a comeback in a gigantic way. But maybe too much time has slipped by. He'd warned her the competition would be fierce, competing against actresses who've had seamless careers like Meryl Streep and Helen Mirren—and even Maggie Smith. *But knowing Toni's determination, I bet she does it. I bet she finds stardom once again on the silver screen.*

He pushed his shoulders back and quickened his stride. *Her role as an alcoholic police detective facing her demons will open the eyes of those myopic producers to the reality that the passage of time can't snuff out a talent like Toni's. Skye Andrews and that plethora of infantile actresses with their over-the-top demands can't hold a candle to her. She's cultured, enchanting, captivating, and . . . utterly fascinating.* He reached for his cellphone but let his hand drop. He'd call Toni after he mollified Skye and put the kibosh on her interminable squabbling.

Thom stepped into his trailer and plopped down onto the couch, reached into the mini-fridge, and pulled out a beer. He flipped the tab and swallowed. A slow smile spread across his face with the realization that the location shoots had finally ended. A very satisfactory end.

A quick knock sounded on the door.

Well, this is a first. Skye must be really eager to see the dailies. She's never responded so quickly to one of my requests.

"Door's open." He took a long gulp of beer, knowing he'd need the fortification.

The door popped open.

"Hey, come in. Come in. Want a beer?" He moved toward the fridge.

"Thanks, but no. I'm excited to see the dailies."

"Always the perfectionist. We still share that trait, don't we?" He didn't wait for an answer and hitched his thumb over his shoulder at the large monitor and several chairs arranged in front of it for screening sessions. "Using digital files saves us a pile of money, but there's nothing like film. The videotape won't be processed and delivered until sometime tonight. Frank and I will be reviewing the film, you know, to check the shots and color."

"I've always admired your eye for detail. Everyone knows you're the best in the business."

A touch of heat mottled his cheeks. "I think you'll love today's shoot." Thom opened his arms and breathed out the tension that'd had an iron grip on him over the past six weeks. A bubbling, deep in his chest, rose, and a delighted laugh filled the trailer as he wrapped his arms around his visitor. The mirthful sound ended as a gunshot filled his ear.

The slug burst through his body, crushed ribs, and exploded his heart.

Chapter Two

Sibéal "Beth" Getty and her husband, Shane Dalton, returned from their tumultuous Italian honeymoon a week ago. While there, she'd lost her lifelong confidante and cherished friend, Deirdre. They'd met as children growing up in their Irish village of Ballynárach and developed an unbreakable bond that only death could rend. To further her heartbreak, Beth discovered that a companion she would've trusted with her own life turned out to be the epitome of evil. As a result, over the past seven days, she'd done a lot of soul-searching.

Sitting across from Shane at the restaurant's linen-covered table, the flickering shadows of candlelight played across his face. He'd been her refuge—her safe place—and his strength had bolstered and encouraged her through many dark days. But now, Beth realized it was time to step up. Do the work she was meant to accomplish. The instant she'd made up her mind, the firm grip of anguish over losing her dearest friend lessened, as did the tight muscles binding her neck and back. But before making any commitments, she hoped for Shane's seal of approval. His okay would make everything perfect.

She took a sip of wine and glanced at the stringed trio composed of two violinists and a cellist as their soothing melodic strains washed over her. She'd decided this would be the best time to spring the news. One of her resolutions, she believed he'd gladly support, but the other she wasn't sure about. *He could interpret it as a threat to our marriage. Well, not a threat, exactly*, she thought, searching for the right word. *Upset. It might upset our routine. But that's been shaken up already with Shane in the process of switching careers.*

She placed the glass on the table ready to share her news. But at that moment, the psychic finger of unmistakable familiarity touched her—not with its usual message of dread—but with something luminous. Shane wanted to tell her something . . . important . . . good . . . fabulous. Her intuition, her sixth sense, her *fey*—the word her granny coined for Beth's gift—alerted her. Beth knew, without a doubt, she possessed a second sight, but Shane, a former Los Angeles Sheriff Department homicide detective, called it superstitious nonsense.

"Well, my darlin' man, there's something you've been keeping from me," she said with the tiniest hint of a smile.

He looked up from his Wagyu ribeye steak and narrowed his eyes. "Have you been snooping around again?"

"Me? Snoop?"

He shook his head but couldn't hide the grin that tugged at the corners of his mouth. "I signed all the paperwork today. It's official. You're looking at the newest detective in the Art Theft Detail of the Los Angeles Police Department."

Overjoyed and confused at the same time, she reached for his hand and squeezed it. "But—but you swore you were finished with police work."

"Finished with being a homicide detective. I applied for the position a month before our honeymoon." Shane scooped up a forkful of garlic mashed potatoes.

"Why didn't you tell me?"

"Didn't your *fey* send you a message?"

"Very funny," she said with a roll of her eyes.

"I don't really know. I guess, after being a bachelor for so long, I sometimes forget to share stuff with you."

She half-nodded. After all, as newlyweds, they were still in the process of making adjustments as a married couple, even after just celebrating their first wedding anniversary. She touched the diamond and ruby locket nestled against the hollow of her neck. Shane's anniversary gift. "Since the police department made their decision so fast, they must be an intuitive lot. And able to cut through a bundle of bureaucratic red tape, no doubt."

He washed the potatoes down with a gulp of India pale ale. "What choice did they have? It's no surprise that I was one of the LASD's top cops. How could they refuse me with my stellar record, skill, and experience?" He said with a wink.

"I always said you're the most incredible detective—"

"I was being sarcastic."

"Sarcastic or not. I wouldn't be surprised if you *are* the best detective in all of Los Angeles."

Despite the soft light, Beth noticed the color rise, blushing his cheeks. He cocked his head, glanced at the ceiling, and then at their table strewn with rose petals. She'd embarrassed him.

"The selection process was thorough," he said. "Since I wasn't sure if I'd even qualify as a candidate, I kept it to myself. I had the initial interview while still working in the sheriff's department. I didn't even tell Collins."

Beth tilted her head, a bit surprised. Gavin Collins and Shane had been homicide partners for years. They were more than colleagues, but best buds, the closest of friends.

"I guess I didn't want to get my hopes up. But then I got a notice for a second interview. I thought it went well but didn't think too much about it since the next day we took off for Venice."

She widened her eyes but remained silent.

"While you were in the hospital—*Ospedale Civile*—for those couple of days, I had a long conversation with Marinello—"

"Marinello," she said with a sigh. "Now, there's a gran' paddy and a deadly detective."

"What?"

It was times like this she used Irish slang to slow him down. Beth wanted to savor every word of his story since it was the answer to one of her most ardent prayers. She believed Shane would never be truly happy being anything other than a detective. "You drummed the words into my head our entire honeymoon that Marinello's analytical, thorough, and an experienced detective. I'm just agreeing with you."

"You didn't think that when he told you to keep your nose out of his investigation."

"Ah, well. In the end, we all became brilliant friends."

"Hmm." Shane rubbed his thumb across the cleft in his chin. "As I was saying, I received an accelerated education from Marinello on how the Italian police keep their vast art treasures safe. You know I'm not exaggerating when I say the entire country is like a giant museum—paintings, sculptures, artifacts, architecture—from the beginning of civilization right up to the present-day."

She offered him a quick nod, hoping to high heaven Shane would refocus on his story.

She didn't want him to reiterate the entire career of his favorite architect, Andrea Palladio. She'd endured that on more occasions than she liked to remember.

"I ran some scenarios by him," Shane said. "Though not an expert in the field of art theft, Marinello knew a lot about techniques and practices. He prepped me for any situation the LAPD could present me with if they called me back for another interview."

"That was really decent of himself."

"I'll say. Then I got a text a few days before we left Venice for home. To set up a time for a final interview. Turned out with my art/architecture background coupled with my previous experience in homicide, they thought I'd be a good fit for the detail."

"Good fit? You'll be amazing."

"There'll definitely be a learning curve. It's only a two-man team, and I'll be doing most of the grunt work. The detail's aim is to target suspects who prey on artists, art dealers, and collectors. I'll help investigate all thefts and burglaries when fine art is the primary object of attack. We'll also investigate fakes, frauds, and forgeries."

"Well then, this certainly is a celebratory dinner. Congratulations, *grá mo chroí*. I don't have the words to say how proud I am of you." She raised her glass. "Art thieves beware, because my Shane will be arresting every last one of ye."

He raised his glass and met hers with a resounding clink.

"I have some news to share, too," Beth said.

"Oh?" He took a swig of the golden ale. "Please, do tell, Betty Getty."

She couldn't help but smile when he said his pet name for her but at the same time, a strange tingling prickled in her chest. *Nerves.* "As you know I've been looking for valuable work to fill my time." She noted his nod but also his narrowed eyes. "I've decided to open Hope's Refuge."

"Hope's Refuge? Wait. Wasn't that the homeless youth shelter ruse the infamous Father Clancy used to trick you into believing his lies?"

She pressed her lips together chasing away the memory of facing a cold-blooded killer within the decrepit walls of a bogus shelter facility. "It was. But I want to make the shelter a reality but with a name change. Hope's Refuge would always remind me of . . ."

Shane nodded, and she cleared her throat.

"It'll be a challenge, but I can't think of a better use of my time or money. I've been burning up the internet searching for information on how to form a charitable organization. I'll have to decide if it's going to be a public or private charity, complete the IRS requirements, establish a board of directors, make and contact a list of donors—"

"Whoa. Seems like you've been doing your research."

She bobbed her head up and down. "I also want to involve the Cute Cat Rescue. My hope is to add a cat café inside the shelter where the kids can learn some real-life skills by running the café and caring for the adoptable kitties."

"Interesting," he said under his breath.

"I'll need to hire a social worker and tutors to help the residents earn their G.E.D.s, offer referrals to drug treatment facilities, and provide employment opportunities. It'll make me feel like I'm making a difference." She couldn't read the expression on his face but noticed that his eyes looked moist. He blinked a couple of times.

"I've always said you have a loving heart. This proves it even more." She felt her cheeks warm.

Still not sure how to broach the other decision she'd made, Beth said, "When do you start your new job?"

"Right away. Tomorrow."

"Tomorrow? They sure aren't letting the grass grow under their feet, so. But that's brilliant, Shane, truly brilliant."

He resumed eating while Beth only stared at the halibut filet on her plate. Just as she'd summoned the courage to tell him the other piece of her resolution, her cellphone jingled. She reached into her handbag, released the phone, and checked the screen. *Skye.* This definitely wasn't the time to listen to another of Skye Andrews' tirades about her movie director. She let the call go to voicemail and dropped the phone back into her purse.

"Who was that?" Shane lifted a forkful of roasted vegetables.

"Skye."

He rolled his eyes.

She guessed he was only playing since he'd accepted Skye despite her foibles. He agreed with Beth that even with all of her professional success as an actress, Skye strived to fill a deep void in her life that her husband and even her little daughter, Emma, hadn't been able to satisfy. Seeking the limelight, becoming a film star with fawning fans and a zillion social media followers, and acting as if the world revolved around her hadn't filled the emptiness inside her soul.

"I received a call from a new television celebrity show a few days ago," she said the words so fast they ran together.

Shane remained focused on his plate. "Oh?"

11

"The host, Mindy Marks, wants to do a feature about me now that I've decided to resume my modeling career." At the time, Beth hadn't told the show's host that her return to modeling wasn't yet a done deal. But now that she'd decided, a small fib in Shane's direction wouldn't be any the wiser.

His fork hitting the plate shattered the restaurant's calm atmosphere. "Resume your modeling—"

"It won't be full-blown."

"I thought you were tired of living in the spotlight. Jet setting around the world. Paparazzi at your heels. Aren't you happy living a more private life? With me?" His brows knitted together as lines sprung to his forehead.

"Ah, darlin'. Of course, I love our life just as it is. But I thought getting back on the international stage would help shine a light on the youth shelter."

She stabbed a forkful of fish and chewed slowly to gauge how he'd taken the news. His face was set like flint, but his eyes seemed to sparkle with excitement. *It could only be candlelight, but no matter.* "It's not like I'll be trying to make a name for myself. I've already done that. I'm in the position to choose the jobs I want. And I promise you, I'm going to be very selective." She raised her glass and took a deep swallow of the sparkling white wine.

"So you won't be putting down roots again in Milan or London—"

"Nothing like that. No."

"Because I don't think I'd do too good with a long-distance marriage."

"No worries, my darlin' boy. There's plenty of work for me right here in LA." She wanted to take him in her arms and reassure him that her work would always be second to their marriage. Instead, she forked an asparagus spear and took a bite. Though he'd never said anything, she sensed a trace of insecurity rising in Shane when fans asked for autographs or snapped photos of her. That's why she'd hesitated telling him of her decision. He'd believe she was slipping away from him and their marriage.

They ate in silence for a few minutes. She wanted a little bit of time before dropping the next bombshell on him.

"I've also kept a secret," she said.

He glanced at her.

"I had an important meeting before we left on our honeymoon. Noelle Cosmetics asked me to resume my role as their spokesperson. They hoped that now that the accident is behind me—"

"Is the accident behind you?" He looked into her eyes.

"You've helped me so much to overcome the trauma, but I'm not really sure. Doing things I love lessens the stress from almost being killed by a drunk driver." She ran her fingertips along the jagged scar that crossed her cheek. "But it'll keep my mind off of losing my dearest friend in the whole world. I don't really know how to carry on without *me ould flower*." She blinked back the tears that seemed to spring to her eyes without warning.

"You have me."

She nodded with an attempt at a smile. "Where would I be without you?"

"You'd be where you are now. A beautiful, kind-hearted woman who can't help but bring joy to everyone she meets."

Now it was her turn to feel embarrassed. "I love you, Shane Dalton, even if you are a bit touched in the head when it comes to me *fey* and me gift for sleuthing."

"Don't get me going on that." He popped a piece of steak into his mouth.

"I think the interest in Sibéal," she said, making air quotes after referring to her public name, "has resurfaced because Skye hasn't been exactly quiet about how I uncovered a phantom killer and saved her life. *People, Elle, Vanity Fair*, and *Cosmo* have contacted me for interviews about my detecting skills."

13

He shook his head. "You never fail to surprise me, Betty." He raised his glass and took a long swallow of beer. "Looks like you're going to be one busy young lady from now on."

"You support me in my new endeavors?"

"As long as it makes you happy. But really, my dear Betty Getty, anything that keeps you from playing detective, I'm all for—hook, line, and sinker."

Chapter Three

Skye paused only a second before tapping on the director's door. She didn't want to believe that Thom Boyle, who she considered a friend, had betrayed her. *But then again*, she thought, *he might not even realize he's been manipulated by a damned stage mother. He's got to be placating Jane just to get her off his back. It's not that her daughter doesn't have acting ability. But the kid's eighteen years old and has a lot to learn when it comes to being an actor. But I kinda feel bad for Isabella Reid. Having to live with a shrew for a mother must be god-awful.*

She lifted her chin and threw back her shoulders. *We're going to settle this once and for all. That little ingénue isn't going to get star billing. If Thom refuses to see it my way, I'm outta here.* She smiled. *There's no way in hell he'll release me from this film. Not at this stage of production. He'll have no choice but to meet my demands."*

Skye hoped to God she wasn't misplaying her hand. *It's no secret actors can be fired and replaced at any given time during the production. After all, it's happened to some of Hollywood's biggest names. Fired for creative differences or for too much drama on—and off—the set. And sometimes, halfway through, the director realizes the actor isn't right for the part. Like what happened to the original male lead*, she thought with a quick intake of air. *Grant Reynolds is a good actor, damn good, but the dailies revealed it as clear as day that he wasn't cutting it in the role of a hard-boiled detective.*

Thom probably saved the film with that decision, but firing me wouldn't only cause havoc, it would ruin the entire project, not to mention the loss of millions of dollars.

Skye's stomach lurched, recalling the rumors flying around the set. The most disturbing of them was that Thom and Jane Reid were having an affair. And that he'd also bedded Jane's daughter, Isabella. But Skye didn't put much credence in rumors. Thom and his personal assistant, Cody Evans, have been intimate for as long as she'd known the director. At least five years. Though she'd never questioned Thom about his personal preferences, it was fairly well-known that Thom Boyle liked to play ball with both teams. A confirmed bisexual. On the set, Thom and Cody were thick as thieves, and she doubted that Thom strayed during the making of *Dark Grace*. Particularly with those two. She made a face.

She shifted from one foot to the other, wondering what was taking Thom so long to answer the door. Granted, she'd told him she'd stop by in fifteen minutes. But she didn't want to seem too eager to watch the dailies, so an extra quarter-hour would confirm that she wasn't at his beck and call. *After all, I'm Skye Andrews. Extraordinary actress in my own right. Married to Golden Globe and Oscar-winning actor, Zach Greyson.* Being married to Zach was her ace in the hole, but one day she swore it wouldn't matter who she was married to. *I'm going to be at the top of the A-list, and this role is going to make that happen.*

"I can't believe it," she muttered. "He couldn't wait a few more minutes?" She turned and descended the steps leading away from the trailer door but then glanced over her shoulder and stopped walking.

Thom really wanted to talk. Unless it was an emergency, he would've stayed put. She shook her head. *It doesn't make sense.*

Skye retraced her steps and this time banged on the door. She waited for what seemed like a whole minute, knocked again before turning the handle, and cracking the door open.

"Thom," she called, pausing in the threshold. She glanced into the long space, took a couple of steps into the main living area, and froze. Halfway down the wide trailer Thom Boyle laid on the floor.

"Thom," she whispered. She wanted to turn and flee but instead moved closer.

She said his name again, louder. He appeared to be sleeping on his back with his head resting on a pillow, arms tucked next to his sides, and his eyes closed. And that would make sense if exhausted from finishing the final shoot, he dropped to the floor out of sheer fatigue. Except. A gash transected his neck that exuded only the tiniest trace of blood.

Her mind flew back to a place she didn't ever want to revisit. She envisioned the body of her former employee, Emma's nanny, sprawled out on her living room floor murdered. "No! No-no-no-no-no! This can't be happening. Not again." She grabbed the cellphone from the pocket of her pencil skirt and pressed nine-one-one.

She answered the dispatcher's questions and ordered her to send the police and an ambulance. Taking another look at Thom, the thread of hope that he had survived the brutal attack snapped. Without checking for a pulse or listening for a sign of breath, his gray pallor told Skye he was dead. It only takes fifteen minutes to steal away any vestige of a once vibrant life. Cold fingers of panic inched up her back. She forced herself to meditate on her breathing in hopes of staving off the fear that would leave her a sniveling wreck.

Common sense warned her to get the hell out of the trailer since the killer could be hiding in one of the rooms. A wave of anger flooded through her, blinding her fear and vanquishing any modicum of trepidation. With hurried steps, Skye moved past the body, walked around the arrangement of chairs, and down the short hallway. She stopped at the bathroom door. Without losing a beat, she stepped inside, glanced at the jetted bathtub designed for two, and pulled open the shower stall's frosted door. Empty. Instead of relief, her heart pounded harder as if it was straining to escape her chest. She paused for a moment and took several deep breaths. She was tired of being afraid. Ever since she came face-to-face with a crazed killer, she hadn't been able to repel the dread that lurked in the back of her brain.

"Enough," she said and continued down the hallway and stopped at the bedroom. With a glance, she took in the king-sized bed, cherry cabinets and dressers, and the mirrored closet doors. The wide window shade, opposite the bed, stood drawn, allowing only a muted light to fill the room. She flipped on the light switch and stepped inside. It only took seconds to pull open the closet doors and peek under the bed. Exhaling, she let out a deep breath and dropped on the bed's edge.

She glanced at the cellphone clutched in her palm. There was only one person she truly trusted on the set. Father Daniel Danbury. He'd been loaned from the Church of the Good Shepherd as a consultant to fact-check the script and confirm that the religious stuff in the movie resonated with the spark of accuracy. Thom, a perfectionist, always insisted that the details be correct, lending a sense of authenticity to his films. Father Dan became a kind of chaplain for the crew and actors on the set.

She scrolled through her list of contacts and finding the priest's number tapped the screen.

"Hey, Skye. I bet you're pleased—"

"Are you still on the set?"

"What's wrong?"

"I need you. I'm at Thom's trailer. I can't believe this but . . . He's dead." She cut the connection.

Skye wanted to curl up on the bed, close her eyes, and forget her director lay dead only yards away. That being impossible, she chewed her lip and debated if she should stay put or leave the trailer. She pulled her red-gold hair back and slipped it into a ponytail holder she'd fished out of a side pocket. The decision dawned easy enough. *Get the hell out of here.* Skye slid off the bed and entered the living area. She didn't want to look at Thom, but her eyes refused to obey as they fell on his severed neck.

"Where's the blood?" she whispered. *Shouldn't he be covered in blood?*

A burst of sunshine filtered through the living room windows. Skye glanced at the pool of light hitting the floor. A flash glinted next to the body and caught her attention. She walked around Thom's body. Wedged under his thigh gleamed a blade mottled with blood. A wave of dizziness hit her, and she fell into a chair. She stared at the floor in the direction the blade pointed. Its tip aimed at a word written in Thom's blood—Cut. Skye covered her mouth with her hand, pressing back the scream that yearned to emerge.

The door flew open, and she shot up. Cody looked at her. "Something wrong? You look like you've seen—" His words died the instant he noticed Thom's body. "What's going on? Thom!" He flew to the body, dropped to his knees, and reached for Thom's hand.

"Don't touch him," Skye ordered, grabbing his shoulders.

He shook her off. "Did you . . . What the hell happened? Thom, my God, Thom," he moaned, crossing his arms against his chest. He rocked back and forth as his sobs filled the trailer.

Skye needed to get outside. Into the fresh air. The sunshine. The walls of the double-wide seemed to be closing in on her. She couldn't breathe. She took a couple of steps toward the door.

Father Dan stepped into the trailer. Their eyes met for a second. Without a word, he squatted next to Cody and placed his arm around the grieving man's shoulders. The sparkle was gone from his eyes, and an unusual solemnity filled the priest's face. He spoke so softly she couldn't make out the words. But they seemed to have an effect since Cody's sobs dropped to a low whimpering.

Dan carried the valise she'd seen him with on the set. He placed it on the couch and withdrew a length of purple cloth. He draped the material around his neck, knelt next to the body, and in a quiet but firm voice began praying. "Holy Lord, almighty and eternal God, hear our prayer for your servant, Thom, whom you have summoned out of this world."

19

e stopped listening, believing the calming rhythm of his words would lure her into a false serenity. She'd been in this position before. Knew she'd be a suspect. If only for a fleeting moment. This isn't fair, her mind thundered. She and her family were only starting to heal from the devastating effects of the nanny's death, particularly her seven-year-old daughter. *How will we manage to withstand fingers being pointed, especially from the damn media? They'll insinuate I had something to do with the murder of Thom Boyle.* She inhaled deeply, trying to wipe the thought away. She glanced at Father Dan as he made the sign of the cross over the dead man.

Who'd want to kill Thom?

The question reverberated in her mind like a sinister echo.

Skye closed her eyes and crossed her arms, hugging herself. She sensed movement but didn't open her eyes.

"Come on, Skye. I'll walk you to your trailer so you can lie down and rest," Father Dan said.

The wail of sirens filled the air. *It took the medics long enough*, she thought with a flash of anger, but the spark died almost instantly. *No amouot of oxygen or medidal procedures would've saved Thom's life. He was already gone when I'd entered the trailer.*

Instead of paramedics bursting through the door, Isabella Reid stepped inside. "What . . . Oh my God. Thom." Terror filled her voice.

Isabella dropped next to Cody and flung her body over the corpse. Father Dan grasped her arm and pulled her away.

"Have you lost your mind?" Skye said, finding her voice.

Tears spilled down the teenager's face. "You wouldn't understand," she managed between wails. "I love him. We're soulmates."

If this wasn't a tragedy, Isa's words would've been laughable. Before Skye could reply, Jane stepped into the trailer.

"Isabella," Jane's harsh voice scolded.

Too many people had invaded the crime scene, and Jane was the last person Skye wanted to see. A new wave of dizziness washed over her. She grabbed the priest's arm as if he was a fortress amid the tempest of anguish that surrounded her.

Jane rushed to her daughter and pulled her upright. "This is no place for you. Out."

"But Momma," the girl whined. "I need to be with Thom."

"Like hell. Out." She pointed to the front of the trailer.

As they neared the door with Isabella attempting to pull free from her mother's iron-clad grip, two paramedics stepped inside. Authority laced the female medic's voice as she ordered everyone out. Skye breathed relief, but Cody didn't budge.

"You better check him out too." Skye nudged her chin toward the personal assistant. "I think he's in shock."

Father Dan, with a gentle touch on her shoulder, urged Skye forward. She hurried outside, onto the tiny porch, and bolted down the handful of steps. Skye looked around, and didn't detect a trace of Jane or her daughter. She did, however, spot a patrol car speeding in their direction.

Father Dan pulled a package of cigarettes from his black shirt pocket, tapped one out, and offered the pack to Skye. She shook her head.

"This is going to be bad. Really bad," Skye said, gesturing toward the cops jumping out of the cruiser.

"What do you mean?"

"You may be able to read souls, Dan, but cops read facts. I was the one that discovered the body. That makes me the number one suspect. At least like for a second or two."

Skye wasn't surprised that the sirens caused a curious group of people to gather near the ambulance and squad car. The cop who'd been driving waved his arm, directing them to move back. Out of the corner of her eye, she spied Antonia Wright circumvent the crowd and hurry toward her. For a second, Skye found it odd that she still wore the dowdy wool pantsuit from the scene they'd just wrapped up. The day had been hot and muggy, and even though the sun was starting to dip toward the horizon, relief from the sweltering heat hadn't materialized. The last thing Skye thought would be for Toni to stay dressed in a sweatbox of a costume.

"Something's happened?" Toni aimed the question at the priest.

Father Dan nodded. "It's Thom. He had a terrible accident." His words held no emotion.

"Come on, Dan," Skye said, "You know that wasn't an accident." She glared at Toni.

"Thom is dead. Someone murdered him."

Toni's eyes popped and her mouth dropped open, but before she could respond, one of the uniformed officers joined their little group.

"Got a call about a possible homicide?"

"I placed the call. He's in there." Skye pointed to the opened door.

The officer flew up the steps and disappeared inside the trailer. A moment later, Cody stumbled out, wiping his hand across his eyes. A burly paramedic sporting a reddish goatee directed him down the steps.

Father Dan moved closer to the staircase. "Can I help?"

"Nah," the paramedic answered. "Said he could make it to the unit on his own. We're gonna take him to the closest hospital. Hopkins."

"What's wrong?" Toni shot the paramedic a concerned look. He pressed his lips into a tight line.

"My heart's beating a little bit funny," Cody said. Fresh tears sprung to his eyes. "I'm not surprised because it's broken."

Skye bit her lip as the paramedic walked the diminutive Cody, who seemed to have shrunk in his grief making him seem even smaller, toward the transport.

Another officer holding a roll of bright yellow tape walked up to them. He informed the little group that detectives were en route and would want to question them. After a curt nod, he began winding the crime tape around the trailer.

Father Dan once again pulled out the package of cigarettes and offered Toni one. "Thanks," she said under her breath and popped it between her lips. He offered her a light, and she leaned into the flame and puffed. "Who found the body?" Toni asked around a mouthful of smoke.

"Skye."

"We agreed to review the dailies together," Skye said.

"What the hell is it with you?" Toni glared at Skye. "You leave one murdered victim in LA only to come here and stumble across another dead body. What are you, some kind of death magnet?"

"I don't like what you're inferring," Skye said.

"Everyone knows, even the good Father here that you and Thom were at each other's throats the whole time we've been in this godawful place." Toni swiped at a bead of sweat rolling down her cheek.

"We had professional differences," Skye said. "Off-set, we were the best of friends."

"Thom told me you're a royal pain in the ass." Toni waved her hand, causing ash to flutter from the cigarette. She took a quick drag, dropped it, and crushed the smoke into the ground. "Everyone on the set knew he felt that way too. You were the only one who had a problem with his directing. And now he's dead."

Skye lunged at the older actress. If Father Dan hadn't jumped in front of her, Skye didn't know what she would've done to that haughty, obnoxious crone. She rested her head on Father Dan's chest and tried to squelch the tears springing under her eyelids as he rubbed the knotted muscles binding her back.

"What the hell's going on?"

Zach's puzzled voice filled Skye's ears. She pulled away from the priest's comforting embrace and fell against her husband. He wrapped his arms around her. She'd completely forgotten Zach had promised to meet her after work. They'd plan to celebrate the completion of the filming by spending the night in a five-star hotel after a romantic dinner.

"It's Thom," she whispered in his ear.

"Thom?"

Father Dan laid a hand on Zach's arm. "Looks like he's been murdered."

"What?" Zach stepped back from Skye, holding her at arm's length.

"Skye found him," Toni chimed in.

"You okay?" He looked into Skye's face.

"Not really. No." Zach pulled her back against his chest and kissed her cheek. Skye swore she heard Toni sigh. "It was bad enough finding Thom like that but . . ." She pulled free of Zach's arms. "Whoever killed Thom is a real psycho." She looked from one face to the other. "He used Thom's blood to write the word CUT on the floor. Next to where he left his bloody knife."

Toni fainted. Before she hit the cement walkway, Father Dan grabbed her with one hand cradling her head and the other around her midsection. As he laid her down, Zach sprung to the priest's side and patted Toni's cheek. "Toni, Toni," Zach said. "Come on, honey."

Toni's eyes fluttered open.

"For God's sake," Zach said, "why are you wearing that heavy outfit? The heat must've gotten to you." He helped her up and wrapped his arm around her waist.

"How gruesome," Toni whispered. "What kind of monster would write a message with his victim's blood?"

"Hmmm. Cut," Zach seemed to say the word to himself. "I guess you could say this is Thom Boyle's final cut. A death cut."

Chapter Four

Beth stood in the doorway of her favorite room. The cozy den she'd furnished with pieces from Ireland. It reminded her of the home she'd left behind to carve out a career in modeling. At age sixteen, she hadn't the slightest idea that decision would skyrocket her to international fame. And now she was about to reenter the world she'd left behind. But this room stocked with memories reminded her where she'd come from—a colleen from a village outside of Dublin—and always grounded her. Especially when she was treated as someone important and deserved special attention. To be honest, she liked the perks but thought much of the VIP treatment went a bit overboard. Not to mention the resentment she harbored toward those who believed her profession reflected the person she was on the inside. But Shane had been able to see through the glitz and loved her for herself.

And somehow, she wasn't surprised to find him camped out in the inviting study.

All during dinner, she hadn't been able to get a word in edgeways as Shane chatted, his voice laced with enthusiasm about his new job. But after his first day in the Art Theft Detail, he realized he'd have to fast-track his efforts on becoming an expert in heists, fakes, and forgeries. This type of detection work was a far cry from investigating a homicide.

Now seated behind her desk, he flipped through pages in a binder, glanced at the laptop screen and back to a stack of papers. Not wanting to disturb him she turned away.

"Beth."

She peeked at him over her shoulder.

He'd slipped his reading glasses down the bridge of his nose and looked at her with questioning eyes. "Do you need me for something?"

"Not really. Well, maybe. But I don't want to interrupt—"

"Actually, I need a break. The cases I've been reading about are fascinating. But, I've been stuffing so much in here," he said, tapping his temple, "I have brain overload." He rolled his shoulders and leaned back in the swivel chair. "What's up?" He laid his glasses on the desk's leather surface.

She stepped into the room. "I've been chatting with Skye."

He raised his eyebrows but kept his lips pressed together.

Beth dropped into a chenille tapestry armchair. Not sure exactly where to start, she chewed her lip and looked at the floor.

"Is something wrong?" He left the desk and squatted down in front of her. Taking her hand, he rubbed the top of it with his thumb.

She blew out a stream of air. "I've told you that Skye's been having a difference of opinion with her director."

He nodded, released her hand, and returned to his seat.

"The truth is, they've had more than a few dragged-out shouting matches. Her scenes were being changed. Cut. Seems that two other actresses' parts were starting to overshadow her role."

Shane fingered his cleft chin as he focused on Beth.

"Just about everyone connected with the film knew about their tiffs," she said.

"Sounds more like all-out war than mere disagreements."

She nodded. "Skye even considered quitting."

"Oh?" Shane narrowed his gray-blue eyes. "That doesn't sound like Skye at all."

"She's always been the utmost professional when it comes to working. But so much was going on while we were on our honeymoon that I could scarcely give Skye two minutes of my time. She's asked me to use my *fey*." She shrugged. "To make a long story short, the director, a Mister

Thompson Boyle, asked Skye to stop by his trailer so they could work out some of their differences. Skye and the director had been friends for years and had worked before with each other. She didn't want to spoil the bond between them. But when Skye reached his trailer, she couldn't believe her eyes. She found Thom dead. He'd been murdered."

Shane sighed loudly. "You're kidding? That's the last thing Skye needed after what she's been through. Have they caught the perp?"

"No." Beth shot up and walked to the far end of the study. She retraced her steps and stopped in front of him. "That's the problem. Rumors began to fly that Skye had something to do with the poor man's death."

"Rumors aren't facts. You know that, and so does Skye. That is, if she's learned anything from the both of you almost losing your lives at the hands of a psycho narcissist."

Not wanting to see his expression, she tore her eyes away from his. It was always the same look whenever the incident from a couple months ago was mentioned. Intense sorrow tinged with a touch of anger.

"Investigators search for evidence, not hearsay," he said. "They're professionals, remember."

"You're right, but . . ." She shook her head. "One day Skye became so frustrated she threatened the director."

"Good God," Shane said under his breath.

"She just shared that little tidbit with me."

"People say things they don't mean when they're angry."

"True, but she did attempt to attack another actress. The woman made sure that bit of info went viral around the set and on her social media pages. The only good news is that a knife, was left behind, near the body." She paused for a second. "According to Skye, the knife didn't kill Thom Boyle. He was shot here," she said, touching her side. "The bullet killed him, but the knife was used to slice open his throat after he died. During the autopsy, the bullet was located under his collarbone."

Shane frowned. "You mean nobody heard the gun fire?"

She shrugged. "Doesn't seem so. At the time, sets were being dismantled amid a lot of noise made by saws, drills—power tools."

"The knife being left behind doesn't make sense." He fingered the clef in his chin. "Pretty sloppy. But if that's the case, I wouldn't be surprised if forensic evidence was left behind too. Skye will probably be ruled out with the wink of an eye."

"That's what I told her."

"But I suggest she works on taming that temper of hers." He turned his direction back to the papers on the desk.

"Everyone on the set believed the location shoots were finished," she said.

He turned toward her.

"They planned to return to LA and wrap up the final studio scenes. But the assistant director who's taken Thom's place announced he wants to reshoot and add another scene. So, it looks like they'll be on location for an extra few days."

He nodded and tapped the laptop's keypad.

Beth brushed a stray lock of auburn hair off her forehead. "I think Skye's at her breaking point."

"Well, Zach's with her, isn't he?" He said, looking at the computer screen.

"Zach and Emma. But Zach's new movie is about to start production and he'll be returning to LA in a couple of days. Skye was hoping I'd fly out there to be with her until the filming is wrapped up."

"Where is out there?"

"Baltimore."

"They're still in Baltimore?" He frowned. "It's not surprising a murder happened there. Charm City hasn't been charming for many a year now."

"What?" Beth scrunched her nose.

"When we were there back in May," he said, pointing from himself to Beth, "we stayed in a luxurious hotel overlooking the Inner Harbor. The

28

only other place we visited was Pimlico. The racetrack. And on the trip to the track, you were so busy texting and talking on your cellphone, I bet you didn't even glance out the window and see the dire state of the city. But then," he said with a shake of his head, "we were on the I-83 for most of the trip—"

"Ah, I do remember passing by a park." She shrugged. "Indeed, I was glued to my mobile screen, so. But I'll never forget the racetrack. Home of the second jewel of the Triple Crown. The Preakness Stakes. And the place where we uncovered an elusive killer."

"I won't forget it either. But along with Pimlico and the Orioles, steamed crabs, and Fort McHenry, Baltimore is best known for its homicides. It's ranked as one, if not the most, dangerous city in the country." He stood, moved away from the desk, and dropped into an adjacent chair. "I imagine Zach will be sending a few of his bodyguards to keep a good watch on Skye while he's away."

"Bruno has been there the whole time, but he's sending the other two just to be sure."

"That's a good thing. Skye needs all the protection she can get. I wouldn't be a damn bit surprised she's irritated a number of Baltimoreans since she's been there. Probably one of them wants to wring her pretty neck."

"Shane, that's not funny."

He shot her a bright smile that held the power to melt her heart.

"I imagine the Greysons are still residing at that fancy estate smack dab in the center of horse country," he said.

"As far as I know."

"And secured, no doubt, like Fort Knox."

She nodded.

"In that case, since I won't have to worry about your safety." He shrugged. "Look, I'm not going to be much company anyway." He jutted his chin in the desk's direction. "Go. Visit Skye and Emma for a few days—and the surprise kitten we brought for her."

"Cloud." Beth smiled. "Emma thought it would be a cute name for a white kitty, especially since her ma is named Skye."

"Real cute," he said, raking his fingers through his sandy blond hair. He looked at the desk and then at Beth. "The murder of Skye's director reminds me of another Hollywood director who was killed way back in 1922. That case has never been solved."

"Oh?" Beth widened her eyes. "I've never heard about that."

"William Desmond Taylor."

He brushed his thumb across his chin, and Beth recognized the look. A dreamy look. The same expression covered his face right before reciting the life story of his favorite architect, Andrea Palladio. But he'd piqued her interest. She wanted to know the details of this mysterious murder.

"William Desmond Taylor was quite an interesting character. Known as 'Bill' to his friends, but 'Billy' to his lovers. Actually, he was one of your countrymen." He raised his sight from his hands folded in his lap and glanced at Beth. "But he left Ireland for a dude ranch in Kansas. He was Anglo-Irish."

"Oh." She nodded with a bit of a frown.

"Eventually, he made his way to 'The Big Apple' with a dream of becoming an actor. He married, had a daughter, and worked at his father-in-law's ritzy British antique store. I guess you could say Taylor pulled himself up, on his wife's bootstraps and became a darling of the social set. He was known to be a heavy drinker and a womanizer. Then one day," Shane said, snapping his fingers, "he disappeared."

"Disappeared?"

"Abandoned his family."

Beth frowned, not liking this William Desmond Taylor one bit.

"He went north. Traveled through Canada and Alaska mining for gold. Even joined an acting troupe. Finished with prospecting, he showed up in San Francisco. He changed his name, being christened William Deane Taylor, and became a producer. Joined the army during WWI and earned the rank of lieutenant, then went to Hollywood."

Knowing how much Shane loved to tell a story, she focused on every word. Still, she knew he tended to be long-winded and hoped he'd get to the point soon.

"Taylor became a film actor. You know, at that time, movies were still silent. And then a top-notch director. He became engaged to Neva Garber, an actress—"

"What about his wife in New York?"

Shane shrugged. "Turned out Taylor didn't marry the starlet. Hints have since been voiced that he was homosexual or bisexual."

She squinted, trying to remember something Skye had told her about Thom Boyle, but it'd slipped her mind. She refocused on Shane.

"On a chilly February morning in 1922, Taylor's body was found inside his bungalow by his houseboy in Westlake, which at the time was a trendy and affluent neighborhood. His murder was never solved."

"Why not?"

"There were plenty of suspects but no evidence. But almost every detective I know has a take on who killed the director and why. Collins thinks it was Charlotte Shelby, a money-hungry stage mother from hell who threatened anyone who had a romantic interest in her daughter, the goose who laid the golden eggs."

Beth smiled with the mention of Gavin Collins, Shane's former homicide detective partner. "Who do you think did it?"

"The general consensus is Shelby. But I'm not completely sold on her. I'm not a hundred percent sure, but I think it had something to do possibly with drugs and sex."

"You seem to know a lot about the director's murder."

A smile touched his lips. "My great grandfather, a grand old gent, we called Greatpa, told me about it when I was a wee little lad."

She inwardly smiled by the way Shane has, on occasion, picked up her speech pattern.

Soon he'll be sporting a brogue.

"That would be a wee bit of a lad," Beth said with a shake of her head and a smile.

"Anyway, he told me all about old Hollywood on sunny days when we went fishing."

"I didn't know you liked to fish."

He ignored her comment. "When Greatpa was sixteen, he'd been working in the picture-making industry for a couple of years mainly as an extra. His goal was to be the next Lew Cody."

She frowned.

"Lew Cody was a suave matinee idol way back in the day. A real heartbreaker. Well, in 1922 Greatpa finally got a break. A small uncredited role in the film *The Top of New York*. Taylor's last film. Greatpa became a bit distracted when the girl he had a gigantic crush on turned out to be a murder suspect. The girl, Mary Miles Minter, was cleared, but today some still think she's a prime suspect."

Beth leaned forward, not wanting to miss a word.

"Somewhere along the line, Greatpa switched from actor to screenwriter and finally wound up becoming an author. He and F. Scott Fitzgerald were contemporaries. Greatpa became well-known for his short stories. One was even made into a movie in the 1940s." Shane paused. "He was an amazing person. He died when I was eleven."

Beth stood and moved next to Shane. She kissed the top of his head.

"I guess you have to make a plane reservation and pack," he said.

"No. That's already done."

"Oh?"

"Well, no use putting things off to the last minute. I would've canceled if you didn't want me—"

"I hear you." He chuckled.

"The airport taxi should be here in an hour or so. I'll be flying out on Zach's private jet."

"Private jet?"

"It'll be bringing him back to LA." She paused for a second, waiting for a reaction. Shane continued to look at the laptop screen. "I was wondering, do you have any of your greatpa's stories? I'd love to read them during the flight."

"In the library. The shelves where I added my book collection. *The Complete Works of Shane T. O'Neill.* A number of the stories are based on his experiences working in the movies."

"Shane? You were named for your great grandfather. That's lovely."

"My mother says they couldn't have picked out a more appropriate name. Swears I'm the spitting image of him. I have a photo of Greatpa when he was my age—there is a resemblance—striking actually. Handsome, suave, debonair." He shot her that smile again. "The photo on the book jacket was taken when he was in his sixties. So, it'll give you a glimpse of what I'll look like as an old codger."

"Old codger. Never. I'll think of you as a distinguished gentleman."

"I meant a cool old codger."

After a playful swat to his shoulder and a kiss on his cheek, Beth headed to the library. His wall of books consisted mainly of thrillers, procedurals, true crime, architecture, and art books. As she searched along the shelves she spotted the book, pulled it free, and looked at the back jacket. Though Shane said the photo was taken when Greatpa was in his sixties, the smiling man looked about mid-forties and could pass for Shane's older brother—if he had one. She pressed the book against her chest and turned toward the door. But then she caught sight of another title. *Jazz Age Deception: The Unsolved Murder of a Hollywood Director.* She grabbed the book as the clock in the main hallway began to chime. Nine rings. *The hackney will be here soon.*

Clutching the books, she exited the library and headed to the master suite to pack Shane's greatpa's book. The other one she couldn't wait to delve into. The five-hour flight would provide plenty of time to read, and the true-crime book might even offer some insight as to why someone would want to kill a movie director.

Chapter Five

Two pairs of eyes stared at Beth. She shifted in the plush leather seat and shot a smile at the bodyguards, Red and Sid, standing in front of her with arms crossed. Their faces remained impassive, even though she detected a slight nod from Red, but it was wishful thinking on her part.

Zach Greyson's bodyguards take their jobs seriously, of course, they're professionals. But who in God's name is going to harm me flying at 41,000 feet?

She swiveled her club chair toward the oblong window. Instead of gazing into the blackness, she glanced at the book resting in her lap. She'd sped through the first chapter of *Jazz Age Deception* and wanted to absorb more info about the hundred-year-old unsolved murder, but feared any second she'd nod off. With each ticking minute aboard Zach's custom private jet, the more she lulled into a state of relaxation. The stress and anxiety she'd been harboring from the merry-go-round she'd been trapped on the last few months seemed to melt away like the last remnants of snow in the spring sunshine. Her shoulders relaxed, the tightness in her back lessened, and her eyelids drooped. She shook her head, trying to revive herself, and realized the glass of wine she'd consumed hadn't helped. She needed coffee.

"How might I get a cup of coffee?" She peeked over her shoulder. The bodyguards hadn't moved.

Without a response, Sid stepped away and headed to the front of the plane. With what seemed only a minute or two, he returned with a steaming mug and handed it to her.

"Thanks," she said and placed the hot cup on the table next to her. "Really, you don't have to wait on me. I can—"

"Not a problem," Sid said, "You're Mr. Greyson's guest, and it's our job to take care of you."

Red nodded in agreement.

"You're certainly not going to stare at me for the next five hours, so." She stood, and the blanket she'd tucked around her dropped to the floor. Sid moved closer to retrieve it, but she shook her head. "I've got my book. Why don't you lads watch a movie?" She gestured to the large screen beyond her. "Or read a magazine. Something—anything but stare at me all night."

"No need getting worked up," Red said, raking his fingers through fiery strands of his military-style haircut. He glanced at Sid. "Heads up poker?"

Within minutes the two burly men sat at a table. Instead of focusing their attention on her, they busied themselves studying the playing cards in their hands.

Beth sipped coffee and realized even the caffeinated drink wouldn't be able to keep her awake. She glanced around the plane's sleek design— all plush white leather and shiny wood. She retrieved the wayward blanket, moved in front of the fireplace, and shook her head in amazement. *Who would've thought, a fireplace in an airplane?*

Even though Zach's bodyguards focused on their game, Sid noticed her looking at the hearth's marble surround. "Would you like a fire?" he asked.

She glanced at the mountain of a man, stroking his salt-and-pepper goatee. "That'd be lovely."

Sid placed his cards face down and moved to the fireplace. He clicked a remote she hadn't noticed before. Orangey-yellow flames shot up, and a stream of warmth blew into the cabin, brushing Beth's legs.

"It's not an actual fire," Sid said, "but a 3-D impression created by combining an illuminated water mist with a simulation of burning wood. The flames are cold, but the heat and sounds are real."

"Truly amazing."

"I can adjust the temperature if it isn't warm enough." He raised the remote control.

"Ah, no. This is perfect." As the simulated flames danced and flickered with the sound of burning wood crackling, she hadn't a doubt the chilliness filling the cabin would be chased away.

"Anything else you need, just give a holler," Sid said, edging back to his game.

"How about more coffee?" Red asked.

"Thanks, but no. I think I'll just relax." She pointed to the comfy-looking divan banking one side of the cabin.

Both men refocused on the cards nestled in their ham-sized hands. She watched Sid move two red chips into the center of the table, adding to the pile of white and green plastic disks.

Leaving them to it, she retrieved the book, stretched out on the white leather couch, and flipped through the pages. She stopped at the section of black and white photographs. For a few moments, she assessed the director, William Desmond Taylor. A dashing-looking fella, she conceded, considering he had the misfortune of being Anglo-Irish. She noted the unfamiliar names printed below snapshots depicting beautiful women dressed in 1920s couture—fur-trimmed coats, cloche hats, shimmering backless gowns: Mary Miles Minter. Mabel Norman. Margaret Gibson. Charlotte Shelby. Beth wrinkled her nose. *Could a woman be responsible for the director's murder?* Though intrigued by the idea, she stifled a yawn. *No use fighting it.* She closed the book and then her eyes.

The moment the jet's wheels hit the tarmac, her eyes fluttered open. Weak light filtered into the cabin. During the night, one of the bodyguards had covered her with a plush blanket. She flung it off and sat up, rolled her shoulders, and raised her arms, stretching her back. She felt ready to face the world. Even Skye's latest crises.

"Breakfast?" Red traveled the length of the cabin holding a tray. He placed it on the shiny mahogany table where earlier he and Sid played cards. She settled in a chair as her empty stomach growled. With a swift motion, he emptied the tray and placed a plate of buttered toast, a cup of fruit salad, and a cheese Danish in front of her next to a large steaming cup of coffee. The delicate porcelain bud vase seemed to disappear in his hand, but after he placed it next to her breakfast dishes, she noticed the vase contained one long-stemmed red rose. Usually, she'd start her day with a piping cup of Lyons, Irish tea, but, today, she suspected she'd need all the caffeine she could muster.

"Thanks," she said, breathing in the coffee's enticing aroma. "This is lovely."

"We'll be disembarking," he said, "in about fifteen minutes."

Sensing motion, she looked away from the table. The captain, dressed in a blue pilot's suit, walked toward her.

"Good morning," Beth said, smoothing back her hair, believing she looked a fright.

"And top of the morning to you," he said with a wink.

Beth wanted to roll her eyes at his lame attempt at an Irish accent. Instead, she offered him a sunny smile.

"We've landed at Frederick Municipal Airport," he said, slipping a hand into the pocket of his neatly creased trousers. "A reliever airport fifty miles west of Baltimore/ Washington International. Mr. Greyson has been storing his jet here while residing in the area. A car will transport you to your destination and should arrive momentarily. Take as much time as you need." He gestured toward her breakfast. "It's been a pleasure, Miss Getty."

"'Twas a lovely flight. Thank you, Captain."

With a quick nod, he turned and walked away as she took a bite from the warm toast. It wasn't until she finished the bowl of melons, strawberries, and mandarin oranges that Beth realized the two bodyguards were nowhere to be seen. She suspected they disappeared in the cockpit, checking on arrangements.

A tragedy had brought her to Maryland, but even so, she looked forward to spending time with Skye. Even if they were polar opposites in almost everything. She couldn't help but feel a bit sorry for the film star who had the world by its tail but often seemed like a lost little girl trapped inside her glittering life.

Beth hoped that stumbling across another body hadn't pushed Skye over the edge. *Even if she's rattled, once Skye's working on the set, she'll be back where she belongs. Work will hopefully banish thoughts of her poor director's murder—at least for a little while.*

She took a quick sip of coffee, focusing on the flower's delicate petals. *I haven't been on a movie set for . . .* Beth counted on her fingers *. . . four years.* A smile settled on her face. *My acting debut. And my only role in a featured film.* She played a minor part but the monotony of repeating the scenes, over and over again, left her exhausted. However, the premiere at Grauman's, the famed Hollywood landmark, now branded the TCL Chinese Theater, with cameras and reporters proved to be a heady experience. One she'd never, in a million years, imagined she'd be a part of. *It would've been perfect, she thought, if Shane had been at my side. But of course, then, we hadn't even met.*

It wasn't the grand affairs like those she'd seen in vintage reels from Hollywood in the 1930s, where throngs of fans blocked the streets a hundred deep to glimpse a peek of a Hollywood luminary. Even so, there had been a sizable crowd, and both Skye and Zach had accompanied her. Their presence offered the eager moviegoers a special treat with the opportunity to catch sight of today's "golden couple" of the silver screen.

Beth had no desire to deviate from her comfort zone of print work and the occasional television commercial. And now, she found herself on the cusp of resurrecting the career she'd walked away from as a cosmetic spokesperson and a "cover" girl.

After finishing every morsel of food, she grabbed her oversized tote bag and headed to the bathroom. It wasn't one of those minuscule affairs found on commercial airlines but was roomy enough to move around in. The marble tiled walls and floor sparkled as well as the gold-plated fixtures. She looked into the mirror and groaned. With a firm rub, she smoothed her T-shirt and Bermuda shorts, washed her face, and brushed her teeth and hair. "I'll truly tidy up when I arrive at Skye's. Even though," she said, turning sideways checking her reflection in the mirror, "considering I slept the night in make-up and clothes, I didn't fare too badly."

When she returned to the cabin, the exit door stood ajar, and the air stairs had been released. She headed to the bodyguards flanking the exit. Red clunked down the jet's half dozen steps in front of her and stood at the bottom of the stairs. When she reached the final metal tread, he grabbed her hands and steadied Beth as her sneakered feet touched the tarmac. With a light touch on her shoulder, Red directed her to the small terminal.

Bruno met her at the door. "It shouldn't take too long to unload the luggage. Why don't you take a seat," he said, pointing toward the waiting area.

"No worries. Don't rush on account of me."

He offered her a curt nod and exited the terminal with a stainless-steel luggage cart in tow.

Beth paused at the expansive window facing the airfield and watched Bruno head to Zach's plane. A light aircraft with a red stripe along its white body caught her attention. The two-seater plane moved down the runway picking up speed, and its wheels lifted off the ground. Beth watched its movement until the plane reached the sky and disappeared from sight.

She turned away from the window, sat on the edge of a cushy tan leather chair, and slipped out her mobile. The glowing time on the phone's screen told her it's the middle of the night at home. *Shane will be fast asleep*, she thought with a smile, *I'll ring him later*. She typed a quick text letting him know she'd arrived safe and sound in Maryland.

When she looked up, Bruno hovered next to her.

"Are you ready to leave, or do you need more time?"

Out of the corner of her eye, she spotted Red and Sid wheeling the luggage through an exit. "I'm more than ready." She dropped the mobile into her bag.

Ten minutes later, they merged onto Interstate 70 as the morning rush hour began to strengthen.

"The trip will take about forty minutes, Miss," Bruno said from behind the SUV's steering wheel.

"Then I'll have time to get back to my reading," she said, freeing the book, *Jazz Age Deception,* from her oversized tote bag. She found her marker, opened the book, and lost herself in the pages that transported her to 1922 Hollywood. When the vehicle pulled into the circular driveway, she wistfully closed the cover of the true-crime book. The pages read like a best-selling whodunit, and she didn't want to stop. After tucking the book away, Sid offered her a hand, and she stepped out of the vehicle.

"Beth!"

She jerked her head and spied Skye jogging toward her. Skye extended her arms and the two women embraced.

"I'm relieved you're here," Skye whispered in her ear.

Stepping back, Beth inspected her friend's face. Beautiful as ever, except for the worry lines creasing her forehead.

"I've had to put on a charade in front of Emma," Skye said. "The last thing I want is to trigger Emma's memory from when that lunatic tried to feed her to Zach's snakes."

"How is the wee colleen doing?"

"She loves it here." Skye moved her arm as if attempting to encompass the entire estate. "There's a lake out back and Zach's been taking her fishing." She shook her head as if amazed by her own words. "C'mon. Let's get you settled." She linked arms with Beth.

She'd been inside the luxurious mansion before, but Beth had only seen the grand foyer, double staircase, and great room. She was eager to explore the rest of the house.

Emma met them in the entry cradling a furry, white kitten with a powder blue velvet ribbon tied around his neck. "Auntie Beth," she said, releasing the cat and wrapping her arms around Beth's hips. "I'm happy you're going to be living with us. Both of us are. Me and Cloud."

As if on cue, the kitten mewed.

Beth stooped down to be eye-level with the little girl. "I've brought you a present."

Emma's eyes grew big.

Beth reached into her tote bag and pulled out a package wrapped in shiny silver paper. "It comes from Venice, an enchanting city, far away from here."

Emma glanced at her mother as if seeking permission to take hold of the gift.

Skye nodded. "I wonder what it could be."

"I don't know," Emma said as if to herself.

"Open it up and find out," Beth said.

Not needing any more words of encouragement, Emma grabbed the package and ripped away the wrappings.

"Oh," she whispered. "It's beautiful."

A few weeks ago, when Beth was keen on the hunt for the "Canal Murderer" in Venice, she'd stopped at a tiny mask shop. Overwhelmed by the beautiful array of handmade carnival masks, when her eyes landed on this particular cat half-mask, she knew Emma would love it.

"I bet you've never seen a cat face like that," Beth said. "It's decorated with a harlequin design." She pointed to the gold mask with its repeating pattern of red, black, green, and orange diamonds."

Emma studied the whimsical cat face and moved her finger across its glossy surface.

"These black ribbons," Beth said, lifting one. "Keep the mask secure on your face. Would you like to try it on?"

Emma nodded.

"This is a baby cat mask, so I'm sure it'll fit you perfectly."

Emma centered the half-mask so she could see through the eye openings, and Beth tied it snugly beneath her ponytail.

"Oh, my," Skye said. "From now on, I'll have to call you my little cat girl."

Emma's lips curved upward. "C'mon, Cloud. Let's go look in the mirror." She skipped out of the foyer with the kitten on her heels.

"That was sweet of you," Skye said. "Why don't we—"

"Welcome, Beth."

Both women turned to the sound of Zach's voice as he bounded down the carpeted staircase.

"It's worked out great that you're going to keep Skye company while I'm in LA." He took Beth's hand and squeezed it.

"It's my pleasure. And how are you fairing, my darlin' Zach Greyson?" She wiggled her hand free.

"Couldn't be better, especially since Emma's recovered from her ordeal amazingly well."

"Daddy . . . Daddy," Emma called.

"Daddy?" Beth raised her eyebrows.

"Yeah," he said with the beginnings of a smile. "Isn't it great? She dropped the Zach the day I found her in the hobby room with that boa constrictor—"

"Look what Auntie Beth gave me." The breathless words flew from the child's mouth.

"Can I wear it when we go fishing today?"

"Of course, you can, kitten." He stroked the top of her head. "Speaking of which, we need to get our gear together. We'll have to make the best of it because soon I'll be going home. I doubt your mom is the fishing type."

"Momma fishing?" Emma's laugh tinkled as the two of them departed hand in hand.

"It's obvious he's crazy about her," Beth said.

"Has been since the moment he first laid eyes on my daughter. Zach always wanted a child of his own, and that just might happen."

"Don't tell me. You're preg—"

"Heavens, no. But if things end up the way I hope . . ."

"What do you mean?"

"I'm working out an agreement with my ex. He's been adamant about not relinquishing his rights as Emma's father. But really, that's not the most pressing matter on my mind."

Beth recalled a conversation she'd had with Zach a couple of months ago. He was on the verge of divorcing Skye. All because she'd deceived him by convincing Zach she couldn't wait to become pregnant with his child.

"You must be starved."

Skye's voice chased Beth's thoughts away.

"Alma has outdone herself by preparing a welcome breakfast for you."

Beth touched her stomach and inwardly groaned. "Well, I wouldn't want to disappoint Alma."

Skye's heels clicked on the shiny floor as she walked across the foyer. "We can discuss this horrid business of Thom's murder over coffee and crepes."

"Right. But first I want to tell you about the amazing book I'm reading."

"Really?" She rolled her eyes toward the ceiling.

Beth ignored Skye's reaction. "It's about a murder that happened in 1922. Of a Hollywood director."

Skye stopped and glanced at Beth over her shoulder. "Who did it?"

"That's the kicker. The murder has never been solved."

Skye blew out a stream of air and linked arms with Beth. "Well then, tell me about it."

43

They walked through the great room and stopped at the breakfast nook right off the kitchen. Beth pulled out a white rush woven chair and sat at the beautifully set Grindleburg table. Beth suspected the place settings were French. Hand-painted porcelain china adorned with delicate colorful flowers. A bouquet of lavender roses in a glass vase sat in the center of the reclaimed pine tabletop.

"Alma," Skye called.

It took a minute for Zach's personal chef to enter the cozy breakfast room. "I was in the pantry organizing spices." Her eyes lit up seeing Beth. "I didn't realize our guest had arrived. Breakfast will be served directly."

Alma left the room, and Skye, sitting across from Beth, zeroed in on her. "Who do you think killed that old-timey director?"

"I don't know. Not yet. But I'm aiming to find out by linking all the clues together. And hopefully, my *fey* will help too."

Alma returned, carrying a silver serving tray, and placed it on the table. Without a word, she filled their two cups seated on dainty saucers with coffee and placed the cream jug and sugar bowl within easy reach. Beth thanked her while Skye lifted the cup and took a sip.

Beth added a dollop of cream and a tablespoon of sugar to her cup. "There's a cast of questionable characters, where any one could be the murderer. For example, one Charlotte Shelby, the stage mother from hell, and her daughter, Mary Miles Minter who supposedly was head-over-heels in love with the director, William Desmond Taylor."

"What?" Skye returned her cup to the saucer. "Is this for real?"

"According to the book, *Jazz Age Deception: The Unsolved Murder of a Hollywood Director.*"

"On my set, we have two similar people. Except, the rumor is both the mother and daughter had affairs with our director. The very idea turns my stomach." Skye waved the air in front of her face as if shooing away the words. "But I doubt it's true. After all, Thom had a long-time boyfriend, Cody. Not to mention a possible romance with that harpy, Antonia Wright, a has-been actress."

"*Janey Mack*," Beth said. "Now this is truly odd. In 1922, it was believed that Taylor had fallen in love with actress Mabel Norman while sexually involved with either his former chauffeur or houseboy. Or perhaps both of them."

"If you solve this cold murder case, I'd bet my last dollar, you'll be able to finger the person responsible for killing Thom. Seems like the two cases coexist in some kind of fantastic parallel universe."

"Except this isn't a fantasy," Beth said. "This is real life. Both directors deserve the closure of their murders being solved. So they can rest in peace."

Chapter Six

Charles "Trey" Blyth Wickham, III, stood in the center of the painting studio. He turned around, taking in the room. Exactly as he'd left it two months ago. Tubes of paints laid out in orderly rows, brushes with bristles pointing upward crammed inside empty coffee cans, stacks of finished paintings leaning against the wall, a canvas nestled on an easel.

As if frozen in time.

Time, he thought with a shake of his head. Not enough time had passed for him to work through his grief, and too much had lapsed from being away from the one thing that could soothe his troubled soul—painting.

His sight gravitated to the portrait hanging on the display wall. Trey missed a breath. He'd almost forgotten how beautiful she'd been. "Lexi," he whispered. He'd nearly met her in eternity that chaotic spring afternoon while enjoying a horse race that could've led to murder—his murder. But when he came to in the hospital after being drugged, an intense determination filled him. He survived for a reason. Not in order to hang out with his buddies at the marina or spend lazy days down the beach. But for his art. To create a sense of beauty for the sake of offsetting, if only a bit, the ugly hatefulness that dwells in so many hearts.

Hope through beauty. A lofty goal—even a bit romantic—or sophomoric. But he believed Lexi would have agreed.

Trey ran his fingertips through his sun-bleached hair and blew out a stream of air.

"There's no time like the present," he said, breaking the silence as he pulled a stool in front of the easel. He studied the landscape painting set in the easel and appraised what needed to be altered. Within an hour, he'd combined several oils for the medium, mixed colors, and reworked a section of the autumn foliage in the background. He stood back, weighing the changes, squinted, glanced at his earlier plein air studies, and nodded.

He squeezed out a blob of yellow ochre and another of French ultramarine blue. With the tip of his palette knife, he blended the blue, little by little, into the yellow. A dull, drabby green emerged. The exact color he needed for a shadow. He grabbed a small, flat bristled brush and ran it through the little pile of paint and was about to lay in the color when his cellphone sounded. Trey cursed under his breath, having meant to mute the ringer before placing it on his worktable. He glanced at the screen and lunged for the phone.

"Mr. Greyson."

"Hey, Trey. Just checking to see if you arrived okay."

"Got here a couple hours ago. The trip went off without a hitch."

"So, that old rust bucket of a pickup made it all the way to LA. I'm impressed."

"Only proves she's not ready for the junkyard yet." Trey paused. "I want to thank you again for allowing me to stay in your guesthouse. With the way things have changed—"

"Look," Zach said. "What's important is that you continue with your painting and get that MFA under your belt. And really, where else would my protégée live?"

"That's real decent of you. I can't thank you enough."

"There is something you can do for me. I won't be back at the house until tomorrow night—late. And with all of my security staff here in Maryland, I'd appreciate it if you'd keep an eye on the property. And drop the appropriate food into the snakes' aquariums. You know the drill, right?"

"Sure. No problem."

"One last question. Are you painting?"

"Yep."

"I thought as much. I'll catch you later."

"Right. Later," Trey said, ending the call.

Trey turned back to the painting and squinted at it again. He wiped out the bristles with a paper towel, having changed his mind about the dull green color.

. . .

Trey checked the time on his cellphone. Almost midnight. He shook his head, wondering how he'd lost track of time—but when in the zone—the hours had a habit of melting away. "I shouldn't be surprised," he said with a yawn.

Grabbing some paper towels, he cleaned the brushes and wiped down the glass palette. The idea of a sandwich crossed his mind, but he nixed the idea, wanting only to collapse into bed. Trey exited the studio at the back of Zach's elegantly appointed guest bungalow and entered the bedroom. He zipped open the backpack where he kept his travel essentials, rooted around in the bag looking for his toothbrush and mint-flavored Colgate. Grabbing them, he entered the en suite, bent over the sink, and splashed a handful of cool water on his face.

Standing upright, he remembered Zach's request about checking the house and feeding the snakes. "Dammit." He reached for a towel and blotted his face. *I really don't need to go over there. The place has a state-of-the-art security system—alarms, surveillance cameras, monitors—only thing missing is the attack guard dogs.*

He sighed. *Zach's been good to be. Damn good. It's the least I can do. Might as well take a quick dip in the pool first. May wake me up a little.* He pulled off his T-shirt and dropped it on the bathroom floor.

He headed toward the sprawling main house, an edifice reflecting the opulence of 1920s Hollywood. Originally built by a silent screen megastar whose name Trey had forgotten, the mansion experienced a succession of owners over the previous hundred years. It took Zach Greyson to bring it back to its initial brilliance. To Trey's way of thinking, Zach sunk at least three times what he paid for the rundown Tower Road property with the refurbishing. *Too bad his wife doesn't appreciate the grand old house*, he thought, wrinkling his nose as if he'd smelled something noxious. She'd rather stay at her ultramodern beach house in Malibu. *That suits me just fine. The less I have to see of Miss Andrews, the better.*

Trey stopped at the pool, kicked off his flip-flops, and eased into the water. He ducked down, acclimating to the water's cool temperature. Popping up, he flicked water from his face and glanced at the fountain spurting jets of spray that sparkled in the soft lights edging the patio. He dived underneath and swam the entire length, flipped on his back, and gazed at the night sky. Clouds scuttled across the black firmament, and only a waning gibbous moon hung low in the sky. After a dozen more laps, he pulled out of the water and toweled himself. He yanked off his soaking wet trunks, slipped into the dry pair of shorts he'd brought to the pool, and headed to the main house.

He paused. Something seemed off, but he couldn't pinpoint what.

Trey hurried around the outdoor kitchen, crossed the terrace, and pulled the keychain from his wrist. Two keys dangled from the yellow coiled band that opened doors Zach always kept locked—his hobby room and a small closet. He punched in the security code on the door's keypad and stepped inside.

Then it hit him. Not one light illuminated the house.

The downstairs lights, set by timers, turned on and off throughout the evening hours. But several rooms always remained lit, including the back entry where he stood. He slapped the wall in search of the light switch, flipped it on, and faced the security control panel. The last thing he wanted was a cadre of police cars descending on the house with him only wearing a pair of ratty cargo shorts. *Zach would probably think it hilarious if I was mistaken for a burglar.*

He shook the thought away and looked at the alarm's display screen. The word "tamper" glowed. Not an expert on security systems, Trey pressed the settings key, perused the list of options, and tapped sensors. He squinted at the screen. It looked like every sensor had been corrupted. He chewed his bottom lip, trying to make sense of the foiled security system.

Well, maybe, he reasoned, in their hurry to get to the airport, Sid or Red had forgotten to set the alarm. *Good Lord, if Zach ever found that out, they'd be sacked in a nanosecond.* He shook his head. *Security is their life's blood. They'd never forget something as basic as safeguarding the house. But even if they did, that wouldn't explain the message shining from the screen.*

When he'd arrived at the guesthouse, Trey automatically pressed the code into the control panel and walked into the studio, never imagining the system was down. But now, a warning blared in his mind that something wasn't right. He had no idea how the system was set up or how it operated. *I guess something could've gone haywire with the wires or the Wi-Fi. But I'm sure as hell not gonna bother Zach—especially in the dead of night— if it's only a glitch in the system.*

His brain told him Zach's house, like a fortress, stood impregnable, but his gut wasn't so sure. He raced through the first floor, inspecting each room. Reaching the library, his fear vanished. *If a thief had broken into the house, the treasures from here would be gone—first editions, valuable rare coins, antiques.* But as in every room he'd checked, nothing had been touched—televisions, computers, sound systems—all intact.

But upstairs, there're different kinds of treasures, he thought with a new wave of uneasiness. *Movie memorabilia. Oscars and Golden Globes statuettes. Artwork.* Trey took the back staircase, two by two, and headed to the master suite. He stepped inside and looked around. Pristine. Even a few hundred dollar bills, seven to be exact, were left on a dresser and hadn't been disturbed. This sealed it for Trey. *Something probably went wonky with the alarm system. I'll call Zach in the morning. Then he can contact the security company and have a technician over within a few hours.*

Trey sunk onto the edge of a chaise longue and breathed out relief. His earlier anxiety had chased away his exhaustion, but now fatigue hit him like a ton of bricks. His goal of crawling into bed spurred him onward until he remembered the snakes. The idea of trudging up to the third floor seemed bad enough but then having to deal with mice, insects, and reptiles . . . *They can wait a few more hours. After I get some sleep.*

When he'd first moved into the guesthouse, Trey thought it curious that Zach Greyson had a dedicated room for snakes and insects. But then he learned the actor earned a graduate degree in herpetology and had begun Ph.D. studies until a different kind of bug caught his interest. The acting bug.

Trey yawned and half laid on the longue. His eyes closed. On the cusp of drifting off, he jumped up. *I need to check the gallery.*

He pulled open one of the massive French doors and entered the temperature-controlled display hall, flicked the light switches on, and the room filled with a warm glow. The soles of his flip-flops slapped against the hardwood floor as he raced along the arrangement of paintings. He noted each painting until he came to a bare space on the wall. The Malibu Coast painting by Grandville Redmond was missing. Trey pushed down a spark of panic, remembering that a couple of months ago, Zach mentioned he might lend the painting to an exhibition showcasing the California impressionist artists.

Is the painting now on display in an art museum?

"Yes." He nodded. "That has to be it. No need to worry." He sucked in a mouthful of air and continued his survey. But this time, he slowed his steps and looked at each painting carefully, allowing its beauty to wash over him. He paused a bit longer at his still-life painting. *Lexi loved this one. She probably persuaded Zach to add it to his collection.* A sad smile crossed his face.

He inched closer to Zach's latest acquisition. A small study of a *Madonna and Child* by the Renaissance master, Il Bacchiacca. Zach decided to have a museum-quality display case built. That way, the front and back of the painting could be viewed through glass panes. He'd spied the case the minute he'd entered the room, standing at the far end of the hall.

Nearing the case, he did a double-take. No painting. His breath died in the back of his throat. *Maybe it hasn't been installed yet.* The hopeful thought evaporated as Trey reached the mahogany case. Splintered wood and a cracked glass panel revealed that the showcase had been jimmied open and the painting stolen.

He stumbled to a cushioned bench and dropped onto it. "I've no choice. I gotta contact Zach. Now."

Chapter Seven

Zach slammed his cellphone down on the bedside table and let out a string of obscenities.

"What's wrong?" Skye blinked her eyes open. She looked at the digital clock. "It's four in the morning."

"I can't believe this is happening." He pulled back the silk sheet and got out of bed. "I have to fly back to LA. I've been robbed."

"Robbed? What do you mean?" Skye pulled herself up and rested against the padded headboard.

He hurried across the room and stepped inside the gigantic walk-in closet. He reappeared, clutching two suitcases. He landed one on the bed, flicked the locks, and opened the aluminum case.

She watched with arms folded. "Don't tell me someone stole your Oscar?"

"What?" He looked up from the drawer from where he was removing clothes.

"What was stolen?"

Not answering, he lifted his cellphone and tapped the screen. "Sid, come to my bedroom. Pronto."

She pressed her lips together, wondering what could've been stolen that was so valuable that Zach would drop everything and head home. A moment later, her eyes widened with understanding. "It's my jewelry."

"Jewelry?" He shook his head. "The most expensive pieces are in a safe deposit box. You know that." He moved to the bed and dropped a bundle of T-shirts and socks into the suitcase.

"So, if not my jewels, what was stolen?"

"Two of my paintings are gone."

"Oh?" She snuggled back down and pulled the sheet up to her chin. "They're insured, aren't they?" She didn't wait for his response. "So, no great loss."

"How can you say that?" His eyes flashed. "How would you feel if one of your abstract expressionistic paintings by your *friend*, Kenny Weston, turned up missing?"

"That'd be no big deal. I'd ask him to paint a new one."

"The artists who painted my pictures are long dead. The Redmond isn't that big of a loss. But the Il Bacchiacca is over five hundred years old." He buried his face in his hands.

Skye worried her lip with a fingertip and slipped out of bed. She walked to her husband, wrapped her arms around his chest, and laid her head against his back. "I didn't mean to sound flip. I had no idea how much you value those paintings."

At first, he tried to shake her off, but then he turned and pulled Skye into his arms. "We must be cursed. Too many terrible things have happened over the past few months."

She couldn't disagree. There was a black cloud hanging over them. "Cursed, indeed. But why, Zach. Why?"

"I don't know. But I swear to you," he said, turning around and holding Skye at arm's length, "whoever stole my masterpieces isn't going to get away with it. I'll hire the best investigative team on the face of the earth. We will find my paintings and Thom's killer."

"Of course, you will, darling." She stroked his bristly cheek. "Just like Beth will uncover the brute who murdered Thom."

"Hey," he said, brightening. "You think she could use that sixth sense of hers to figure out who stole my paintings?"

She shrugged. "It's worth a try. But I'll ask at a more reasonable hour."

"Do that. Not that I really believe in that kinda thing. But . . ." He moved back toward the dresser. "It's weird that when Trey entered the house, the alarm was on the fritz. All the sensors were tampered with. The thief knew how to disengage a complex alarm system. But who with that know-how would realize those two paintings mean the most to me?"

"Are you suggesting somebody we know broke into our home?"

"I don't know what to think." He glanced at his Rolex. "I'm gonna call the pilot. Let him know there's been a change of plans. I want to return to LA as soon as possible." Before he could tap the screen, a knock sounded at the door.

Skye opened it. Sid stood there with a worried look on his face.

"Don't just stand there. Come in," Zach said.

Sid took a couple steps into the room.

"Trey called." Zach slammed the suitcase shut. "The Beverly Hills house has been burglarized."

"What the hell?" Sid's eyes popped open as a maze of lines crisscrossed his forehead.

"The sensors have been tampered with. How could that happen?"

"The tech company checked it last week. Red and I wanted to be certain there'd be no problems with the security systems while we were here. I checked it myself right before we left. Yesterday."

Zach's face turned a reddish color. "Don't be playing me, dammit. Two of my irreplaceable paintings have been nicked. I can't believe this."

"Like I said, Boss, the system was working fine." He brushed thick fingers through his tangled black hair. "Unless—"

"What?" Zach stepped closer to the man.

"Unless one of those technicians is behind it. The company has all the security codes. It would've been a snap for one of those guys to reenter the estate and disarm the system."

"Makes sense," Zach said. "Because these kinds of things are mostly inside jobs. I've used ACE Security for years. Those guys have been through the entire house installing motion detectors and surveillance cameras. If one of them is behind it, I bet my last dollar the outside cameras are out too. Dammit to hell."

Skye doubted either man realized she was still in the bedroom. "I'll make you two some coffee," she said. "And a bite to eat before you head back to LA."

Zach and Sid looked at her, a bit startled.

"Thanks," Zach said. He grasped his buzzing cellphone. "The pilot. Hopefully, we can leave within a couple of hours."

Skye, slipping into a filmy robe, padded out of the room. *Though I don't have a sixth sense,* she thought, *my intuition tells me the alarm company is above board.* She tied the robe's delicate sash, wondering who hated Zach so much that he'd steal his prized possessions.

Chapter Eight

Shane couldn't quite believe that his first assignment in the Art Theft Detail would be at Zach Greyson's mansion. He dimly recalled Beth mentioning something about Zach being a collector of fine art but at the time hadn't paid too much attention. What he did remember was that Zach's home resembled a Palladian villa—impressive, symmetrical, stately—obviously, a vehicle to flaunt his immense wealth.

The sun began to brighten the morning sky as he turned his unmarked police sedan into Zach's driveway. The gate stood open, so he didn't slow down and continued to travel along the concrete pavers beneath a canopy of leafy trees. He shook his head. *How could Zach's security be breached? It has to be state of the art. Plus, he has a security force. Could one of them be the culprit? Or a member of Zach's extensive staff?* From reviewing the initial police investigation notes, he'd learned that the house staff was on paid leave for as long as Zach and his family were out of town. The groundsmen continued to work, but they were independent contractors. He parked and stepped out of the car. "An inside job?" he muttered to himself. *Possibly.*

At the front entry, he spied his partner, Esma Flores, talking to Trey Blyth-Wickham. He strode toward them.

"This is Detective Dalton," Flores said.

"Shane?" Trey's eyes widened. "Wait. Don't you work for the Sheriff's Department? Homicide?"

"Not anymore. Art Theft Detail with the LAPD." He shot out his hand, and Trey shook it.

"I guess you'd like to forget the last time we met inside a Baltimore hospital. Anyway, weren't you planning to spend the summer at your family's home on Gibson Island?"

"That was the plan." Trey shrugged. "But I decided to resume working on my MFA. I arrived yesterday, never imagining something like this would've happened." He rubbed his eyes.

"Man, you look beat."

"Haven't slept in . . ." Trey shrugged. "I really couldn't tell you."

"Do you know which specific paintings are missing," Flores asked, interrupting their conversation.

"A Redmond landscape," Trey said. "Granville Redmond was one of the original California impressionist painters from the early part of the twentieth century. The other one is an Il Bacchiacca. *Madonna and Child.* He was an Italian Renaissance master, Mannerist in style—"

"I'm familiar with the artists and don't need an art history lesson," she said, waving the air in front of her face. "Are those two the only valuable paintings Mr. Greyson owns?"

Taken aback by her outburst, Shane raised his brows and offered Trey a shrug.

"Not by a longshot." A hardness edged Trey's voice. "He's compiled one of the best private collections in the country. Paintings, sculptures, manuscripts, and even a handful of ancient artifacts."

She pressed her lips together and looked directly at Trey. "Only two paintings were stolen?"

"As far as I could tell. When Zach gets here, he'll be able to—"

"Are the paintings displayed throughout the house?"

"Not really. Most of his paintings are in the gallery. Located in the original ballroom, he redesigned it into an art salon. That's how Zach refers to it. A couple times a year, he hosts a soiree. He invites leading figures in art and literature to discuss trends and creative developments. Usually, there's an art historian who analyzes one of Zach's pieces along with a stringed quartet for background music."

Shane let the air slip out between his teeth. He knew Greyson was into art, but he had no idea he'd taken it to the level of entertaining intellectual bigwigs. But then, he wasn't really surprised. *The guy overcompensates for being a matinee idol by amassing expensive collections and pursuing intellectual interests. As if he's some kinda academic snob.* He brushed the thought away in time to hear Trey say that Greyson wanted to reignite the concept of hosting the most influential and illustrious talents in his atelier much like the famous 1920s Parisian salon hosted by Gertrude Stein.

"So, he has shared his art pieces with the public," Flores said.

"A limited public," Trey said.

Flores glanced at the pad in her hand. "You said you arrived here yesterday. Why? Are you some kind of caretaker?"

"Uh, no. I don't work for Zach. I'm a student. I live in the guesthouse."

"A student?"

"Trey is Mr. Greyson's protégée. An amazing artist in his own right," Shane said as the color rose on Trey's cheeks.

"Uh-huh." She jotted on her pad. "Is anything missing from the guesthouse?"

Trey narrowed his eyes. "When I arrived yesterday, I went directly into the studio. I didn't inspect the place. And I've been here," he said, motioning toward the mansion, "all night. Zach wanted me to take care of his snakes—"

"Snakes?"

"He's a herpetologist."

"A what? I thought—well, never mind," she said with a frown. "So, you stayed in the main house all night?"

"Except when I drove to a 24-hour Arby's and got some food. I was too antsy to sleep. I basically hung out by the pool."

"Does Greyson have any paintings in the guesthouse?" Shane asked.

"The art there is mostly mine. But there are a couple Dutch landscape paintings and a fairly rare Picasso etching in the living room."

"Well then, we'll walk with you to the guesthouse," Shane said. "Have a look around. You can tell us if anything is missing."

"Okay," Trey said with a yawn.

Shane and Flores followed behind Trey as he led them to the bungalow. He pulled the door open, and the detectives entered the living room. Trey stepped inside and faced the eggshell-colored plaster walls.

"Oh, no," Trey whispered.

"What?" Flores sidled next to him.

"The Picasso." Trey pointed to a space between two sleek leather chairs. "I can't believe I didn't notice it. *Le Modèle Nu*. It's gone."

Chapter Nine

Beth awoke as streams of early morning sun filtered into the guest bedroom. She blinked her eyes open and patted the space next to her. For a moment, she'd forgotten that twenty-six hundred miles separated her from Shane. She was missing him already. She rolled her shoulders, feeling as if she'd slept a full twenty hours. After a quick trip to the bathroom, she puffed up the pillows and scooted back into the bed. A soft tap sounded on the door. "Come in," she said with a singsong lilt.

The door opened wide enough for Skye to peek around it. "I didn't wake you, did I?"

Beth shook her head. "Come in." She combed her fingers through her auburn hair. "I'm ready to take on the day. And by the looks of it, it's going to be a glorious one." She motioned toward the Palladian window and the sapphire blue sky beyond it.

Skye handed her a mug of tea.

"Ah, my darlin' girl, truly sweet of you." Beth blew across the hot liquid before taking a tiny sip. "What's on the agenda for today?"

Skye plopped down on the edge of the bed, bowed her head, and stared at the carpeted floor. "I've been up since four in the morning. The Beverly Hills house was broken into."

Beth bolted upright, causing the tea to slosh in the cup. She wanted to grill her friend for details but waited for Skye to continue.

"Zach left for LA two hours ago. Sid went with him."

"How did you discover—"

"Trey called. Broke the news that two of Zach's prized paintings have gone missing."

"Trey? The poor lad. He's back in Los Angeles?" Beth's brow furrowed.

"Must be. After what happened to Lexi, I thought he'd stay away for good. There's got to be sad memories for him in California."

"True," Beth said as a fleeting image of her best friend flew through her mind. She didn't want to remember Deirdre's murdered body submerged in a muddy Venetian canal. Instead, Beth imagined her vivacious spirit and bright, friendly smile. "I'm guessing sometimes being at the same place where you lost a loved one brings cherished memories. The idea of visiting Venice isn't on my imminent agenda. But I will return there, and remembering times spent with *me ould flower* will bring only happiness. Sure to be the same way with Trey."

"Could be." Skye looked at her manicured nails as if trying to find a flaw in the rosy polish. "I was wondering, actually, Zach and I hoped your *fey* could shed some light onto who's the slimeball that stole the paintings. According to Zach, they were downright masterpieces."

"I've told you before—"

"I know. I know. But I thought maybe that elusive sixth sense of yours had contacted you or something. Offered a clue about who had invaded our home."

Our home. Beth had often longed to hear Skye say those words. Their marriage had been tumultuous, to say the least, with both breaking their marriage vows—perhaps multiple times. Apparently, the weeks they spent as a family here had strengthened their nearly broken relationship. *Just like my granny says, there's always a silver lining. Something good had come out of the harrowing experience when Skye had been terrorized by a phantom killer. Her ailing marriage restored.*

"Haven't had a single nudge from my *fey*. Sorry."

"I guess that was wishful thinking. Zach's under the impression that one of the techs at the security company who checked the system is responsible. But I suspect it's someone who has a grudge against Zach. I've been wracking my brain trying to come up with a suspect. Then it

dawned on me. Ranald, or maybe it's Renaldo, I don't really remember. He was a chauffeur Zach hired last year. He admitted to having a few minor scrapes with the law, but Zach's personal assistant vouched for him. Said he was a friend of a friend. He'd been working for us only a few weeks when one of the maids—you know the one with the Russian accent—"

"Sofia?"

"I guess. Well, she complained to Zach that Renaldo came on to her. When Zach questioned the chauffeur, he didn't deny it. Said something like the maid was hot, and why shouldn't he try to get a piece."

"Are you kidding me? That was stupid."

"That Renaldo character was under the impression that he and Zach were buddies. Thought it was okay to talk about his sexual exploits. Zach hates that kind of thing. So, he ended that real quick and fired Renaldo's ass. I was glad too, because the guy gave me the creeps. The way he stared at me with a big, old smile."

"You think the chauffeur did it."

"He could have. He seemed sneaky enough. Somehow he could've gotten the code to one of the doors, let himself into the house, and pulled out the wires of the alarm system."

Beth wrinkled her nose. "I imagine it'd be a wireless alarm."

"Whatever." Skye tossed her head. "He was furious when Zach fired him. Well, Bruno did the actual firing. Renaldo made a whole lot of threats before Bruno and Sid escorted him off the estate."

"There's no denying it, some of my sleuthing ability has rubbed off on you."

"You think so?" A smile crossed Skye's face.

"When you talk to Zach, tell him your theory."

"That's exactly what I plan to do."

Beth nodded and took a sip of tea. It had turned cold.

Chapter Ten

The sound of heavy banging filled the guesthouse. *No. NoNoNoNo.* Trey pulled a pillow over his head and pressed it tight against his ears. *Come back later. I need sleep.* The pounding grew louder.

Trey groaned, slipped out of bed, and grabbed the T-shirt off the floor. He hadn't showered, combed his hair, or shaved for two days. Stubble peppered his face. He stumbled out of the bedroom, pulling on the shirt, and hurried down the hall into the living room.

He considered leaving the guesthouse. *Book a room in a nearby cheap hotel. Then I won't have to deal with the police. And the press. God only knows how they found out.*

He pulled the door open. Zach stood in front of him.

"Mr. Greyson . . . um, I mean Zach," he said, ranking his fingers through his tangled hair. "Come in. I was trying to catch some Z's."

"I see," Zach said, not moving beyond the threshold. "I won't keep you long." His eyes riveted on the wall, and a scowl jumped to his face. "Damn whoever stole my prized artworks. That Picasso etching was one of my favorites. Most of my guests who've stayed here," he said, pointing inside the doorway, "don't know a whit about art but, everyone knows Picasso. So, that," he said, jerking his chin, "was the perfect spot for it."

"I didn't realize it was gone until the detectives checked the place. When I arrived, I just dropped my stuff." He pointed at a canvas duffel bag and a couple of suitcases a few feet away from the door. "And went into the studio. I was, you know, in the zone. It was like midnight when I remembered to check the house."

"It's not your fault that some damn thief—"

"The hobby room wasn't touched. The snakes, insects, mice are good. Except—"

"What?"

"Might not be anything, but when I checked the third floor, the hobby room door stood wide open. You always keep the door locked, so I was kinda surprised."

"How the hell? That door is always locked." Zach took a deep breath. "I don't mean to take it out on you. I'm just damn frustrated and pissed. Totally pissed."

"No problem."

Zach blew out a stream of air. "Thanks for taking charge. Checking the house and dealing with the cops." He reached into his pocket and pulled out a pack of Marlboros. "This thing's got me back to smoking." He fished a gold lighter from his pocket, tapped out a cigarette, and lit up. "I've spent thousands of dollars on security, and now this. Why didn't the alarm company contact me? That only fortifies my suspicion that someone from the security outfit is responsible for the break-in and theft."

Trey reached into the leg pocket of his rumpled cargo shorts and pulled out a card. He handed it to Zach. "The detective in charge of the investigation."

Zach glanced at it for a split second. "Dalton? Since when did he start working art thefts?"

Trey shrugged. "I guess he got tired of looking at dead bodies."

"His wife is staying with Skye in Maryland." Zach took a long drag then tossed the cigarette onto the pavement. "I can't wrap my head around all the crap that's going on. Things were getting back to normal with Skye working and Emma smiling again. Then Skye's director wound up murdered. And now this."

"Murdered?" Trey's heavy eyes widened.

"Yeah. Thom Boyle. Looks like overkill. Shot in the back, and his throat sliced open. The killer left a message written with Boyle's blood. Cut. Whatever the hell that means."

"Damn. That director must've messed with the wrong person."

"To top it off, Skye found the body."

Trey let out a soft whistle. "That's the last thing she needed to see. After Lexi—"

"Yeah." Zach patted Trey's shoulder a couple of times. "It's a mess. Boyle was a standup guy and a hell of a director."

"Thom Boyle," Trey said to himself. "Didn't he direct that trilogy of superhero movies? Mega Man. I saw all of them, and they rocked."

"He made a fortune on those three. But he's done serious work too. Won an Oscar for a noir film, *Dangerous Allies*.

"I must've missed that one."

"It'd brought him the gold once. I guess that's why he revisited the genre. Now the assistant director, who I regard as a giant pain in the ass, has taken over the production. The producers thought it a smart move. Reluctantly, I agree."

"Excuse me," Trey said in the middle of a yawn. "I haven't had more than two hours of sleep like in the last forty-eight hours."

"I won't keep you. Just wanted to let you know the security system is being upgraded. Don't be concerned if you hear people walking around the grounds and inside." Zach motioned toward the living room.

"Okay." Trey swiped at a strand of blond hair that fell over his forehead. "That reminds me. Yesterday when the gate was open, a nosy reporter showed up asking all kinds of questions. I ended it by saying 'no comment' and walked away. But I think she's gonna be persistent. Wanted to give you a heads-up."

"Got a name?"

"Don't remember. Micki or Markie. Something like that."

"Mindy Marks?" Zach frowned.

"Could be."

"She's the host of *Celebrity Files*. A new entertainment show. She's a lightweight and shouldn't be a problem. But thanks for the warning. Now get some sleep."

"Will do," Trey said, offering Zach a salute. He shut the door as Zach headed down the paved walkway toward the main house.

Zach stopped at the pool, dropped into one of the woven chairs, and stared at the spraying fountain. A jumble of thoughts bounced around his brain, making his head ache. He tented his fingers under his chin and tried to conjure up additional suspects. In case the cops clear his former security company.

Someone on my staff. Nah. Couldn't be one of them. I treat them like gold. But . . . There was that driver I canned. Bruno reported the guy left with a mouthful of threats. Which I didn't pay any attention to at the time. But maybe I should've.

He drummed his fingers against the chair's vinyl armrests. "What the hell was his name?" Zach muttered. Though he tried, he couldn't recall the name of the former chauffeur. He pulled out his cellphone and tapped his personal assistant's number. The call went to voicemail. "Jay, I guess you heard about the robbery. I'm gonna give the cops the name of that driver that turned out to be a jerk. But I need his name. Also, have you heard anything about that Boyle film I'm contracted to do? Now that he's dead, is the project dead too? Give me a call."

Zach was still looking at the phone's screen when he heard his name. He glanced over his shoulder. "Dalton," he said, standing.

"One of your maids let me in. Nice spread," Shane said, taking in the expansive yard with its grove of orange trees, tennis court, and the view of the hazy city in the distance. He stretched out his hand, and Zach shook it.

"So, what's up?"

"I've got a few questions," Shane said.

"Shoot," Zach said, pointing to a nearby chair.

Shane moved the chair around to face Zach, and sat. "You have any ideas about the burglary?"

"Haven't been thinking about anything else." Zach's cellphone pinged, and he checked the screen. "Hold on a sec. My personal assistant." He scanned the text and refocused on Shane. The detective's scowl showed he didn't appreciate the intrusion. "You might want to look at a driver I fired. Renaldo Jones. He was pissed off when I fired his ass. Here's his information." He handed Shane the cellphone.

On his opened pad, Shane jotted the name down along with the DOB and SS number. "Anyone else?"

"Yeah. The security company. Last week they sent a couple of techs to inspect the system and it winds up completely disarmed. I suspected those guys first."

"Names?"

"I don't know any individual names, but the company is ACE Security. Stands for something like A+ Certified Electronics, which I now believe is a total crock."

Shane again scribbled on his pad.

"Who knows about your art collection?"

Zach pursed his lips. "It's not exactly a secret, if that's what you mean. A couple years ago, there was a spread in an art collector magazine when I put several pieces up on auction. But very few people knew about my latest acquisition which is missing. A painting by Il Bacchiacca, *Madonna and Child*. It's a study for a larger work housed in the Baltimore Museum of Art."

"That's quite a coincidence since you've been living in the Baltimore area."

"Coincidence?" Zach shrugged. "It was thrilling to see the larger, final version displayed at the BMA. Emma's face lit up when she spotted the painting and recognized its similarity to my small *Madonna and Child.* She's becoming quite an aesthete."

Shane raised his eyebrows.

68

"You know, someone who appreciates art. Anyway, I acquired the painting from the oldest, and in my opinion, the most esteemed auction house in Europe. You may have heard of it, Dorotheum, located in Vienna."

"Can't say I have. But, believe me, we'll check out every possible angle. So, try not to worry too much. The Art Theft Detail has recovered over 122 million dollars' worth of stolen property since its inception."

"I'm not doubting your ability to locate my stolen works of art. I'm betting on that. The fact is these pieces may not be my most expensive, but they are my most cherished."

"I gotcha. And you've got my word. We'll pursue every lead. Check out galleries, museums, auction houses, art dealers. It may take some time, but—"

"Time? How much time?" Zach shot up from the chair.

"Trust me, the investigation will be thorough." Shane shook his head. "It could take years."

Zach paced along the paved deck edging the pool, trying to work off rising anger. Afraid he'd blow his top, he inhaled a few times and slowly released the breaths. He'd always prided himself on his self-control and certainly didn't want Shane Dalton to see a rare display of temper.

He felt Shane's gaze following his every step. When their eyes met, Shane looked at the pad in his hand.

"If there's nothing more," Shane said.

Zach stopped pacing. "There is, actually. A reporter was snooping around here yesterday. I hope the LAPD will keep the investigation quiet."

"Can't do much about that. It's already been reported. But it's not a major story, so you shouldn't be concerned about too much traction."

Not a major story. Like hell. "You might be surprised. I have a huge fanbase. I'll be all over social media. Mark my words."

"We'll be checking that too."

"Checking what?"

"Social media. Is there anyone you've come across that seems hinky?"

"What?" Zach crossed his arms.

"Someone like Dot Barnett. A person who's obsessed with you."

"You don't think she's behind this?" Zach stepped closer to Shane.

"Not in the least. Last I heard, Dot's back on her meds living in Seattle. Her niece hired a live-in assistant to keep a good watch on the old gal."

"That's good news, I guess." The last thing Zach ever wanted was to face poor, demented, "crack-pot Dot" ever again. *It was bad enough when she showed up as a candidate for the nanny position with her declaration of love for me.* A smile longed to form with the memory of Skye's reaction. *She about had a cow.* He dropped his arms. "Keep me updated."

"Will do." Shane rose, but after a couple steps, he stopped. "How's Skye doing? I understand she's pretty upset about the murder. Poor kid can't seem to get a break."

Zach read genuine concern in the detective's eyes. "I didn't want to leave her. Thanks to your wife, Beth will be the best medicine she could have. She may not show it, but Skye's nerves are shot. And now this robbery, on top of everything."

"You guys sure are going through a tough time. Beth told me the Baltimore shoots are almost finished."

"Yup. The rest will be shot at a studio in LA. Filming will wrap up in about six weeks."

"When it's in the can, you two should plan to get away for a while. A vacation."

"I heard all about your disaster of a honeymoon. Wouldn't want to take a chance knowing our luck lately. Something terrible would probably happen." Zach paused for a second. "But we could pile into Skye's beach house and let the sun, sand, and the sound of the Pacific soothe our worries away."

"Sounds like a plan."

"It'll have to wait until I get some downtime from my new film. I'll be on the set tomorrow."

"Work is good. It'll keep your mind off of—"

"I hope to God, it does. If only we could catch a break."

Shane's cellphone rang. He whipped it out of his shirt pocket and looked at the screen. "Your prayer might just have been answered."

Chapter Eleven

Detective Jeremy Fox sat at his desk in the Baltimore City Homicide Unit, knowing he should go home. He willed his eyes to stay open, gulping down a mouthful of coffee. *Cold.* He wanted to spit it out but swallowed the bitter-tasting liquid. For what must've been the hundredth time, he looked at the notes strewed around his laptop and shook his head.

The detailed interviews had been numerous and painstaking since everyone on the movie set of *Dark Grace* had to be questioned. Most were winnowed away as suspects, but a handful remained. He grabbed his pen, tapped its shaft against the desk's edge, and scanned the list of names in front of him.

He dropped the pen, ran his fingers through his blond hair, and stared at the wall.

"You're still here?"

As if woken from a deep sleep, Jeremy Fox jolted in his chair, startled by the unexpected words.

He glanced over his shoulder and spied Tamera Stevens, a fellow detective, and a friend. He'd worked numerous cases with her and valued her expertise and advice. "I'm working. But why the hell are you still here," he said, tapping his watch. "Don't you have three kids at home missing their mom?"

"Missing me?" Tamera shrugged. "I doubt it since Brandon's watching them. He took the kids to dinner at McDonald's and bought them ice cream at Soft-Serve. Forgetting all about the leftovers in the fridge. He spoils them. Rotten." She looked at her hand where not too long ago a wedding band encircled her ring finger. "He's great with them." A hint of a smile touched her face. "So, everything's cool." She dropped into the chair behind her desk.

He'd met her new boyfriend, Brandon, a few times and pegged him for a stand-up guy.

Tamera deserves it after the hell her ex-husband put her through.

She'd met her former husband, Darnell, when they were both patrol cops. Not long after, they tied the knot and had three kids like stairsteps, one after the other. Then little by little, things started to go haywire. The stress of them both being city cops. Odd work schedules. Tamera promoted to detective and making more money. Darnell spending more time with his buddies. It all cumulated into one gigantic meltdown when he started cheating on her.

One thing Fox couldn't stand was a cheater. Especially one that would cheat on a good woman like Tamera.

"Actually, I came in here to cool down," she said. "Just had a run-in with Darnell. Even though our marriage is over, that man can still get my blood boiling." She shook her head.

"You were over in Narcotics?"

"Uh-huh. Wanted to find out if Redding's death was drug related. You know, the homicide victim found near that Old York Road stash house."

Fox nodded even though his eyes were fixed on the paper in his hand.

"Turned out it was. Apparently, he was killed by another gangbanger. He had a couple vials of blow on him. So, we can scratch Tavis Redding off our roster of open cases. Damn shame, the kid was only eighteen." Tamera shook her head. "Well then, I'm outta here." She stood and walked past his desk. "Hey, J., when was the last time you were home?"

Fox dropped the sheet and looked at her. "I think it was yesterday . . . morning." He picked up the pen and resumed tapping.

"That Hollywood Case," she said, making air quotes, "ain't going nowhere. Give it a rest. In the morning, you'll see it better with a clear mind."

"I know you're right, but—"

"No buts about it," Tamera said, stopping at the unit's doorway. She peeked over her shoulder. "Hear?"

Agreeing with her was the only way she'd leave without worrying about him. "I'll be heading out in ten to fifteen minutes. See you tomorrow."

"See ya."

The clicking of her high heels faded as she moved away from the office. He shook his head. He'd never known a detective who wore shoes like Tamera. She can do just about anything in them, too. He once witnessed her outrun a suspect in heels and then had the satisfaction of arresting the perp.

Fox raised his arms and stretched. *Tamera's right.* He started to gather his notes together when his eyes fell on a name. Skye Andrews. He leaned back in his chair. *No matter how you look at it, everything points to her. Granted, there's no physical evidence yet, but too many statements attest that Andrews and the director were at each other's throats. That she threatened him. Discovered the body or too slow on the getaway after committing murder?* He yawned. "Damn shame," he said under his breath. "Not only a looker but one heck of a good actress."

Chapter Twelve

Beth stretched on the pool lounge, eager to delve into the pages of *Jazz Age Deception*. During stolen moments between listening to Skye's complaints about her job and playing with Emma, she'd been able to move forward, racing through the pages, chapter by chapter. The riveting account transported her back to the jazz age. That decade wasn't just about fast and syncopated music. But, actually, the Roaring Twenties was a period of carefree hedonism, wealth, freedom, and youthful exuberance. And movies. Silent until nearly the end of the decade, the moving pictures showcased actors the public considered more than mere celebrities; they were stars. And like ethereal beings, they sparkled and shined in the limelight and glowed on the silver screen. Idolized, emulated, fantasied, and dreamed about by throngs of young people who flocked to Hollywood in hopes of joining the celestial constellation. She opened the book, but before reading a single word, she heard voices. Happy, excited voices.

Beth dropped the hardback into her lap and slipped her legs over the side of the lounger into a sitting position. She spied Emma, wearing the cat mask and heading in her direction. Alma Perez, Zach's personal chef and Emma's temporary nanny, followed, wiping her hands on her apron.

"Hello, Emma. Alma. Glorious morning," Beth said. She noticed Cloud walking behind Emma, secured with a collar and leash. "How clever of you, darlin', teaching Cloud to walk on a lead. Truth be, I've never seen that before. Cloud must be a brilliant kitten."

A smile broke across Emma's face. "He is Auntie Beth. The smartest kitten in the whole world."

"His brothers and sisters won't like hearing that."

Emma lifted the half-mask to her forehead. "Well, I haven't met them yet. But I think they're pretty smart too. I got a letter from Miss Kathy at the Cute Cat Rescue. She sent me pictures. I'll get them for you." She slid the mask down and skipped toward the house, while Cloud romped behind the little girl with the leash dragging across the pavement.

"Take a load off, Alma." Beth gestured to the pool chair next to her.

"Now that's a good idea. I'm not as young as I used to be." Alma dropped into the chair, pulled a pair of sunglasses from her chef jacket, and placed them on her face.

"You must be *fierce* exhausted taking care of Emma and preparing all the meals. Oh no, you're not cleaning the house too, are you?"

"Miss Andrews hired a cleaning service."

"Thank heavens for that," Beth said with a nod.

"What are you reading?"

"A fascinating account of an unsolved murder that happened in Hollywood a hundred years ago. The victim was William Desmond Taylor. A movie director."

"Is that so?"

"The more I read, the more it seems to parallel the murder of Skye's director. It's uncanny."

Alma shifted in the chair and faced Beth. "Parallels?"

"There's a cast of characters, each with his own motive that could've driven any one of them to commit the deed. Much like the situation on the *Dark Grace* movie set. Well, that is, according to Skye. Regarding the 1922 case, the expert consensus is that a stage mother, Charlotte Shelby, killed the director even though there isn't any hard evidence. But my Shane doesn't think she was the culprit, and I'm having doubts too."

"Who do you think murdered this William . . .?"

"Desmond Taylor." Beth paused. "I really don't know. Not yet."

"Sounds intriguing." Alma removed her sunglasses and wiped the lenses with the hem of her white short-sleeve jacket.

"Have you heard of Isabella Reid?"

"The child actress?"

"She's not a child anymore. Skye believes her mother would like Isabella to remain pubescent for the next decade. She's eighteen."

Alma shook her head. "It seems like only yesterday she played the baby of the family, Amelia, on that cute sitcom."

"The truth is," Beth said, leaning closer to Alma. "Isabella's mother, Jane Reid, is a real piece of work. She threatened to sue the last director Isabella worked with, and the rumor is," she paused, "she had an affair with Skye's director. As was Isabella."

Alma's eyebrows shot up, nearly touching her hairline.

"Just like in the 1922 case." Beth tapped the book's cover. "Ingénue, Mary Miles Minter' love letters and nightgown were found in Taylor's bedroom. Rumor had it that Mary's mother, Charlotte, was also having an affair with the director. That's why the detectives back then thought Charlotte killed the director. They just couldn't dig up any evidence that stuck."

"Discovering your daughter was having an affair with your lover could very possibly drive someone to murder," Alma said.

"I want to get Skye's take on Jane Reid, Isabella's ma, but she's gone back to bed," said Beth.

"I heard her and the Mister moving about early this morning. When I entered the kitchen to start breakfast, I was surprised to see them up. Unless she has an early morning shoot, Miss Andrews usually sleeps past noon."

"That's understandable. I know first-hand how grueling filming schedules can be. The good news is the location shoots are about completed. Hopefully, when you return home, the agency will have found Emma a new nanny."

"We can hope," Alma said, raising her hands, crossing stout fingers. "But in all honesty, Beth, I'll be a happy camper when this film is finished. It's been miserable living with Miss Andrews. Nothing but complaints."

Beth frowned. "I thought Skye loves your cooking."

"Oh no, not about the cooking. About the movie. It's been nonstop. The director this and the director that. Mr. Greyson does his best to calm her down but . . . Isn't it wonderful the way he and Emma have become so close?" Alma didn't even take a breath allowing Beth to respond. "It's always been obvious how much he cares for the little girl, but now he's taken on the role of a real dad to Emma." She raised a finger to her lips. "Now, keep this hush-hush, but I overheard Miss Andrews talking to Tim, her ex-husband, on the phone last week."

Beth knew she should stop Alma from sharing any back fence talk. But gleaning a juicy bit of gossip was one of her weaknesses. A habit she wanted to break . . . sometime. But even so, eavesdropping and bits of gossip had served her well in her escapades as a sleuth.

"Well . . ." Alma leaned her considerable girth over the chair's armrest closer toward Beth and lowered her voice. "Seems like Tim is willing to accept Mr. Greyson's offer and allow him to adopt Emma."

"Really?"

"Tim is the shoe manager at the Walmart in Torrance. They're barely scraping by living in a rented one-bedroom house. The children sleep in the tiny living room." Alma shook her head. "His wife is pregnant again. They already have three kids of their own, all under the age of five. Well, the last two were twins. Precious baby girl and boy." A soft smile crossed her lips. "One day Lexi, God rest her soul," Alma said, making the sign of the cross, "had to study for an exam, so I took Emma to her father's for visitation. His new wife is hardly as beautiful as Miss Andrews but is pretty and so very nice. She's a stay-at-home mom. Which, of course, makes their financial situation even more difficult."

"Truly a sacrifice nowadays for mothers to stay home with the wee ones."

"If I've understood correctly, Mr. Greyson is willing to buy the family a three-bedroom house. And give them a bundle of cash, you know, for taxes and new furniture."

"How do you know this?"

"I overhear a lot when I'm serving dinner."

"Does Emma know?"

"Heavens, no." Alma shook her head. "She rarely eats with the adults. We usually have our dinner an hour before and in the kitchen."

Beth tilted her head and spied Emma galloping toward her. She'd changed into her bathing suit but still wore the mask. There was no sign of Cloud. She waved a manila envelope in her hand.

"Here are the pictures, Auntie Beth."

With a radiant smile, Emma dumped the envelope's contents into Beth's lap and grabbed the top photograph. "I've named this girl kitty Ginger. You can tell she's a girl because she has long eyelashes." Emma pointed to the little furry red and white kitten's bright green eyes.

"Ah, indeed."

"And this one—"

"I might as well give up on getting any sleep," Skye's voice boomed. "Sounded like a herd of elephants racing through the house."

Emma jumped, and Beth turned in Skye's direction.

"Alma, take her somewhere," Skye said. "All of this ruckus has disturbed my serenity. I'll have to spend at least an hour meditating to reclaim my sense of well-being."

Alma rose and grasped the little girl's hand. Emma looked downward as if studying the pavers beneath her feet.

"And you young lady," Skye said, eyeing Emma, "should know better. I have to work tonight. If I give a miserable performance, it'll be your fault."

"Skye," Beth said. "Don't be so harsh with the wee one. She only wanted—"

"I don't care what she wanted. My interior serenity and well-being override any silly thing that Emma wants."

"Sorry, Momma," Emma said, still looking downward.

Beth's blood boiled. *This little tirade proves Skye hasn't changed. The world still revolves around Skye and her needs.* Without realizing it, words flew from her lips. "That's no way to be talking to your precious daughter. Are you aiming to steal away Emma's joy? Have her transform into a glum little girl? Make her feel dejected. Alienated. Unloved. Because from what I've just seen, you're doing a bang-up job."

Skye covered her eyes with her hands. "Of course not," she whispered. "But Beth, you know how important this movie is. I have to be on. Flawless in my delivery. My acting brilliant."

"Your job is more important than your daughter's love?"

Skye dropped to her knees, lifted Emma's face, untied the mask, and placed it on the ground. "Forgive me? I'm sorry for being mean. Sometimes even mommies make mistakes." She wiped away the tears slipping down Emma's face. "I love you, my little cat-girl." She brushed Emma's cheek with her lips.

"I love you too, Momma." Emma threw her arms around Skye's neck and kissed her.

After giving the child a quick hug, Skye stood. "I see you're ready for a swim. I'll change into my suit," she said, touching her silk robe, "and I'll join you. Afterward, how about you and me go fishing?"

Though her cheeks were still wet, Emma laughed. "You want to fish?"

"Why not? I think you'll be an excellent teacher."

"Are you afraid to put a worm on a hook?"

Skye made a face.

"Don't worry, Momma. It's not hard. Fishing just takes practice." Emma raced to the pool and jumped in.

Skye barely looked at Beth before hurrying away.

Beth remembered how Skya as an unwanted child bounced from one foster home to another. And winding up in a group home that she escaped by marrying her first husband. Emma's dad.

Even if Skye had never experienced her own mother's love, her behavior had been inexcusable.

"I thought Skye had changed, but I guess—"

"It's the movie and the murder of the director that's got her on edge," Alma said. "I'm certain that's it."

"You're probably right," Beth said, watching Emma doggie paddle across the width of the pool.

"So, you think that Isabella's mother killed the director?"

Alma's words startled her. She'd been replaying the scene in her mind between Skye and Emma. Skye had bent over backward to make amends with her little daughter. So she couldn't really stay angry at Skye.

"Miss Andrews certainly didn't do it," Alma continued, "though sometimes she seems angry enough to commit a murder."

For an instant, the thought of Skye committing the murder didn't seem so impossible. *Could the stress caused by working on the movie set have pushed Skye over the edge?* Beth chewed her lip and wondered.

Chapter Thirteen

"I'm not a fan of Hugo Daines," Skye looked straight ahead as if talking to herself.

Beth sat next to her on the Lexus SUV's center row, directly behind Red, who was at the wheel. She reached over the console and placed a hand on Skye's arm.

"I don't like him at all."

Earlier in the day, Beth considered Skye a suspect. But abandoned that outlandish idea, chalking up to what Shane called her "flights of fancy". *Skye murdering her director? Impossible. After all, through the movie, Dark Grace, Thom provided Skye the opportunity to claim her spot at the top of the A-list.* But then, Beth thought, the director began to diminish her role infuriating Skye. *Enough to commit murder?*

"Don't like who," Beth asked, chasing her thoughts away.

"Of course, you wouldn't know him," Skye said with a shake of her head. "Hugo Daines started off working with Thom as a college intern. But after Hugo graduated college, Thom hired him. The guy is like twenty-four years old." Skye pressed her lips together and pulled a mirror from her Gucci gray snakeskin shoulder bag. She studied her reflection.

Beth believed Skye purchased expensive snakeskin bags to infuriate Zach, whose graduate studies focused on reptiles. *But then it could be a weird type of revenge on the species. Particularly the constrictor that tried to consume Emma.*

"His job as first assistant director took on an expanded role. Instead of managing the schedules and coordinating the cast and crew so the shoots ran smoothly, he started telling Thom how to do his job. The job of the first AD is to handle the logistics, not the creative part—that belongs to the director."

"I see." Beth nodded.

"But now," Skye continued, "he's been promoted to director in an attempt to finish the film on schedule."

"How can that be? He's extended the location shoots."

"But he's trimmed the studio shoots."

"Ah." Beth twisted her neck and looked out through the passenger window. The sun dipping lower on the horizon promised only a couple more hours of daylight. "A bit of a coincidence, I'd say, since I once knew a family named Daines." She glanced at Skye. Half of her face lay hidden in shadows. "They lived on the outskirts of our quaint, lovely village. I thought the family was peculiar. A standoffish lot. You'd never find a blessed one in the Green Clover, our local pub. Perhaps he's a relation of theirs."

Skye raised her eyes toward the vehicle's headliner. An exasperated look crossed her face. "He's not Irish, Beth."

"Of course not. Daines is an English name."

A smile flashed across Skye's face brightening her sour expression. It disappeared as quickly as it surfaced. "But now that you mention it, Hugo is a bit of an oddball. He wears the same clothes for like a week at a time and douses himself with so much cologne it's enough to make you choke. I mentioned his hygiene issues to Thom, but he shrugged my concerns away. He explained that geniuses tend to be eccentric."

"Thom Boyle thought him a boy wonder?"

"Thom might've thought he was brilliant, but I think he's creepy. Hugo wears dark sunglasses. You never know where he's looking when he's talking to you. But the thing that irks me the most is his unbridled ambition. Don't get me wrong, I'm all for ambition. But I think this guy was using Thom for his own purposes. It didn't take him too long to stab Thom in the back."

"What do you mean?" Beth shifted in the seat to see Skye better.

"He went straight over Thom's head to one of the producers. Told him a load of crap in an attempt to have Thom fired. It was all dumb stuff like Thom never should've replaced the original male lead. That he was wasting money building elaborate sets and renting actual landmarks to film scenes instead of using stage sets. But what really burned me up was that Hugo dared to suggest that Toni should play the female lead. My role. Thank God, Thom put an end to that nonsense. For all of Hugo's talent, I think Thom threatened to fire him."

"How do you know all of this?"

"People talk."

"So it's hearsay?"

"Not exactly. That same producer Daines went running to with trash about Thom has a thing for me. He wined and dined me one night a couple of weeks ago. Before, he attempted some half-assed sloppy moves, but, really, by then he was pretty soused, he spilled the fact that Thom was madder than a hornet with some of the underhanded tactics Hugo was pulling. Like trying to have me replaced."

"If that's true—"

"You think Hugo had something to do with Thom's murder."

"I wouldn't go that far. But it definitely needs to be considered."

"That's why I wanted you to come to the set tonight. To see if your *fey* gives off some vibes or whatever. Because if it's not Hugo, then it has to be someone else involved with the film. I mean, who in Baltimore would have a vendetta against an LA director?"

Beth had the same reason for wanting to visit the set. But she didn't want Skye to get her hopes up that she'd be able to finger the murderous culprit.

"Now, you mentioned a Toni—"

"Antonia Wright. Don't get me started talking about that witch."

Beth raised her eyebrows, surprised by the venom filling Skye's voice.

"Apparently," Skye said, "she agreed wholeheartedly with Hugo. Toni's been dying to steal my role. On top of that, she was bending Thom's ear in a major way." She took a sip from her water bottle, emblazoned with the movie's title. "The rumor is they were a couple but wanted to keep everything hush-hush until the filming ended. I have no idea what Cody thought about that. Not to mention Isa Reid, who made it clear she was gaga over Thom."

"Sounds like a real-life Peyton Place." All the names Skye was throwing out seemed overwhelming. Beth pulled a pad from her tote bag and jotted down the names. Once I'm on the set, she decided, I'll be able to figure out the players. *Or should I say, suspects?*

"I believe Thom hired Toni out of pity. Granted, she made a splash on Broadway and used to be an A-lister, but that was like a hundred years ago."

Beth squinted, trying to remember something about the actress. "Antonia Wright. The name sounds familiar, but I can't quite pinpoint—"

"It was in all the celebrity magazines. They were even guests on a bunch of those boring talk shows."

"Who?" Beth frowned.

"Zach and Antonia. Don't tell me. You don't know?" Skye's eyes widened in disbelief. "I thought the whole world knew that Zach and that woman had been an item."

Now the real reason for Skye's vitriol became crystal clear. She was jealous of one of Zach's former relationships.

"It's hard to imagine, but they were together for over two years. But in Zach's case, he became involved with a has-been who couldn't give him want he really wants. A kid."

Was that the real reason she'd changed her mind about allowing Zach to adopt Emma? To placate Zach and keep her marriage intact?

"Toni's at least twenty years older than him." Skye continued. "What the hell Zach ever saw in that obnoxious, overbearing, decrepit woman, I'll never know."

"Who knows why people are attracted to each other," Beth said with a shrug.

"Please." Skye shook her head. "It makes me want to barf that my husband ever found that troll sexually appealing. He might as well have hooked up with Dot Barnett." She squinched up her face in disgust.

A light began to shine in Beth's mind. It's no wonder Skye felt threatened by Dot's affection, misplaced as it was, toward Zach. *She might even believe her husband harbors some type of weird fetish for older women. But even if that's true, he married Skye, who's at least a half-dozen years younger than he. Could he have only married Skye believing she'd present him with children making him the father he longed to be?*

Beth remembered a conversation she'd had with Zach. His angry words about how Skye had concealed the fact that she'd had a fallopian tube ligation. Her tubes tied after Emma was born.

"I'm not some kind of an idiot," Skye said, "even if Zach swears he was only attracted to Toni's mind. She's some kind of engineer. Taught at UCLA." She clamped her teeth together.

"I'll let you off here," Red said, looking at them over the top of the seat. "After I park the vehicle, I'll meet you at your trailer."

"Whatever," Skye said, grabbing her water and opening the door.

Beth pursed her lips. *How many other celebs blather in front of their personal employees? And how many of their workers keep their mouths shut? After all, Red must've heard, if not all, bits and pieces of their conversation. Especially when Skye raised her voice in irritation. The Greysons must trust their security team implicitly. Or Skye is just plain clueless and doesn't care.*

Beth alighted from the SUV and caught up with Skye. "Are you prepared for your scene?"

"Surprising as it might seem, fishing with Emma earlier seemed to realign my equilibrium. I was stressed out wondering why the "boy wonder," as you called him, wants to redo it, thinking he didn't like the way I interpreted the scene. But I know I was good. Really good. So that can't be the reason why."

"Skye."

A man Beth didn't recognize hurried toward them.

"Hey, Cody. How are you holding up?" Skye didn't wait for an answer. "This is—"

"Sibéal." Cody shot out his hand, and Beth grasped it for a moment. "I recognized you from your public service announcements. They're sure to make a difference. Causing people to think before getting behind the wheel after having too much to drink."

"That's my intent. Thank you."

"I was Thom's personal assistant, but more than that we were, um, close friends. Partners, actually."

"I'm sorry," Beth said with a light touch to the man's shoulder. Towering over him, she detected emotion clouding his face.

He swiped the back of his hands across his eyes. "Physically, I'm fine," he said, focusing on Skye. "The irregularity in my heartbeat was due to the stress of seeing Thom that way." He cleared his throat. "I'm here to collect some personal items from the trailer. The police have completed their crime scene investigation, so I have permission to enter it."

"If you like, I could go with you," Beth said.

"I was kind of dreading entering the trailer alone."

"No problem. I'm happy to help out."

"That's so kind. Thanks."

"Why don't you go on then," Skye said. "Hugo is headed this way."

Beth glanced at the young man moving in their direction. Tall with a slight build, dressed in a T-shirt and faded jeans, aviator sunglasses covered his eyes. He stopped a good six feet in front of Skye and crossed his arms.

"Late again, Skye."

She shrugged.

"There's been a change in plans." He glanced at Beth. "Sibéal?"

Skye turned to Beth. "Hugo Daines. Director."

Daines' thin lips curled upwards. "Like this is fantastic. I can use you in the scene. I was starting to stress out over who was gonna play the role of the nurse. I just wrote that character into the scene and was planning to hire an extra who qualifies but now—"

"Nurse?" Skye frowned.

Ignoring Skye, he kept his focus on Beth. "You're still a SAG member? Or will we need a waiver? By the way, you were fantastic in *Roll of the Dice*. Why haven't you done anything else since it's obvious the camera loves you? If my opinion counts for anything, and believe me, it does, you've got *it*. Real talent."

Beth felt as if she's been caught up in a whirlwind.

"Look, let's get you to wardrobe and have makeup take a look. In the meantime, I'll review the script with you."

A whiff of Daines' aftershave caused Beth to cough. She held up her palm, signaling him to stop. "I'm about to head out with Cody. And truth be, I'm not interested," she stopped short as an idea took hold. *Being part of the production could allow me an opportunity to search for clues.* "Umm, well, maybe. A nurse, you say?"

He pulled the sunglasses up to his forehead. She saw sparks of eagerness in his dark eyes. "Well?"

"Sounds lovely. But first," Beth said, gesturing to Cody, who stood staring at the ground with hands stuck into the pockets of his khakis.

"Fine. Fine," Daines said, stepping away. "When you're finished, have him direct you to wardrobe."

Chapter Fourteen

For being a short man, Cody's gait was surprisingly long. It took Beth a few quick steps to catch up. When they reached the trailer, he pulled out a key and unlocked the door. He held it open so Beth could enter first.

She glanced around the trailer. Though impressive, it wasn't over the top like some she'd seen during her brief foray into the movie-making industry. Practical. Warm. Comfy.

"This is where his body was," Cody said, pointing at the floor. "And the knife." He took a few steps. "Here," he said, tapping the floor with the tip of his brown tasseled loafer. "As soon as the detectives released the trailer, I hired a cleaning crew to," he paused for a second, "to eliminate any traces of Thom's blood." With hurried steps, Cody headed to the rear of the trailer.

Beth detected the anguish in his hushed voice. She hoped her *fey* would offer an image or a semblance of who committed the crime. If she was really lucky, a clue. She closed her eyes and concentrated. Nothing.

She dropped onto the edge of a chair and ran her fingertips over the wooden armrest. *Perhaps if I touch something belonging to the director, the power of me fey will be released.* She turned in a tight circle taking in the trailer with one glance. She stopped in front of the mini-fridge and ran her fingertips across the stainless-steel door. *Nothing.* Not giving up, she moved to the couch and lifted a pillow, and pressed it to her chest. Beth chewed her lip, as a malicious shiver climbed along her spine. A vague sense of evil wasn't enough. After releasing the pillow, she hurried to the dining table and pressed her hand against its shiny surface. She closed her eyes again and waited for a sign.

"Are you okay?"

"Fine," she said, flashing her eyes open.

Cody held a book tucked under his arm and several framed photographs. "I've gathered what I came for." He jutted his chin toward the still opened trailer door.

Beth didn't want to leave just yet. "Photos? Of the two of you?"

He nodded.

"I'd love to take a peek. That's if you don't mind?"

"Mind?" He shook his head and placed them on the table as if they were a handful of precious jewels.

She pulled out a chair and sat. Cody followed her lead. The item on top turned out not to be a photograph but a framed certificate.

"What's that?" She attempted to read the parchment's heading penned in elaborate calligraphy. Before she could make out a single word, Cody dropped his hand and rested it on top of the glass surface.

"A commendation from the mayor of Los Angeles."

Beth opened her mouth, a question on the tip of her tongue, but Cody didn't give her a chance.

"Thom sat on the board of directors for an anti-drug commission. A handful of additional celebrities accepted that honor too. But for the majority, it was in name only. But unlike them, Thom took it to heart. He'd seen too many friends become addicted to that crap. A couple even died. He visited schools and other public events, giving presentations on the perils of drug use. I think he was more proud of this certificate than his Oscar."

Beth nodded, recalling how many of her friends had chosen drugs instead of food to maintain the perfect model weight. In the long run, it hadn't turned out well for many of them.

"Oh, well," Cody sighed, handing her a golden framed photograph. "This is a special one. I'd only recently become Thom's assistant, and the attraction between us was magnetic. This was our first date at the premiere of *Dangerous Allies*. With that film, he won the Oscar for best director."

"I remember. What a suspenseful movie. I nearly jumped out of my seat a couple of times." She gazed at the photo and zeroed in on Thom. Compared to Cody, who stood next to him with a wide Pepsodent smile, Thom looked gigantic. And dapper, dressed in a tux. His face looked kind and intelligent. He must've been quite a handsome man when he was younger, she decided.

"This one," Cody said, handing her another framed photograph, "was shot in Tahiti. We spent one Christmas there."

She smiled, seeing the two of them dressed in tropical shirts and Brooks Brothers shorts, raising cocktails as if offering a toast. She handed back the photograph and spied the book he'd laid on the table. "Was that his favorite book?"

"This?" He lifted the hardback protected by a dust jacket. "I don't know. It's Toni's book. He was reading it when." The words died as he shook his head. "I need to return it to her."

"Toni? Oh, Antonia Wright?"

He nodded. "The two of them had been spending a lot of time together." He motioned to the coffee-colored chenille couch. "They'd be snuggled there all cozy-like talking and giggling. Sharing books, discussing art, watching films. After work, they'd visit galleries, piano bars, the best restaurants in town."

"How did you feel about that?"

"I wasn't very happy." He shook his head. "Truthfully, I was a bit jealous. No. A *lot* jealous."

"I understand they've been friends for years."

"I suspected their relationship had long passed the friendship stage. There was talk," Cody said, folding his hands on top of the table, "that they'd become a couple. That Thom had proposed."

"Marriage?"

"Yeah." He raked his finger through his thick wavy hair. "I confronted him about it. Thom hemmed and hawed and never gave me a straight answer. But I had a feeling he'd fallen for her and didn't know how to tell me."

Now we're getting somewhere. "Were you angry?" *A jilted lover could be capable of committing murder in a fit of rage.*

"I wouldn't call it anger exactly. More like a crushing feeling of profound sadness. I didn't understand why Thom couldn't come out and tell me the truth. I believed that out of respect for what we had, I was at least entitled to know that much."

She closed her eyes for a couple of seconds trying to conjure up her *fey*. But it never seemed to work when she needed it the most.

"Sibéal?"

Both of them looked toward the doorway upon hearing the voice. A young lady stood there with a clipboard in hand. "Hugo sent me here. I'm Jean from wardrobe. Would you mind coming with me so I can fit your costume?"

"Sorry, Cody, but I have to go."

"That's alright. I have to return this book to Toni."

The little voice in her head told her that Antonia Wright was the last person Cody wanted to see.

Chapter Fifteen

Shane glanced around the family-owned restaurant. Beside a few glossy framed photographs of the Acropolis and Santorini, the stucco walls were plain and the lighting too harsh. He lifted the card menu and perused the list of sandwiches. He'd worked through lunch and didn't want to eat something heavy since he planned to return to the office afterward for a few more hours. It'd been a pleasant surprise when Gavin Collins texted him about them getting together for dinner.

"How's that plum job of yours going?" Collins asked.

Shane looked over the top of his menu at his former partner. For nearly six years, they'd investigated murders in the Los Angeles Sheriff's Department and had become close friends. "Started working on my first case."

A waitress, who couldn't be older than sixteen, stopped at their table. "Hi. I'm Amara. Are you ready to order?" She smiled, and the metal braces on her teeth glinted in the artificial light.

"Yep," Shane said, handing her the laminated list of à la carte offerings. "I'll have the burger with a side of *fasolia giganies*."

"The rack of lamb on the rare side and an order of the *broccolini*, for me," Collins said. "And please add a fresh truffle." When the waitress walked out of earshot, he said, "You order a burger at a Greek restaurant? A burger and baked beans. Really?"

"Hey, the burger is made with a mixture of lamb and beef. Can't buy one of them at McDonald's." Shane took a swallow from the chilled mug of IPA he'd ordered from the bar before sitting at the table.

Collins followed suit and took a sip from his glass of Pinot Noir. "Art theft must be a whole different ballgame from homicide."

"Yeah. There're no stiffs."

Collins patted the top of his taper fade haircut. "How do you like the new look? Chic, don't you think? Bonita likes it."

"Bonita?" Shane squinted. "You mean that woman from the domestic placement agency?

The one who sent Dot Barnett on a nanny interview with Skye Andrews?"

"Right. Bonita Garett. And you can't blame her for that."

"I can't, huh?" Shane noticed how Collins' hazel eyes seemed to sparkle. "So, you two dating?"

"Uh-huh. We went skydiving last weekend."

Shane raised his eyebrows.

"We've been seeing each other for only three weeks, but man, this might be the one."

"Look, when Beth gets back from Baltimore, let's all go out to dinner because I need to check out this girl before you do anything rash."

"I'll bet my last dollar you'll agree. She's damn amazing." Collins raised his glass. "Hey, why's Beth in Baltimore?"

"Holding Skye's hand."

Collins' skin, the color of milky coffee, crinkled on his brow. "Something happened?"

"You can say that. Skye stumbled across the murdered body of her movie director."

"You're kidding me? She found another body?"

"Hard to believe but true. Listen, it gets even better. My first case turns out to be three stolen works of art that belong to Zach Greyson."

"Now I know you're pulling my leg."

Shane raised his hand as if taking an oath. "God's honest truth."

"Any leads?"

"Looks like a professional heist. No forensic evidence yet. We're making routine inquiries with art dealers, local collectors, and galleries. That kind of thing."

"No pawn shops?" A playful smile slipped across Collins' face.

"Really?" Shane rolled his eyes upward at the ceiling. "I'm thinking it's an inside job. But the perp would have to be some kind of electronics expert. Not only was the alarm system disarmed, but so was the control panel that opens Greyson's fancy gate leading to his mansion."

"Hmmm." Collins swiped his thumb across his chin. "Have you considered that a big shot actor like Greyson might have staged the robbery? He hasn't been in a movie for a couple of years. And as the saying goes, 'There's no such thing as bad publicity except your own obituary'."

Shane pressed his lips together and considered Collins' suggestion. "A few days ago, I would've said that was plausible. But now," Shane said, shaking his head, "I don't think so, no. It was something Greyson said about the missing paintings not being his most valuable but the ones that mattered the most to him. That told me that the robbery was personal."

"Sounds like it," Collins said.

"Greyson believes a tech from his security company was behind the robbery. But my gut says that isn't right. Even so, I interviewed the techs that worked at the Greyson spread. Turns out the same two guys have been working his security systems for years. So, I did a bit of digging and the techs came up clean. No priors. And no complaints from customers. Of course, their financial records were a no-go, but it seemed unlikely they'd become art thieves out of the blue. Plus, both guys have air-tight alibis."

Collins tapped his fingers on the wooden tabletop. "Does Greyson have any disgruntled employees?"

"Yeah," Shane nodded. "A driver, he fired."

"Oh?"

"But, I don't know. Would a chauffeur have the know-how to dismantle a sophisticated security system?"

Collins half-shrugged. "Good point. But you are gonna check him out? Because he could have connections." He looked past Shane at the waitress moving in their direction.

"Here you go," Amara said, placing a large bowl of salad on the table along with two smaller dishes. "Um." She looked at Shane. "Weren't you on the six o'clock news yesterday? The detective investigating a robbery at Zach Greyson's place."

Shane squinted at the pretty teenager. "Yeah. You have any leads?"

The girl giggled. "No. But, I thought you might want to know that my mom thinks you're good-looking enough to be a movie star just like Z.G." She hitched a thumb over her shoulder.

Shane followed the direction of her gesture and spied a stout, heavily made-up lady with curly black hair. She offered him a pert smile and a finger wave. Then blew him a kiss.

Collins' eyes sparkled with mirth.

"Ah, tell your mom thanks." Shane lifted his mug and took a gulp of beer.

"Sure will. She was also wondering." Amara paused for a second. "Is that a wedding band?"

"Yes."

"Oh well, never mind." After a quick smile, she left their table.

"It's not funny," Shane said before Collins could comment.

"Hey, if it was me, I'd take it as a compliment that the owner of a successful restaurant has the hots for you." Collins tapped his index finger on his chin. "I always thought Dot Barnett had a bit of a crush on you. The way her face lit up when you walked into her room in the psych ward. You must really turn on the older set." He shook his head. "It still amazes me how you managed to marry a woman like Beth." The smile faded from his face. "I'm just hoping some of your luck rubs off on me."

"Speaking of luck, I can't imagine anyone having more rotten luck than Skye Andrews.

Stumbling across two stiffs in almost as many months."

Collins scooped a plateful of salad. He stabbed a chunk of tomato and raised his fork but held it mid-air. "What are the odds of that?" He shook his head and placed the fork on his plate. "But, I'd say she has nothing on Beth. Didn't she find a couple of waterlogged corpses in Venice?" Not giving Shane a chance to respond, he said, "How is she doing?"

"Good, considering. I'm kinda glad she's in Baltimore with Skye. Being there will keep her mind off of the tragic loss of her best friend."

"That's rough." Collins picked up his fork. "Maybe Beth will work through her grief by trying to figure out who killed the movie director. What's that thing called that guides her—her sixth sense whatsit?"

"*Fey.* Her grandmother filled her head with that nonsense, and Beth thinks she's got the gift."

"Maybe she does. 'Cause, it's just too damn coincidental that she's been able to finger two killers when the cops were at a loss."

"Don't tell me you buy into that hocus-pocus stuff?" Shane asked.

"The department has been known to bring in a psychic when all other leads have fizzled out."

"Maybe that's what it's gonna take to locate Greyson's missing art if the driver doesn't pan out. Because if we have to start interviewing Greyson's list of acting buddies, the investigation will take on the aspect of a three-ring circus."

"The media would love that. Not to mention those Hollywood tell-all TV programs."

"They've already started." Shane shook his head. "A reporter was sniffing around the Greyson estate. I read her the riot act, but I doubt that had much of an effect."

"Yeah. Those people are like a bulldog with a bone." Collins popped the tomato into his mouth and chewed while Shane filled his plate with salad. "Don't look now, but your admirer is heading this way."

Shane glanced over his shoulder and spied Amara's mother balancing a tray on her opened palm with a bright smile lighting up her face.

Chapter Sixteen

Beth stopped near the front steps of the Church of the Good Shepherd as a flurry of excitement swirled around her—tool belted men transporting equipment, little groups of extra players strolling around, wardrobers checking costumes, cameras flashing. In search of a quiet spot, she hurried along the cement walkway and discovered a grotto dedicated to the Blessed Mother. She sat on a bench and hoped the serenity offered by the flowering garden would calm her building agitation.

Even though she was supposed to memorize the lines, she couldn't get Skye out of her mind. *Fierce thick, she was.* Skye's eyes flashed daggers while she brooded during the entire ride to the church for the location shoot. Beth opted to leave her in peace, knowing any interference would make matters worse. *Let her cool down a wee bit. When Skye's ready, she'll share what's bothering her.* Hopefully, she won't cause an ugly incident by unleashing her pent-up anger. She was nearing the point of explosion.

"*Janey Mac*," she whispered, facing the statue's tranquil face. "I don't have much time to learn these lines." It turned out to be more words than she'd imagined, causing a flutter in her belly. She looked at the typed dialogue filling the pages. She didn't want to stumble over the words making a fool of herself, especially since the principal actor in the scene turned out to be Antonia Wright. She was anxious to meet this woman, who Skye considered a troll. *And hated because she'd been Zach's lover?*

She glanced away from the script, silently mouthed a line, and quickly checked the words on the page. When she looked up, a nun approached her. "Good evening, Sister." Beth jumped to her feet with a hint of a curtsy. Childhood habits were difficult to break.

"Oh, no. I'm not a real nun." The woman moved her hand in front of her habit. "I'm Louise Wilson. I'm portraying Sister Anna Catherine."

Beth's cheeks warmed even though it was an understandable faux pas on her part.

"You must be Sibéal. I recognized you from your ads for Noelle cosmetics. By the way, I love their products. But I wasn't aware you're an actor as well as a model."

"I'm far from being an actress. I've only one film under my belt. Apparently, I'm doing this," she said, holding up the script, "as a favor to keep the filming on schedule."

"By the way, call me Willie. Everyone does."

"And I'm Beth." She noticed the woman's smile was easy and warm. "Truth be known, I was roped into playing this part since I'm a SAG member, and the director had no one else." She gestured to the pale blue scrubs of her nurse costume. "I'm trying to learn these lines though I'm feeling the pressure, and I'm afraid—"

"Let me take a look," Willie said.

Beth handed her the script.

"The best thing to do is forget about the actual lines."

Beth wrinkled her brow, not hiding her confusion.

"What's important is to visualize the scene. As if it's a picture playing in your head. Here it says," Willie said, pointing at the page. "You're the first medical personnel on the scene. After a quick check of the victim's pulse. That would be this," she said, tapping her wrist, "since I'm playing the murdered nun. You determine the nun is dead. So, when the detective questions you about what happened, how would the character respond?"

"Well," Beth said, brushing her hand against her V-neck cotton shirt. "I guess the nurse would say something like . . . um . . ." She closed her eyes and took a deep breath envisioning the crime scene. "When I arrived at the chapel, something seemed wrong. The altar wasn't prepared for the morning Mass."

"How did you know that?" Willy said, taking the role of the detective.

"I attend the morning service before I start my shift. Sister Anna Catherine and I were friends. She considered her position as sacristan a sacred duty."

"Go on."

"I found the altar cloth on the chapel's closet floor surrounded by candles, which was odd enough, but it was draped over something. Without thinking, I lifted a corner of the material. And there lay Sister with blood pooled around her head. I checked her pulse, and she was alive. But the beat was weak. And then it stopped pulsating altogether." Beth flashed her eyes open.

"BINGO." Willie smiled. "You nailed it."

"I did? But that's not in the script."

"But it is the heart of what's written there. It's your personal expression. Your voice as an actor bringing the scene to life."

"Ah, lovely. I understand. My job is to make it feel real, not just repeat words written on a sheet of paper."

"Exactly." Willie looked over Beth's shoulder and made a face. "Here comes the director's pet. I'm in no mood to make nice to her. It's bad enough we're in the same scene. But at least, I'll be playing dead." She glanced at Beth. "Don't worry. You'll do fine. I'm sure of it."

She gave Beth two thumbs up before hurrying away.

"Are you Sibéal?" Beth turned toward the sound of her name.

"Yes?"

"I'm glad I found you. I'm Antonia Wright."

Antonia Wright was nothing like Beth imagined. The actress, who according to Skye's calculations had to be nearing sixty, belied that fact by her youthful appearance: her skin smooth and creamy, chestnut hair thick and shiny, and blue eyes bright and inquisitive. Beth couldn't help but chide herself for accepting Skye's description of the woman. *By now,*

I should know that Skye is prone to exaggeration, especially when it's about someone she dislikes.

The petite woman shot Beth a dazzling smile and held out her hand. Beth shook it. "Pleased to meet you, Antonia," Beth said.

"No need to be formal. I'm Toni. May I call you Beth?"

She nodded, wondering how Toni knew her anglicized name. She noted the plain navy pantsuit and suspected in real-life Toni would never dress so conservatively. No, she sensed the actress was used to glitz and glitter, not a working woman's attire.

"I know this isn't the ideal space to practice, but the crew is still inside the chapel, doing last-minute adjustments with the stand-ins. We could move into the main church."

Beth shook her head "It's quiet enough here."

Toni agreed and pointed at the ground. "Imagine the body there. A couple of extras will be portraying forensic investigators checking the corpse. I'll be facing you. So move here." She motioned to a spot in front of her.

In her new position, Beth caught a glimpse of Willie talking on a mobile. She looked up, and Beth caught her eye. Willie waved by moving her entire arm.

Toni twisted her neck to see what had gotten Beth's attention. "Look at her. Probably trying to score some drugs."

"Drugs?"

"Louise Wilson had a promising career years ago but threw it away in favor of cocaine."

Beth pursed her lips.

"With her career in the tank, she left Hollywood behind to live with a former boyfriend who is probably her supplier. Don't get me wrong. I'm not trying to belittle her. It's public knowledge she spent time in prison on drug charges in Baltimore. She didn't serve the full four years. Good behavior. But I wouldn't be surprised if she winds up behind bars again."

The warmth evaporated from Toni's voice, and the coldness replacing it, left Beth with a shiver. Antonia Wright couldn't hide her disdain for Willie.

"But Thom, soft-hearted Thom, felt bad for her," Toni continued. "When she came begging him for a part, he couldn't say no. Granted, the role may be pivotal to the story, but it's a minuscule part for an actor."

Toni's words struck Beth. *Could it be true? Because if Toni Wright is telling the truth, Willie's plight is similar to that actress in the book I've been reading. Margaret "Gibby" Gibson. She was mixed up in the 1920s drug scene and turned to prostitution. Hopefully, Willie hasn't stooped that low.*

"Shall we?"

"Oh, yes, of course."

After running through the scene only two times, Toni shook her head. "You're not half-bad. Your expressions are believable. You've managed to create an authentic sense of grief. It certainly won't be lost on the big screen."

Beth wasn't surprised. A cutting sense of anguish still clung to her after losing her dearest friend to murder last month. "I received excellent advice from—"

"Skye Andrews."

Beth wanted to correct her. Tell her the woman she'd disparaged had assisted her. Instead, she kept her mouth shut. She crossed her fingers in hopes Toni would share her opinion of Skye.

"I'm not surprised at all. Skye is a marvelous actor. Mark my words, it won't be long until she is awarded the coveted little statuette. That would make Zach so proud. Not that he isn't proud of her already, that is."

"You and Zach were close once—"

"We still are the best of friends. But what you're alluding to, I suspect, is our romance." Toni shrugged. "It was one of those autumn/summer affairs. I think both of us knew deep down it wouldn't last forever. Skye, on the other hand, is his springtime love." She tilted her head. "Speaking of the devil," she said, "here she comes."

Beth glanced away and spied Skye arm in arm with a priest dressed in a cassock. *Unusual dress for such a young priest. A touch of the theatrical, so. I'm certainly not going to make that mistake again. Handsome as he is, the priest must be an actor.* She turned to ask Toni, but the woman had slipped away. Beth caught a glimpse of her turning the corner, heading toward the front of the church.

"Beth," Skye called, waving her arm. It was then she noticed Red trailing behind them. A no-nonsense guise colored his face. She took a few steps toward the couple, and a moment later, they met up.

"This is Father Dan," Skye said, "and this is my BFF, Beth Getty, formerly known as Sibéal."

"Glad to know you," Beth said. "But a quick question. Are you truly a priest or one of the actors?"

"I guarantee you," Father Dan said, "I'm the real thing. Ordained eight years ago at Mt. St. Mary's Seminary located in Roland Park. Not far from here."

Beth exhaled a stream of air. "'Tis a bit perplexing trying to distinguish the actors from the authentic religious."

"In a story like this, I understand how it can be confusing. You know, Beth," Father Dan said with a shake of his head, "*Dark Grace* is based on an actual event. That's why I've been called in as a specialist. I spent a couple years training under Father Gabriel Amorth, the famed chief exorcist in Rome. I'm an expert when it comes to beliefs and practices of the occult."

Beth sucked in a breath of air. *Father Dan an exorcist. How can that be? He's too young—to engaging—a parish priest, yes. But . . .* "You're an exorcist?" She squeaked the words out.

"Every diocese in the country has a priest who's been trained to perform the Rite of Exorcism. I was assigned that privilege. But mainly,

I'm the associate pastor at," he said, tilting his head in the direction of the church.

"I'm a bit ashamed to admit it, but truth be known, I'm a bit fuzzy when it comes to the movie's plot." Beth shot a glance at Skye. "Never thought to ask anything more than if it was a crime film."

"Check the internet," Father Dan said. "You can locate information about the actual case. Type in Father Gerald Robinson. For anybody, it would be shocking but especially so for a Catholic."

"I'll do that." Beth reached inside her pant pockets where she'd slipped her mobile.

"Dan's been a rock," Skye said, still hanging on his arm. "I was furious that Hugo replaced me for Toni in that scene you're playing. My character was supposed to interview the nurse. But Dan was able to calm me down, as usual."

"It seems, Father, you truly are gifted." Beth shot Skye a smile. "But, in all honesty, I'm grateful you've been a pillar for Skye. She's been through so much—"

"He's heard all about it," Skye said, "and has helped me to come to grips with my recent losses."

She knew Skye was referring to her personal assistant who'd lost her life after a brave struggle to survive the machinations of a lethal killer a handful of months ago.

Willie approached them. "Daines is about to have a conniption fit. He wants you on the set like now."

Skye huffed. "That man," she said under her breath.

Willie lifted her long black skirt and turned from the little group. Beth watched her jog away as the rosary clipped to her belt bounced up and down.

"I wonder what's going to happen to Willie now that Thom won't be able to help her," Skye said. "She's had quite a rough patch. Drugs. Most directors won't even give her the time of day. Believe me, Hugo Daines tops that list."

"A shame," Beth said. "She seems lovely. Willie helped me learn my lines."

"I didn't know that about Willie," Father Dan said. "I'll keep her in my prayers along with you, Skye."

"I'll take all the help I can get. Especially since you have a direct line with—" Skye pointed to the sky streaked with wisps of pinks and violets. "Come on." She linked her arm with Beth's and hurried toward the church.

When they entered the narthex, Beth's stomach flip-flopped. She couldn't keep her hands from shaking. *Jitters.* The exact sensation she experienced as a new model about to take the runway. But once all eyes were on her, the nervousness fell away. She hoped as much would happen now.

Beth glanced at the main sanctuary and murmured a prayer under her breath. Alongside Skye, they approached the side altar that substituted for the hospital chapel. A crowd of people spilled into the church where an array of wires ran along the floor. With a quick sweep, she noted Hugo stationed behind a camera, a bank of lights, and the boom operator holding the mic. Willie took her place on the floor and assistants huddled around her preparing the scene. One of them covered her with a crisp white cloth dotted with red drops that Beth imagined were supposed to be blood.

Daines left the camera and approached Beth. "Looking great. How do you feel?"

Beth's stomach tightened. "Okay," she murmured.

"Good. Good. This is what I want you to do." He moved close and his breath brushed her cheek. She stepped away.

He pulled off his sunglasses and pointed toward the side-chapel. "Walk in there, frown, and then with slow, tentative steps approach the shrouded body."

"Right."

"I want to see hesitation. Your nerves on edge. A tremor would be good when you crouch over the body and lift up the edge of the altar cloth."

The nervousness bit won't be acting.

"Gasp. Reach for her wrist. Got it."

"Yes," Beth said, waiting for the word that would alert her to begin.

He moved back behind the camera. "Action," Daines firmly said.

She did as instructed. Once, twice, three times, and then she lost count. Though Daines praised her again and again, stating she was a natural, he wanted shots from different angles. After what seemed half the night, the director moved on to the next scene. Where she'd say her lines to Toni Wright.

Adrenalin pumped through Beth. She'd been down that road before and knew how it felt to discover a dead body. Daines hustled Beth to her mark. It wasn't until then that she realized Skye was to be in the scene—though silent—standing next to Toni. Once the camera started rolling, the words flowed naturally, as Beth slipped into the zone, assuming the persona of a nurse discovering a murder victim. She was surprised when after only doing her bit four times, Daines called, "Cut. Print."

Beth stepped away from the chapel, walked down the nave's main aisle, and slipped into a pew a bit disappointed that her scene had ended. *It couldn't be that I enjoyed acting? Could it?* Not wanting to analyze her feelings, she shifted on the padded bench and caught a glimpse of Red seated across the church, ever diligent in protecting Skye.

She closed her eyes as a flood of exhaustion washed over her. Fighting the desire to sleep, she plucked out her mobile, hoping that pulling up the information on Father Robinson would keep her awake. Beth read the account of an ordained priest linked to a cult of sadomasochistic clerics who dressed as nuns when they allegedly sexually abused and tortured children. The words shocked her. Any vestige of weariness dissipated as she sat ramrod straight in the pew. Never had she heard of such a horror. She scrolled down the list of articles attempting to digest the words glowing from the mobile's screen.

The piercing sound of a siren jolted her. Blaring alarms were commonplace in cities, but this one sounded like it was right outside the church. She looked in Red's direction, but he'd left his spot in the pew. A couple of police officers entered the church behind a man she gathered was a detective. Then it dawned on her. *They're shooting a new scene.* She resumed her search on her mobile's internet.

Before Beth could read another word, a loud commotion filled the sacred space. She twisted in her seat as agitated voices bounced against the sanctuary walls. She stood, exited the pew, and moved closer to the side-chapel in time to witness Skye being escorted out. Her wrists handcuffed.

Chapter Seventeen

Shane rolled over in the bed and reached for the ringing telephone. He glimpsed the time on the nightstand clock. 1:47. He was used to getting calls in the middle of the night when he worked Homicide, but he'd figured the Art Theft Detail would keep more regular hours.

"Dalton," he said, jamming the receiver against his chin.

"It's me. Something terrible has happened."

"Beth? Are you okay?"

"No worries, I'm fine. It's Skye. I'm afraid she's been arrested. For the murder of Thom Boyle."

"What?" Shane tore off the sheet, flipped his legs over the mattress, and sat upright.

"I'm at the precinct. Been here most of the night. The detectives are still interviewing her. This insanity has done my head in."

"Skye couldn't be arrested on suspicion. There has to be forensic evidence."

"Evidence?"

"Something at the crime scene that links her to the murder."

"She found the body, for heaven's sake."

He heard the strain touching her words.

"Look, Beth. There's no use trying to imagine the reason why she's in custody. We'll have to wait—"

"The officer on the desk told me if Skye is booked, she may not be arraigned for forty-eight hours."

"Sounds right."

"I haven't spoken to her. So I have no idea if she's contacted Zach or not." Beth paused. "She should've contacted her lawyer, who probably told her not to say a word. But knowing Skye, she didn't pay any mind. She's been in the interview room for hours. Her outrage at being considered a suspect has probably clouded her good judgment. Causing her to fight tooth and nail to persuade the detectives she had nothing to do with the murder."

"Which isn't the smartest move."

"I'm scared for her."

Shane swallowed hard. He wanted to offer reassuring words but didn't want to give Beth false hope. "We can only wait and see what happens."

"If she didn't contact Zach, and I've got a sneaking suspicion she didn't, he needs to know."

Shane guessed what was coming next.

"Red, one of the Greyson bodyguards, was about to ring Zach. But I stopped him. You're experienced in delivering bad news from when you worked Homicide. So, I thought—"

"No problem. I'll phone Greyson."

"A call? Really, Shane?"

He rubbed his eyes with the heels of his hands. "You want me to go over there?"

"Ah, darlin' that'd be lovely. Zach's sure to benefit from the support you can offer."

"Alright, then. I'll drive over to the mansion and give him a heads up. Before the media makes Skye's arrest into a public spectacle. But knowing how those vultures operate, I might be too late."

"The news reporters have been camped outside the station for an hour just hoping, I bet, for a scandalous story to break."

"I'm not surprised."

"This is a nightmare. And there's Emma to consider. If the police detain Skye, how will I break the awful news to the wee child?"

"You'll do what you do best. Explaining the situation with a gentle touch and a glimmer of hope."

"Thanks, but—"

"You sound exhausted."

"Dead on me feet."

"Have one of those bodyguards take you to the house. And then get to bed."

"Won't matter. How will I be able to sleep?"

Shane cursed the miles separating them. He wanted to hold Beth close and chase her fear away. "I can't promise things are gonna work out for Skye."

"But Shane, you know she isn't capable of murder."

"Truth is Betty, we really don't know what a person is capable of. Look, there's a homicide detective I worked with when we were in Baltimore last spring. Jeremy Fox. I'll contact him. See if he knows anything."

"That's a brilliant idea."

He detected a trace of relief in her voice.

"This Detective Fox might even be questioning Skye as we speak," Beth said. "If he's half the investigator you are, he'll come to the conclusion that Skye had nothing to do with the murder."

"But there must be evidence linking her to the crime."

Her sigh filled his ear.

"Skye's been angry about her role being altered in the film," Beth said. "She harbored ill feelings toward Thom Boyle, but truly Shane, I don't think Skye is capable of murder. Not really."

"So, you think she might have—"

"Not actually. No. You know how my imagination has a way of—"

"Leading you to flights of fancy. So your *fey* hasn't offered any insights." He wanted to swallow the words the instant they'd escaped his lips.

"It hasn't."

He blew out a puff of air. Luckily, Beth hadn't detected the trace of sarcasm lacing his comment.

"I better go," Beth said. "I miss you *a chuisle mo chroí.*"

"Miss you too, my darlin' Betty Getty." The sound of the phone's soft click sounded in his ear. He entered his walk-in closet, reached for a pullover and a pair of jeans, and dressed.

Twenty minutes later, he sat in his cruiser directly outside the closed wrought iron gates blocking entrance to Zach Greyson's estate. Shane drummed his fingers against the steering wheel as the dashboard clock read two-forty-five. He hated the idea of waking Greyson in the middle of the night, but it would be way worse if he found out about his wife's arrest by some pesky reporter on the morning news. He looked in the direction of the mansion and couldn't see much more than the roofline. He tapped his cellphone screen and waited. A groggy voice sounded in his ear.

"What?"

"Greyson. This is Dalton."

"Dalton?"

Dead air filled the connection for a couple of seconds. Shane imagined he was trying to shake off sleep.

"Did you recover my stolen art?"

"We need to talk. I'm at your gate. Let me in."

"Okay. Right."

Shane slipped the phone away and waited for the gate to swing open. It happened quicker than he'd imagined. He drove down the long driveway and focused on the house lit up like a Christmas tree. He parked in the semi-circle, jumped out, and headed to the front door. When he got there, Zach leaned against the doorframe, smoking a cigarette, dressed in a cashmere sweater and a pair of faded jeans.

The only time I show up at Greyson's mega-mansion is during times of crisis. First, Emma, then the stolen paintings, and now Skye's arrest. Hopefully, a false arrest, Shane thought with a sigh.

111

"What's up that you had to barge over here in the middle of the night?" Zach threw the smoke to the ground.

"Let's go inside."

Zach moved away from the entrance, and Shane stepped past him. The foyer set the stage for the entire house. Way over the top.

"You've never been the bearer of good news, so I take it this isn't good," Zach said, ushering Shane down a windowed corridor and into a vast library. "Have a seat." He dropped on top a leather hassock. "Well?"

Shane stood facing him. "This isn't official business. But I need to discuss a serious situation."

Zach frowned. But as if remembering something, he stood and moved toward a group of bottles arranged on a glass-top liquor table. "Bourbon?"

Shane nodded. He remained silent until Zach handed him a tumbler, and he took a reasonable swallow. "It's about Skye."

"Skye?" He narrowed his eyes. "She's okay?"

"She's been taken into custody—"

"What?"

"For the murder of the movie director."

Zach sunk back onto the hassock, his face a mask of confusion.

Shane looked into the glass he clutched, allowing Zach a few moments to process the news. "We didn't want you to hear it from an unreliable source."

"You mean the damn media."

"I'll contact a Baltimore detective I know and get to the bottom of this." He wasn't sure if Zach had comprehended the severity of the situation. "Skye's arrest means the cops have moral certainty that she's the prime suspect."

"Moral certainty?" Zach narrowed his eyes. "Skye's not capable. No matter how pissed off she was at Boyle. Skye wouldn't hurt him, let alone do him in. No, never."

"I understand. But perhaps some kind of accident led—"

"I was there. Right after she found the body. She didn't have a speck of blood on her hands or clothing." Zach began pacing. "Skye may be a lot of things, but she's not violent." He paused for a second and squinted as if trying to remember something. "I swear to you, Dalton," he said, as his voice rose filled with emotion, "Skye didn't kill Boyle."

A young woman clad in a silky robe entered the room. "I heard voices."

Shane looked from the woman to Zach with a question on his lips. *He couldn't be cheating on Skye again?*

"Go back to bed, Sofia," Zach said.

She turned to leave.

"Wait. Make us some coffee."

She padded out of the room.

Shane stood and stuck his hands into his pockets. *How stupid can I be? Sofia's one of the maids. Involved with that bodybuilder who was a suspect in the Lexi Horne murder.* "I'll get back to you as soon as I know something."

"Don't go."

Desperation colored Zach's face. Shane hadn't seen that look since the life had almost been squeezed out of Emma. But a second later, his jaw tightened, and he pinned Shane with a penetrating stare. "I want you here. That way, I'll have immediate access to the information you get out of that Baltimore detective."

"Alright." Shane downed the remainder of his drink. "I'll stay."

With his lips pressed into a tight line, Zach nodded, moved to the arrangement of bottles, and refilled his glass.

Shane wondered why Zach had ordered the coffee. But he figured that learning your wife is being interrogated for murder would drive even a teetotaler to drink. He glanced at the actor who seemed preoccupied gazing into his glass of bourbon.

Leaving Zach to his thoughts, Shane walked along the edge of the library. The scent of leather and wood polish filled the air as he looked at the cherry wood shelves checking out the book titles. "Ah," he said under his breath and freed a large volume from a shelf. *The Four Books of Architecture* by Andrea Palladio. Cradling the hard-covered tome, he sat at Zach's massive desk and gingerly turned over the ancient leather case. The architectural treatise had been translated into English and published in 1715, according to the date printed on the title page. He squinted at the archaic words and, after a few minutes, gave up reading and instead studied the magnificent illustrations.

Sofia entered the library, but this time dressed in a maid uniform. Shane took the cup she offered him. He sipped the piping hot coffee prepared to wait for the hours to pass until he could contact Jeremy Fox, the Baltimore detective. He placed the cup on the desk's mahogany surface and stared at the book's browned brittle page.

Chapter Eighteen

Skye sat in the small windowless room and waited. The intensity of her initial outrage had dulled due to exhaustion. And frustration. *How many times do I have to tell that idiot detective I didn't do it?* She crossed her arms on the table and laid her head down. She'd drifted off, but the sharp slam of a door jolted her upright.

"Sorry to keep you waiting. I'm Detective Fox. Jeremy Fox."

A different detective. Skye looked at the tall, thin man with sparse blond hair but said nothing. *Maybe this one will be reasonable.*

"Can I get you something to drink? Water, coffee, a Coke?"

"I just want to get out of here. I worked most of the night and need to go home. So whatever it is you want to ask me," she said, "make it quick."

"I understand," he said with a tiny nod. "But the length of this interview is up to you." He glanced at the legal pad he brought with him, laid it on the top of the circular table, and pulled a pen from his shirt pocket protector. "You *do* understand why you're here."

She stared at him.

"Miss Andrews, we suspect you had something to do with the murder of Thompson Dale Boyle."

"That's ridiculous."

"We have physical evidence."

"Evidence? What are you talking about?"

Fox pursed his thin lips and stroked his pointy chin. "You discovered the director on the floor in his trailer, but you didn't try to revive him?

Didn't the dispatcher instruct you to perform CPR? But you refused. Is that correct?"

"For good reason," she spat. "Thom was already dead. His skin was gray. And I know from experience that happens fifteen minutes after someone dies. Anyway, his throat was cut. He wasn't breathing."

"You knew he was dead because you shot him?"

Her mouth dropped. "I shot Thom? You must be out of your mind. I had nothing to do with Thom's death."

As if ignoring her, Fox said, "The slice across his neck was only superficial. The word—CUT—painted with blood on the floor next to the body was what? For theatrical effect? You are an actress, after all."

She stood and walked toward the door.

"We're not finished." He jumped to his feet, moved next to her, and gestured toward the table.

"I have nothing more to say."

"Like everyone else on the set, you gave us a sample of your DNA."

"So?"

"Your carelessness doesn't make sense. Answer me this. Why did you leave the knife behind? We found traces of your DNA on its handle."

She spun around, faced him, and placed her hands on her hips. "That's absurd. I didn't go near that knife. I barely looked at it, let alone touched it."

"I've talked to a number of your associates."

She stepped closer to the door.

"Please," Fox said, ushering her back to her seat.

Skye jerked her shoulder away from his hovering hand and flumped into the hard chair with her arms clasped against her chest.

"Time after time," he continued, reclaiming his spot across from her, "every single interview eventually wound back to you."

He widened his eyes. Skye noticed they were a dark, chocolatey brown. She couldn't understand why they seemed warm and kind. A bit sad. And at odds with his words. She didn't want to listen anymore, now utterly disgusted by his charade. But he kept talking. His chatter made her head spin.

"I need something to eat. A bag of chips from the vending machine. Anything. I feel woozy."

"No."

"How can you refuse me something to eat? A candy bar then."

He shook his head.

Skye wasn't used to her requests being denied. She pouted.

"Other forensic evidence was found at the murder scene—hairs and fingerprints—that we suspect belong to you," Fox said. "In addition, Hugo Daines, along with others, attested that during the entire filming, you and the deceased were at odds with each other. That you made a threat on Mr. Boyle's life."

She rested her head against her opened palm. "Yes, that's all true. Thom and I had several disagreements. Artistic differences. And words said in the heat of anger. No. Words voiced in frustration. But, Detective, words are only words." Skye lifted her head and looked directly into his eyes. "I've heard what you have to say, but now you're going to listen to me. If you want a viable suspect, I suggest you grill Daines."

His face remained set like granite.

"Hugo Daines is ambitious. He'd do about anything to become a successful director even, I suspect, kill for it. He's the director now. Doesn't that prove something?'

Fox didn't answer.

"There are others just as suspicious."

"We've looked at all—"

"Then look again," Skye said. "Something was brewing between Thom and Antonia Wright. They always had their heads together, laughing as if sharing some inside joke. Constant chatter about books and authors as if they comprised their own private book club. And the kissing. Seemed like they were always kissing. Foreheads, cheeks, lips."

"Friends do kiss." Fox pulled his eyes from her and jotted on his pad.

"Have you checked Thom's computer? Read his emails? Texts? I'd bet my last dollar he was falling for her. So, then. Where does that leave Cody Evans—Thom's lover? He's mild-mannered and a bit mousy, but jealousy makes people do funny things, including murder. Revenge, Detective Fox. Isn't it always about revenge?"

He tented his fingers under his chin but made no move to stop her.

"Then there's the teenager, Isabella Reid, whose mother keeps a tight rein on her. I don't know how the girl breathes. But she escaped once. Had a clandestine affair with a leading man nearly two decades her senior."

"You would know this," he said, tapping his pen against the pad, "because Reid was involved with your husband."

Angry words sprung to her lips, but she swallowed them. "I know because she told me. And it wasn't my husband. As a result, she became pregnant. Isa wanted to keep the baby, but her mother forced her to have an abortion." Skye took a deep breath. "And speaking of her mother, Jane, it's public knowledge she attacked a director last year. He'd become a little too chummy with Isa. Jane would do just about anything to put an end to any romance involving her daughter. The thing is, the kid didn't keep it a secret that she was crazy about Thom." Skye shrugged. "Maybe the rumors were true about the two of them. If they were planning on marrying, she's of age even though Isa looks like she's fourteen. Then the goose that lays the golden eggs would be out of *Mommy dearest's* greedy little hands." She pursed her lips a second. "Still, there's a chance Jane was also having sex with Thom."

Fox folded his arms across his chest but moved closer to the table as if not wanting to miss a word.

"I assume you know that much by talking to Isa."

Fox's lips parted as if he was about to speak, but Skye didn't give him a chance.

"The bigger question is that if Jane was having sex with Thom, what if little Miss Isabella Reid got wind of that? She wouldn't be the first person to kill out of jealousy. Actually, I heard Thom was having sex with all three of them. Jane. Isabella. Toni." She counted the names off on her fingers. "Oh, and Cody too."

Fox moistened his lip with the tip of his tongue, uncrossed his arms, and leaned back in his chair. "Interesting. But, Miss Andrews, how do you explain your fingerprints on the knife that slashed the victim's neck?"

"Not that again," Skye's voice rose. "No." She shook her head. "You're lying. Trying to make me crack. Admit to a murder I didn't commit. I've watched those crime shows on TV and have picked up on the games you detectives play. But it's not going to work this time."

She stood and brushed her fingertips across the blazer, part of the costume she still wore. She could barely wait to discard the pantsuit and get into her own clothes. An image crossed her mind of snuggling in her king-sized bed with Emma and the kitten. She raised her eyes and riveted them on Fox. "I demand to speak to my attorney. Now."

"That's your right. If you do spend time watching those true crime programs, you know what's coming next. Skye Andrews, I'm arresting you for the murder of Thompson Dale Boyle."

Chapter Nineteen

Too tired to sleep, Jeremy Fox stared at the television screen, but his mind was elsewhere. He left the notes he'd scribbled during Skye Andrews' interview at the office, determined to forget about work. But he couldn't erase her from his mind. The anguished look of despair on Andrews' face haunted him as he handed her over to the patrol cop who'd transport her to Central Booking. Or was it a look of indignation, he wondered, closing his eyes.

About to drift off, the jangling of the phone startled him. He muted the TV, pulled the recliner into a sitting position, and grabbed the receiver from the nearby end table. "Fox," he said.

"Just checking to see if you're home," Tamera said. "You've had too many all-nighters."

He shook his head. *That woman treats me like I'm one of her kids.* He couldn't hold back a smile. "Yes, Mom. I made it home before curfew."

"You think you're funny, don't you?" She didn't wait for a response. "Did you catch the news?"

"Nah. I turned on a sitcom instead. An old rerun of *Seinfeld*. Kinda funny though," The fib slipped out easy enough. He'd never been untruthful to Tamera before, and to lie over something as stupid as the late-night news made little sense.

"Top story on all four local news stations," she said. "Even had footage of Andrews being led out of the station, handcuffed, and put into the patrol car. But I guess you can't blame the media. A Hollywood murder taking place in Baltimore is a once in a lifetime story."

"Seems some people get a thrill out of seeing celebs fall. Probably makes them feel better about their ho-hum lives." He yawned.

"Could be." Look, you're probably ready to hit the hay, so I'll let you go."

"Maybe we made a mistake."

"What do you mean?"

"About Andrews."

"I take it she didn't confess," Tamera said.

"Hell, no. She pointed the finger at people on the set that had a beef with the director. Except—"

"There wasn't any evidence to consider them suspects. You recovered touch evidence from the knife that matched Andrews' DNA."

"Well, yeah. But all that proves is she handled the knife. It was a gun that killed the movie director. A gun we don't have. The only evidence collected was Andrews' cells found on the knife handle and a strand of her hair located on the body."

"That's more than enough evidence needed to lock her butt up. You know, some of those damn celebrities think they're above the law. And Skye Andrews won't be the first to have committed murder. She'll be joining the ranks of the rich and famous killers from Claudia Longet and Phil Spector to Oscar Pistorius and dozens of others."

"Not if she didn't commit the murder."

"It's pretty obvious she's responsible."

"It's the knife that's bothering me."

"Give it a rest, J."

"It's too perfect. Only one set of prints and Andrews' DNA. Looks to me like she might've been set up."

Tamera sighed. "You're overthinking again."

"Maybe. Maybe not. Once the prints are analyzed, we'll know for sure if they belong to Andrews."

"And if the prints come back a match?"

"I don't know." He imagined Tamera rolling her eyes.

121

"It doesn't matter one way or the other," she said. "She's been booked. It's up to her lawyers to prove her innocence not you. You did your job, so forget about it already."

"But—"

"But nothing. What you need is a good night's sleep."

"Spot-on as usual."

"Alright then. See you in the morning."

"Night." Fox unmuted the set and dropped the receiver in his lap. He hoped the sports headlines would get Andrews out of his mind. He focused on the announcer's words. The Orioles had creamed the Yankees, always a reason to cheer. But when the story switched to the qualifying teams for the Euro Cup, he shut off the set. *Tamera's right. They'd done their investigation, and now it's up to the judicial system to find justice for the slain director.*

He walked into the kitchen and pulled open the refrigerator. Not much interested him until he remembered the leftover sub he'd placed in the crisper. He grabbed it, pulled loose the wrapper, and took a generous bite while still facing the opened fridge. He snatched a Natty Boh, twisted off the beer bottle cap, and took a long swig.

Fox made his way back to the recliner sofa with sandwich and beer in hand. But even before he sat down, his mind began replaying the interview with Andrews. He rewrapped the sub, placed it on the end table, and took another gulp of beer. His gut told him he'd made a mistake arresting her. *After all, a couple of months ago, I helped thwart an attack on her life.*

Fox shook his head. He'd only caught a glimpse of Skye Andrews that day at the Preakness Stakes. Heart-stopping beautiful, she exuded glamor and Hollywood glitz surrounded by adoring fans. *Well, mostly, one was aiming to kill her. And now she's suspected of murder.* "Life sure is stranger than fiction," he muttered.

He focused on the beer bottle, attempting to eradicate the images of Skye Andrews that had taken his brain hostage. He dropped down on the pebble gray chenille couch and took a sip of beer. His mind refused to shut down.

Granted, he considered, when the fingerprints taken from the knife were run through the system, there wasn't a match. *But, they were identified as likely belonging to a woman because of their size. And the only woman who seemed to have a beef with Boyle was Skye Andrews.* He paused, pressing his lips into a tight line. *According to Andrews, all wasn't well between Boyle and the assistant director, Hugo Daines. Plus there's the possibility of a jilted lover. Not to mention the stage mother, Jane Reid. Could the fingerprints belong to her and not Andrews?* He rubbed his eyes with the heels of his hands. "We'll know that much tomorrow when we get the fingerprint results," he said as if seeking affirmation from the empty room.

Fox stood, grabbed the beer bottle tighter, and started pacing. *If only we could've located the murder weapon. I wouldn't be surprised if it was tossed into the harbor, washed out into the Chesapeake Bay, and lost for good. We have the slug but no cartridge.* He chewed his lip, noting the recovered bullet was lodged beneath the director's collarbone, meaning the barrel was tilted upward when fired. Ironic, he thought, that the bullet was a .32 ACP and likely discharged from a Walther PPK. The pistol made famous by James Bond in the novels and the movies. He took a couple swallows of beer, thinking how apropos the weapon seemed for a real-life Hollywood murder.

Fox pursed his lips. *That's a small gun. The piece could've been concealed in a pocket or a pocketbook. Dammit. Should've done a gun residue test on Andrews but at the time . . .* He raised the bottle, surprised to find it empty. He walked to the kitchen for another one. A stupid mistake, he thought, twisting off the cap and raising the bottle. But before it reached his lips, he placed the beer on the kitchen countertop and rubbed his temples. *We need to get our hands on Andrews' clothing. Doesn't matter if they'd been laundered. Washing doesn't remove all particles of gun residue, but if she tossed them, they could be rotting away in a stinking landfill, God knows where.*

"Of course, she denied owning a gun," he said under his breath. "That claim will be easy enough to verify if the gun surfaces. Fat chance," he muttered. *If by some stroke of luck the gun shows up, the ATF will do a gun trace on the piece. And discover the owner. But then again, maybe not. There're countless ways to get hold of a "hot" firearm. Andrews' big brute of a bodyguard probably has connections. He could've picked one up with no questions asked.*

Though only conjecture, Fox sensed he could be onto something. The bodyguard. He searched his memory for the name. "Oh yeah," he whispered, "Bruno Ricci." *He could've ditched the pistol for her. Need another chat with him. First thing tomorrow. He glanced at his watch. It's already tomorrow.*

He returned the beer and sub to the fridge and headed to bed, hoping the case wouldn't haunt his dreams.

Chapter Twenty

Startled by an unexpected movement, Shane looked up from the architecture book. Sofia ushered a man inside the room. He looked familiar, but Shane couldn't place him. Sofia closed the door behind her with hardly a sound as the visitor strode toward Zach.

Not wanting to intrude, Shane stood and backed into a shadowy corner. But then, in a sudden flash and a turn of his stomach, he realized where he'd seen this man before. *Marc Hammond.* It wasn't only on the flashy TV commercials entreating undecided voters to elect him as California's newest state senator—he'd seen him in person—in court. Suave, smooth-talking, persuasive. A real showman.

"I've talked to Skye," Hammond said.

Zach jumped up from a cushy leather chair and reached for the lawyer's outstretched hand.

"I wanted to meet with you face to face," Hammond said. "Before flying to Baltimore."

Zach lifted the cigarette burning away in an ashtray, and inhaled the smoke.

"There's no easy way to say this." Hammond dropped his head for a moment as if studying the hand-woven carpet covering the floor.

Shane moved nearer to the two men.

"Zach, the truth is . . ." Hammond slammed his mouth shut, spying Shane. "I didn't realize you have a guest." He nodded in Shane's direction before refocusing on Zach. "What I have to say is extremely sensitive and needs to be discussed in private."

"He's okay," Zach said. "This is Detective Shane Dalton."

Hammond stroked his goateed chin. "Hmmm. Dalton," he said under his breath as if attempting to place the name.

Zach gestured toward Shane. "This is—"

"I know who he is," Shane said. "Lawyer to the *stars*. From what I've seen, you manage to get your clients off with only a slap on the wrist. I don't care who the hell you represent; superstars or working stiffs. Justice shouldn't be able to be bought."

"Not a fan, I gather," Hammond said with a lop-sided smile. An instant later, as if finally understanding Shane's charge, his expression went stone cold. "If you're suggesting some kind of bribery, Detective, you're sorely mistaken. The undisputed fact is that I'm a brilliant criminal defense lawyer. Which brings me back to Skye. She's been arrested. For the murder of Thompson Boyle."

"Tell me something I don't already know," Zach said. "Like how you're gonna get her out of that hellhole." He reached for the burning cigarette, placed it between his lips, pulled it out, and crushed it into the ashtray crowded with half-smoked butts. "Skye won't last even a few minutes in jail. She'll lose her mind," he said, raking his fingers through his dark, tousled hair. "You gotta get Skye out of there."

"Don't underestimate her. She's tougher than you think," Hammond said. "Look, she's okay. Really. Fuming mad, but that's to be expected. And she doesn't want you to worry. Skye wants you to concentrate on your work. She mentioned something about stolen paintings."

Zach waved his hand as if swatting away the lawyer's words. "That doesn't sound right. Not like Skye at all. My wife would want me to fuel up the jet immediately to get to her side. And that's what I'm going to do."

"Okay, okay. You're right," Hammond said. "But I talked Skye into agreeing that you need to stay put. It would be foolish for both of your reputations to be tarnished. After all, you were with Skye after she found the body. If you butt into Skye's case, you'll be scrutinized like a specimen under a microscope. That's the last thing we need."

"Makes sense," Zach said. "But—"

"But nothing. I won't have you encouraging the investigators to put two and two together. Not to mention the media will have a field day if there's even the slightest hint that you're involved. It's bad enough what this will do to her career. Probably destroy it." Hammond shook his head. "Why flush your career down the drain too."

"Skye didn't do it. She's innocent."

Hammond shrugged.

"What the hell? You think she killed that man." Zach's face flushed an angry red.

"I didn't say that. Look, I've got a plane to catch. Fingers crossed I'll reach Baltimore before her arraignment. Bail will be set. I'm sure of that. But it may be upwards of one-two million. Depending on the judge."

"I don't care how much it is. Just get her out of that damn jail." Zach wiped his hand across his face. "And when she's home, we'll go to a place like Morocco where there's no extradition."

Hammond narrowed his eyes. "You're not suggesting—"

"That she skips bail? Absolutely." Zach folded his arms across his chest. "Ever since Dalton broke the news, I've been weighing all the options. I need to get Skye somewhere safe. Where the law can't touch her."

Shane stepped closer to Zach believing the strain had broken him. "Skye on the run would only confirm she's guilty."

"What other choice is there? The media is gonna play this for all it's worth. And no offense," Zach said, glaring at Shane, "but I think the cops must be framing her."

"You're exhausted," Shane said. "After a solid eight, you'll sort things out rationally."

"I agree with the detective," Hammond said. "Even if Skye settled in Morocco where she'd be swathed from head to toe in one of those burka things, she wouldn't get away with it. Because of you." He puffed out a mouthful of air. "Zach, my friend, you'd lead the cops right to her doorstep. Because you couldn't bear being separated from her."

"What about Emma?" Shane asked. "She'll need you more than ever."

"Oh my God, Emma," Zach whispered. "How will the kid deal with losing her mother? My God—"

"Hold it." Hammond raised his palms, urging Zach to calm down. "If I do my job right, which I will, Skye will be exonerated of all charges. Free, to come home," he said, waving his arm as if attempting to encompass the room, "where she belongs with you and her daughter."

Hammond doesn't know the state of their marriage, Shane thought with pursed lips. Even if he couldn't abide the lawyer with his underhanded tactics, at least Hammond was committed to the welfare of both Skye and Zach.

"What if we lose?" Zach said.

"I know how to win over a jury. Especially if my client is innocent."

Zach dropped into a chair and buried his face in his hands. "When I talk to that cop in Baltimore, he better give me the whole story."

Zach's words were muffled, but Shane understood his meaning. He wanted to badger Fox. Force him to relinquish confidential information regarding Skye's case.

"What cop?" Hammond asked.

Zach lowered his hands. "Dalton knows a Baltimore detective. When he contacts him, I'm gonna demand an explanation for why they arrested my wife. And demand—"

"Like hell." Both men voiced their objections at the same time.

"But—but I need to do something. I can't just sit here."

"Your lawyer has offered sound advice," Shane said.

"I'd never steer you wrong, Zach, my boy," Hammond said. "Follow my instructions. Go to work, attend those Hollywood parties, and golf. But keep your lips cemented when it comes to Skye. Even when the media hounds you. Your response, no comment. Got that?"

"Yeah, I got it. But how the hell am I supposed to act like nothing's happened?"

"Don't you have a couple of Oscars around here?" Hammond asked.

"I hear you. Act like everything's cool. Gotcha."

"You look like hell. I mean, it's understandable. Hey, where's that maid?" Hammond said. "I'm going to have her warm up some milk and tuck you into bed." He strode out of the room, calling, "Maid. Maid."

Shane glanced at Zach, and he looked whipped. Shane guessed that he looked the same way. They'd probably both gotten about the same amount of sleep. "Try to rest. I'll talk with Fox, and if he knows anything, I'll contact you right away."

Zach nodded as Sofia entered the library with a puzzled look on her face.

Chapter Twenty-One

Skye stood in the overcrowded women's holding cell, believing she'd entered the bowels of hell. She rubbed her temples realizing the jammed-packed bench offered the only place to sit. A couple of women, who'd fallen asleep, rested their heads on the person's shoulders crammed next to them. But the majority of prisoners, waiting for their hearings, moved around the closed-in space like caged animals. Others, tired of standing, had dropped to the floor and sat on the varnished concrete surface. Skye shuddered, glancing in the direction of the toilet. A rail-thin woman hugged the stainless-steel bowl. The person crouched next to her couldn't wait and vomited on the floor.

Skye clapped her hand over her nose and mouth, not wanting to breathe in the fetid air, as she scanned the women around her. Their complexions ran the gamut from deep brown to pale pink. Some were scarred, most were tattooed, and a few sported fresh wounds—bruises, busted lips, scratched cheeks, eyes swollen shut. A number, she imagined, were prostitutes. Not dressed in slinky outfits, fishnet stockings, and fingerless gloves, these women wore flip-flops, shorts, and low-cut T-shirts stained with God knows what. Their eyes stared like lifeless hollows, and their arms a telltale story of drug addiction.

Disgust mixed with pity, but mostly, disgust filled her.

"Hey, hon," said a dark-skinned woman with hair shaved close to her skull, "What *you* in for?"

"It's a mistake," Skye said, not looking into the woman's eyes. "I won't be here long."

"Yeah, sister," said a heavyset woman who smelled like a brewery. "That's what everyone says. You look like a schoolteacher. Did you have sex with one of the kiddies?" Her laugh drowned out the sound of a woman retching.

Skye wanted to refute the woman's words but kept her mouth shut. If they knew who she really was . . . She thanked God for her conservative costume, hairstyle, and bland jewelry, which worked wonders in subduing her usual sense of glamor.

One of the women sitting on the floor piped up. "Real fancy earrings. Them real diamonds?" She rose on her knees and reached toward Skye. "Would look good on me."

Skye wanted to scream, "Leave me alone." Instead, she pulled the baubles from her earlobes and gave them to the woman. "Here." Even if they'd been diamonds instead of rhinestones, she would've gladly handed them over.

The woman stared at the earrings then looked into Skye's face. Tears streamed down her cheeks. "Ain't no one ever give me something so fine as these. Thank you," she murmured. "Thank you."

Skye turned away as her name was called. At first, she thought someone had figured out who she was. But no one, save the lady on her knees affixing the earrings to one of many vacant holes running along the side of her ear, looked at her.

"Andrews," the taut voice called again.

Skye circled around, waved her hand at the guard standing by the barred door, and headed toward her. The door swung open, and Skye stepped into the brightly lit corridor. She breathed relief, looked into her savior's face, and met a blank stare.

"Follow me," the guard ordered.

Skye did as she was told.

Freed from the holding cell, Skye thought things couldn't get any worse. It didn't take long to realize being booked for a crime was a lengthy process. Dead on her feet, she didn't care if they locked her up in a cell just as long as it had a mattress.

Skye loved having her picture snapped. And for the most part, didn't mind the paparazzi—sometimes she even posed—so they'd have a good shot for their celeb magazines. But having a mugshot taken rattled her. She could barely keep from shaking, holding the identification placard beneath her chin. That was nothing compared to being strip searched. As if she hadn't been humiliated enough, this did the trick. After being fingerprinted, she received permission to make a phone call.

Before being carted to Central Booking, Detective Fox had allowed her to telephone Marc Hammond. Marc wasn't her personal attorney. Her lawyer specialized in contracts. But according to Marjorie, her friend, and Marc's wife, he was a top-notch defense attorney. Skye's voice quavered as she'd explained her situation. Marc had been able to soothe away her fears with the assurance that he'd start the ball rolling for her release and exonerate her good name.

This call was pegged for Beth. Under pressure to keep it quick, Skye explained she'd been arrested but the nightmare would end soon since Zach would certainly pay bail, no matter the cost. After hanging up, a different female guard directed her to another wing of the building.

"To tell you the truth, I've never seen anything like it," the correctional officer said.

"Like what?"

"A prisoner moving through booking as quick as you. I guess this is what's meant by 'star treatment.'"

Skye tried not to but couldn't help but roll her eyes.

"I was wondering." The woman, dressed in a mannish uniform, pulled out a small pad stamped with the jail's name and a pen from a side pocket. "My daughter is a huge fan and would love an autograph."

Skye tamped down the profanity that wanted to burst from her lips, gulped a mouthful of air, and forced a smile. "I doubt that's appropriate considering the situation. But, give me her name and address. When I'm out of here," she said with a shake of her head, "I'll send her an autographed picture."

"Oh, okay." The officer's face fell.

Just as I suspected, Skye thought. *There probably isn't even a daughter. If I'd signed that page, it would've been up on eBay in a split-second. Skye Andrews' authentic signature from prison probably coupled with my mugshot.* "Where are you taking me?"

"Bail review. It's a hearing to determine if the bail that's been set for your case ought to be changed. Or if you should be released on your own recognizance under the conditions set by the Court."

"You mean I might be released. Tonight?"

"In your case," the officer shook her head, "I doubt it. Even if you can pay the bail. I mean, it's not like you offed some drug baron, which the judge would probably be grateful for." She smiled, revealing yellowish-brown stained teeth. "That would merit a medal. But you're accused of killing a bigwig movie director. A whole lot of people will want to see justice for that."

"Believe me, I'm one of them. Because I sure as hell didn't kill my friend." Skye wiped her sweaty hands on the prison uniform. She'd been ordered to wear the orange jumpsuit, and the outfit turned her stomach. Orange, she'd long suspected, wasn't her color. When this farce is exposed and the real killer caught, she swore to herself she'd never wear the garish color again. It would only remind her of the injustice she suffered at the hands of an incompetent police force.

"Here we are." The officer escorted Skye through a security door and down a corridor.

They entered a room where a middle-aged man dressed in a suit sat behind a Plexiglas wall.

"I've read the charge, Miss Andrews. How do you plea."

"Innocent. I'm innocent. I didn't do it, Judge."

"I'm not a judge. I'm a court commissioner."

Skye frowned.

"My job is to evaluate your case to determine if you're eligible for bail."

Skye chewed her lip.

"I don't consider you to be a danger to the community, so your bail is set at two million dollars. If you cannot make bond, you will be held at the Detention Center. However, I do deem you to be a flight risk. Therefore, if you leave the state of Maryland, you will be extricated and detailed in this jail. Do you understand?"

She'd agree to just about anything to get out of the ghastly place. She lifted her chin, looked him straight in the eyes, and said a resounding, "Yes, sir."

He motioned for the officer to step forward. Skye tapped her foot, wondering what would happen next.

A handful of minutes later, the officer directed Skye out of the hearing chamber. "You lucked out," she said. "The commissioner decided not to assign you to the general population but to the protective custody unit."

Not knowing what that meant, Skye didn't ask for details, but with a broken spirit followed obediently. They walked down a labyrinth of hallways until they stopped at a metal door.

"Here you go," the officer said, swiping a key card and opening the door. She escorted Skye into a small cell and pointed at the amenities. A bed with a lumpy mattress and a commode.

Skye stumbled to the bed and sat on its edge. The minute she heard the door shut, she jumped up and began to pace. Though her body ached for sleep, she forced herself to move back and forth across the cement floor. She'd stay awake until she was released. Since the very prospect of being locked up in a cage for the rest of her life would undeniably haunt her dreams.

Chapter Twenty-Two

Seated behind Zach's impressive library desk, Shane checked the time on his cellphone. *Four o'clock. Meaning it's seven in Baltimore. Any detective worth his salt would be at his desk. Unless he was already in the field. Only one way to find out.* He freed the business card from his wallet and tapped the numbers into his phone.

The phone rang twice.

"Homicide. Fox speaking."

"This is Detective Dalton from Los Angeles."

"Dalton? Oh, yeah, the attempted Preakness Stakes murders."

"Right. Fortunately, only the perp wound up dead."

"It's great when that kinda thing happens. So, what's up?"

"As you might recall that case centered on Skye Andrews. She's a family friend, and I was hoping you'd be able to give me an update on her status."

"Turn on the TV," Fox said. "The arrest has been made public, but I guess it might not've hit the airwaves on the west coast yet." His voice trailed off, and Shane heard papers being rustled. "I understand your concern. But, I'm not at liberty to divulge any specifics. All I can say is that the individual evidence collected at the crime scene points directly to the guilt of Miss Andrews. "

"I'm not doubting the veracity of your crime scene investigation. But she did discover the body and would've left trace evidence behind."

"There was a lot of traffic in the victim's trailer once the body was discovered, which could have contaminated the crime scene. But our CSI team was able to collect forensic evidence. Look, I get it, Dalton. Andrews is a friend of yours. Even so, there's nothing more I can tell you."

"Yeah, I understand. Thanks," Shane said.

"No problem."

The phone clicked off in his ear. "Our problems have just begun," Shane said, looking at the darkened screen. He glanced away from the cellphone as Sofia entered the room. "You're still up?"

"Can't sleep," she said.

Her voice held a touch of an accent he couldn't quite place. "I'm worried about Miss Andrews. Being arrested under false pretenses is frightening." Sofia shook her head. "I've heard stories from my grandparents. Of how people were thrown into prisons and never heard from again. Not to mention the horrors of the Holodomor."

Shane frowned.

"In my homeland. Ukraine. Never have I imagined such a thing could happen here. In America."

For a moment, he didn't know what to say to the young woman facing him. But he wanted to assuage her fears. "We have due process, so there's nothing to worry about. Skye will have a fair trial. A jury will determine her fate."

"Yes. But how is it that she would even be considered capable of doing such a terrible thing?"

He rubbed his eyes with his fingertips. "Evidence."

"Evidence," she spat the word. "Evidence can be planted."

He sighed. "Perhaps, but not in this case, I'm afraid."

Sofia let out a little gasp. "I can't believe—"

"Believe what?" Zach stood in the doorway, then strode across the floor and stopped in front of them.

"I think we could use some strong coffee. Do you mind?" Shane asked Sofia.

"Forget the coffee," Zach said. "Get some rest. You look exhausted."

After a quick nod, she crossed the library and exited the room.

"Smart girl," Zach said. "Completing a master's degree while working in the engineering department as a teaching assistant. I hired her as a downstairs maid, but, really, all she does is answer the door and fix coffee for guests. Leaves her plenty of time for studying and working in the university lab."

"Beth's told me how you're big on education."

"One of my chief interests." Zach walked to the arrangement of liquor bottles. "I imagine," he said, lifting the bottle of Woodford Reserve, "this will be necessary since you have news?" He poured the caramel-colored liquid into the crystal tumblers. He handed one to Shane.

"I contacted Detective Fox." Shane raised the glass and took a quick swallow. "I'm afraid it's not good. Skye's arrest wasn't some kind of mistake. There's forensic evidence."

"Evidence. What do you mean?"

Shane shrugged. "DNA. Fingerprints."

"Of course, they'd find biological evidence. She'd been in Thom's trailer countless times."

Zach's cellphone rang. He yanked it free from the pocket of his rumpled shorts and checked the screen. "Hammond," he barked at the screen. "Oh, Skye, it's you." he said, his voice softening. "Are you okay?" He tapped on the speaker icon and placed the phone on the desk.

"No. It's horrible. I'm being treated like some kind of criminal. You know I had nothing to do with Thom's death."

"Of course, you didn't."

"The detective said, oh, it's impossible. Insane, really. Said my DNA was on the knife that slit Thom's throat. Marc told me not to worry. That he's going to make things right." She whimpered but then cleared her throat. "Bail's been set. Get me out of here. Please, Zach. Please."

"Don't worry, my love," Zach said. "I'll wire the money. Just think good thoughts. With a little patience, you'll be out in no time. I'm gonna do whatever it takes to clear your name. I'll hire a private detective—"

"No. No, detective,"

To Shane's ears, her voice sounded stronger.

"Beth will find out," Skye said. "I trust her *fey*. Hold on." Her muffled voice offered unintelligible words. "I have to go. I love you."

The click of the phone dotted the final period of the conversation.

"I can't believe Skye thinks your wife's sixth sense is going to get her off of murder charges," Zach said. "That's ridiculous."

"Skye's under a lot of stress. Probably sleep-deprived."

"Yeah." Zach paused. "You know any good private investigators?"

"One or two I could hook you up with."

Zach nodded.

"Smart move on your part. Because if Skye is expecting Beth to uncover some new evidence, she'll have a long wait. I don't deny that Beth's been damn lucky, but it had nothing to do with some paranormal sixth sense, as far as I'm concerned." He shook away the idea that Beth had been too lucky and that maybe some mysterious force *was* directing her steps.

Before Zach could respond, his cellphone rang, and he picked it up. "A text from Hammond." It took only a second for him to read the message. "Says Skye's holding up like a trooper." Zach looked at Shane. "Really?" He glanced back at the phone. "Bail's been set at two million."

Shane whistled under his breath.

"It's gonna take time to get that much cash together. Most of my assets are tied up. I'll have to sell some stocks, bonds," he said as if talking to himself. He scrolled down on his cellphone screen. "I'm contacting my financial advisor."

"Your advisor won't be able to do anything until the banks open."

"Well, maybe."

They both looked up when Sofia entered the room dressed in a blue striped T-shirt and a pair of navy Capris. A backpack hung from one of her shoulders. "I can't sleep. So, I'm heading over to the lab. I have an exam to proctor later this morning. But," she said, shaking her head, "it's on television. Miss Andrews' arrest is being shown on the news." She blinked a couple of times as if to keep from crying and rushed out of the room.

Chapter Twenty-Three

Beth watched Alma measure a cup of flour, hoping that observing the classically trained chef would help her in the kitchen. Alma placed the cup down when the smacking of feet hitting against the hardwood floor interrupted her. Emma raced into the kitchen, holding a squirmy Cloud.

"Can I help?" Emma dropped Cloud, and the kitten scurried away.

"Of course, you can," Alma said. "I'm making a special surprise for your mom. Her favorite. Sugar cookies."

Emma crouched on the floor in search of the wayward kitten. "They're her favorites because Momma's sweet like sugar." Giving up, Emma popped up. "Do you like sugar cookies, Auntie Beth?"

"Love them. Where I come from, we call cookies biscuits."

"Biscuits?" Emma squinched her face. "We have biscuits with gravy mixed with tomatoes, don't we, Alma? But that's not a cookie?" She looked up into the chef's face. "Isn't that right?"

"Our biscuits aren't cookies. Aunt Beth grew up in Ireland, where they have different meanings for some of our words." She lifted an egg and cracked it on the side of the bowl.

"That's right," Beth said. "For instance, a French fry is a chip, and a potato chip is a crisp."

"That's funny, Auntie Beth." A smile crossed the child's usual serious face.

"Funny, indeed, but true." Beth couldn't help but worry. *The child has been through so much—terrorized and almost murdered—and now this. Her ma arrested.*

Emma pulled a stool around the work island and placed it next to Alma. She climbed up, rested on her knees, and reached for an egg. She imitated Alma, but instead of a gentle tap, Emma banged it against the bowl. Slippery egg white and bits of shell slid over her hand while the unbroken yolk plopped onto the countertop.

"Oops." Emma sucked in her lips as a tear gathered in the corner of her eye.

"'Tis nothing to fret about," Beth said.

"Of course not, sweetie." Alma reached for a wet wipe and cleaned Emma's hand. "For a first try, you did great. Look," she said, pointing at the yolk. "I'll add it to the flour while you check on Cloud. When you come back, your job is to mix the ingredients. I'll also need your help dropping the batter onto the cookie sheets."

"Okay," she said, scooting off the stool and skipping out of the room.

"That poor child," Alma said, shaking her head. "It's like she's walking on eggs. No pun intended. The poor lamb is afraid she's going to disappoint someone. Her mother mostly. But when Emma is with Mr. Greyson, she's at ease. Giggling. Relaxed. As if the burden of perfection has been lifted from her shoulders. I hate to tell tales out of school, but Miss Andrews insists Emma be the perfect little miss. Her schoolwork, riding lessons, even the child's playdates." She looked into the bowl of wet ingredients. "Lexi was wonderful with her too. I hope the next nanny will have a similar effect on Emma."

"Shame that Skye's quest for excellence is rubbing off on the colleen. My old aunt Ealga was much the same way. My aunt basically raised me after *me ma* died. Because of my father, her fussiness didn't make too much of an impression. *Me da* thought it comical the way Auntie bustled about complaining about everything from the good Father's homily as to why the neighbor's hogs didn't get a fair price at market."

Emma hopped on one foot reentering the kitchen. She'd located Cloud and held him pressed close to her chest. "Cloud wants to help too!"

"We'll let Cloud help by licking up what's left of the egg." Alma grabbed a spatula and scrapped the egg white from the granite countertop into the cat's dish. She placed it on the mat where Cloud ate his meals. The kitten wiggled out of Emma's grasp and trotted to the bowl.

Alma handed the girl a wooden mixing spoon. "Mix all the ingredients like this." She pantomimed the stirring action.

Emma stirred under Alma's watchful eye but looked up when Bruno entered the room.

"Mr. Bruno. I'm making cookies. For Momma."

"Cool," Bruno said with a wink. "Save one for me, okay?" He smoothed away a dusting of flour from her cheek. "I'm heading out to hopefully pick up . . . umm . . . that item," he announced to no one in particular.

Beth understood. He'd be off to the Detention Center with hopes of collecting Skye. Her first reaction that Zach would post the cash bail was heartfelt relief. But now, she worried how being accused of murder and spending nearly two days in prison had affected Skye's psyche. On a good day, Skye could be a bit of a challenge.

Bruno passed through the kitchen and crossed the great room before disappearing down a wide corridor.

"While you two bakers finish your cookies, I'm going out by the pool and finish reading my book."

"Is your book about a cat?" Emma looked up from the bowl.

"A cat? You could say that. It's about a fat cat who got caught by a sneaky little mouse."

Emma giggled. "That's not right. Cats catch mice."

"Right you are, Emma." Beth headed toward the patio doors and muttered, "A conniving rat is more like it. If only my *fey* would wake up."

Beth grabbed the book from the teak coffee table and headed to the patio. The sun's ray bore down and reflected off the marble pavers, so she settled in the shade cast from the retractable awning. She stretched onto a cushioned lounge and flipped open *Jazz Age Deception*. The similarities between the murder case of the 1920s director and that of Thom Boyle seemed more and more curiously aligned. *A murdered director, an established actress, an ingénue and her overbearing stage mother, a down and out drug-addicted actress, and a houseboy.* She pressed her lips together. *Thom didn't have a houseboy, but there's his personal assistant, Cody. Proving all of the 1922 suspects can be matched up with individuals on the set of Skye's movie. But there's not a match-up for Skye because she isn't involved in the murder at all.*

Beth snatched the pad and pen she kept with the book and flipped to the pages full of her jotted notes. She started a list.

1922	Today
Director – Wm. Desmond Taylor	Thompson Dale Boyle
Actress /Friend – Mabel Norman	Antonia Wright
Ingénue – Mary Miles Minter	Isabella Reid
Stage Mother – Charlotte Shelby	Jane Reid
Has-been actress – Margaret "Gibby" Gibson	Louise "Willie" Wilson
Houseboy – Henry Peavey	Personal Assistant – Cody Evans
Chauffeur – Edward Sands	Assistant Director – Hugo Daines

She tapped the Bortoletti pen against her opened palm. Someone on the 1922 list murdered Taylor. *But who? And would that shed light onto who killed Skye's director? Many individuals have tried, experts and amateurs alike, but the riddle surrounding the murder has never been solved.* She shifted her sight to the present-day column. "Are one of you responsible for the murder of Thom Boyle?"

Beth closed the pad. Tempted, she opened the book to the final chapter. Those pages explained the "who, what, and why" of the probable person responsible for Taylor's murder. Ever since reading the first page, she decided not to peep at the last chapter. She wanted to draw her own conclusions. Much like what she wanted to do with the Boyle murder. She flipped through the pages and found her marker stuck a little past the middle of the book.

"No," she whispered, shaking her head. "I can't speculate about who committed the murder. I have to solve the Boyle case. If I don't, the real possibility is that Skye will spend the rest of her days locked behind cold steel bars."

Chapter Twenty-Four

Shane glanced at Zach, nursing yet another drink, slouched on the edge of the hassock. *He's doing well, considering the situation. If the shoe was on the other foot, I'd be boarding a plane this very minute to be at Beth's side. Make sure she hadn't been traumatized out of her freakin' mind. But, of course, Zach's loaded. He has people to take care of things. Like Hammond.*

He checked his watch. The sensible thing would be to go home and collapse into bed, but he was too wired to even think about sleep. Shane picked up the abandoned architectural book, returned it to the shelf, and moved closer to the dejected figure.

If only Zach's fans could see him now. Would they be shocked or impressed? Perhaps, Shane considered, he's not as worried about Skye's plight but how her situation might affect his career. *Is he trying to devise a plan for damage control? A way to distance himself from his wife? Or is he considering becoming Skye's champion by taking a page from the myriad of characters he's portrayed on the big screen?*

Shane assumed that Zach's stolen artworks had taken a back seat on his list of priorities. It would be callous otherwise. *After all, a painting, even if it holds great monetary and artistic value, is only a canvas or wood panel where paints have been manipulated on the surface. It can't compare to someone's life whose freedom has been stolen away. But even if the theft dropped from the top of Zach's list, it remained a prime concern within the Art Theft Detail.*

For a split second, he wished he was working homicide again. *Those police in Baltimore don't know Skye and could care less if she's innocent or not. But like all detectives, they have heavy caseloads, and an open and shut case makes their jobs a helluva lot easier.* But for all her irritating traits, his gut told him Skye was incapable of committing murder. *Artistic differences as a motive pale next to lust, loathing, or loot. Plus, according to Beth, she liked the director. Considered him a friend. Or at least someone who could further her career.*

"I'm gonna hit the road." Shane's words shattered the silence binding the two men.

Zach looked at him, a bit startled, as if he'd forgotten Shane was there. He downed the remainder of his drink, stood, and extended his hand. Shane grabbed and released it after a quick squeeze.

"Thanks," Zach mumbled, dropping back onto the ottoman.

"No problem."

"Did you see the look on her face? She's petrified. I should be with her."

During the previous hour, the two of them had been glued to the large television screen, revealed from its hiding place behind an ornate wooden panel. All three major networks, plus Fox News, MSNBC, and CNN reported on Skye's arrest. Shane wouldn't have been too bothered except for the announcers. They presented the story with smug expressions and eyes gleaming as if they'd already pronounced Skye guilty of murder. So much for the presumption of innocence in the media's mind. Especially if there's a chance that fair reporting would reduce the salacious aspect of the account.

"Look," Shane said. "You're worried sick, but Beth is there. She'll be a rock for Skye and Emma's protector, shielding the child from any negativity ."

Zach squeezed his eyes shut.

"You're beat," Shane said. "Get some sleep. And take your lawyer's advice. Making a decision now could jeopardize your career—"

"I don't give a tinker's dam about my career. I'm considering chucking the whole acting thing to finish my Ph.D. I could do a lot more good as a neurobiologist than mouthing someone else's damn words."

But you mouth them so well, Shane thought. "Neurobiologist?"

"Yeah." Zach flashed his eyes open like he'd been hit with a bolt of electricity. "Not all of us actors are dimwits." He balled his hand and pounded the hassock. The leather surface muted the sound of the strike.

"I'm outta here." Shane took a couple steps when tinkling chimes filled the air.

"Dammit. Who the hell is that?" Zach jumped to his feet.

"Bad news travels fast."

"How many times do I have to tell Sofia to make sure the gate is closed when she leaves the house?" Zach stomped across the carpet, his eyes blazing as if ready to pummel the poor dope ringing the bell.

Shane intercepted Zach before he exited the room. "Pour yourself another drink. I'll take care of whoever's at the door." Not waiting for a response, he sidestepped Zach and hustled to the massive entrance. The doorbell rang nonstop, as if the finger pressing the bell was on some kind of instant replay. By the time he pulled the bronze sunburst door open, irritation sparked through him. A diminutive blonde-haired woman, looking as if she'd just stepped out of a magazine ad, faced him.

"Oh, hello," she said. "I'm Mindy Marks." She paused as if giving him a second to acknowledge her.

He couldn't place the name, but for some reason, it sounded familiar. Even so, he didn't know who the hell she was. "Yeah?"

"I'm here to see Zach Greyson."

"He's not seeing anyone." Shane started to close the door, but she placed one high-heeled foot over the threshold.

"He'll see me. I'm the host of *Celebrity Files*."

Ah-ha. Beth has an interview with this woman. "Good for you. But I said—"

"Whoever you are, get the hell out of my way," she hissed.

"Listen, lady," Shane whipped his identification out of his pocket. "Do I need to take you in for trespassing?"

She moistened her glossy lips with the tip of her tongue. "Maybe you can help me, Detective? I didn't get your name. You flashed your ID so fast."

"It's Dalton. Detective Dalton. And I repeat, leave the premises, or I'll haul your . . ."

He caught himself. "You down to the station."

"There's no reason to be rude about it." She stepped back onto the cobblestone pavers facing the entrance.

"Sorry, miss. Let me make it up to you."

A glint of excitement crossed her face.

Piranha, he thought. "I'll walk you to your car and direct you out of here."

"That won't be necessary," she huffed and stamped away.

Shane couldn't help but laugh as he headed to his unmarked cruiser. He pulled around the parking circle and wound up behind the reporter in her Mercedes Benz SUV. He followed her down the long driveway. Reaching the opened gate, she paused only a second before turning south onto Tower Road. "Good riddance," he said under his breath.

He wished he could do more to help Skye. But it wouldn't make sense for him to do the legwork as a detective in the Art Theft Detail. Collins, on the other hand, could make a few calls and maybe squeeze a few more details out of Fox.

Ten minutes later, he pulled into a diner parking lot. He reached into the console and pulled out a container of eye drops. Years ago, he learned to always carry two items with him, a bottle of antacids and Visine. One to settle his tense stomach and the other to soothe his tired, red eyes. He brushed his fingers through his blond hair and hustled toward the building. *Probably not too busy this time of day.*

He entered the t-shaped diner, surprised it was more crowded than Shane anticipated. He plopped down at the counter and focused on the television screen on the wall. The sound was muted, but the picture shone clear. He fingered his dimpled chin and watched Skye being led to a patrol car. He'd seen the image a half-dozen times already but was relieved that he couldn't hear the perky, wide-eyed reporter's words. She reminded him of that Mindy Marks.

"What can I get you?" The waitress said with a smile.

"I'll start off with coffee."

A second later, she landed a mug in front of him. "Cream. Sugar?"

"Black is fine."

"Looks like you've been up half the night," she said, handing him a menu. "Haven't I seen you before with that model? Sibéal."

Shane narrowed his eyes. *She's fishing for something.* He raised the mug and took a sip.

Not waiting for an answer, the stout, gray-haired waitress hitched a thumb over her shoulder. "All morning the news has been reporting the arrest of Skye Andrews. Can you believe it? The cops think she murdered a movie director. My, my, what's this world coming to? I just loved Skye in *The Imposter.* Well, anyway, some time ago, I'm not exactly sure when I read an article in one of those celebrity magazines that Sibéal and Skye are best buds. So, I was wondering—"

He raised his hand to stop her droning. "I don't know any Sibèal." He had no qualms lying to the hotpot, believing his personal life was none of her business. He looked back at the menu and said, "I'd like the number three. But instead of toast, I'd like an English muffin. And extra butter on the flapjacks."

She scribbled on her pad. "I'll get that right in for you. But I could've sworn you and that model. And I thought, 'What a beautiful couple.'" She was still muttering as she headed to the kitchen.

At least no one will bother me at work. They're in the dark that I'm married to supermodel "Sibéal." Thank God. He took a gulp of coffee and it tasted a touch bitter.

149

He pulled out his cellphone, checked the texts, and read one from his supervisor, Esma Flores. Technically, she wasn't his supervisor, but because of her seniority and experience, she gave the impression she was in charge. He admitted they weren't equals—yet. He read the message twice and placed the phone screen side down on the Formica countertop. He stared at it with knotted brows.

The waitress placed a plate brimming with food in front of him. "Something wrong?"

"Wrong? Not at all. Looks delicious."

She swiped the countertop with a cloth and moved on to another customer.

The truth was, something didn't feel right between him and Esma Flores. He'd been getting weird vibes from her. During conversations, she stood a little too close, brushed her fingers across his arm, and did that hair flip thing. Flores didn't have to tell him she's married since the glittery diamond on her finger advertised that fact.

He took a bite of the buttered English muffin and chewed slowly. The odd behavior started when they'd interviewed Zach about his stolen artwork. Before that, she'd been professional, helpful, and efficient in bringing him up to speed in the department. *Why the change?* He poured a dollop of maple syrup over the last few pancake bites. *And now she wants to have breakfast together? If it's to discuss strategies on how to proceed with the Greyson case, we can do that in the office.* "Oh well, too late for us to have breakfast," he muttered, texting her back.

He scooped up the last bit of eggs. *I'll run Flores' behavior past Beth,* he thought, and see what she thinks. *Thankfully, my Beth's not the green-eyed monster type that'd accost Flores with the message of leave my man alone or else.* He'd seen more than enough murders whose catalyst had been old-fashioned jealousy.

Flores should be busy all day with the Feds. He squinted, noting the meeting revolved around a crate of *alebrijes,* sculptures depicting ancient Aztec symbolic creatures, from Mexico. The shipment inspected by the

CBP at the border revealed that the hollowed-out wooden figurines were stuffed with heroin. The *alebrijes'* bases had been plastered shut and painted in matching vibrant colors. Their first supposition placed the smuggling operation with the Sinale Cartel. But the authorities quickly nixed that idea believing they'd never be that sloppy.

A light flashed in Shane's overly tired mind. *That's why Flores wanted a breakfast meeting. Innocent enough. Just wanted to discuss the case of the drug-packed sculptures conveyed into the US by a private transport company.* He downed the last mouthful of coffee. *The most curious part of the crooked enterprise was the shipping address didn't pan out. Posted to the deceased son of an elementary school principal in Minnesota.* He wondered if the drug smugglers were just damn stupid and had affixed the wrong address on the crate of contraband.

Shane wiped the napkin against his lips and left a tip next to his empty plate. He strolled toward the cashier when his cellphone rang. He pulled it out of his pocket and swiped the screen.

"Hey Beth."

"Oh, my darlin', Shane. I'm missing you."

The sound of her voice acted like a tonic.

"Me too, Betty Getty. You holding down the fort okay?" He handed the cashier a credit card.

"I'm doing my best."

"Hold on a sec." He signed the receipt, pocketed his card, and walked into the lobby. "I'm back."

"Things here are as good as could be expected. Alma is teaching the wee one how to bake cookies. Getting ready for a mighty homecoming for Skye. I came up with an excuse that Skye had to spend an overnight at work. Emma's used to that kind of thing, though I told Alma the truth. I hope they're not disappointed if Skye doesn't make it back today."

"Once he juggles his assets around, Zach will be wiring the bail money."

"That's a relief."

"As you'd say, it's costing a *fierce* amount of money. Two million."

"*Janey Mack*. A lot of money to free Skye from a crime she didn't commit. How's Zach holding up?"

"Not great. Skye's arrest has taken his mind off the stolen artwork. He's anxious to put together the bail money so that welcome home party might happen today. I'll keep my fingers crossed for Emma's sake."

"Wouldn't that be brilliant?" She paused for a moment. "But knowing Skye, she's sure to be more than a bit rattled. I can't imagine what her emotional state will be like. Reunited with Emma and the wee kitten should help spring Skye back to her old self."

"We can only hope. But from my perspective, her old self wasn't one to write home about."

"Ah, speaking of writing, I'm about finished reading the book."

"Book? Oh, Greatpa's short stories."

"Ah, no. The book about the unsolved murder of the silent screen director. *Jazz Age Deception*."

"William Desmond Taylor? I didn't realize that piece of Hollywood history caught your interest. Greatpa wrote a story based on the Taylor murder. Have you have read that one yet?"

"It's next on my to-do list."

Her words flowed so fast, he almost missed what she said.

"Have you come up with who murdered Taylor?"

"Not yet. But the more I read, the more there seems to be some kind of cosmic connection between the two cases. It's uncanny."

"Cosmic connection?"

"I'll explain later how they link up. If only I could channel my *fey*. That way, I'd be able to finger the killer of Skye's director and clear her of this horrible injustice."

"The case is being handled by a Baltimore Detective named Fox. Jeremy Fox. Leave it to him."

"*Rawmaish*," she said under her breath.

"Huh?"

"I'm sure this Jeremy Fox is a lovely detective, but this is serious. And if my *fey* guides me, I might be able to solve two murder cases at the same time. Oh, my darlin' boy, I have to ring off. Bye."

The sound of a kiss filled his ear before the call disconnected.

Shane walked out of the diner shaking his head. *Her meddling and undeniable belief in a sixth sense will get Beth seriously hurt one of these days.* He screwed up his face recalling how her past snooping ventures landed her in the hospital. But this time, his gut told him, it could turn out to be even more dangerous.

He pulled open his car door and slipped behind the wheel. *I've no choice but to put a stop to her interference.* He reached for the bottle of antacids and flipped the lid open. *How in God's name am I ever going to squelch Beth's stubborn belief that some profound intuitive power is guiding her to solve crimes?* He tapped a couple of the chalky tablets into his mouth and chewed. "Even by some slim chance her *fey* is legit," he said under his breath, "I still don't want Beth to place herself into a dangerous situation that doesn't concern her. Because I'd bet my last dollar, Boyle's death isn't what it seems."

Chapter Twenty-Five

Shane sat at his desk reviewing old cases. He wanted to understand how the pros had tackled major art heists and recovered stolen artworks. He still had a lot to learn to meet his goal of becoming a top-notch art theft investigator. But more than once, he found himself staring into space, wondering what Beth meant about solving two murders. If she hadn't hung up abruptly, he, sure as hell, would've asked. But he guessed that's why she'd ended the call. She didn't want him to question her motives. *I'll do more than question her actions, I'm gonna make sure she keeps her nose out of the Boyle case. If only I knew how.*

He could always forbid her. The thought brought a smile to his face. Forbidding Beth to do anything would only cause her to dig in her heels and proceed no matter how dangerous the situation. If Beth truly has some kind of psychic ability, and he wasn't sure she did, it could lead her into trouble. It was his job, after all, to keep his wife safe.

He'd hoped with the launch of her new projects, she'd forget about police investigations. She wasn't a cop, detective, or even a damn private investigator. *She's a model who's paid a preposterous amount of money to smile and have her photo snapped.* He'd happily support her effort in just about anything from volunteering at a cat rescue to working the souvenir shop on Hollywood Boulevard. Any activity that would steer her clear of behaving like she's a sleuth straight out of an Agatha Christie novel. Granted, he conceded, Beth does have a knack for stumbling across leads that even law enforcement failed to uncover. *She's got good gut instincts. But physic powers? Why can't I persuade her to stick to what she does best and leave murder investigations to the professionals?*

"You're here early."

Shane shook his head, dispelling his concerns about Beth, and focused on Esma Flores.

She stood in front of his desk with a trace of a smile. "I'm catching up on some old cases." He hoped she wouldn't bring up breakfast. "I thought you'd be tied up with the Feds all day?"

"Most likely." Flores shrugged. "The more I learn about this case, the more fascinating it becomes. I'd love to discuss the details with you. Are you free for dinner?"

Dammit.

"You mentioned your wife is out of town. But even if she weren't, I'm sure she's used to your unpredictable work schedule."

"Well, yeah. But, um . . ." He couldn't come up with an excuse as a wave of exhaustion washed over him. His eyelids drooped. "I was up most of the night. A friend's in trouble. I tried to help."

"Legal trouble."

"You could say that." He pressed his lips together, determined to keep his personal life private.

While working in the Sheriff's Office, he'd experienced some good-natured ribbing until his colleagues met Beth. She thoroughly charmed them, and they fell over themselves whenever she stopped by the station. Except for Collins. He saw past her physical beauty and recognized her generous and kind heart. When Beth opened the house to them with her potlucks and pool parties, they all became friends. But it took time. He certainly didn't want to have a replay at his new job.

"Well then," Flores said, "since you'll want to call it an early night, I have a lunch break at noon. We can grab something to eat, and I'll bring you up to speed."

He nodded.

"So," she said, looking through a folder on her organized desk, "what's on your agenda today?"

"I'll be meeting with a couple gallery owners and a private collector." He moved the opened file on his desk and slipped a pad free. "Steven Polachek."

"Good. Keep me updated." She grabbed a couple of binders and left the room.

The door barely closed behind her when his office phone rang. "Dalton," he said into the receiver.

"Detective Fox."

Shane straightened up.

"A Detective Collins at your previous job gave me your new number. I don't mean to interrupt—"

"No problem. Can I help you with something?"

"Regarding our earlier conversation, I left out one important detail."

Shane heard him take a deep breath.

"Though all the evidence points to Skye Andrews, my gut is telling me she may not of killed Boyle."

Shane rubbed the clef in his chin, allowing the detective's words to sink in.

"The case is, of course, out of my hands," Fox said. "But I've got a nagging feeling that a piece of the puzzle is missing. Anyway, I couldn't live with myself if I caused an innocent person to be found guilty of a crime she didn't commit. I'm taking a few days off from work for a quick trip to Los Angeles. You think we could meet up and discuss this further?"

"Sounds like a plan. Contact me when you get here."

"Will do. Thanks."

Shane leaned back in his swivel chair and pursed his lips, not sure what to think. He did know, however, that he had a thief to catch. He grabbed his sports jacket from the back of his chair and headed out the door.

Chapter Twenty-Six

Beth clicked off the TV news as Bruno entered the great room. Red followed on his heels. They didn't look happy, but they always seemed to keep their faces impassive, masking any trace of emotion.

"Afternoon, Beth," Bruno said, walking past her. She'd had enough of their formality, and unlike Skye, insisted the bodyguards address her by her given name.

She twisted on the sofa and faced his fleeting back.

"Is there a problem?" She stood and moved closer to the two men.

"Problem?" He looked at her over his shoulder.

"Is Skye out?" she whispered.

"Bail's posted. Miss Andrews is in the living room with her attorney."

"She can't leave the state," Red said. "Looks like I'll be staying on with Miss Andrews. I'm not sure what's gonna happen with her daughter. But Alma," he said, crossing his fingers, "will hopefully stay put. That lady is a food magician."

Beth nodded absently. She hadn't seen Emma for hours and she didn't want the girl to inadvertently disturb Skye's meeting with her lawyer. *Whoever he may be.*

It took a moment for Red's statement to register. Beth frowned, looking into his pale blue eyes. "Did you say Skye can't return to Los Angeles?"

Both men nodded.

"For how long?"

"Until her trial," Bruno said. "From what I, um, overheard, when Miss Andrews was on her cellphone, the judge didn't seem to be a fan of movie people. Especially one that's supposed to have offed someone."

"The judge was prejudicial?"

"Beats me," Bruno said, scratching the back of his head. "All I know is Miss Andrews has to stay put. And man, she ain't happy about it either."

"I can imagine." Beth sat on the edge of the couch, grabbed a pillow, and squeezed it. *How could a judge be so coldhearted keeping Skye a prisoner in her house—her rented house.* She took in the massive room with its stone fireplace and contemporary furnishings. "Well," she conceded, "it's truly a beautiful place to be sequestered. But she's lost her freedom. 'Tis a shame she won't be able to return to Malibu. The lulling rhythm of the ocean would tame her worries sprouting from this farce of an arrest."

"I guess. But the digs here ain't bad at all," Red said. "Not foo-foo fussy as the Beverly Hills house and not stark like the Malibu house. Sorta like a meeting in the middle. But, Miss Andrews doesn't have to stay inside the house. She has to stay in the state. Maybe," he said with a shake of his head, "she'll buy the place. She seems happy enough here."

Beth pressed her lips together. That would be the last thing Skye would want. A charming, traditional house amid Maryland horse country. "Ahh," she said, remembering that Alma had taken the wee one to her riding lesson. One of the first things on Skye's list, when they relocated to Maryland, was to enroll Emma in the local Pony Club. Besides kittens, Emma's other love is horses. Beth breathed relief, realizing that Skye's meeting would continue without any unforeseen interruptions.

"All of us will probably stay here. So no worries, Red. You won't have to depend on fast food and pizza," Beth said with a wink.

"Except me," Bruno said. "I gotta get my gear together. I'll be flying back to LA tomorrow. Mr. Greyson wants extra security at the house because of the break-in." He sauntered off, and after a quick nod, Red followed him.

Beth tossed the pillow and picked up her book. The narrative had done a splendid job of laying out the background information regarding the Taylor murder and introducing the players. One of which, Beth felt certain, had to be the killer. *But who would have thought that the dawn of Hollywood would've been overrun with drugs, illicit sexual liaisons, and murder? It hasn't changed much over the past century*, she thought with a shake of her head.

She flipped to the spot where she'd left off but then closed the book. *The movie. Dark Grace. How will Skye finish the studio scenes if she's stuck here?*

"Beth!"

She jerked around. Skye hurried toward her.

For a brief moment, she stood facing Beth. It was enough time for Beth to make a quick impression. Skye had lost weight. Her normally glistening red-gold hair hung around her shoulders, lackluster and limp, and a sprinkling of acne had blossomed on her chin. After only two days, prison pallor had already invaded her.

Beth jumped to her feet and opened her arms. Skye fell within the warmth of her friend's embrace. "I'm relieved. Truly relieved you're out of that awful place. Emma will be thrilled you're home. Now that you're free—"

"Free?" Skye pulled out of Beth's hold. "I'm stuck in this stupid state for God knows how long."

"But the trial—"

"Could be years." Skye's shoulders sank. "At least they didn't clamp one of those ankle monitors on me," she said with a face. "That would've been pure hell."

Beth took Skye's hand and led her to the couch. Skye sat while Beth dropped onto the teak coffee table and waited for her to say something. Skye's usual lively eyes seemed hollow and tiny lines etched into her forehead. It stung Beth's heart to see her vivacious and glamorous friend reduced to a shadow of her former self.

"Please, help me," Skye whispered. "You have to channel into that *fey* of yours. Two days of being locked up inside a cage just about killed me. Please."

"Of course, I'll help. But I don't know how. I haven't had a single premonition since your arrest." Beth exhaled loudly. "I was born with the gift, and now I don't understand what's happening."

"You saved me once before." Skye's eyes pleaded. "Isn't there something you can do to turn it back on?"

How naive of her, Beth thought, as if my sixth sense worked like a spigot. "I can't control it, Skye. But the good Lord willing, I'll be able to identify the actual killer."

"That's what you need to do." Skye leaned forward, only a couple of inches away from Beth. "I've had a lot of time to think, and the killer has to be Hugo Daines. That's why I want you to contact him. Make up a story about how much you'd love to be on the set and watch a genius at work. Play up to his tremendous ego."

"I see," Beth said, bobbing her head up and down. "On the set, I can nose about a bit.

Ask a question here and there."

"Right."

"You're certain Daines is the culprit?"

"Who else?"

Chapter Twenty-Seven

"Look who I found. A little equestrian." Marc Hammond entered the great room holding Emma's hand. Beth shot up from the coffee table and eyed the distinguished-looking lawyer, dressed in a three-piece suit, who seemed vaguely familiar.

Emma's face lit up seeing Skye. "Momma." She broke free of Marc's grasp and ran into Skye's open arms.

Skye kissed Emma's cheeks, forehead, and the tip of her nose. "I missed you so, so very much," she whispered into the child's ear. After another hug, she released Emma and took a backward step. Her eyes locked on her daughter as if trying to drink in every inch of the little girl. A smile broke across Skye's face brightening it.

Skye looks like herself again. Well, almost, Beth thought.

"Run upstairs," Skye told the child, "and get out of your riding outfit, wash-up, and then we'll—"

"Okay, Momma. Alma and me made a surprise for you. Cloud . . ." She shifted her head from side to side as if looking for the kitten. "Well, he tried to help. I need to find him. He missed you too." Emma offered a snaggletooth smile and skipped through the room,

Once sure that Emma was out of earshot, Skye said, "You know Marc Hammond, don't you, Beth?"

"Can't say I've had the pleasure." Beth took his outstretched hand and shook it.

"So, we finally meet," Hammond said. "You're friends with my Marjorie. She insisted on coming along to comfort Skye. But with the

161

campaign in full throttle, I had to remind her about a couple current commitments. She's been a tremendous help rallying the troops, as they say. To top it off, she's quite a talented speaker."

Beth wasn't surprised. She'd known all along that Marjorie loved to talk. Her long-winded conversations consisted of mostly gossip. Even so, she couldn't be more pleased Marjorie had stepped up and agreed to assist in her husband's senatorial campaign. *Hopefully, becoming the wind behind Marc's sail has settled her nerves about losing his affection. Must be difficult being married to a charismatic man with a roving eye, particularly when you're his third wife, who may be warming the bench for number four.* Nevertheless, Beth wasn't going to hold that against Marc Hammond, especially if he'd prove Skye's innocence.

"I sincerely hope that I can count on your vote," Marc said.

His melodic voice scattered her thoughts. Beth glanced at the middle-aged man. He stood tall with a deep tan and a bit of gray at the temples. *I wonder how many female jurors have been persuaded not only by his arguments but because of his dashing looks.*

"You'd have it in a heartbeat, that is, if I were a citizen."

"You have mine," Skye said, "providing I'm home in time for the election."

"I wouldn't bet on it," Marc said. "I suggest you request an absentee ballot."

"You mean . . ." Skye's face fell.

"Now, Skye. There's no reason to look defeated," he said. "I promise, the minute I get back to my office, my team will be working tirelessly on your defense."

"Team?" Skye's eyebrows squished together.

"Is that a problem?"

"I thought you would be preparing my defense." Skye thrust her hand in his direction.

"I haven't personally been to court since the political campaign has revved up. But, rest assured, all the lawyers in my firm are persuasive, organized, aggressive, and, of course, experts in the law. They wouldn't work for me if they lacked those basic skills. Top-notch. Each and every one of them. So, my darling Skye," he said, patting her arm, "don't worry."

Marc glanced at his watch, which Beth imagined a Rolex or a Patek Philippe since she pegged him as only owning the best.

"I've got to run," he said. "I've scheduled a press conference at the airport. Too much time has slipped by without an official statement. The public needs to know the truth. Skye Andrews is one-hundred percent innocent of the murder charge. I'll be in touch soon. Goodbye, darling." He brushed his lips against Skye's cheek. After a quick nod to Beth, he breezed out of the room.

"Wow," Beth said. "He's brilliant. You'll have no worries, so."

"But how is he," Skye rolled her eyes upward and said, "his team going to explain my fingerprints on the knife?" She sank into the sleek leather couch.

Beth didn't want to sound like a Pollyanna and fill Skye's head with false hope but needed to crush her defeatist attitude. "It's his job to prove to the jury that you're incapable of the charge. That's why Marc Hammond gets paid the big bucks. And from what I understand, he's worth every penny. His record of acquittals is impressive." At least according to Marjorie, it was, and Beth believed she hadn't been exaggerating.

"Momma. Momma." Emma raced into the living space. "I can't find Cloud."

"He's got to be around somewhere," Beth said, noticing the lack of interest written on Skye's face. "I'll help you look for him, darlin'. But first, I'm thinking your ma needs to get herself to bed." She glanced at Skye. "A nap will do you a world of good."

Emma grabbed Beth's hand. "Come on." Almost instantly, she released it, ran to Skye, and kissed her cheek. "After your nap, we're going to have a party." Emma's hand shot over her mouth. "It's supposed to be a surprise." She shrugged. "Everyone's going to be there. Auntie Beth, Alma, Bruno, Red, and Cloud. A tea party." She ran to the far side of the room, dropped to the floor, and peered under a loveseat. "Cloud. Cloud," she said in a singsong voice.

"Just what I need. A surprise tea party. As if I haven't had the surprise of my life," Skye said with a shake of her head.

"Have a lie-down," Beth urged.

"I wish I could close my eyes and never wake up."

"Don't be an *eejit*. You have everything in the world to live for. To fight for. Especially . . ." She gestured toward Emma, who now cradled Cloud in her arms.

"I found him." Joy filled not only Emma's words but also her face.

"If only it was that simple to find the damned killer that framed me." Skye crossed the room and disappeared down the corridor leading to the back staircase.

Chapter Twenty-Eight

Beth believed the tea party was an altogether grand idea, a sweet and touching homecoming for Skye. Her eyes widened in surprise as she entered the formal dining room. The table looked as if it had been transported from Victorian England dressed elegantly with a floral ruffled tablecloth and lacy overlay. Two sets of flickering candlesticks nestled in crystal holders framed a floral centerpiece composed of pink and peach roses, blue hydrangeas, and lavender chrysanthemums. Place cards, handwritten by Emma, sat next to each setting.

She found her seat and noticed the arrangement of food. Three-tier dessert trays arrayed with golden sugar cookies and pink frosted cupcakes and finger sandwiches artfully grouped on serving trays sported a variety of bread: white, wheat, and pumpernickel. The traditional fare of creamed egg, cucumber, and smoked salmon rounded out the fillings except for the selection of peanut butter and jelly sandwiches, which she imagined were made especially for Emma.

Garbed in a silky teal frock, Skye arrived last at the party. The men rose from their seats not dressed in their usual black suits but in pastel-colored shirts and contrasting silk ties. Lively enthusiasm returned to Skye's face, and she smiled as Emma, in a sky-blue party dress, showed off Cloud, who wore a matching blue ribbon around his neck.

Alma served the tea dressed in a formal double-breasted white chef coat and black slacks. She hadn't gotten very far with the tea pouring when Skye took the pot from her hand. "This is lovely," she said. "Thank you, Alma." She gestured to a vacant seat.

As Skye continued pouring tea, Beth headed to the Georgian-styled china cabinet, located another place-setting for Alma, and set it on the table. Emma held the kitten in her lap and moved Cloud's front paws together in a clapping motion. After laying Alma's place, Beth removed another teacup from the breakfront and filled it. "We can't forget about Cloud. He's a party guest too."

"Cats don't drink tea," Emma said wide-eyed.

"Sure they do. Tea makes their coats shiny."

Emma released the kitten, and Cloud leaped to the floor. Beth spread a dishtowel over the plush Oriental carpet, and the kitten brushed against Beth's legs in anticipation of the unusual refreshment. She sat the cup down alongside tidbits of Cloud's favorite treats that she'd grabbed from the sideboard. A few seconds later, the kitten lapped the tepid liquid.

"He likes it. Cloud likes tea," Emma said, placing down her cup filled with more milk than tea. "Can he eat a cookie too?"

Beth shook her head. "Cloud's treats are his cookies."

"They are? Oh, good." Emma said, biting into one of the PB&J sandwiches.

Bruno launched into a funny story about the cat, Felix, his childhood pet. Skye laughed, and Alma fussed making sure everyone had enough to eat.

Red sat back and laid his hands on his belly. "I'm stuffed. It was delicious, Emma. Thanks for inviting me." He shot her a rare smile. His usual steely blue eyes lit up, and the skin around them crinkled.

"Great tea party, kiddo," Bruno said. He picked up the last smoked salmon sandwich and popped it into his mouth. "Delish," he managed between chews.

The color in Emma's cheeks blushed. She pulled her legs into a kneeling position then stood on the chair's satin seat. "This party for my Momma is to show her how much we love her." She waved her hand in the air. "Everyone here loves you," she said, looking at Skye. "And if

Daddy Zach didn't have to work, he'd be here too." She jumped off the chair, ran around the table, and, reaching Skye, kissed her cheek.

Tears sprung to Beth's eyes, but she brushed them away, not wanting to act like a sentimental schoolgirl. Proud as punch of Emma, she knew the child had warmed her mother's troubled heart. While Beth suppressed her emotions, Skye allowed the tears to gather in her eyes. She hugged Emma and whispered into the child's ear.

"The tea party is officially over," Alma announced.

"I'm going to help clean up." Emma beamed as she reached for her mother's Limoges gold-edged plate.

"Hold up," Alma said. "Collecting the silverware is your job. Make sure to put them into the dishwasher while I stack everything else."

Dutifully, Emma reached for a serving knife.

Skye rose and looked around the table. "Before we go our separate ways, I want to thank my precious daughter and Alma. A beautiful surprise," she said, gesturing toward the table, "that touched me deeply. This tea party will always be one of my most cherished memories," she said, laying a hand over her heart.

"What are you practicing for? The Academy Awards?"

All eyes turned toward the familiar voice.

"Daddy." Emma dropped the Stieff Rose server onto the table and ran to Zach. He lifted Emma and swung her around in a circle and her laughter filled the room. After kissing her cheek, he landed the child gently on the floor. He moved to Skye and took her hand.

"Everyone shoo," Alma said, flicking her hands back and forth in a brushing movement.

The bodyguards were the first to slip away while Beth lingered long enough to see Zach pull Skye into his arms. Emma ran ahead and called, "Daddy, I'm gonna find Cloud so you can see how much he's grown."

After leaving the dining room, Beth slipped into a tank top and a pair of Bermudas. She grabbed both of Shane's books and headed outside. Beth lounged by the pool for a few minutes gazing at the spray from the pool fountain. She lifted the book on top and studied its glossy cover. A montage composed of 1920 photos of the prime suspects circled a portrait of the slain movie director. The similarities between the two murder cases separated by a century intrigued her. Even though Shane had introduced her to the hundred-year-old mystery, she believed her *fey* opened her eyes to the uncanny parallels.

How am I supposed to interpret the information?

Beth's sixth sense remained dormant, which infuriated her. She tapped down her building frustration, holding on to the belief that her *fey* would return when she needed it the most. Even so, her patience, now frazzled, wore thin.

"Beth," Skye's voice rang out.

She looked away from the cover of *Jazz Age Deception* and half-rose but plopped back on the lounge when Skye joined her. "Sure has been a day of wonderful surprises for you."

"It brought home all the things that may be stolen from me." A touch of sadness filled Skye's eyes. "There are so many things I've never appreciated. Little things like brushing Emma's hair, playing with a kitten, laughing with friends." She glanced at Beth. "And the big things like freedom." She dropped into a nearby chair.

"I'm guessing the old adage is true. You don't appreciate what you have until it's gone."

"I don't want to lose what I have." Tears welled up in Skye's eyes, and she blinked them away.

The last thing Beth wanted was to see Skye upset. *It's my duty, as Skye's friend, to calm her anxiety.* "Where's Zach?"

"Getting the gear together. He's taking Emma fishing." Skye waved in the vague direction of the lake located at the far back right corner of the four-acre property. "Emma's wearing the cat mask for luck. She came up with that idea by realizing that cats like to eat fish."

"That darlin' girl. And Zach—"

"Zach will be staying with us for a week," Skye said

"Ah sure, you'll have some family time, you will. Lovely."

"Thank God his director gave him the time off. Zach has a photographic mind or something like that. He zips through rehearsals and rarely, if ever, flubs up his lines." She twisted in the chair to face Beth. "But I think Zach called in a favor. And that's what I need from you." Skye stuck her hand into a side pocket, pulled out a business card, and handed it to her.

Beth scanned the brushed matte silver card. The name, Hugo Daines, printed in fancy lettering, eclipsed the added image of an old-fashioned movie camera. His job title, embossed in bold script, caused Beth to frown. She looked at Skye. "It says, film director." She tapped her fingertip against the call card's shiny black letters.

"Are you surprised? Just another sign of his overreaching ambition. Calling himself a director when he worked as an assistant."

"What do you want me to do with this?" Beth shook the card in her hand.

"I want you to contact Daines."

"On the set, right?" Beth slipped the card into the pages of her book.

"I have a better idea. If we don't find Thom's killer soon, they'll stick me in a damn cell for the rest of my life. That's why I need you to meet with Daines as soon as possible. They've finished the location shoots and are working in LA. Empire Studios. Soundstage 16."

"Okay. I'll call the airlines—"

The tiny lines crossing Skye's forehead softened. "I knew you wouldn't let me down.

There's no need to call the airlines. Zach's jet will be ready to take off tomorrow."

"That's right. Bruno's returning—"

"You can fly back with him. And find the proof to nail Daines. I wouldn't be surprised if Hugo planned to kill Thom so he'd become the director and frame me. So that his darling Antonia Wright could take my place."

"That seems a bit excessive."

"Excessive? You don't know him like I do."

"That still doesn't answer the question of how your fingerprints wound up on the knife."

Skye sighed. "The only knife I touched was the one used in the shoot, and I was wearing those awful latex gloves. Detectives wouldn't touch a piece of evidence with bare hands."

"No, they wouldn't." Beth pursed her lips.

"If a prop knife wound up missing, the property master would know. He's amazing. Spot on with the locations set-ups. Thom had Willie join his team because her role is so tiny, and he wanted to help her out. Her regular job is working as a waitress or a barista in some rundown dive to make ends meet."

"Pity." Beth shook her head.

"Willie brought it on herself, didn't she?"

Skye's harsh response told Beth she held little compassion for Willie's plight. "That prop knife—""

"What about it?"

"Did it have an actual blade?"

"Duller than a butter knife." Skye squeezed her eyes shut. "There was one time I

might've touched the knife. But it wasn't real. Oh, I can't remember— my mind is jumbled up. I can't chase away the thought that I could be locked up again like a common criminal."

"Your deep breathing meditation will help—"

Skye flashed her eyes open. "I can meditate from now to kingdom come, and what good will that do? Make a jury find me not guilty?"

"It'll help you de-stress."

"You really think I can relax with a murder accusation hanging over my head?"

Beth placed her hand on Skye's arm. "I'll ring Daines the minute I arrive in LA."

"Be careful around him. Daines likes you. That much was obvious when you played that scene. He has hands like an octopus."

Emma skipped toward them wearing the half-cat mask, holding an orange sand pail in one hand and a flower in the other. "Momma," she called. "This is for you." She held out a lavender mum that had been part of the tea party centerpiece. "Wear it in your hair."

Skye dropped to her knees, and Emma slipped the flower behind her ear. "How do I look?"

"Pretty," Emma said.

"My Emma," Skye said. "Whenever I see a purple flower, I'll think of you."

"You won't have to think about me cuz from now on, me and Cloud are never going to leave you. You get sad when you're away from us."

"What's that?" Beth asked, pulling the child's attention away from Skye, who fought tears.

Emma held the pail under Beth's nose. It was half-filled with dirt. "Worms." She poked a finger into the damp soil, scooped out an earthworm, and held it for Beth to see. "Alma's gonna fry up the fish we catch for dinner." She flicked the worm back onto the moist dirt.

"Ah, I love fresh fish. My last dinner with you for a while." Beth said, glancing in Skye's direction. "I'll be going home to California."

"Do you have to, Auntie Beth?"

"I do. But I'll be back, my darlin' slip of a girl." Beth lifted the cat mask from Emma's face and rested it on the top of the child's head. The sparkle faded from Emma's eyes. "I'll tell you what. Since you'll be here living here a bit longer, when I come back to visit, I'll bring the rest of Cloud's brothers and sisters."

"Really?" She looked at Skye. "Can she? Can she really, Momma?"

"We'd have our hands full with six kittens. But why not? It'll be fun to watch them zoom around the house."

"Oh, it will, it really will," Emma said.

"You better get Cloud on board," Beth said. "I be thinking Cloud has become a wee bit spoiled. He'll have to be learning how to share."

Emma nodded solemnly. But an instant later, the seriousness vanished from her face. "I've gotta tell Daddy. He's gonna be surprised. And happy too." She skipped away.

"Hopefully, the kittens will stay put at the shelter since we'll all be home soon. Once your *fey* reveals how to nail Daines."

With no thanks to her *fey*, the little voice in Beth's head told her Hugo Daines had nothing to do with the murder of Thom Boyle.

Chapter Twenty-Nine

Settled in the plush SUV, it seemed to Beth that the bodyguards had forgotten about her. The two men's conversation, though sparse, revolved around a Dodgers baseball game. Sid drove, and Bruno, seated next to him, had finally stopped looking over his shoulder, asking if she needed anything. Being left to herself gave Beth time to devise a game plan of her own. *It'll be lovely to see my Shane again*, she thought. *But he'll be steaming mad about me poking around a movie set trying to uncover a killer.*

But helping Skye was her first priority. Beth realized other obligations had piled up and feared she'd spread herself too thin. Before Skye's arrest, she contacted Noelle Cosmetics and agreed to renew her contract as spokesperson. Not wanting to waste time, the company emailed her the agreement. Luckily, she was able to slip into a canceled appointment slot with her contract attorney, and with his okay, signed the form and sent it on its way.

Within six weeks, the cosmetic company would begin production for a new advertising campaign. During that time, the creative concept, storyboard, and scripts would be hammered out, including specifics as to the location for the shoots, background music, wardrobe, and every other detail needed to produce a dazzling advert. Their products, once again coupled with Beth's star power and a bit of luck, would send millions of women to their local department stores to purchase the newest products by Noelle Cosmetics. Beth wasn't privy to what product she'd be hawking— she imagined perfume—since the commercial's time frame was slated to air during the Christmas shopping season. That gave her plenty of wiggle room to launch her own investigation into the murder of Thom Boyle.

There's the interview scheduled for next Wednesday, she thought, chewing her lip. *Celebrity Files.* She couldn't quite put her finger on it, but something about the host rubbed her the wrong way. Even so, she hadn't met the interviewer in person and wanted to give Mindy Marks the benefit of the doubt.

Taken aback when Mindy Marks had contacted her by phone, Beth wondered why her longtime agent hadn't handled the scheduling. No doubt, she decided, Mindy Marks went over his head, which Beth considered unprofessional. The host rattled off topics she wanted to cover during the interview: Beth's resurrected modeling career and new projects she might have lined up. At first, Beth believed the show's segment would offer a wonderful opportunity to speak out about the homeless situation facing so many young people. It took Mindy a nanosecond to nix that idea. Mindy huffed that the program wasn't a reality show and political and social issues were strictly forbidden.

But now, with Skye's arrest, Beth had a sneaking suspicion Mindy would renege on her initial guidelines and center the interview on Skye's plight. She'd leave it up to her agent to set that perky, little blond reporter straight. *Any discussion about Skye Andrews is off-limits.*

She snuggled deeper into the plush leather seat and pulled out her cellphone. Taking advantage of the three-hour time difference between the east and west coasts, she figured the newly promoted director would probably be lunching in some posh LA eatery. She glanced at Daines' business card, tapped his number, and prayed the call wouldn't go to voicemail.

He answered the phone on the first ring and sounded testy with a curt, "Yeah."

"Mr. Daines. This is Sibéal. I have a tremendous favor to ask you."

"Oh, Sibéal." His voice softened. "I'll be only too happy to oblige. If I can."

"I was hoping to drop by the sound stage tomorrow. I'd love to see a true artist at work."

"You flatter me."

She heard the smile in his voice.

"I might be able to swing something." He paused for a second. "Say, are you free for dinner tonight?"

She glanced at her watch and converted the time change in her head. "Eight o'clock?"

"It's a date. How does *Bella Giardino* sound?"

"Lovely." Beth wasn't surprised that he'd selected a ritzy Beverly Hills restaurant frequented by top celebrities. "I'll see you there at eight."

Chapter Thirty

Stumped, Shane tapped a pencil against the edge of his desk. The normal contacts had fizzled out. Big time. Art dealers, galleries—private and public—nothing. He even popped into a couple of pawnshops out of desperation. Not expecting much, that's what he ended up getting. The only promising angle left was Greyson's former driver. Renaldo Jones. A real longshot. Most times, threats, said in anger, faded away once emotions had a chance to calm down. But since both Zach and Skye had zeroed on this guy, Shane figured he'd have nothing to lose.

He turned to his computer and logged into the department's secured database to run a criminal background check. Chances are the guy's clean, he guessed as he plugged Renaldo Jones and his personal information into the system. "But then again . . ." Shane pumped the air, locating Jones' record. He scanned the list of offenses, including misdemeanors, which paled in comparison to the felony that sent Jones to the slammer. Dealing cocaine. He walked out of the Men's Central Jail after fourteen months due to good behavior.

This enlightening data led Shane to call the county's probation office. A short conversation with Jones' probation officer resulted in a report of good behavior while under supervision. Jones maintained gainful employment and hadn't any subsequent brushes with the law.

Hurling revenge threats at Greyson wasn't gonna earn Jones the Model Citizen of the Year Award. Could be he's just gotten better at not getting caught. Shane kept his thoughts to himself and jotted down the address of the lube shop where Jones worked. According to Shane's calculations, the shop in West Hollywood was less than six miles away from the Greyson spread. Shane grabbed his jacket from the back of his chair. As he neared the door, his cellphone beeped. He pulled it out of his pants pocket and glanced at the screen. A text. From Flores. He scanned the message. *Can't do lunch. Tied up with Feds. TTYL.*

NP, he texted back. After questioning Jones, he'd pick up lunch—a late lunch, he decided, glancing at his watch—a couple of minutes past one o'clock. He was about to step out of his tiny office when his cellphone rang. "Now what?" Expecting to see a text from Flores, he smiled at seeing Beth's face fill the screen. He swiped it, retraced his steps, and sat on the edge of his desk.

"Hey, babe. What's up?"

She sighed.

"That bad, huh?"

"Marc Hammond thinks he can sway any jury. Except he's so wrapped up in his senatorial campaign, he's delegated Skye's case to his subordinates."

"Can't say I'm surprised. Even though I hate to admit it, the firm is top-notch. So, rest easy. Skye will have the best defense money can buy. And believe me, Hammond ain't cheap. He'll charge Skye a fortune in exchange for a defense that, with a dose of luck, will win her freedom."

"We have to stay positive and have faith the truth will be brought to light."

"I had an interesting conversation with Fox, that Baltimore detective I told you about. I'll fill you in later."

"Grand. We can talk tonight because I'm coming home."

"Best news I've heard all day." He tapped the speaker and held the cellphone like a microphone. "Is Skye coming with you?"

"She's barred from leaving Maryland until her case is heard."

"That could be a year or longer."

"Probably longer, according to Marc. But, Skye's trying to make the best of a bad situation. She's enrolling Emma into a private school that fosters academic excellence, has wonderful art programs, and to top it off, an on-grounds stable. Emma loves horses, and riding is part of the curriculum."

Shane glanced at his watch, knowing how Beth loved to chitchat. He didn't want to cut her off, but he was anxious to question Jones.

"Skye is thinking about a brief getaway to either the beach or the mountains to clear her head. And Zach will be flying out for visits as often as he can. So considering, she's doing remarkably well. It was Skye, herself, that insisted I get back to my lovin' husband."

"That's generous of her." He tried to keep the sarcastic tone from his voice but feared he'd failed.

"Darlin'." She cleared her throat. "I won't be home until around ten or eleven. It depends on how quickly the pilot and the airport can figure out the flight plans and such. Don't feel like you have to wait up—"

"Of course, I'm going to wait up. Look, Betty Getty, I've been neglecting you since I started this new job. But I swear, my new position isn't gonna rob us of the time we need to be together. Seriously, I've missed you."

"Me too. But don't be worrying too much about your hours at the office. Soon I'm going to be busy *meself* setting up the shelter, modeling, and my pet project—the drunk driving PSAs. So, don't be expecting me to be a housewife much longer."

"A housewife?"

"Oh, and I can't forget, I have an interview next week with Mindy Marks."

"Mindy Marks." He frowned. "I met her snooping around Zach's place trying to get a scoop, or whatever it's called, about Skye's arrest. Believes she has the right—that she's entitled to barge into a private residence during a crisis because she works for a celebrity show. Damn snowflake."

"I haven't met her in person, but your take is interesting because I got a sense, well, there's no other way of saying it; I think she's pushy."

"That's putting it mildly. But, knowing your kind heart, I'm not surprised."

"The interview is supposed to center on my modeling career. But Mindy might try to waylay it in Skye's direction."

"I'd bet on it."

"I won't allow her to sensationalize Skye's plight by grilling me about it."

"Of course not."

"Here I am going on and on. I'm guessing you're still on the hunt for Zach's stolen paintings. Any luck?" Beth asked.

"I'm about to interview a person of interest."

"I won't be keeping you, so."

"*Mo chroí*," he said in Irish. "My darling, until tonight."

"*Tá me chroí istigh ionat.* I love you too. Until tonight."

He held the cellphone for a couple of seconds before slipping it away. He recalled the day they met when she literally ran into him at the courthouse. The impact caused her to spill a steaming cup of coffee that would've splashed on him if he hadn't been quick on his feet. Love at first sight. A soft smile crossed his face. He pulled out of his reverie, slipped into his sports jacket, and hightailed it out of the office.

Several motivating factors drove him to wrap up the case. The foremost reason being, Shane wanted to prove to Esma Flores that he was a damn good detective, and it hadn't been a mistake hiring him. Reason number two was personal satisfaction. He could almost taste the victory when he'd inform Zach Greyson his prized pieces of art had been recovered. He wanted Greyson to realize that though he's made a mountain of money pretending to be someone else, the great movie idol hadn't the slightest idea of how to recoup his prized possessions. Lastly, and most importantly, he wanted Beth to be proud of him.

An hour later, he pulled into the Swifty Lube parking lot. A man in a short-sleeved gray work shirt with the company's logo emblazoned above the breast pocket approached him.

"Full service?" The lube technician asked.

"I'm Detective Dalton. LAPD." Shane stepped out of the sedan with his badge hanging from a lanyard around his neck.

The tan skin tightened around the man's mouth.

"I'm looking for Renaldo Jones."

"You're looking at him."

"Mr. Jones. I've got a few questions for you."

Jones' black eyes shifted warily. "Whatever you think I did, I didn't do nothing. So, I guess that answers all of your questions."

"I hear you, man. But this won't take but a few minutes. That is unless you'd like to go to the station?"

Jones shook his head.

"Someplace around here where we can talk?"

Jones turned toward the building, and Shane followed on his heels. They walked through the garage, into a small waiting area, and into an equally small break room. Two vending machines stood jammed against a wall and two tables, one round and the other rectangular, filled the rest of the space. Jones pulled out a folding chair and dropped into it. He rubbed his wisp of a mustache and stared at Shane.

"Can I buy you a soda? Bag of chips?" Shane asked.

"Nah."

"Okay, then." Shane pulled out a rickety chair and sat. He folded his hands on the plastic tabletop. "Zach Greyson's place was robbed a few days ago. You know anything about that?"

Jones' eyes bore into him. "Yeah, I heard about it. On the news." He stroked the mustache a couple more times before dropping his hand on top of the table. "What's it to me?"

"You worked for Mr. Greyson as a driver. Correct?"

"Before I got this job, which is like a million times better. I don't have to deal with that stuck-up bitch who thinks she's so high and mighty but is only a maid."

Sofia.

"I know how it is having to work with difficult people," Shane said, trying to warm up to Jones. Gain his trust. "So, this maid did what? Complained to your employer about you."

"Worse than that. She got me fired."

"Bummer."

"Just because I told her she was hot, and you know, I'd like to get a piece. It was a damn compliment, man. But she got insulted."

Shane refrained from explaining his comments had been degrading, relegating Sophia to an object of sexual gratification.

"For that, I got fired."

No, Shane thought he really wouldn't understand. "Tough break."

"Yeah." Jones nodded. "It was a cushy job too. Got to drive movie stars around in cars like you wouldn't believe. Bentleys, Benzes, Jags."

"You ever spend time inside the Greyson mansion?"

"Nah, not really. Only in the kitchen. That cook was real nice. Even if you wasn't hungry, she'd load up a plate, and the food," he said, "out of this world good."

"You ever go into any other part of the house?"

He shrugged.

"Maybe to the bowling alley or art gallery."

"You're kidding me. There's a damn bowling alley in there?"

Shane's gut told him that Jones was lying through his teeth.

"Do you know anything about the stolen artwork?"

"Wait. You think I had something to do with them stolen paintings?" His face hardened once again.

"The thought crossed my mind. We both know you weren't exactly a happy camper when you were fired. Made a number of threats."

"I was royally pissed. But I swear, I don't know nothing about no stolen paintings." He shot up and turned away from the table.

"Say I believe you."

Jones turned around with his arms folded, his face a mask of distrust.

"You know there's one way to rule you out as a suspect," Shane said.

"You already got my fingerprints. DNA." A slow smile spread across his face. "You got nothing then. If you want to give me a lie detector test, you can forget it. I know my rights." He sauntered out of the room, whistling a tune Shane had never heard before.

Chapter Thirty-One

Beth hated lying to Shane but wondered if she had a choice. *If I tell him about the dinner date with Hugo Daines, he'd want to know why I'm meeting with the director.* She could hear his questions ringing in her ears. *Does this have something to do with the murder? Don't tell me, you're sticking your nose into the investigation? Questions. Questions. Questions. All of which I wouldn't be able to answer to his satisfaction and that would lead to more lies. If I'd been truthful, he'd hit the roof effin' and blinding so loudly he'd disturb the neighbors.*

"Please fasten your safety belts. We'll be landing shortly," the pilot's voice sounded in the cabin of Zach's well-appointed jet.

She attached the belt and took a sip from her wineglass. *If only Shane believed in my fey, I wouldn't have to sneak behind his back to conduct my investigation. Investigation.* She used the word lightly since her involvement aimed at uncovering the truth. "My *fey*," she whispered. *How can I clear Skye's name without my fey?* A wave of anxiety triggered her stomach to flip. She took a few deep breaths, fighting off the sense of dread that somehow her gift—both a blessing and a curse—had abandoned her.

Beth leaned her head against a soft cushion, closed her eyes, and massaged her temples. She hoped the gentle motion would unblock the channel and allow her *fey* to flow.

"I'll be happy to drop you off at your house," Bruno said.

With her fingertips still moving, she glanced at him. "That'd be lovely. Instead of my home, could you drop me off at a restaurant? Bella Giardino. It's in Beverly Hills."

"No problem."

"I have another tiny favor. Would you mind holding my luggage until tomorrow? I'll swing by Zach's and pick it up around noontime."

"That won't be necessary."

Beth wrinkled her nose, not understanding his response, but let it slip. "You're a darlin' man. Even if you have a fearsome look about you," she said with a wink. "No use trying to hide the fact. I saw you cradling Cloud and rubbing his belly."

Color rose to his cheeks. "I'm fond of cats."

"Once things settle back to normal, Zach's house will be filled with kittens. A clowder of littermates. Six in all. You'll be able to cuddle them to your heart's content."

His face remained somber, but she caught a glint of light softening his eyes.

"We'll be landing in about twenty minutes. Can I get you anything?" Bruno asked.

"Thanks, but no. I've only a few more stories to read," she said, tapping the cover of Greatpa's anthology of short stories. She adjusted her seat into an upward position and locked the club chair in place while Bruno moved to his spot outside the cockpit.

In truth, she'd read only a couple of the short stories. Every time she opened the cover, her mind wandered to the theories discussed in the other book, *Jazz Age Deception*. She couldn't shake the notion of how the 1922 love triangle between Taylor, Mary Miles Minter, and her mother, Charlotte Shelby, aligned with the players on Skye's set. *But with the Dark Grace crowd, it's more like a love diamond composed of Isabella Reid, her mother, Jane, Antonia Wright, and Cody with Thom in the middle. I'll have to wade through this confusing tangle of possible lovers tomorrow on the set.* She'd considered scratching Cody off her suspect list. *If he's feigning anguish, then Cody's the one who should be acting tomorrow on the soundstage.*

Beth pulled a notebook from her oversized tote bag and flipped through a few pages.

She stopped, locating the sheet with the name, Hugo Daines, written in capital letters. *Blind ambition has led to worse things than striving to be a movie director.* She tapped her chin. *After all, countless wars have been fought in the name of honor or patriotism but, in reality, were spurred by lust for supreme domination. Granted, Hugo Daines only wanted to dominate the production of a film. But regardless,* she thought with a tilt of her head, *power is power, and he craved to be a director. Now he's got his wish. But did he achieve it through orchestrating Thom's murder?* She looked through the window and noticed they were flying below the clouds. Her notebook slipped to the floor. Beth reached for the pad, and a more daunting problem crossed her mind. Skye's fingerprints on the knife. *If I can unravel that riddle, Thom Boyle's murder will be all but solved.*

The wheels jolted against the tarmac, and she tucked the notebook into her bag. Beth believed tonight she'd discover if Daines should be the one behind bars. Even if she had to resort to her most powerful tool: her feminine wiles.

On the way to the restaurant, Bruno's concern for her comfort surfaced as he pointed out the beverage cooler, offered to blast the air conditioning her way, and inquired about her music preferences. Otherwise, he remained silent. That's why his question inquiring if she was meeting her husband for dinner startled her as they pulled into the eatery's driveway. He'd said it so offhandedly that she almost told him she was meeting with Daines to wheedle the truth out of him. Bruno pulled to a stop, and she checked her watch. Five minutes until eight.

Perfect.

She stepped out of the Bentley and smoothed the black silk sheath dress she'd slipped into before they'd landed. Her stilettos clicked the pavement with hurried steps, not wanting to keep the director waiting. A moment later, the maître'd ushered her to the table Daines had reserved. He wasn't there.

Figures.

She thanked the head waiter for pulling out her chair. Instead of checking the time, she pushed down her impatience by scanning the room. With its sleek lines, twinkling lights, and leafy foliage the décor created the appearance of dining within the walls of an Italian garden. The restaurant is perfectly named, she mused, Beautiful Garden.

"Sibéal."

Daines' voice made her heart skip a beat.

"Sorry, I'm late. A meeting with the DP—"

"No need to apologize. And please, call me Beth."

"Beth? Okay." He pulled out the chair opposite her.

She took a quick inventory. He'd ditched the sunglasses and swapped out his usual jeans and T-shirt for a gray chambray suit.

"We got everything squared away regarding Skye's scenes."

"Oh?"

"She'll play her part against a greenscreen in a Baltimore studio. Then the film will be superimposed, making it appear as if she and the other actors are sharing the screen. Filmed separately but combined using chroma-keying."

Questions ran through her mind, but desiring to avoid a discussion on the technical aspect of filmmaking, she squashed them. "This is a lovely restaurant. I've never been here before."

"The food's great, plus it's a real hotspot. People eat here just to catch a glimpse of celebs."

Beth raised her brows. "Must be tourist, so. Locals don't seem to be affected much by film actors."

He half-shrugged.

A waiter in formal wear approached their table. With a small bow, he handed them leather-bound menus. "May I get you something to drink?" He spoke with a slight accent. Beth pegged him for an Italian.

"*Il tuo vino della casa migliore e più costoso.*"

The waiter's face lit up. "*Bene. Si, signora.*"

"Whoa," Daines said under his breath. "You speak—what was that? Italian?"

"I picked up some of the local lingo when I modeled in Milan."

"Oh, that makes sense. I was confused because I thought you were Irish—"

"You're right about that. Born and bred."

"I visited Ireland once as a kid. Don't remember much about the trip except for the rain and eating lots of potatoes and lamb. Lucky for me, those are two of my favorites. We visited relatives in England, and my parents decided to meet with another strand of the family that had moved near Dublin."

"Really, now?" She suppressed the smile that wanted to form. *He has to be related to the Daines family from my village.* "And where might they live? Ballynárach?"

He shrugged. "Speaking of lamb," he said, closing his menu. "The basil stuffed lamb here is delicious."

"Is that so? I was looking for something lighter. The salmon over a bed of greens, I think."

"You don't know what you're missing."

The chit-chat drove her mad. She longed to ask him point-blank if he was responsible for Thom's death. But of course, that wouldn't fly. He'd laugh it off.

The waiter returned with the bottle of wine. Daines did the honor of sniffing, swirling, tasting, and accepting the exorbitantly expensive bottle. She had requested the house's finest. The waiter poured the two glasses and asked for their order.

"We'll start with the antipasto platter. The lady will have the salmon salad. I will have the lamb."

"Very good, sir," The waiter said and slipped away.

"I hope you didn't mind me ordering for you," Daines said.

Mind? If Shane had done that, he'd gotten a swift kick to his shin under the table. But with Daines, she was beginning to see the micromanager surface. *He probably had a near fit when I ordered the wine.*

"Not at all, Hugo."

"My dad always orders for my mom. I picked it up from him."

She took a sip of wine, keeping her eyes focused on the director "The film is almost complete?"

"In six weeks. It's going to be amazing. A blockbuster. No doubt about it."

The waiter re-emerged with a platter stocked with sliced meats, cheese, olives, raw vegetables, and a half loaf of sliced focaccia bread. He deposited the appetizer in the center of the table and set plates in front of them next to gleaming silver utensils. "Anything else I can get for you?"

"We're fine," Beth said before Daines could answer and the waiter departed.

"If you don't mind." Daines grabbed her plate and filled it with a sampling of each selection.

"Don't tell me, your father," she said, looking into his face.

He nodded and placed the overfilled plate in front of her.

What is he going to do next? Spoon-feed me.

Intent on his plate, Daines cut the salami, prosciutto, and bresaola into small pieces and poured a couple of tablespoons of pinzimonio dipping sauce onto his plate. Then he moved on to the vegetables and chopped the grilled red pepper, carrot sticks, fennel, celery, and cherry tomatoes into tiny bite-sized portions. He took a slice of bread, cut it into quarters, dipped the edge of one piece into the sauce, and popped it into his mouth.

She'd never seen so much knife work before. Beth moved the container of pinzimonio next to her plate, lifted a piece of the Parmigiana Reggiano with her fingers, and moved it to her mouth. She held the cheese between her teeth for a split second before chewing it, believing he'd be shocked by her lack of manners.

"You have beautiful teeth," he said.

If he was appalled, it didn't show. "Thank you, Hugo." She lifted a carrot stick and dipped it into the sauce as he began slicing the baby mozzarella cheese balls. "Who's going to be credited as director for *Dark Grace*?"

He widened his eyes. "That's a tricky one. However, I believe that both Thom and I will be recognized as co-directors." He stabbed an olive with his fork. "You know," he said, placing the fork on his plate. "Chances are, I'm going to be directing a romcom later this year. You'd be perfect for the part of Hannah. It's not the lead. Skye Andrews was slated for that, but her replacement hasn't been decided yet," he said with a shrug, "but it's the BFF's part."

"Sounds intriguing." She popped another piece of cheese into her mouth.

"I'll definitely put in a plug for you with the producers and the casting director."

"That's kind of you, but you shouldn't bother."

"This I can promise you." He placed his hand on top of hers. "I'll make you a star."

She slid her hand free, picked up her wineglass, and took a sip. "That's very nice, Hugo, but I am an internationally renowned model."

"Of course. That's why it's going to be easy."

"I can't commit—"

"No problem." He dipped another square of bread into the sauce.

She decided to take the plunge. "Who do you think killed Thom?"

"The person arrested. Skye." He popped the bread into his mouth and chewed slowly.

"The police are grasping at straws."

"There must be evidence linking Skye to the murder."

"Artistic difference is a slim motive for murder."

"You'd think." He focused on his plate and sliced the olive cutting around the pit.

This is going nowhere. Beth stabbed a slice of salami but then rested the fork on her plate. "There was talk the night of Skye's arrest. I didn't put too much stock in it at the time." She didn't want to point the finger at him, so she chose a safe bet. "Cody's responsible."

"That's interesting." He chewed a forkful of sliced olive. "Because I kinda suspected him at first, too. Not to add to the rumor mill, so this is strictly between us." He pointed his knife from himself to Beth. "Antonia Wright, a magnificent actress, by the way, came to me with a problem. We're kinda close, so she wanted my take. Turned out that Thom proposed. She hadn't seen that coming and was perplexed about the whole idea of marrying him."

"Really?"

"Yup. She told him she'd have to think about it. You know, with Thom being bi and all. She worried that he'd eventually drop her for a man. Nobody needs publicity like that."

"But perhaps Toni did accept Thom's proposal, and that's why Cody—"

"Killed Thom." Daines slipped onto the chair next to Beth and reached for his plate. "Hey, I've got an amazing idea." He dropped his hand under the table and laid it on Beth's thigh.

She wanted to slap away his unwanted advance. As she suspected, he'd suggested their dinner meeting as a prelude to sex. *Fat chance of that ever happening. But I'll have to play along for a little while, at least.*

"Why don't we finish this conversation at my place?"

"What about our dinner?"

"They'll box them for us."

"I am a married woman."

He shrugged.

Beth knew one way to change the direction of the conversation fast. *Accuse him.* But at that moment, the waiter carrying a silver platter stopped at their table. He deposited their plates in front of them.

"May I get you anything else? Fresh ground pepper? Cheese?"

"We're fine," Daines said, not taking his eyes off of Beth. "However, we need some to-go boxes."

After the waiter departed, Daines' fingers started to move toward the inside of her thigh.

She'd had enough. "I was thinking."

"Uh-huh." He moved closer so that his lips brushed her cheek.

"Maybe you wanted Thom dead."

He jerked his head away. "What?"

"The young, creative, ambitious genius," she said, removing his hand from her leg, "who doesn't want to pay his dues, murders the director to assume his place. That scenario makes sense to me."

A slow smile crept across his face. "That detective, what's his name? Oh yeah, Fox. Had the same idea. But as you see, I'm free and poor Skye." He shook his head. "Look, I understand you want to help your friend. But you have to face facts."

She pressed the side of her fork through the salmon filet. "Facts?"

"Sometimes people are driven by strong emotions to do things. Like Skye murdering Thom. And me wanting to make love to the most beautiful woman I've ever known. Even if she is married."

Beth looked away, wondering how she'd wiggle out of this mess. She'd been a fool to think he'd admit to murder. But then she did a double-take seeing a mountain of a man heading in their direction. *Bruno.*

"Oh my," she gasped.

Daines looked up from the lamb roast he was cutting into tiny pieces.

She gestured toward the bodyguard.

"Who's he?" Daines asked, holding his knife mid-air.

"My husband," she said, hoping to the good Lord that Bruno would play along. "He's prone to jealousy and has a temper. That's why I kept our dinner a secret."

Bruno stopped a few feet away. Before he could say anything, she blurted, "Darling, this is the director." She noticed a mild look of amusement cross Bruno's face.

"Hugo Daines," he said, jumping to his feet with an outstretched arm.

Bruno made no attempt to shake his hand but only stared at Daines with his usual intimidating expression. "I'm taking you home."

"Is there a problem?" The waiter said, returning with the take-out boxes.

"No," Daines said.

"If you could pack my dinner." Beth motioned toward her plate.

The waiter filled two boxes. One with her dinner and the other with the leftover antipasto. Three pairs of eyes stared at him in stony silence.

With one hand, Bruno grabbed the boxes while Beth grasped his arm. She glanced over her shoulder at Daines and mouthed, "See you tomorrow."

Chapter Thirty-Two

Unable to concentrate, Jeremy Fox shut down his laptop. The aim of Baltimore's Police Homicide Unit was to work and resolve cases by sending the bad guys to jail. But he, like everyone in the city, knew that didn't always happen. Not even half of the time. The number of open murder cases topped sixty-five percent and never seemed to shrink. He often reminded himself not to dwell on the stats but to do the necessary work and close one case at a time. Still, there remained a myriad of innocent dead, murdered in streets that resemble war zones, and he longed to be their voice and find justice for them. That's what kept him doing an often thankless job.

Even if the murder case of the Hollywood director was one for the books, it wouldn't let go of him. Mainly because of who he'd arrested. *Maybe talking with Dalton in LA will . . . What? Offer confirmation or reinforce the fact that I made a big mistake?*

"Skye Andrews," he mumbled the name, tossing his pen on the desk. It hit the metal surface and did a summersault in the air before landing on the worn carpeted floor.

"What's up with you?" Tamera Stevens looked at him from behind her desk.

"Can't focus." He retrieved the pen.

"You need to go home, eat a decent meal, and get a good night's sleep. Because in all honesty, you look like a wreck. Don't tell me it's that ex-girlfriend of yours? You guys haven't reconnected—"

"No, nothing like that. It's this." He lifted a file from his desk. "The Thom Boyle murder."

"What about it?"

"That's the problem. I don't really know. But something seems off. Like why was there only one set of prints on the knife belonging to Skye Andrews? Seems hinky. That's all."

"It was enough to convince the DA's office."

"True. But what about motive? Seems thin. Andrews disagrees with the director and offs him. It's hard to believe that a big star like her would throw everything she ever worked for away over how some movie scene is to be played."

"I'm still trying to understand why people do the things they do. No matter how crazy it seems."

"You and me too. But," Fox said, resting his chin in his palm, "Andrews believed killing the director was more important than her career?"

"Who knows? But anyway, there's not much you can do about it. You did your job. It's not up to any of us," she said, waving her arm as if encompassing the room, "to make a judgment. We're here to do the grunt work."

"Right, right. I know."

"Besides, a woman like Skye Andrews is loaded. And her husband is more loaded than she is. Zach Greyson." A dreamy look covered her face. "That is one, damn, sexy man. The way he plays a love scene," she said, shaking her head. "Anyway, Skye Andrews has the cash to hire one of those super expensive lawyers that are sharks in the courtroom. Hey, remember O.J.?"

"I guess you're right. But—"

"Look, if you have reservations, some of the jury members are bound to feel the same way. So don't lose any sleep over it." She took a quick sip of coffee. "Because from the look of things, you may have lost too many Zs to catch up."

"I hear you. I guess I do need a break. That's why I put in for some time off. Racked up a few weeks of vacation, I've put off using. Should know today if it's approved. With it being summer and all, I might not get it." He shrugged.

"How many weeks did you ask for?"

"Days. Four days."

"Sheez, that's like asking for a long weekend off."

"It's enough time to do what I need to take care of."

"It's too short for a trip to Aruba. That, by the way, would be a good place for you to unwind. So, you planning to go down the ocean?"

He grabbed a few papers and stepped next to her desk. "I just printed these. Take a look."

She sat up a bit straighter and took the pages. She thumbed through the sheets then gave him a sideways glance.

He read the amused look that had a habit of making her eyes sparkle.

"So, you're going Hollywood."

Chapter Thirty-Three

Beth slid into the back seat of Zach's Bentley Flying Spur. The soft hum of the engine filled her ears as she looked through the window into the darkness. She'd sent up a quick prayer of thanks for her rescue from "hot to trot" Daines. Even so, she still hadn't gotten over the shock that Bruno had shown up in the restaurant at the pivotal moment.

She crossed her fingers that Bruno's intimidating presence had discouraged any idea of romance from Hugo Daines' warped mind. She pursed her lips. *The opposite reaction might arise if Daines is open to a challenge. But,* she thought with a shake of her head, *I bet he doesn't have the nerve to go toe to toe with my surrogate husband just for a roll in the hay.* She wanted to pin Daines, all the more, for the murder due to his brazen behavior. But, she knew being a sleaze didn't necessarily qualify someone as a killer.

"He might be a damn good director, but I don't like that guy," Bruno said, breaking the silence between them.

"Me either." Beth drew her attention away from the window and focused on what she could see of Bruno from the back seat. "I'm confused. Why did you enter the restaurant in the first place?"

"Mr. Greyson instructed me to take you home. Make sure you arrived safe and sound. Including your luggage."

His earlier comment now made sense. "So you returned to *Bella Giardino*—"

"Never left. I parked in the lot until I figured your dinner would be over. Then I hung out in the lobby 'cause you were still eating. But when that director what's his name—"

"Hugo Daines."

"Yeah. When Daines made a move on you, it was time to act."

"Truth is, you're a lifesaver." She imagined her compliment brought a blush to his cheeks. "I hope you didn't mind that I pretended you were my husband."

"Heck, no. Didn't mind one bit. Kinda made my day."

"I'm glad to hear that. If my darlin' Shane had walked into that scene, it would've been—I shudder to even imagine. You handled it brilliantly."

"All in a day's work."

"Um, Bruno. Has anyone checked Skye's beach house to make sure it too wasn't burgled?" She hadn't the slightest idea why the oceanfront property zipped through her mind. Skye hadn't mentioned concern about her ultra-modern house, even though she considered it her prized treasure and the source of solace whenever she needed a break from Zach.

"I don't think so. No."

Now that the idea had taken hold, Beth couldn't relax until she knew the beach house hadn't been tampered with. "You think we could swing by there? I keep Skye's emergency key in my change purse."

"It's an hour away."

"But this time of night, traffic won't be so bad?" Normally, she wouldn't insist. But now that she'd made the request, a rush of adrenaline coursed through her. If it hadn't been dormant for so long, she would've sworn her *fey* had sent the message.

"The caretaker hasn't contacted me about any pressing issues. But whatever you want. I'm at your service, courtesy of Mr. Greyson."

"Ah, that be grand altogether. Truly, Bruno, you're bleedin' massive."

"That would be a good thing?"

"A *fierce* good thing."

197

Beth yawned. Still on Eastern Time, she realized it must be nearing midnight in Baltimore. She hadn't slept much on the flight back to LA, so she snuggled against the cushy leather seat and closed her eyes.

$$\cdot \quad \cdot \quad \cdot$$

"Miss, we're here."

Bruno's voice sounded far away. Beth fluttered her eyes open, seeming as if she'd only closed them. The passenger door opened, and he offered Beth a hand as she stepped out of the car. She rolled her shoulders and glanced at the contemporary-style house. Light filtered from the facade's three-story wall of glass. She chided herself for worrying. Nonetheless, Beth hurried to the front door, slipped in the key, and turned the handle. She stepped inside with Bruno behind her.

The elevator door stood to the left of the foyer but Beth opted for the grand staircase that swerved like the movement of a bird in flight. While Bruno faced the alarm, she ran upstairs, energized from her brief nap, and stepped into the main living area. The previous owners used the airy space with soaring ceilings and windows walls as a rec room equipped with a hand-carved pool table and an array of vintage pinball machines. Skye, on the other hand, furnished the space with leather, glass, and metal. A handcrafted chandelier with natural brass and descending crystal drops hung from the ceiling and large canvases splashed with bright colors filled the walls. It gave off an aura of cool elegance, which usually left Beth longing for the coziness of her little den.

She clicked on the lights and froze.

Cherry red paint splattered the pristine white wall. Streams of dried paint had dribbled downward and settled into shiny pools on the wooden floor. The large abstract paintings created by Skye's former lover, Kenny Weston, lay in a jumble slashed and covered with trails of red paint. Beth covered her mouth and turned around, taking in the devastation.

"Bruno!" she shouted, finding her voice.

"Charlie up there with you?" he called as his heavy footsteps sounded on the metal staircase.

"Charlie?" she whispered.

"Holy crap!" Bruno said, stepping into the room. "Good God Almighty!" He moved among the debris, walked the length of the massive room, and peeked into the kitchen. "Don't come over here," he raised his palms in an attempt to stop her.

Beth ignored his directive and moved to the kitchen. She cringed, not believing her eyes. The blender, coffee maker, and toaster looked like they'd been smashed with a sledgehammer. The cabinets stood empty and marked with red paint, while crockery lay in ruins on the ceramic tile floor. She crossed her arms, trying to take in the carnage. It'd been only a month since the main living area had been refurbished—walls painted, floors replaced, custom window treatments, and new furniture Skye handpicked. After finding the murdered body of Emma's nanny in the great room, Skye wanted a new look. That way, she wouldn't be reminded of the tragedy that had transpired inside her beloved beach house.

"I'm gonna check the rest of this floor and upstairs. You stay here." Bruno said. "Where the hell is Charlie?" He glanced at Beth. "The caretaker."

She couldn't stand around waiting for Bruno to check the house. After a few seconds, she crept down the staircase and moved along the wide corridor, peeking into rooms. Nothing looked disturbed. A cold shiver ran through her body when she reached the screening room. She inhaled as a wave of both gratitude and foreboding filled her. Her *fey* had resurfaced by issuing a warning. Something ominous took place in the mini theater. She debated running upstairs to locate Bruno or to enter the dark room.

It took only a split-second to decide. Beth stepped into the theater, flicked on the light switch, and walked down the aisle, stopping on the second riser. "Dear Lord," she whispered, scooting in front of the plush seats toward a figure slumped over the armrest console. "Charlie?"

"Beth, are you down here?" Bruno called.

"In the theater. Come quick," she yelled. She pressed her fingers against the man's neck in a mad search for a pulse.

It seemed like an eternity until Bruno appeared at her side. "What the hell?"

"I can't find a pulse."

She moved away to give him room. Bruno touched the man's face and checked his carotid artery.

"He's alive."

Relief flooded through her.

"He might've suffered a TBI."

She chewed her lip, not understanding.

"Call 911. I have paramedic training, but I can't do anything without equipment. We'll need police and a medic unit."

Beth pulled the mobile from her clutch and tapped the emergency number. "Someone's hurt." she said. "We need an ambulance and the police." Doing her utmost to remain calm, she answered the dispatcher's question about their location but then handed the phone to Bruno.

"Got a male, mid-thirties, comatose, most likely a TBI," he said.

Beth sunk onto a step. It seemed likely the injured man wasn't responsible for the desecrated rooms upstairs. Bruno handed back her mobile.

"Charlie?"

"Yeah." Bruno sucked in a mouthful of air. "I recommended Charlie for the job."

She rose and touched Bruno's arm. "Will he be okay?"

"Hard to say. Traumatic brain injuries can be fatal. Looks like a two-by-four bashed his head." Bruno pointed to the clot of dry blood on the back of Charlie's head. "Could've been watching a movie and didn't hear the perp coming behind him."

"The poor man."

"I discovered the point of entry," he said. "A window in the mudroom off the garage."

"None of this makes sense." Beth shook her head.

"The theater is pitch black when a movie is playing. The thug could've mistaken Charlie for Miss Andrews."

Beth's temples throbbed. The idea that Skye might've been a target in a murderous scheme rang true. Whoever trashed her house and attacked the caretaker possessed a deep hatred for Skye. Stars are loved, emulated, revered, but also stalked, judged, and envied.

How could it be that Skye's the target of another madman?

She looked at the mobile in her hand. If ever she needed Shane, it was now. She tapped his number and waited.

Chapter Thirty-Four

Tamera Stevens couldn't sleep. She threw off the sheet and headed to the kitchen, opened the refrigerator, and pulled out a take-out box containing a slice of cheesecake. Earlier that evening, her dinner date with Brandon had been perfect. For a few hours, the stain of co-parenting vanished. Her ex had been getting on her last nerve by refusing to follow the set rules and routines they'd established for the children.

She filled a mug with water, placed it into the microwave, and paced across the ceramic tile floor, waiting for it to heat up. Usually, work kept her up late at night but not this time. Two men—Brandon Greene and Darnell Stevens—had stolen her sleep. The beeper sounded. She removed the mug, dropped a chamomile tea bag into the water, and waited for it to seep.

Tamera hoped the tea would soothe her worries away. She grabbed the mug, the cheesecake, and sat at the peninsula separating the kitchen from the family room. She lifted the creamy cake and took a generous bite. It melted in her mouth, and she took another quick bite. She licked the remains off her fingers and took a sip of tea. Spying her cellphone, she fought the urge to check for texts. Plenty of detectives kept their phones bedside, but she didn't. There's no way she'd leave her sleeping kids tucked in their beds while she poked around a murder scene. And in this city, there were far too many of them.

"That's why J is a great partner. He takes all the night cases so I can work mostly during the day." Her voice, barely above a whisper, sounded like a bullhorn in the silent house.

She glared at the cheesecake, debating whether to pop the remaining piece into her mouth. After a few seconds of indecision, she decided against it. She'd gained ten pounds since the divorce. She had no one to blame but herself, having turned to food when she couldn't deal with Darnell's nonsense. She grabbed the mug, took a sip, and walked the length of the kitchen. On the return trip, she released the cable from the cellphone charger, remembering she hadn't checked the photos the waitress snapped of them at the restaurant. The screen lit up, and Brandon's smiling face greeted her. A soft sigh escaped her lips. "Darnell can't compare to you."

The two men couldn't be more different. Darnell, the epitome of tall, dark, and handsome, and Brandon—well, she admitted with a shrug of her shoulder, he's got the dark part down pat. Brandon stood only a couple inches taller than she and sported a spare tire around his middle, but his laugh was music to her ears, and his smile warmed her heart. Darnell, on the other hand, had broken it.

Still holding the phone, she resumed pacing. *How many times has Darnell disappointed the kids for not showing up for his weekend with them? And when he does take the kids, he loads them up with expensive toys and electronics and always returns them way too late with a different bimbo on his arm.* Too many times to count, she'd bitten her tongue around the kids. *They adore him.* She shook her head. *And then there's the child support.*

She stopped at the counter and took a sip of tea. *Darnell seems to be rolling in money. Or else he's up to his eyeballs in hock. A brand-new Mercedes. And what the hell is he thinking, buying a house in Federal Hill? Some of those houses sell upwards of eight hundred thousand dollars. No Baltimore City cop can afford to live like that.*

She tapped the darkened cellphone screen and scrolled through a group of photos. She stopped at one of Brandon and she, clinking champagne glasses for a toast. The six-month anniversary of their first date. All thoughts of Darnell vanished.

I like Brandon. But things are moving too fast. I don't want to be committed to any man now. She swallowed a mouthful of tea and made a face tasting the tepid liquid.

"Mom."

Tamera looked away from the phone and into her eight-year-old daughter's questioning eyes. "Why aren't you in bed?"

"Can't sleep." The girl shrugged.

"You have school tomorrow. C'mon. I'll tuck you in."

"Can you lay on my bed with me?"

Tamera nodded. Snuggling with her daughter seemed the only way she'd fall asleep tonight.

Chapter Thirty-Five

Beth, along with Bruno, waited outside for the detectives to arrive. Spotlights illuminated the beach house's exterior as bright beams streamed through every window of the glass and stucco edifice. Beth willed the minutes to fly as she looked for Shane's car to turn into the driveway. She covered her mouth, trying to suppress a yawn, willed her eyelids to stay open, and inhaled a couple gulps of sea air.

She glanced at Bruno, leaning against one of the decorative stucco walls enclosing groups of native shrubbery bordered by clusters of palm trees. He'd done most of the talking when the first responders arrived.

While the paramedics worked on the injured man, Beth attempted to channel her *fey* and unlock the perpetrator's identity. Wiping all thoughts from her mind, she hoped a message would surface. A soft breeze caressed her face, and the briny air moistened her skin. Distracted, she raised her hand and touched her hair, not surprised that the humidity had crimped the auburn locks into wavy curlicues. Beth sighed, not receiving the slightest insight, and dropped onto the step with her back facing the double glass front door.

"Hello?" A familiar voice sounded.

Marjorie? Marjorie Hammond.

Beth wasn't the least surprised. Marjorie lived for a juicy piece of gossip.

"Beth? I thought you were in Baltimore helping Skye out." Marjorie pointed to the array of police vehicles lining the street. "What in God's name is going on?" She didn't pause for a response. "I had a grueling day on the campaign trail for Marc and come home to this."

Though weighted by fatigue, Beth stood and stepped closer to the woman.

"You can't imagine how exhausted I am," Marjorie chattered. "Not only did I have a speaking engagement at a women's club and a blog interview, we attended a dinner at a lawyer event which thankfully, I bailed out of once the speeches began. Marc is still there."

"You have been busy."

Marjorie nodded. "Soaking in my tub, the tension gripping my body started to melt away as I sipped a glass of champagne—then bam. It sounded like all of Malibu must've burst into flames with the deafening blare of sirens. So, like what choice did I have? I jumped out of the tub, threw on some clothes, and rushed outside to find out what happened."

Beth squeezed her lips into a tight line.

"And once again," Marjorie said, jutting her chin toward Skye's house. "I knew better than to like just knock on the door. I did that once before, and it got me no place." She gave Beth a sidelong glance.

Marjorie referred to the murder of Emma's nanny a few months ago. Beth wanted to ask Marjorie if she'd really expected Shane to divulge the details of a crime scene to a nosy neighbor. But she didn't have the strength.

"As you know, my statement turned out to be vital," Marjorie said. "If the case had gone to court, I would've been one of the star witnesses." A smile shot across her face.

Witness? The only thing Marjorie witnessed was sending poor Lexi on an errand a couple of hours before she was killed. And slipping the nanny's diary into one of her kitchen drawers. Knowing Marjorie, she'd elevated her role in the investigation to bolster her sense of inadequacy. Compared to her overachiever attorney husband, Marc Hammond, Marjorie truly believed she couldn't measure up with only a high school diploma and her former profession as a restaurant hostess.

Beth felt a bit sorry for Marjorie, driven to putting on airs to convince herself she was good enough to be married to a brilliant lawyer. But besides being nosy and a bit flighty, her major flaws, Marjorie possessed a good heart. She'd stayed by Skye's side, comforting her during her previous ordeal—when Skye faced two murders that had hit close to home.

'Tis no surprise Marjorie has been working herself to the bone on Marc's campaign.

It doesn't take a sixth sense to grasp the depth of Marjorie's trepidation. And truly, I wouldn't be surprised if Marc eventually dumps her like his previous three wives. That would destroy her. In Marjorie's eyes, her Marc shines like the sun, the moon, and the stars. She adores him.

"Well?" Marjorie asked.

"Huh?"

"What happened?"

"Nothing to be concerned about. A break-in. Probably adolescent hijinks." There was no way on God's green earth Beth would divulge even a sliver of information about the wreckage and the injured caretaker.

"Like this is what Skye needs. Especially now. When she's . . . in *jail*," Marjorie whispered.

She's trying to wheedle information out of me, Beth decided but wasn't going to play into her little game. After all, she imagined Marc would have told her Skye had been released from custody.

Beth glanced at Bruno. He hadn't moved but had folded his arms across his chest. She offered him a half shrug and linked arms with her inquisitive friend. "I'll be at Marjorie's house," she said. "Over—"

"I know where she lives," Bruno said.

As they walked away, Marjorie said, "I don't know why Zach has that brute for a bodyguard. He's so gruff. Rude, even."

"Bruno's job description doesn't require a pleasant personality."

"Whatever," Marjorie said with a shrug.

"It's been only a few hours since I arrived home from visiting Skye," Beth said.

"How's she holding up?"

"A bit fragile. But at least she's back with Emma and Zach in the beautiful house where they've been staying."

"Oh, that's right. Marc did mention Skye got bail. But tell me," Marjorie said, leaning in close to Beth, "do you think she did it?"

"Did what?"

"You know. Did Skye kill the director? Bill Boyle or whatever his name was."

"Thom Boyle. And seriously, you really think Skye's capable—"

"No. But I've been watching a lot of those true crime shows on TV. Some of those people commit murder for the stupidest reasons." She shrugged. "You hungry?"

"Now that you mention it, I didn't eat much dinner."

Marjorie ushered Beth into her house, led her into the kitchen, and opened the refrigerator. She pulled out a handful of containers. "I've got mashed sweet potatoes, roasted chicken, peas, and cornbread."

"Sounds wonderful, but do you have anything lighter? A cup of soup?"

"As a matter of fact, I have a quart of hot and sour soup from that amazing Chinese restaurant, Golden Lantern. You've ever eaten there?"

"Not yet." Beth shook her head. "The soup sounds wonderful."

Marjorie grabbed a plastic take-out container and placed it into the microwave while Beth sat at the marble-topped work island.

"I was thinking about visiting Skye," Marjorie said. "Marc said she's not doing all that great."

"She'd love it."

"Really?" Marjorie's eyes widened.

"Of course. You'd be just the tonic needed to raise her spirits."

The microwave buzzed. Marjorie removed the soup, poured it into a ceramic bowl, and placed it in front of Beth. A second later, she handed her a spoon and a linen napkin. "I have some news." She sat on the swivel barstool next to Beth.

"Oh?" Beth raised a spoonful, blew across the steaming liquid, and tasted it. "You're right. It's delicious." She fought the urge to drink the soup directly from the bowl.

Marjorie took a deep breath. "I haven't told Marc yet."

Beth read the hesitation on her face. "Is something wrong?" She rested the spoon in the soup bowl.

"No. Not really—like—um—well, I'm pregnant."

"Pregnant!" Beth threw her arms around Marjorie and squeezed her. "How wonderful. How far along are you?"

"Three months."

"And you haven't told Marc?"

"He already has two kids from his first wife. They're grown. One is married and is a top-notch realtor, and the other is in medical school. Marc always says he's glad the kids are out from under his feet and living on their own." Tears filled her eyes. "It's not fair. I always wanted a baby— kids—a house full of them. But now, with his job and the campaign, I know he's gonna say a baby doesn't fit his lifestyle." A stray tear slipped down her cheek.

Beth handed her the napkin. "You might be surprised. I can't imagine Marc not wanting a darlin' baby with you."

She patted her eyes. "You think so?"

"I do. And no more champagne for you."

"Oh, that. I mentioned champagne because it sounds sophisticated. Actually, it was actually sparkling blush, you know, apple and raspberry cider."

Doorbell chimes filled the air.

"It's probably Bruno," Beth said. "The detectives might've arrived and want to question me. You stay put. I'll get the door."

Beth left the kitchen, crossed through the newly decorated living area, and raced down the staircase. She expected Bruno, but a wave of relief rippled through her seeing Shane fill the doorway. She fell into his arms.

"Bruno told me you were here," he whispered in her ear. "Can we leave before—"

"Beth," Marjorie called.

"It's Shane. I have to go now."

Marjorie appeared at the top of the landing. "Hey, Shane." She didn't wait for a response. "I'll talk to you soon, Beth. And thanks."

"Goodbye, God bless," Beth said and grasped Shane's arm. Once outside, she realized the air had cooled. A dry breeze had arisen and blew tendrils of hair off her forehead.

"Marjorie didn't storm over to Skye's like last time, did she?" Shane asked.

"I intercepted her. But she was all ears wanting to know what happened."

"Same old Marjorie."

"Indeed."

They took a few steps in silence.

"Have you been inside Skye's house?" Beth asked.

"Not yet. But I shouldn't have trouble gaining access since paintings are involved."

"Brace yourself. It's devastating. Will probably send Skye over the edge. I'm guessing that was the purpose of trashing her house. But the poor caretaker. An innocent victim in a vicious game. Luckily, he's still alive and hopefully reached the hospital in time." She looked at Shane. "Who would do this to Skye?"

"You, of all people, should know that sickos become obsessed with celebrities. Sometimes they stalk them, other times they kill, believing the celeb will be impressed, or sadly even kill the object of their obsession. Why do you think Greyson has bodyguards? This could just be par for the course."

"I don't think so. No. This is personal. A message of pure hate."

They reached the end of Skye's driveway. Beth noticed Bruno engaged with a man, a detective, she imagined, dressed in a sports jacket and tie with a stoic expression that matched the look on Bruno's face. Tugging on Shane's arm, Beth hurried her stride, and they joined the little group. The detective glanced at Beth and introduced himself.

Before Beth could respond, Shane said, "I'm Detective Shane Dalton, LAPD, Art Theft Detail. I understand some valuable works of art were destroyed."

"Go on in. You know the drill."

Shane knew it only too well. Before entering Skye's house, he fished out latex gloves from a pocket and pulled his hands into them. He stepped into the foyer, nodded at the officer by the door, and signed the login sheet. Taking the steps, two by two, he flew up the wide staircase—one of the few features in Skye Andrews' oceanfront house that impressed him.

Shane had been inside the house several times, most memorably when Skye surprised him and Beth with a pre-wedding party. He'd hung out mainly in the downstairs den. But did spend time admiring the unique staircase while Skye flitted among her movie star friends, Beth mingled, and Zach held court. Though he wasn't a fan of the ultramodern structure, he believed the beach house exemplified an excellent standard of modernist architecture. Perfectly suited for Skye's love of functional and minimalist elements.

Shane moved from the second-floor landing into the great room, where a forensics team meticulously worked the scene. They'd examine every square inch, searching for any traces of evidence from the tiniest thread to fingerprints. Shane let out a sigh, taking in the room. Even though Beth had described the vandalism, the destruction looked worse than he'd imagined. Large splashes of red paint defaced the walls, and Skye's prized paintings lay in irreparable heaps on the floor. The only good thing was that Kenny Weston could create new ones, whereas Zach's stolen artworks could never be reproduced. He fingered his cleft chin, attempting to

211

discern a connection between the two incidents. If forensic evidence was found, it could offer a clue to Zach's stolen pieces. But his gut told him that whoever did this trash job had been careful and betted not a vestige of evidence would be found.

Shane walked around the perimeter, glanced at the kitchen area, and shook his head. He reached for his cellphone, scrolled down his contact list, and, with a touch of dread, tapped Greyson's number. The ringing filled his ear. Just as he was about to cut the connection, he heard a sleepy "hello."

"It's Dalton. I've got some disturbing news."

"What?" Zach paused. "About my stolen artwork?"

"No, not that. It concerns Skye. Her beach house's been was vandalized, and it doesn't look random. You need to get here ASAP."

"You've got to be kidding. Dammit. What the hell is going on?" Any vestige of sleep coloring his voice had vanished.

Shane didn't know how to answer. "I think your stolen art and Skye's ruined paintings share a common link."

"You mean the Weston paintings—"

"Completely trashed."

"Look, I'm in Maryland. It'll be hours before I can get there."

"Alright. Shouldn't be a problem. I'll tell the detectives you're on your way."

"Hold up. What about the caretaker? Is he responsible for—"

"Ambushed. Been transported to the hospital. If he regains consciousness, he might be able to offer up something. "

Silence filled Shane's ears. He doubted the signal had failed but believed Zach needed a few seconds to digest the information.

"Beth's the one who thought of checking the house. Bruno brought her here and they discovered—"

"Look, Dalton. I don't want Skye to know about any of this. Make sure no one from the LAPD contacts her. Okay?"

"Yeah. Sure. I'll notify the investigator and give him your cell number."

"Right then. I'll be in touch. And thanks."

"No problem." Shane ended the call.

Turning his back on the ravaged upper level, Shane went downstairs and moved along the hallway into another living area. Less formal than the room upstairs, it housed a bar, an arrangement of cushy-looking chairs, and a travertine fireplace set between floor-to-ceiling windows. A lone greeting card sat on the fireplace mantel. He squinted, thinking the card seemed out of place stuck between two abstract ceramic vases. He walked around the edge of the room and grabbed it. The cover seemed overly decorated with a pink floral design and a lacy overlay for Skye's taste. He flipped the card open. Instead of a printed greeting with fancy calligraphy, a jumble of pasted cut-out letters and words from magazines filled the inside spread.

"What is this? Some cheesy take on a fifties noir TV show. Weird," he whispered. He read the words, and his stomach tightened.

Don't sit alone in the dark watching yourself try to act, or else, you'll be sorry.

Chapter Thirty-Six

Shane pulled into their driveway, unable to expel the cryptic message from his mind. Beth slept most of the trip home, so the ideas bouncing around his head weren't interrupted. He shut down the engine and glanced at Beth, rubbing his dimpled chin. *Greyson's stolen art and Skye's destroyed paintings couldn't be a coincidence. The paint splatter, ruined furniture, and wrecked kitchen prove a deep-seated loathing for Skye. But why target works of art?* He shook his head. An attack on social media or in the press, he guessed, wouldn't do as much damage as the loss of their prized art treasures. *A blow directly to the heart?*

"We're home." He kissed Beth's cheek.

She twisted in the seat, keeping her eyes closed.

"I'll guide you to the bedroom. You won't have to open your eyes."

"I didn't get a chance to tell you," she mumbled. "My *fey*—"

"Tell me in the morning." He alighted from his Audi, ran around the car, and opened her door. Leaning inside, he unfastened Beth's seatbelt.

She turned her head and kissed him squarely on the lips.

"Hey, I thought you were sleeping."

"I woke up," she said, slipping out of the car and throwing her arms around him. "I missed you so much, but what a homecoming."

"You can say that again." He touched the silky bodice of her dress. "And you gussied up for the occasion. Pretty fancy for a flight."

"I changed outfits on the plane." She swiped a lock of frizzy hair behind her ear. "I wanted tonight to be romantic, hence the new evening dress. Bruno stopped at that lovely Italian restaurant, Bella Giardino, where I picked up dinner. I intended to set the table by the pool, and after we ate well, I was going to let you," she said, slipping the strap off her shoulder. "Oh well, my plans are ruined, but the food is in with the luggage."

He ran his fingertips across her cheek, brushing her jagged scar. "We could always go for it another time. Tomorrow night?"

"Lovely. That'll be grand altogether."

He moved to the trunk, and she followed a step behind. "Bruno is a very accommodating guy driving you all over the place."

"Bruno is devoted to the Greysons. Zach instructed him to oblige me. And it's a good thing too. If he hadn't, that poor man—the caretaker—might've died."

"He's not out of the woods yet. It may be touch and go for a while. Brain injuries are tricky."

"I'll say a decade for his recovery before going to sleep." Beth grabbed her carry-on from the trunk and walked through the opened garage into the house.

She didn't pause to check the pile of mail stacked on the table off the mudroom and took the elevator to the second floor. Her stomach clenched. *The lying has to stop.* Her twisting of the truth and outright deceit seemed like a sickness she couldn't shake. *I swear, I'll turn over a new leaf tomorrow. No more dishonesty when it comes to my Shane.* She walked across the expansive bedroom and took a quick look into the mirror, made a face, and undressed. Since her facial cleansers lay buried somewhere in a suitcase, she grabbed a bar of soap. After washing her face and using Shane's mouthwash, she bunched up a couple of pillows and slipped into bed.

The hour-long nap on the ride home revived her and Beth sought guidance from her *fey.* The welcomed return of her sixth sense bolstered her confidence and ensured she'd pinpoint the culprit who'd murdered Thom. And, fingers crossed, lead her to the despicable person responsible for vandalizing Skye's house and attacking the caretaker. She reached for her rosary on the nightstand.

The perp's soul must be inflamed with blistering hatred toward Skye. What on earth could she have done to trigger such hostility? Beth blew out a stream of air and glanced at the beads wrapped around her fingers. She raised the crucifix about to begin her prayer when Shane entered the room.

"Still awake?" Shane asked. "I thought by now you'd be out like a light."

"The awful scene at Skye's got me thinking. Murdering the caretaker wasn't the perp's intent. It was ransacking Skye's house."

Shane sat on the edge of the mattress and rubbed his dimpled chin with his thumb.

"That deduction was easy," she said. "Who carries buckets of paint with them when they plan to murder someone?"

"Uh-huh."

"Are you even listening?"

"We're both exhausted. It'll keep until morning." He leaned over and kissed her.

"You're right." She scooted down the mattress. "Except, there's something I have to tell you about Marjorie."

"I cringe to think what the outcome would've been if you'd told Marjorie what happened in Skye's house. Half of Los Angeles would know by now."

"I wouldn't be surprised. But, the truth is, Marjorie can keep a secret. She's keeping a doozy from her husband."

Shane's eyebrows lifted, widening his eyes.

"She's going to be a mother."

"Oh," he said under his breath. "Did that upset you?"

The fingers of depression hardly touched her anymore because of Shane. He'd helped her embrace life again after learning she'd never conceive a child.

"No worries, love. I'm thrilled for Marjorie. Even so, 'tis a shame, she has reservations about sharing the news with her husband."

"You mean because he's a self-centered jackass."

She ignored his comment. "Marc's children are grown and out on their own. He's content with the way things stand. Meaning no more kids."

"I'm not surprised. A baby would certainly cramp his style, especially if he's planning on becoming the newest US senator from the state of California." Shane pulled his tie loose and unbuttoned his shirt.

"She didn't come right out and say it, but I think she's scared Marc might divorce her or try to talk Marjorie into an abortion. The thought of that breaks my heart."

"What will she do?"

Beth shrugged. "Marjorie loves her lifestyle and the idea of being a senator's wife. Let's hope Marc welcomes the idea of being a father again."

"You know, I feel kinda bad for the kids of celebrities. With their parents' constant need to feed their egos, I doubt much time is left over for the children."

"Not all celebs. Zach is desperate for a child. Looks like he's going to get his wish. Skye is hammering out the details so he can adopt Emma."

"Those two probably share a close bond. After all, Greyson saved Emma's life."

"She adores Zach."

"Speaking of Greyson, this may sound crazy, but my gut's telling me there's a connection between the stolen paintings and Skye's destroyed ones," Shane said. "I'm at a loss, though, when it comes to what that correlation could be."

She pursed her lips. "That has to mean you're on the right track." *Is this what my fey's been wanting to tell me?* She closed her eyes, intent on emptying her mind to allow her sixth sense to surface. But, after only a half-minute of concentration, she drifted off into a dreamless sleep.

Chapter Thirty-Seven

Jeremy Fox stared outside the airplane window. A sheet of puffy clouds resembling a mass of giant cotton balls stretched for miles. *Convective clouds.* The knowledge surfaced from a repository of data, stored away from a cloud computing class in college when Fox majored in meteorology. Air escaped his lips like a whistle, remembering how many years had passed since he traversed the halls of academia. *Seven.* After graduating, the idea of settling into a nine-to-five seemed suffocating, so he'd opted to pursue another line of study. The interdisciplinary major of criminal justice piqued his imagination, and he'd never looked back.

He shifted in his seat, flipped the tray forward, and adjusted his earbuds. The choral strands of Mozart's Requiem in D filled his ears. The music's doleful melody, beautiful and haunting, did little to quiet the fluctuating thoughts that had him wishing he'd never left Baltimore. *What the hell am I doing? The Boyle case is closed tighter than a drum.* He recalled the confusion filling Skye Andrews' blue-green eyes during the interrogation. Sure, sure, he assured himself, she's an actress. Her innocent demeanor could've been an act. *But still . . ..*

With a concerted effort, Fox returned his gaze to the book he'd planned to finish during the flight. He'd scarcely read a full paragraph. After only a couple of sentences, he gave up. The printed words didn't compute, so he closed the true-crime paperback, and glanced at his watch. In about an hour, the plane would be landing at LAX.

He hadn't been to California since his family relocated from the Golden State to Maine when he was fifteen. It'd been tough leaving behind his friends, high school, and his very first girlfriend, who on rare occasions crossed his mind. One afternoon, struck by a sense of nostalgia, he typed her name into Facebook. She'd been the most popular girl in school with a following of wannabes and he believed she'd have a long list of followers on social media. Nothing showed up. Probably married and changed her last name, he supposed, hoping that her childhood dreams of becoming a veterinarian had come about.

Now another woman crossed his mind. Tamera Stevens. *Tammy.* Before his flight, he'd stopped by the office to check emails and drop off paperwork. Tamera sat at her desk, with a furrowed brow and pursed lips. Instead of a smile or good-natured ribbing, she offered him a half-hearted hello. It didn't take a detective to realize something troubled her. At first, he thought she'd hit a glitch with one of the investigations. It turned out he was off-base since her ex-husband proved to be the cause of her consternation. *Darnell Stevens.* The badge pinning ceremony for Darnell's promotion to sergeant commenced in a few days, but that wasn't the cause of her curious mood. He replayed the conversation in his mind.

"What's up?" he'd asked.

Facing her laptop screen, she shrugged.

"Got the green light for my vacation."

Tamera peeked around the computer and faced him. Her deep brown eyes looked sad. "Have a great time. I'm gonna miss you, J."

This wasn't like Tammy. Normally, she'd wish me a fun time, not to do anything she wouldn't do, and to be sure to send her a postcard.

"Look, Tam. I can tell something's wrong. What's going on?"

She exhaled and leaned back in her swivel chair. "It's Darnell. And Brandon."

He raised his eyebrows but remained silent.

"Brandon's great. Maybe he's too good for me. I don't know. The kids love him, and maybe I do too." She lifted a take-out coffee and took a sip. "One of the best things about Brandon is that he's not a cop."

"He's a teacher, right?"

219

"An associate professor at Morgan State. Teaches chemistry."

"Oh, yeah. Right."

"Lately, he's been talking about our future," Tamera said. "Planning a long weekend at Deep Creek Lake to see the leaves turn color. And a skiing vacation next winter in PA. Since he's never been married, he's crazy about the idea of a ready-made family. That's the problem."

"You don't want to marry—"

"Brandon would be a fantastic husband and an amazing stepdad, but I don't want to be tied down, not now anyway. The very idea of getting married again could make me hyperventilate."

He nodded.

"But I'm afraid he won't wait until I'm ready. A guy like Brandon doesn't come around too often. Could be, I'm a fool."

"Never."

"If that wasn't enough for me to deal with, I'm worried about Darnell."

"Darnell? He's not your husband anymore."

"But he is my kids' father." She squeezed her eyes shut. "The problem is he's like rolling in money. It doesn't make sense."

"Could've won the pick four?"

She flashed her eyes open and shot him one of those you're kidding me looks. "He's never played the lottery a day in his life."

"I guess inheritance is out too?"

"He didn't have no rich relatives, that's for sure."

"So, what're you thinking? He's gone rogue?"

She scrubbed her face with her hands. "I don't want to think Darnell crossed the line. But how else to explain a brand-new Mercedes sports car? And a house contract on Federal Hill. Expensive clothes, the diamond pinky ring he's been wearing, and all the high-priced toys and electronics he's been buying for the kids."

"Hmm," Fox said, sitting on the edge of his desk. "Does sound hinky."

"Damn, J. I don't even want to consider that he'd be involved with . . ." Her words trailed off, and he noticed her eyes looked wet. "I was up most of the night trying to devise some logical explanation, but I couldn't. I think." She shook her head. "I can even say it out loud."

"Nannery's Raiders?" Jeremy said under his breath. Every cop he knew was familiar with the infamous NYPD sergeant and his cohorts that participated in unlawful activities, including seizing drugs and large amounts of cash. And reselling the drugs at half the market price during the mid-1990s.

"No. NoNoNoNo. Not Darnell. He's a cop's cop. Once his nephew ran a red light over on Charles, and Darnell pulled him over. Wrote him a ticket. Hoped it would teach him a lesson. Darnell couldn't be doing illegal searches and seizures. Protecting drug dealers. Selling that crap."

"Except that's what you think he's doing."

"I don't know what to think." She chewed her lip. "But yeah. I'm afraid of the lure of all that money. But at what price, J?"

"Look, Tam. I'm only going to be gone for four to five days tops. Try to forget about your suspicions. Spend time with the kids and Brandon. Don't think about the past, and don't look to the future. Just enjoy the present day. And when I get back, I'll do a little investigating of my own and get to the bottom of where Darnell's money is coming from. Okay?"

"Yeah. Sure." She half-shrugged. "There's something on your desk you've been waiting on."

He spied a manila envelope lying in the center of his tidy desk. He unwound the red string holding the mailer shut and fished out the paper inside. He scanned the information typed on the page. "Dammit." He looked at Tamera. "Fingerprint results. Perfect match to Skye Andrews."

"So, you gonna cancel that flight to LA?"

He slipped the form into his center desk drawer. "What?"

"Your vacation. You still planning on going to California?"

He nodded. "Do me a favor. Put Darnell out of your mind and hold down the fort." He squeezed her shoulder and left the office.

For most of the drive to the airport, Fox couldn't stop dwelling on the fingerprint results. Hard evidence that Skye Andrews handled the knife.

But did that prove she killed Boyle? He pulled onto 295 North and shifted his thoughts to Tamera's concern over her ex. Fox questioned himself, wondering why he'd never told Tammy he disliked Darnell Stevens.

Before he made detective, Fox worked with Darnell in the Western District. Word was, Darnell's a player and even offered prostitutes a pass in exchange for sex. That was before Fox met Tamera, and since then, he'd kept that information to himself. The last thing he'd ever want for Tamera was to be hurt by that rat of a husband. But thankfully, she wised up and divorced his ass. *But now this?*

He moved the lever and reclined the plane seat, closed his eyes, and breathed in the melodic strains spilling into his ears. He allowed the somber beauty of the *Lacrimosa* to lull him into a quiet sense of tranquility.

That sense of calmness turned out to be a brief interlude. Within minutes the plane landed, and the passengers debarked. He made his way to the rental office and picked up the sedan he'd leased online. Before driving out of the lot, he pulled out his cellphone and texted Dalton. He wanted to meet with the detective ASAP.

Chapter Thirty-Eight

Beth woke up a little after five. The sun wouldn't rise for at least another forty-five minutes, but instead of closing her eyes and turning over, she slipped out of bed. She glanced at Shane, sound asleep with a trace of a smile on his face. She wanted to kiss him but refrained, knowing even that gentle touch would wake him. He needed all the rest he could muster. *Solving the riddle of the party responsible for the artwork situations will keep him busy searching for an answer to the perplexing puzzle.*

Ever since her wayward *fey* made a comeback, a sense of confidence buoyed her. She believed the loose threads of the divergent crimes would eventually become one neatly woven tapestry. Soon, she hoped, crossing her fingers.

An image of Skye's ransacked house flicked through her mind, and her stomach tightened. *Has Skye, once again, become the target of a crazed sociopath?* She padded down the corridor to a guest bathroom. Even though the shower water ran warm, she shivered as the message from her sixth sense became clear. *The person who'd destroyed Skye's cherished paintings, ransacked her house, and attacked the caretaker must be the devil who'd murdered Thom Boyle. And is responsible for framing Skye. It has to be*, she thought, stepping out of the shower and towel drying her hair. She dropped the striped ocean blue and white Turkish towel, and tiptoed down the hallway headed for her walk-in closet.

Beth wanted to reach the movie studio before the start of the day's shoot. Most importantly, she needed to save Skye from a disastrous miscarriage of justice. She was positive, thanks to her *fey*, the killer had to be a member of the *Dark Grace* set. The biggest obstacle to overcome, she believed, would be ingratiating herself with the other actors and enticing them to discuss the director's murder. Especially those actors whose names appeared on her suspect list.

She hoped Louise "Willie" Wilson would be on the set. The friendly actress would surely introduce her to the others. Beth particularly wanted to question Jane Reid, the mother of the ingénue, Isabella. Isa Reid hadn't kept her love for Thom a secret. Perhaps Jane feared a love affair would distract her daughter from acting or even cause Isa to quit it altogether, putting an end to multi-million-dollar contracts.

Beth recalled an important fact she'd written in her notes. *According to the Coogan Law, now that Isa is eighteen, she has access to fifteen percent of her earnings kept in a trust.* Beth wondered what Jane had done with the other eighty-five percent. *The money Jane should've used to pay taxes, fees, and commissions that Isa owed, as well as cover any job-related expenses. Has Jane used Isa's millions for her own benefit?* Beth pursed her lips. *Could Jane have sought a court order to be awarded her daughter's guardian much like Brittany Spears' father? That would ensure Jane the bulk of her daughter's earnings. That alone could be motive enough for Jane to kill Isa's object of affection.* Beth's imagination might've easily led her to various scenarios of how Jane had framed Skye but logic told her anyone on the set could've killed Thom.

She stopped outside of their bedroom door. An image of Skye's slashed paintings flitted through her mind. Beth imagined her friend, while on the set, trying to overcome her innate feelings of inferiority by rattling on that Zach wasn't the only art collector in the family, and that she collected original abstract paintings by the celebrated artist Kenny Weston. *But how does Zach's stolen artwork fit into the scenario?* She entered the bedroom with a frown.

"Something wrong?" Shane sat with his back against the bed's cushioned headboard, pad in hand.

"Oh, darlin', I didn't mean to wake you."

"You didn't. It's this damn case that's making sleep nearly impossible."

"You're a brilliant detective. I'm sure all the pieces will fit together before you know it. It'll be grand altogether when you return Zach's paintings to him."

"It's more than just Greyson's missing artwork."

"Isn't that the truth? Well then, I'll leave you to your work. I want to arrive at the studio in about forty-five minutes anyway."

"Studio?"

She dropped the monogrammed shower wrap from her body. She paused a couple of seconds to allow Shane to take in the sight of her. Then she scooted onto the bed and eased on top of him. She's missed Shane about every minute of their separation. It didn't take long to realize that he'd missed her just as much.

He ran his fingers along her spine. She quivered in anticipation and found his mouth with hers. His strong hands gripped her waist and pressed her close until her longing was satisfied. The lovemaking failed to offer the sense of solace she craved to quell the anxiety of her soul. Instead, it instilled a whiff of exhilaration like the last flicker of a flame before the fire dies.

"You have that interview today with Mindy Marks?" Shane asked.

"That would be tomorrow. I'm heading out to the set of *Dark Grace*." She slipped off him, now feeling a touch of exhaustion. She rested her head on his chest. "I want to make sure Skye's role isn't reduced to next to nothing."

"My dear Betty Getty, you're always on the lookout for the people you care about." He ran his fingertips along the damp skin of her belly. "But, babe. Skye's career is probably kaput, so you traipsing over there is most likely a moot point."

"I can't believe that, Shane." She pulled the covers across her body.

"Detective Fox called me. Skye's DNA is on the knife."

"Does that matter? After all, it was a bullet that killed Thom Boyle. And provided the blood needed to write that macabre message."

"Don't tell me you think Skye found the murdered director, slit his throat, and wrote the message."

"Now, wouldn't that be ridiculous?" Beth said.

"Even in Skye's book, that'd be carrying a grudge a bit too far. But then how—"

"The killer planted the knife and wrote the message. There's no other explanation."

"Uh-huh. Even if that's true, how did he manage to get Skye's DNA onto the knife?"

"That's what I'm aiming to find out."

"Beth," he said, exaggerating her name. "This doesn't concern you. It's up to Marc Hammond to save Skye's butt."

"I know, darlin', and of course, you're right," she said to placate him. "But, the director, Hugo Daines, has family that lives in Ballynárach."

A flash of confusion crossed his face.

"My hometown."

"Oh, yeah. Of course," he murmured as his cellphone pinged. He glanced at the text message.

"Just being around that dynamic man reminds me of folks back home. I'm so missing Ireland." She hoped the Irish connection would soften his objections.

He nodded as he tapped the phone's keypad.

"Work?" She nodded toward his cellphone.

He looked up. "Indirectly. You were saying something about Ireland?" He placed his finger under her chin and turned her face toward his. "Because of my job, I won't be able to whisk you to Ireland for our make-up honeymoon. Anytime soon, that is."

"Don't be fretting, my darlin' boy. I could invite Carmel to visit us along with the wee granddaughters. Might help them to forget their loss for a bit."

"That's a great idea. With me busy at work, entertaining Deirdre's family would keep you out of trouble," he said with a wink.

"I still have those," she said, gesturing toward a stack of papers next to the laptop sitting on the chaise longue, "to finish translating for Carmel."

"Deirdre's short stories?"

Beth nodded. "The ones I discovered in her make-shift parlor and written in Italian." She glanced at the clock set on the nightstand. "*Janey Mac*, the time. I need to be taking another shower and—"

He leaned over and kissed her lips, quieting her. For an instant, she forgot about everything but the touch of his lips on hers.

"We can save time by showering together."

She arched her brow. "Now tell me, Shane Dalton, just how will that be saving time?"

"Four hands are quicker than two." He jumped out of bed, crossed the wide expanse of a room, and stepped into the rose marble en suite. It took Beth only a moment to catch up.

After blow-drying her hair and dressing, Beth clattered around the kitchen long enough to put on the kettle for herself and prepare coffee for Shane. She considered cooking him a hearty breakfast of eggs, bacon, and toast. But changed her mind, fearing she'd lose track of the task by envisioning her mission at the studio. She certainly didn't want to burn another one of Shane's meals. It was bad enough he seemed to take delight in telling people that she was an awful cook. Though he was only joking, Shane said it with such seriousness that most people believed him. Instead, she prepared a bowl of minute oats in the microwave, toasted some whole wheat bread, and poured the coffee. She placed the meal on a tray and carried it to their bedroom, where he still lay in bed, looking at his pad. A perky voice sounded from his cellphone, reciting the weather report.

"Enjoy your breakfast, darlin'," Beth said, landing the tray on his lap.

A smile replaced the consternation covering his face. "Don't tell me. I've forgotten it's my birthday," he said, glancing at his watch.

"Don't be silly. I'm only trying to be a good wife."

"Of course, my darlin' Betty Getty. You're the most thoughtful wife a man could have. How did I get so lucky?"

"Only the best for my lovin' man," she said and kissed his cheek. "I'll be heading out now. Luckily, the studio is nearby on West Pico Boulevard. Summit."

"Oh, that studio. Well, I'm glad it's only four miles away because, according to the news, traffic is already building. If you don't leave soon it'll be bumper to bumper."

"No worries. I should make it there in plenty of time."

"You will be home for our postponed reunion dinner out by the pool tonight?"

"Nothing will keep me away." She blew him a kiss and moved to the door.

"I'll be meeting with Greyson this afternoon at Skye's house. Greyson wants to see the devastation."

She faced him. "I haven't the slightest idea how Zach's going to break the news to Skye. It's sure to push her over the edge."

"Maybe it's a good thing she can't leave Maryland. By the time her trial is over, Greyson should have the house back in order. And new paintings by Weston on the walls. Provided she isn't found guilty."

"Now, that would be a crime. Putting an innocent woman behind bars."

"There's something I haven't told you." He dropped his spoon into the bowl of cereal.

She stepped closer to him, her eyes wide and lips pressed together. An icy chill made her clasp her arms. Her sixth sense. *What does it want to tell me?*

"My case is more than stolen paintings," Shane said, fingering his cleft chin. "I found a note in a greeting card off of Skye's home theater threatening her."

Questions filled her mind, but Beth pressed her lips together.

228

"It wasn't a handwritten note or even typed, but one of those B-Hollywood movie-style threats made from cut-out letters clipped from newspapers and magazines."

Beth waited for him to continue.

"Your theory that Skye is being framed for the murder may not be far-fetched. In fact, this new piece of evidence insinuated a blatant threat to her life. I'm trying to connect how stolen paintings, a murdered director, and a threat on your friend's life tie together."

She nodded, remaining quiet.

"I'd be surprised if any forensic evidence is found on the card. But I'm afraid the detectives will limit the investigation to a home invasion. My gut is telling me it's more than that. I have to discover how all the links fit together."

"If anyone can do that, it's you," Beth said. She knew better than to say, with the help of my *fey*.

"There's another thing."

Beth stepped closer to the bed.

"That Baltimore detective, Fox, contacted me. He wants to meet and discuss Skye's situation."

She squished her face, wrinkling her nose. "Does that detective want to explain why he arrested her? That's the cart before the horse, I'm thinking."

Shane shook his head. "Something's not sitting right with him about Skye's arrest."

"Is that so?" Beth whispered. Knowing not to say a word about it to Shane, she'd made a decision. Somehow she was going to meet with Detective Fox, too.

Chapter Thirty-Nine

Beth pulled her Volvo out of the garage and inched across the pavers arranged in a scalloped design. She glanced in the rearview mirror and caught sight of her L-shaped house. The realtor had called it the Chateau of Baroda Drive. But the dwelling reminded Beth not of a French country estate but of the castles of Ireland with its soft gray and terracotta stones and the two-story turret housing the main entrance. Before she'd met Shane, she'd decided to put the house on the market and planned to move into a city penthouse apartment. She'd stepped up her efforts after the accident when her dream of motherhood shattered due to internal injuries sustained, all because of a drunk driver's recklessness.

It had been a sin of pride owing to the success of her modeling career that Beth had purchased the upscale property. All the while, she knew the house and grounds were too expansive. Once she'd settled inside, she ignored the grand staircase and the elevator and remained on the first floor. She slept in the bedroom off the kitchen, which she imagined had been designated for a cook.

But everything changed with Shane. The house took on a new life as his police buddies, especially Gavin Collins, dropped by for cookouts by the pool. Soon their wives, husbands, and kids bustled throughout the house with casseroles, crockpots, burgers to grill, and most importantly, laughter. And Skye, too, had found a warm welcome and mingled, forgetting, seemingly, of her "star" status. Contented, Skye watched as Emma splashed, ran, and played with the other children. Beth came to believe that Skye thought of their house as a refuge. Another home actually, second only to her Malibu beach house, which didn't say much for Zach's Beverly Hills mansion.

As she neared the white wooden gate crossing the driveway, Beth took another look in the mirror and noticed Shane. Jogging toward her, he clutched something at his side. She pressed the brake, shifted into park, and opened the window, wondering if something was wrong. But the instant she saw his face, she smiled.

"I almost forgot," he said, handing her a bouquet of flowers through the window. A riot of color and fragrance filled her senses. "A little token to welcome you home."

"They're beautiful. Lovely, indeed." The stems, wet to the touch, told her Shane removed them from a vase. He'd probably placed them in the foyer, but last night she was too exhausted to have noticed anything but their bed.

"All your favorites from the garden."

Her heart swelled with joy as she thanked God for her lovin' man.

"I wanted you to see them while they're still fresh. They may be wilted by tonight."

"They'll be fine if you put them back into water. And a perfect centerpiece for our special dinner tonight." She stepped out of the SUV, kissed him hard on the lips, and almost squashed the flowers as she pressed against him. Beth wanted to forget about the unsolved case of the murdered director, Zach's stolen paintings, and Skye's ransacked house. She only desired to soak up the warmth found within her husband's embrace and didn't want to release him. But soon enough, he'd be leaving for the office, and her *fey* wouldn't give her a moment's peace until she moved forward in uncovering the scoundrel who stole Thom Boyle's life.

"I better be going," she managed to say as he pulled her close, kissed her cheek, and found her lips. The intensity of his kiss took her breath away. Her resolve weakened.

He released her, and she handed him the now crushed bouquet.

"Oh, the blossoms," she said.

"No worries," Shane said, trying to revive the damaged petals with his fingertips.

She couldn't help but laugh, spying the stricken look on his face.

"I'll take care of the flower situation, and you have fun at the studio."

"I forgot to tell you. I was railroaded into playing a part in Skye's movie. A nurse."

"You're planning to take up acting?" He frowned.

"Now, don't be fretting. Isn't it the God's honest truth, I have me hands full just taking care of you?" she said with a wink. Beth hopped back into her vehicle and blew him a kiss. A smile remained on her face as she pressed the gate remote and made a right turn onto the road.

Tall hedges camouflage the stately houses lining the road. The first action Beth took after moving into her home was to have the shrubberies cut back, therefore, opening the view from her property. The tall growth had been confining. And after spending the last ten years of her life in hotel rooms, photography studios, and cramped apartments, she wanted to experience a sense of freedom. It didn't take long to believe she'd made a mistake. Open-air tour buses stopped in front of her house several times a day, offering their customers a grand view of her property. She wanted independence and privacy—nice work if you can get it, she often told herself—but that goal remained elusive for her.

She braked at the corner of Sunset Boulevard and flicked the left turn signal. Before departing, Beth planned to take the shortest route to the studio, only a hair over three miles and a drive time of no more than fifteen minutes. She glanced at the steady stream of vehicles beyond her when cold fingers of fear crept along her spine. Her heart pounded, and her breath clung heavily to her lungs. She tried to shake off the paralyzing anxiety holding her captive. Her *fey* sent a strong warning.

"What? What are you telling me?" She whispered as an alarming notion took hold that Skye could be responsible for the murder. The unsettling thought danced in her brain and caused Beth's vision to blur.

She forced air through her nostrils and exhaled slowly. She repeated the deep breaths until her heart stopped hammering.

A light toot sounded from a silver convertible Rolls waiting behind her.

Though her temples throbbed, she took a swallow of air, blinked a few times, and focused on the traffic. Not believing her luck, a break in the line of vehicles opened. She pressed the gas and stopped in the median for only a second before merging into a driving lane.

"No. NoNoNoNoNo," she said. "Skye can't be involved. The very idea is downright mad." She swallowed hard. *The house-sitter's brutal attack was meant for Skye. Plus, she was nearly three thousand miles away, locked behind prison walls.* "How in God's name does Skye make people angry enough to want to kill her?"

If it hadn't been for the voice sounding from the dashboard GPS interrupting her musings, she would have driven beyond the right turn onto Greenway Drive. She shook her head, banishing all distractions, and focused on the road stocked full of quick turns as she navigated through Beverly Hills.

Two minutes before seven, Beth pulled up to the Summit Studios gate. "Hello, I'm expected at the *Dark Grace* soundstage. Beth Getty."

The guard's forehead wrinkled.

"Perhaps it's under Sibéal?"

"Here it is," the guard said with a smile as she flipped a sheet of paper over. "Stage 16." She handed Beth a visitor's badge, a parking pass for Lot A, and a map. The guard pointed in a general direction, urging Beth to continue driving.

The studio lot unfolded before her, impressive in size but also intimidating. Relief trickled through Beth as she glanced at the map. A yellow star marked the location of the car park a stone's throw away from the *Dark Grace* sound stage. She hoped, at some point, for a chance to explore the grounds. The backlots boasted of a modern city street, a medieval castle, and a western town.

After scooting into a parking spot, she stepped out of her Volvo. Disoriented, she looked around. The victim of a poor sense of direction, Beth wondered which way she should head. She chewed her lip, turned in a tight circle, and spotted a man beyond her. Without a second of hesitation, she hurried in his direction.

"Excuse me," she called.

"Sibéal?"

"Ah, yes, hello," she said.

"Hi. Jason Warner. We met at a fundraiser a few years ago."

"Of course," she lied, not recognizing him from Adam. "Oh, Jason, hello. So nice seeing you again."

"Call me Jace. Everyone does. "

"Right. Jace." She looked away and frowned. "Forgive me, I'm so turned around, I don't know where—"

"This place can be overwhelming. Where you headed?"

"Stage 16."

"Hey, me too." He offered Beth his arm, and she took it. "Are you a cast member?"

"My part is so small that, if you blinked, you'd miss it. How about you?"

"The male lead," he said, looking down at the paved ground. "I portray the police partner and love interest of the leading lady, who in real life was arrested for murdering our director. But I guess," Jace said, catching Beth's eyes, "you've heard about that."

She nodded, saying nothing, anxious to hear his take on the murder.

"We were dumbfounded when they hauled Skye Andrews off to jail. Surreal is the only way to describe it. I guess the arrest makes sense but . . ." He shrugged.

"But what?"

"When I heard Thom had been killed, the first suspect that jumped into my mind was the guy whose place I took. Grant Reynolds. Grant was like crazy mad when Thom fired him. It wasn't that he's a lousy actor—no, he's damn good—but not the right actor for the part."

"You think this Grant Reynolds is responsible?"

"That was my initial feeling. But then I remembered Thom had a meeting with Frank Daniels, the DP, you know, Director of Photography. They were meeting in Thom's trailer when the film dailies arrived, giving Daniels means and motive."

"Motive?"

"Everyone knows Thom and Daniels are famous for their obsession with perfection and mulish stubbornness. They've had more than one big blowout over the fine details. Hot and heavy shouting matches heard by everyone on set."

"Is that so?"

"Uh-huh. Anyway, since I knew about the meeting, I pointed the finger at Daniels. Turned out to be a big mistake. I wounded the guy with my rush to judgment. Thom and Daniels were long-time buddies, and their outbursts and angry words were par for the course. Plus, Daniels' had an air-tight alibi. After that, I left the sleuthing to the professionals."

"Probably a good idea. But tell me, getting back to Grant Reynolds, is he the kind of person to hold a grudge?"

"Wouldn't know." Jace shrugged.

"If the actor was angry enough, maybe he wanted to get back at Thom for firing him."

"Good point. But no." Jace stopped walking, freed his arm, and stuck his hands into the back pockets of his jeans. "After the murder, the news surfaced that Thom felt rotten about letting Grant go. Turned out Thom did a little PR work. He suggested Grant for a role to a director buddy of his. A terrific part in a WWII action flick starring Zach Greyson. He's got the second lead in the film. So, that would clear him of hard feelings toward Thom."

Beth sighed. "I imagine so. Of course."

They continued walking. Jace stayed silent and Beth, now disappointed that two good leads she never considered, hadn't panned out.

"You still modeling?"

"Modeling? Ah, no. Not since my accident." Without thinking, she touched the scar crossing her cheek. "But I've renewed my contract with Noelle cosmetics and will be part of their Christmas campaign."

"Cool." He stopped walking and motioned to the building facing them. "Stage 16."

"I doubt I would've found it on my own. Thanks."

"No problem. I'm gonna head to wardrobe. I'll catch you later."

"Thanks again." She offered him a quick wave, but he'd already taken off with a quickened pace, which a couple of seconds later turned into a jog.

Chapter Forty

Beth glanced at the bronze plaque affixed to the exterior wall of Stage 16. The plate's raised engraving highlighted a list of movies shot on the soundstage. The first title, a film she must've missed on the classic movie channel, dated 1938. She perused the list. Many of the titles had been honored with at least one of the coveted Oscar statuettes and showcased the talents of Hollywood luminaries from Tyrone Power to Johnny Depp, Mae West to Julia Roberts. Amazing, she mused, that an extraordinary measure of movie magic happened within these four walls. And the impact of these films, which have entertained and delighted people, young and old alike, over eight decades, is mind-boggling—impossible to imagine. And to think, if *Dark Grace* turns out to be the kind of movie Skye believes it to be, I won't be surprised if its title earns a spot on the impressive list.

Beth looked away from the turquoise-painted wall, took a deep breath, and sent up a quick prayer. She peeked through one of the windows of the black double doors. Unable to see much, she pulled it open and entered. It took a couple of seconds to take in the scene. The enormous room, divided into different sets, lined the walls.

But the aroma of breakfast wafting through the air caught her full attention. Tables stocked with food warmer trays chocked-full of scrambled eggs, bacon, sausages, and pancakes greeted her. Beth moved along the buffet and stopped in front of the toast bar. A variety of bread tucked into stainless steel racks sat alongside toppings from avocado cream and smoked salmon to berries, vegetables, and nuts. Beyond the arrangements of toppings sat a large metal bowl stocked with fruit and platters filled with pastries and doughnuts. At the end of the table stood urns of coffee and pitchers of juice and water. She'd forgotten how well the actors and crew were fed on a movie set.

"Hey, Beth?"

She spun around and faced Louise Wilson. A pink apron smock with two large pockets covered Willie's casual attire consisting of jeans and a T-shirt.

"Oh, Willie. Hello." Beth couldn't believe her luck. Exactly the person she'd hoped to meet.

"I didn't realize you had more scenes."

"Truth is, I don't. I'm here to observe."

"Well, then," Willie said, pointing at the buffet, "load up a plate, and we can eat there." She jutted her chin at a group of long tables and chairs filled with crew members and actors enjoying their breakfast.

Beth selected a slice of whole-wheat toast, covered it with a layer of peanut butter, and added a couple wedges of apple, a sprinkle of granola, and a spurt of honey. She moved along the table to the coffee urn and filled a cup to the brim.

Beth hurried, holding her plate and trying not to slosh the coffee. She pulled out a chair next to Willie and across from a couple of crew members. The men looked familiar. They must've worked on the chapel shoot in Baltimore, she imagined, when one of the men excused himself.

"Beth, this is Sam. He's the property master for the film."

"Nice meeting you."

He grunted a "hey" over a mouthful of food.

"He's my boss," Willie said.

"Boss?" Beth took a sip of coffee.

"A terrific boss, if I say so myself," Willie said, beaming at Sam.

A flush of color rose to his cheeks.

"That's right. Skye told me you worked in the props department."

"Thom thought Sam could do with an extra pair of hands, not that he really needed the help," Willie said. "But, knowing Thom, he wanted to bring me back into the business even if it's behind the camera."

"Regardless of the reason, you've been a godsend," Sam said, pointing his fork at Willie. "Most directors do everything in their power to keep costs down to please the producers. You see," he said, focusing on Beth, "I lost one of my staff due to maternity leave, and most directors would've just said, deal with it. But not Thom. Willie slipped nicely into her place."

Willie modestly lowered her eyes, though a flicker of a smile touched her face. She fiddled with her fork before shoveling a mound of scrambled eggs into her mouth.

"I've got to get going," Sam said, standing up, looking at his cellphone screen. "I'll meet you on the courtroom set at seven-thirty. Double-check the props. Everything needs to be perfect."

Willie nodded and offered him a coy smile. Sans makeup with her hair pulled into two pigtails sticking out above her ears, Willie resembled a teenager.

"Later," Sam said. "Oh, and nice meeting you, Beth." He pushed in his chair and with quick strides headed toward one of the sets.

"Sam's great to work with. The lady whose job I took over was the weapons master. But really, there's not a whole lot of weapons in the movie save for the cops' guns and the murder weapon—a knife. And they're not even real. The toy guns stay inside the detective holsters, and the knife, well, I think a butter knife is sharper. So instead of checking guns to ensure they're cold, I've been more like Sam's assistant. Working with the script supervisor to maintain set continuity. Luckily, Sam's been dealing directly with Daines." Willie squinched up her nose, making a face.

"I take it, you don't like Director Daines," Beth said.

"Hell, no. He hits on just about every female on the set. We all think he's a creep, that is, except for Toni Wright. I wouldn't be surprised if the two of them are having an affair."

"An affair? I thought Thom and she were a couple."

Willie shrugged. "It would be somebody's full-time job to keep track of who is with whom at any given moment on a movie set. But for Thom's sake, I hope he hadn't gotten involved with the witch. Not that it matters now." She moved the leftover eggs around on her plate. "If Skye is really innocent, I bet Toni killed him. She acted like they were best friends, but behind Thom's back, she'd badmouth him. Said he was a rotten director. Didn't know what he was doing. Crap like that."

"Really?"

"Uh-huh. Then she'd be up in his face smiling and making nice. Toni's nothing more than a two-faced bitch."

"Skye isn't fond of Toni either but she believes Thom had a soft spot for her."

"Knowing Thom, he probably did. He and I go back a long way," Willie said. "We met working on a made-for-television movie. One of those fluffy romances I was over the moon thrilled to star in. It was my first big break." A tiny smile pulled at her lips. "I believed my career was beginning to take off, and the future looked amazing." She shook her head.

"I didn't know Thom directed TV."

"Directed? Oh, no. Thom acted back then. During the making of that movie, *Beach Time Romance*, we became lovers."

Beth widened her eyes and twisted in her chair to face Willie.

"I was nineteen, portraying a lovesick teenybopper. Thom played the wise father, trying to keep his daughter from falling for the wrong guy. Sort of an updated Gidget type of chick flick." A faraway look filled her face. "Believe me, there wasn't anything fatherly between us off the set." She lifted her coffee, looked into the mug, and placed it back on the table. "It wasn't long after that film Thom started directing. I was just a young actor trying to break into the business and Thom took over my career. He'd been acting on stage and screen for years. Twenty-two years older than me, he had a lot of experience. And with his guidance and clout, it wasn't long before I found myself on the A-list."

Beth scooted to the edge of her chair, not taking her eyes off Willie.

"But being a dumb and young celebrity went to my head. Thom tried his damnedest to keep me on the straight and narrow. But I'd found new friends, new lovers, new pastimes. Blow, snow, flake, coke—whatever you want to call it—cocaine took over my life. My career went down the drain."

Beth chewed her lip, not knowing what to say.

Willie folded her hands in her lap but then shot Beth a bright smile. "No use crying over spilled milk, especially since everything's changed for the better. And I mean, way better. There's a new guy in my life who I'm crazy about. Wedding bells are right around the corner."

"Ah, lovely. I'm truly happy for you, I am. Is he a member of the crew?"

"Nah. I met him in Baltimore. I moved there a couple of years ago to take care of my mom. She died of cancer last year, and I decided to stay put. It's a good thing too. Otherwise, I never would've met my fiancé."

"Tell me about him."

"Well, he's handsome and smart. And rich. The perfect package in my book."

"That's grand altogether. I take it, he's helped you kick your drug habit."

"Oh, God. Look who's heading our way."

Beth glanced across the table and glimpsed Antonia Wright.

Willie checked her watch. "Thank God, I've gotta go. Sam's gonna be looking for me." She pulled a pair of latex gloves from one of the apron pockets.

"What are the gloves for?" Beth asked.

"Sam's a perfectionist. Doesn't want any fingerprints or smudges to wind up on the props." Willie pulled her eyes away from Beth and shot out of her chair.

"I hope you'll introduce me to some cast members," Beth said.

"Sure. Let's meet for lunch at the commissary. Everybody hangs out there during breaks." Willie grabbed her plate and the orange she hadn't eaten and hurried across the soundstage.

Beth took a bite of toast as her cellphone pinged. She freed it from her oversized tote bag and checked the screen. Skye. Before she could check the text, she noticed the time. *Seven twenty. Hmm. Did Willie hightail it out of here because she saw Toni Wright or . . . Maybe Sam isn't who he seems to be. Is she scared of him? Could he be responsible for the murder? Because—*

"Beth."

She landed the phone next to her plate. "A good morning to you, Toni. Take a load off, why don't you," Beth said, gesturing to Willie's vacated seat.

"I can't believe you're eating that. Don't you know carbs can ruin your figure in less time than a New York minute?" Toni placed a script on the table but held onto the clear shaker bottle.

Beth took another bite of her peanut butter and apple toast.

"Don't tell me, I didn't warn you." Toni dropped into the chair. "Have you talked to Hugo?"

"Hugo? Ah, no. I haven't seen him this morning." Beth placed the remaining bit of toast on the plate. She gazed at Toni, outfitted in a stuffy suit, which Beth took for her costume, believing the vivacious actress would hardly choose to dress that way. She noticed the fine network of wrinkles skirting the actress' startling blue eyes and the slight lines alongside the corners of her mouth. "What's up?"

Instead of answering, Toni took a sip of the green liquid from the shaker bottle.

As Toni sucked from the straw lid, Beth recalled Skye's animosity toward the actress and wasn't surprised that Skye's jealousy would be aimed at one of her husband's ex-girlfriends. Especially one highly accomplished and, for her age, still quite beautiful. The fluttering of her heart, as if skipping a beat, shattered Beth's thoughts. A sure warning that her *fey* was going to unveil a message. She closed her eyes, blocking out the surrounding activity.

"I told Hugo last night, not to worry, you'd probably be agreeable."

Toni's words interrupted Beth's attempt at concentration. A bit startled, she refocused on the actress. "Did you say something?"

"Here he comes now." Toni stood, clutching the bottle, and grabbed the script. "We'll see each other on the set." Her heels clicked against the wood floor as she strode away.

Beth pressed her lips into a tight line. The opportunity to glean the directive from her *fey* vanished. She lifted the toast and chewed the final bite. From the corner of her eye, she spied Daines moving in her direction. She had plenty of questions for him, but her intuition nudged against the possibility of Daines being a killer. But she needed to make sure, if only to ease Skye's suspicion aimed at the newly appointed director.

Daines pulled off his sunglasses and looked at her with a silly grin plastered on his face. "I'm real glad to see you. I thought maybe because of what happened last night, you wouldn't show. But that doesn't matter because you're here." He pulled out the chair opposite her and sat. "I don't know how this slipped my mind. I guess with all the drama revolving around Thom's murder and your husband barging in on our date—"

"Date?"

"Dinner-date. Anyway, I meant to tell you earlier. I need you to say a few lines today."

"A few lines?" Beth narrowed her eyes.

"We're shooting the courtroom scene. And, of course, the nurse who found the body would be called to testify." He showed her a rolled-up paper he'd pulled out of the back pocket of his jeans. "Here. It's not much to learn, but I need to see a lot of emotion. Look, I gotta run." Not giving her a chance to respond, Daines shot out of the chair. With a quick finger wave, he headed toward one of the sets.

Beth unrolled the sheet and glanced at the highlighted sentences. *Now, what have I gotten myself into?* She sighed. After scanning the words, she realized Daines hadn't exaggerated. Her part consisted of only a handful of words.

"Excuse me, Miss Sibèal?"

Beth looked up from the page.

"If you could come with me to wardrobe, I have your costume ready."

Beth tossed the paper and her cellphone into her bag, grabbed her coffee mug, and followed the young woman with flaming red hair. The costume lady, a chatty type, talked about the weather and her plans for the weekend. Not wanting to be rude, Beth murmured an occasional uh-huh. The costumer's lively words didn't shake away the image, crowding out everything else from Beth's mind—Skye dressed in striped black and white prison clothes, standing behind a door of bars.

No, she vowed, I'm going to find Thom Boyle's killer if it's the last thing I do. An icy chill took her breath away. She had no idea what her *fey* wanted to tell her, but she hoped to God, it didn't mean finding the killer *would* be the last thing she ever did.

Chapter Forty-One

Shane raised his hand, gesturing for Flores to hold her thoughts until after he answered his pinging cellphone. He glanced at the text from Fox. The Baltimore detective was waiting in the lobby. Shane typed in a quick OMY and refocused on Flores.

She stood with her arms crossed. Her foot tapping against the blue-gray tile floor filled the minuscule office with the sound of clipped slaps.

"Sorry about that. As you were saying," Shane said.

"Those *alebrijes* turned out to be touristy souvenirs. Which didn't surprise me. On the other hand, the heroin inside them was the real deal. I wasn't much help to the Feds. They're trying to detect the location of a new start-up drug trafficking enterprise. Those wooden *alebrijes* could've originated from any holiday spot. You know, places like Oaxaca City, Cancún, Cozumel, or Puerto Escondido." She counted off the locations on her fingers. "Where the sculptures were purchased doesn't mean that's the location of the undetermined cartel. The two may not be connected at all."

"I wouldn't be a bit surprised that's why they used the *alebrijes* to smuggle in the drugs. Those folk art sculptures originate in the south, so the logical assumption is that the drug kingpins are working in that region of Mexico. But, I'm thinking, whoever's responsible is probably located north of Mexico City."

"My thought, exactly." She paused for a moment. "It doesn't concern us anymore. The investigation will proceed under the jurisdiction of the DEA offices in Mexico."

Shane nodded, trying to think up an excuse to duck out of the office.

"Any updates on the Greyson case?" She asked, dropping her arms.

"Not much. I had a chat with Greyson's former chauffeur. He was fired and left with a mouthful of threats. According to his probation officer, the guy's been on the straight and narrow. But I've got my doubts. I think it's time for a formal interview." Shane glanced at his watch. "I was about to head over to his workplace."

"Don't let me keep you. It'd be a stroke of luck if we could wrap up the case this afternoon. That is, if this . . ."

"Renaldo Jones."

"If Jones admits to the crime and leads us to the stolen art. That would be a feather in your cap." Her face softened, and she shot what Shane took to be a seductive smile. A second later, she'd reclaimed her professional mien. "The damn media is having a field day with that family. Zach Greyson, king of the box office, is robbed of priceless art, and his movie-star wife has been arrested for murder. If I wasn't involved with the case, I'm cynical enough to think it's all a publicity hoax."

"It's gotten worse."

"What do you mean?"

"Skye Andrews' house was ransacked, her million-dollar collection of Kenny Weston paintings destroyed."

Flores sank into her chair. "Why wasn't I notified?" Her eyes narrowed as she thrust out her jaw. "I'm the senior detective."

Shane wasn't about to enlighten Flores. Still adamant about keeping everything Sibèal-related out of the office. "One of the investigators reached out to me last night. I surveyed the scene, but," he said with a shrug, "they're treating it as a home invasion. So, as of now, our department isn't part of the investigation."

"One less thing on our plate, thank God. I've got my hands full with those missing Jack Armstrong paintings. They were tucked inside a Lincoln MKZ that had been stolen a few months ago."

"I was working homicide for the sheriff's department when that robbery occurred. But I'd heard about the theft on the news."

"We reached out to the public and got the usual kind of response. Nothing of value. But a new lead surfaced so I'm gonna check it out." As if dismissing Shane, she focused on her laptop and tapped the touchpad.

Shane stood and grabbed his jacket off the back of his chair. "I hope it pans out. Those paintings are worth millions." Though not a fan of the artist's work, there are plenty of rich people who wouldn't think twice about shelling out the big bucks for one of Armstrong's canvases. Just like the work of Kenny Weston. "Later," he said and exited the office.

He hustled to the elevator eager to meet up with Fox. But reaching the lobby, Fox wasn't there.

Dammit. Fox couldn't wait a few minutes, he thought, reaching the glass doors leading outside. If he couldn't locate the detective, Shane decided to go with his original plan of bringing in Renaldo Jones for an interview. And, God willing, getting a confession out of the guy.

Shane glanced at the Memorial Wall of Fallen Officers located in the public plaza adjacent to headquarters. From a distance, the monument appeared like a solid golden wall. But up close, the two thousand individual brass plaques looked to be afloat in air and light. Over two hundred of the distinct pieces glistened with inscribed names of police officers who made the ultimate sacrifice. Whenever Shane stood in front of the wall, his throat dried, his pulse sped, and a heaviness filled his heart. It wasn't out of the realm of possibility that if his luck went south, his name could be etched into one of those brass rectangles.

Shane glimpsed a lone figure on the memorial's raised platform. He didn't relish heading there, but common sense told him that if Fox was nearby, he'd be at the wall. He hustled to the plaza. By the time he'd climbed the steps leading to the platform, a couple, hand in hand, and an elderly lady stood before the golden memorial. Shane zeroed in on the tall, thin man with sparse blond hair and hands stuck into the pockets of his khakis—his sight riveted on a plaque where a single white rose had been slipped above it. Shane swallowed a couple of times, wishing he'd grabbed the water bottle from his desk.

"Detective Fox?"

"Yeah." The man turned his head and shot out his hand. "Dalton. Good seeing you again."

Shane shook the Baltimore cop's hand. Without commenting on the memorial since no words seemed necessary, he said, "Let's head over there." He pointed in a diagonal direction.

After descending the platform and reaching the sidewalk, Shane, a half-step ahead of Fox, turned right. He wanted to get to the point of Fox's visit. But vying with the screeching brakes of transit buses, droning hum of car engines, and the distant wailing of police sirens, walking along W 1st Street did not offer a sufficient environment to discuss a homicide. Small talk was needed. Shane hated small talk.

"So," Shane said, "First time in LA?"

"No. I grew up in the Valley. Sherman Oaks. In one of those three-bedroom, 1800 square foot houses that now sell for a million bucks."

"You still have family here?"

"My sister. She teaches algebra and trig at Whitney High School in Cerritos."

"You'll be able to visit her?"

"Wouldn't you know it? She and the kids are in Maine visiting our folks. And I'm not especially close to my brother-in-law. But, this trip isn't about family or site seeing."

Shane turned onto N. Hill Street, intent on reaching Grand Park, a twelve-acre strip of greenery squeezed between government buildings. A calmer place to discuss the pressing matters on Fox's mind.

"I'd appreciate your insight," Fox said. "Officially, the Boyle case is closed. We conducted a thorough investigation. Now it's up to the DA's office to prove Andrews' guilt. Except, I'm the one feeling guilty."

The park came into view, and Shane motioned to a wide cement walkway. Shane shielded his eyes from the bright sunshine and spied an empty table positioned in the shade cast from a group of Mexican Fan palm trees. "Over there," he said, jutting his chin in the direction of the lone table. A few seconds later, Fox pulled back a bright magenta metal chair, sat, and folded his hands on top of the matching table. Shane sat opposite him.

"What do you feel guilty about?" Shane asked as if no time had elapsed from their earlier conversation.

"All the evidence points to Andrews." Fox ran his long, tapered fingers through his sparse hair. "But I've got a gut feeling something isn't right."

Shane waited for Fox to continue. But instead of elaborating, he bore into Shane with questioning eyes.

"I understand your dilemma. But as you said, it's out of your hands," Shane said.

"I want to find answers. Do you think Skye Andrews killed Boyle?"

"It doesn't matter what I think."

"Do you?"

"I don't. No."

"Who do you think is responsible?"

"You got me."

Fox rubbed his temples. "I assumed when you called the other day that maybe we'd overlooked something."

"If I had evidence Skye didn't commit murder, I would've been on the first plane to Baltimore. But, I've got nothing."

Fox nodded.

"We have to trust the facts," Shane said. "No matter how much our instincts say they don't make sense."

"You're right." Fox paused as two women in business suits walked by. "That said, I'm gonna do a bit of nosing around."

"I'm afraid my wife is doing the same thing."

Fox raised his eyebrows as if asking a question without words.

"Beth believes she possesses a sixth sense. I don't buy into that kinda stuff. But I gotta hand it to her, she's got the best gut instincts than any cop I know."

"Our department has used psychics. A couple of times, they hit the proverbial nail on the head. I wouldn't totally disregard your wife's premonitions."

"To be honest, I'm starting to wonder if there is something to that hocus-pocus stuff." Shane shrugged. "So, where you headed now?"

"Summit Studios. With the slim chance, I might turn up something we missed."

"That's where my wife is. Beth Getty aka Sibèal."

"Sibèal? The lady on those public service announcements against drunk driving?"

"Among other things. Yup. That's my Beth."

"Maybe I'll run into her at the studio."

"If you do, give her a message. Don't forget about our dinner date."

"No problem." Fox stood.

"Good luck. I hope to God, you find something. Seeing the charges dropped would make a whole lot of people happy. And I'm not just talking about Skye's fanbase."

"I hear ya." Fox nodded. "As I said, I'm looking for a way to ease my guilt. The truth is, I'm looking for evidence that will nail Andrews' butt to the wall. Because fingerprints on a knife left at the scene, in my book, don't prove a damn thing. Especially when the victim was shot in the back."

Shane rose with such force he knocked the chair over. "You're not on Skye's side?"

"Side?" He stroked his pointy chin. "The only side I'm on is that of the truth." With a curt nod, he headed down the white sidewalk, all but sprinting in the direction of city hall.

Chapter Forty-Two

The air, thick with humidity, left Tamera wilted, but the typical summer Baltimore weather was the last thing on her mind. She sat on the edge of the bench where a slice of shade cast from an old oak tree shielded her from the late afternoon sun. A couple of joggers passed by, their feet slapping against the running trail encircling the reservoir. *How can they run in this stifling heat?* she wondered, swiping the dampness from her brow with a tissue she'd fished out of her shoulder bag. She grabbed her bottle, sweaty with droplets of condensation, and gulped a mouthful of cold water.

One of the oldest parks in the nation, Druid Hill, held special memories for her. She gazed across the reservoir. The blocky buildings in the distance appeared tiny, belying the crime and poverty running out of control along many derelict and dangerous Baltimore City streets. Boarded-up rowhouses, burnt-out hovels, drug dealings in broad daylight, and the seemingly endless shootings. Homicides. But here, amid the oasis of greenery, she enjoyed a hiatus from the ugliness that filled her nine-to-five.

She'd asked Darnell to meet her. What seemed like a lifetime ago, they used to sit on this bench and talk for hours. As if they were the only pair of lovers to have wholly connected, agreeing on just about everything. Tamera believed their love was something that only happened in fairytales.

As the sun edged the horizon, they'd drive the park road to the zoo. They'd walk hand-in-hand along paved pathways and chuckle at the antics of the prairie dogs, stand a bit awestruck before the Siberian tigers, and

251

pause in front of the chimpanzee enclosure. With their noses pressed against the glass barrier, they'd study the knuckle-walking primates. The chimps' antics seemed humanlike with their grooming, play, and even squawks of anger. Inevitably, they'd wind up at the polar bear exhibit and watch the giant creatures dive into the pool and paddle after blocks of ice filled with fish treats their keepers tossed into the water.

A trace of melancholy gripped her. If only she knew then their relationship was destined to crash and burn. "Ended more like a gruesome fable than a beautiful romantic tale," she breathed. The day Darnell jacked her up against a wall, screaming obscenities and finishing his tantrum by striking Tamera's face and busting her lip, had ended it. All because she hadn't had a chance to iron a shirt he wanted to wear.

"Tam."

She raised her head. A sad smile crossed her face. "I was just thinking about how we used to sit here for hours. Talking. Laughing. Our walks through the zoo."

"That was a long time ago." He sat next to her and focused on the packed, brown dirt beneath his feet. "You wanted to talk?" He glanced at the Omega watch on his wrist. "I'm kinda pressed for time."

"Like that's a newsflash." She took a deep breath. "Well, then. I'll get right to the point. I'm worried. About you." She shifted on the bench and looked at his handsome profile.

"Worried? No need to be concerned about me." His eyes again drifted to the bare ground.

"No? Then how do you explain that expensive watch, your fancy new car, a mini mansion in Federal Hill?"

"Oh. That's it." Darnell raised his head and shot her a smile. "You're wondering how I can afford to live the good life on a detective's salary. It's simple. And for God's sake, it's nothing for you to stew over."

"I'm concerned for the kids. You're trying to buy their love. And how can they respect you with a different floozy in your bed every other weekend?"

He laughed. His mirth sounded hollow to her ears.

"I'm flipping houses."

"You're what?"

"Haven't you ever watched HGTV?"

"Like I have time to sit in front of the television."

"I've been remodeling out-of-date houses in the city and the county. You know, knock down some walls to make an open living area, upgrade the kitchen, add a coat of fresh paint and tiling."

"When did you learn to do that? You never made any improvements to our house. I painted all the walls and hung the curtains. Changing a light bulb seemed to tax your ability."

"You know damn well I'm no handyman." A touch of irritation laced his words. "I don't do the reno. I work with a contractor, and he hires crews to do the actual grunge work. And I've got a realtor that sells the properties. What I do is make the investments."

"So, where does the money come from to *flip* these houses?"

"I get a short-term mortgage. A bridge loan."

"You planning on this becoming your full-time job?"

"Hell, no. It's only a side gig. Anyway, you know I just got a promotion. So why would I leave the department? I get a rush every time I lock up one of those knuckleheads for dealing that garbage."

Not knowing why, she reached for his hand and squeezed it. He placed his other hand on top of hers.

"You're a good woman," he said. "I admit, the credit for wrecking our marriage is mine. I took you for granted. Treated you like crap. Sorry."

Tamera chewed the corner of her lip. He seemed sincere, but she wasn't sure. She braced herself, waiting for the other shoe to drop.

"But you're off base accusing me of having sex with a bunch of different babes. You may not realize it, but I learned a lot during our marriage. The biggest thing—my temper—way outta control. I don't blame you for kicking me out and divorcing my ass."

Where the hell is he going with this?

"What I'm trying to say. . . Look, Tam, I'm getting married."

"Married?" She jumped up from the bench and faced him.

"Yeah. And I don't plan to screw it up like I did with you." He paused, gauging her reaction. "I wanted to tell you first. Before breaking the news to the kids."

What is he talking about? Getting married? WTF? A bolt of anger flew through her. She took a deep breath, attempting to suppress her spiraling emotions "Have the children met her?"

"Yeah. And she loves them—and me. I'm gonna give her a big diamond ring and make it official as soon as she's back in town."

"Well, then," Tamera said, her voice cold as ice. "I wish you luck."

Tamera left him and hurried to her car. With the back of her hand, she wiped away the tears streaming down her face. She didn't know why she was crying. Pulling open the driver-side door, she slipped behind the wheel and headed back to the station.

Chapter Forty-Three

Jeremy Fox flashed his badge at the guard manning the studio gate. After a quick call on the cubicle's phone, she handed him a parking pass and visitor's badge for Stage 16. He pulled into the lot, stepped out of his rental, and looked around. Not sure which direction to take, he spotted a map kiosk and hurried to it. "Whoa," he said under his breath. *This is a huge place. Must be fifty or more acres.* A mark on the map stated, "You are here." It took him only a second to detect the route that would lead to the soundstage. After a short walk, he stood at the building's door.

He hesitated, knowing he didn't have the authority to question anyone regarding Thom Boyle's murder. *But if Skye Andrews told the truth and she didn't kill the director, then there's a good chance the killer is in this building.*

Fox pulled the door open and stepped inside. He walked past a long table with a line of empty stainless steel chafer dishes and moved deeper into the cavernous space. The unnatural quietness led him to imagine the proverbial pin dropping. Careful his rubber soles didn't make a sound, he swallowed his discomfort and headed toward a courtroom setting.

He stopped behind a cluster of people, a grouping of umbrellas and lights, a camera operator, and a guy sitting in a director's wooden frame chair minus the name printed on its canvas back. Fox scanned the scene before him, absorbing every detail. In the gallery area, players filled the benches, and beyond the bar, a man in a black robe sat on a judge's bench. He lingered on the familiar-looking woman in the witness chair near where a boom operator held a microphone aloft.

"Cut," a voice called out. The guy in the director's chair stood. Tall and lanky with a backward baseball cap on his head, the director wore ripped faded jeans that looked like they belonged in a rag bag. A pair of sunglasses covered his eyes.

"I need more emotion," he said.

"Look, Hugo. I wasn't expecting to act in another scene." Beth stepped off the platform.

"I understand you didn't have much time to prepare—"

"That's not the problem. If I'm supposed to be a nurse, I'm used to seeing dead bodies."

"That's true, Beth. But the murdered nun was your friend. A friend killed in a satanic ritual."

She sighed and returned to her previous position.

"Beth," Fox said under his breath. *Dalton's wife. The one with the sixth sense.* With newfound interest, he watched Beth replay the scene. Clipped words hesitated on her lips as tears spilled down her face. The acting came across as raw, emotional, and authentic. Whatever the director had objected to about earlier perplexed Fox. *She's a damn good actress.*

"Cut. Print," the director said. "That's what I was looking for. I knew you had it in you." He turned and faced the assembly of staff and crew members. "We'll take a lunch break. Meet back on the set at two o'clock."

After Beth left the witness chair, Fox moved through the bar's swinging door. A woman cut him off. She threw her arms around Beth, giving her a quick hug. "You were amazing," the woman said.

"'Tis kind of you, Willie. I had a wee bit of trouble getting into the character's head. But when I recalled the sorrow I'd felt after losing someone special, it clicked."

"That's what acting is all about. Putting ourselves into the mind of the characters we portray." Willie took a backward step and banged her shoulder in Fox's chest.

256

"Oh, sorry," Willie said, facing Fox. "I didn't realize—oh, it's you." With a sharp breath, she twisted at the waist facing Beth. "I'll be at the commissary."

The soles of the woman's high-top sneakers squeaked as she hurried away. Her hasty retreat struck Fox as odd. But then he remembered. He'd questioned the woman in Baltimore about the director's death, but at the time, she'd been dressed in a nun's habit. When she'd removed the veil and coif, her short pigtails stuck out from her head. But she, like everyone else he'd question, hadn't been able to provide any useful information.

Remembering Beth, he faced her. She stood with her arms crossed against her chest.

"I'm Detective Jeremy Fox and—"

"I'm Beth Getty."

Fox had never been one to keep up with who's who in celebrity circles. He'd only glanced at the PSAs during commercial breaks during televised ball games and assumed the pretty woman urging drunks not to drive worked for MADD or another anti-drinking/driving organization. But now, looking into Beth's face, a flush of heat surged through him, and a bead of sweat popped onto his forehead. He'd seen attractive women before. Skye Andrews, for one, but Beth took it to a new level. Even the ragged scar crossing her cheek couldn't mar her beauty.

"You're the one who arrested Skye."

The accusing tone of her words wasn't lost on him. Fox feared his pale skin had bloomed pink. He gulped a mouthful of air and banished the weird reaction the woman triggered. He wanted to offer her his hand but feared it would tremble. Not the impression he'd want to portray as one of Baltimore City's finest.

"Your husband says you have a sixth sense."

Beth's eyes narrowed, and her brow creased.

"Maybe we can work together," Fox said. "My gut tells me that your friend, Skye Andrews, may not have committed murder, no matter what the evidence suggests. I'm here to uncover the truth wherever it may lead."

Fox noticed the tension drain away from her face.

"You believe in my *fey?*"

"I've worked with psychics in the past without prejudice. Mainly as a last resort. The truth is," Fox said, pulling his sight away from her emerald eyes. "It boils down to this. We need someone with your gift to uncover the person responsible for the murder of Thom Boyle. Be it Skye Andrews or someone not on our radar."

Beth grabbed his arm. "Well then. What are we waiting for? We'll have an hour to scope out the main suspects during the lunch break."

Chapter Forty-Four

Beth glanced around the studio commissary, waiting for Fox to pick up his lunch order. *The art deco-style room has to be original to the studio, spanning back to the dawn of Hollywood.* The splendid wall murals, elegant and luxurious, reminded her of the Polish deco artist, Tamara de Lempicka, a woman way ahead of her time. *The paintings must be nearing a hundred years old, still, they shimmer with the exuberance and glamor of that golden age.* She focused on the portraits of long-ago stars, vintage movie cameras, and cubist-style buildings.

She wondered if William Desmond Taylor had eaten a meal here with a young starlet hanging on to his every word. Peering into the empty dining room, she imagined the restaurant bursting with beautiful women in bias-cut dresses, their softly waved hair beneath Garbo slouch hats seated beside dapper men in sober colored suits with double-breasted lapels and wide shoulders. The talk would be about auditions, upcoming roles, and, of course, Hollywood gossip.

"You ready?"

Fox's voice shattered the image playing in her head.

Holding her lunch plate and a bottled water, she motioned with her chin to the door leading to the outdoor lawn seating, "Let's eat al fresco."

He glanced at the dining room. "Smart choice after being cooped up in that dreary courtroom set." Fox opened the door, and Beth stepped outside.

He motioned toward one of the gray tables with umbrellas next to a neatly trimmed hedge. Beth placed her lunch on the table, and Fox pulled out her chair that glided across the manicured lawn.

Beth took a quick bite of her grilled vegetable sandwich on focaccia bread. "We'll have to nose around a bit. And determine who the actual killer is." She twisted the bottle cap off and took a sip of water.

"The evidence points to Skye Andrews." Fox lifted his hamburger smothered in mayo and grilled onions.

"We'll have to prove she's innocent by uncovering the actual killer." A slice of bell pepper slipped free from Beth's sandwich and landed on the paper plate. She popped it into her mouth.

Fox set his half-eaten burger down and looked into Beth's face. "I'm not here to prove your friend's innocence."

She stopped eating and dropped her hands into her lap.

"I'm good at my job. When I make an arrest, in here," he said, tapping his chest, "I know they're guilty. This time, something's off. The motive's weak, and we still haven't located the murder weapon. And that damn knife seems too convenient."

"You think it was planted to frame Skye?"

"I honestly don't know. Maybe it's ridiculous for me to come all this way when the case is outta my hands." He looked at his plate then pushed it aside.

"I can tell you're a good man, Jeremy Fox. A seeker of the truth, you are. Well then, with your expertise and my *fey*, we're bound to find the culprit." She took the final two bites of her sandwich.

Beth looked across the rows of tables searching for Willie but didn't see her. She settled on Sam seated with three other men and grabbed her water bottle. "I'm going to touch base with Sam, the prop master. See if he knows where Willie is. She promised to introduce me to the actors." Beth left him to his burger and headed to the nearby table.

She felt Sam's eyes on her as she moved closer. He stood, and Beth slowed her pace.

"Beth," Sam said. "Please, join us." He swept his hand toward his vacated chair.

"Ah, sure, that's kind of you, but I'm looking for Willie. Do you know where she'd be?"

"Willie came down with a migraine, and I sent her back to the hotel. The Sunset Tower." Sam shook his head. "Thom's favorite hotel. Built way back in 1931. The old gal still imparts a touch of the old Hollywood glitz." He glanced downward as if studying the blades of grass beneath his feet. "It's hard to believe Thom's gone."

"'Tis a terrible shame. From what I've gathered, Thom Boyle wasn't only a top-notch director but a kind and generous man."

Sam raised his head. "And always ready to give back to the community. Thom volunteered hundreds of hours working as an anti-drug advocate. I think he blamed himself for what happened to Willie. You do know—"

"Uh-huh. Willie's quite open about her addiction. Former addiction."

"Ruined her career. Then you know, she waitresses in a two-bit bar in Baltimore. Damn shame."

"Oh? Yes, of course. An awful turn of events for the colleen."

"Thom thought so too. Gave his best shot to help Willie out. That's why he came to me, searching for a position for her. Turned out to be a smart move since she's done great. And I'm happy to keep her on my staff. But I suspect Thom wanted to resurrect Willie's acting career. He would've been thrilled if that'd happened." Sam blew out a stream of air. "And to think Skye Andrews . . ." He shook his head. "I still find it hard to believe Skye's responsible for Thom's death. Doesn't make sense."

Beth tapped her chin with her forefinger. "Can you think of anyone who might've wanted to see Thom dead?"

"To be honest, my first impulse pointed to Jane Reid." He flicked his thumb at a table occupied by two women. "Rumor is Isabella had the hots for Thom, and they were involved. Jane would do her damnedest to squash something like that. But murder?" Sam shrugged.

Beth eyed the two women at the adjacent table. The older woman sat with her arms crossed against an ample bosom while the younger one wore dark sunglasses and held a cellphone against her ear.

"I think I'll introduce myself," Beth said, gesturing toward the Reids'. "Lovely chatting with you." From the corner of her eye, Beth saw Fox walking toward her.

Beth met him, grabbed his arm, and whispered, "Jane and Isabella Reid. Over there." She waved her hand in the direction of the mother and daughter. "Come on." She took a deep breath and moved toward the table with Fox at her side.

"You're Isabella Reid," Beth said, "and this must be your ma, Jane?"

"Yes, I'm Jane Reid." She dropped her arms and looked at Beth with narrowed eyes.

"Oh my God," Isabella said, placing her cellphone on the table. "You're Sibèal. I love your perfume." She stretched out her arm in Beth's direction. "I'm wearing it now."

"Lovely," Beth said, recalling the successful ad campaign for the perfume Noelle cosmetics named after her. "Do you mind if we join you? This is my friend, Jeremy."

"Please, do," Isabella said, sliding the sunglasses onto her head.

"I didn't realize you act," Jane said. "Aren't you famous for being a walking clothes-hanger?" A smirk claimed her face. "But then you had an accident." Jane squinted as if trying to recall something. "You had a bit too much to drink—"

"It was the other way around. I was hit by a drunk driver." An instant dislike for the woman overtook Beth. Suppressing her reaction, she sat next to Jane while Fox remained standing.

"You'll have to excuse my mother," Isabella said. "She's furious with Hugo."

"Oh?" Beth said, focusing on the young woman.

"With Skye's arrest, we hoped I'd get top billing. But Hugo insists Skye's not out of the picture. She's going to finish her role long-distance or something." Isabella turned her attention to Fox. "Just don't stand there. Sit down." She patted the empty chair next to her.

Fox sat and folded his hands on top of the table.

"I'm not upset," Isabella continued. "Hugo offered me the starring role in his next film. A rom-com. Should be fun."

"Lovely," Beth said. "But speaking of Skye, I don't think she murdered anyone."

"Is that because you two are friends?" Not allowing Beth to respond, Jane said. "Skye Andrews is nothing more than a stuck-up bitch who murdered one of the industry's greatest directors. She threatened Thom and then carried that threat out. Simple as pie. Good riddance to her, I say."

Beth shot a questioning glance at Fox. He pressed his lips together and offered her an almost imperceptible nod.

Seemingly bored with the conversation, Isabella turned her eyes toward Fox. "You look familiar, but I can't quite place you. Have we met before?"

"I'm a police detective from Baltimore. I investigated the murder scene."

"Oh." Isabella pursed her lips for a moment as if thinking of what to say. "That was the worst day of my life. I couldn't believe it, actually, I refused to believe that my Thom was dead. I was a wreck when a police lady started asking me a long list of questions. I didn't want to talk to her or my mom, or anyone, really. I only wanted Thom to be okay. But he wasn't." She lifted her cellphone, glanced at the screen, and slipped it into her skirt pocket. "I wish you would've questioned me. I bet you could've calmed my nerves." Isabella placed her hand on top of his folded ones.

"The detective that questioned you is my partner," Fox said, sliding his hands free of Isabella's. "I handled the crew, and she talked to the actors. Until later on—"

"I think policemen are so strong and sexy," Isabella said. "Walk with me to the commissary."

"Miss Reid, I—"

"My friends call me Isa. I hope you'll be my friend." Isabella widened her doe-like eyes and pouted. "I'm awfully parched. Please, Jeremey." She stood.

Fox's cheeks flushed. "Of course, Miss," he said, rising.

"It's real cute the way you blushed." Isabella snatched his arm.

Isabella's words became muted as they walked away. If it wasn't such a serious matter, Beth would've chuckled watching a police detective being lassoed by a teenage girl. But now that she was alone with Jane, Beth had questions she wanted answered. But, just like when it came to Daines, her *fey* remained silent. She longed to banish the sinking feeling that Jane Reid hadn't murdered the director. No matter how much she'd wished the woman had committed the crime.

"So," Jane said, looking at Beth. "Because of your friendship with Skye Andrews, you were handed a trivial role in the film. And now she's locked up for murder." Jane shook her head. "Too bad Skye allowed her passions to overtake her common sense."

Beth pressed her lips into a tight line, sensing Jane had more to say.

"God knows how hard I've tried to reign in Isabella's passions. I'm afraid I'm losing that fight. Her flirtations with older men have only led to heartbreak. If only she'd consider boys her age. But no. I blame it on her father—the no-good bum. He ran off with some bimbo before Isa was born. Haven't heard a peep from him since. It seems her entire life, Isa's been looking for a daddy to love her."

"Ah, the poor colleen."

"But Thom was a whole different story."

Beth leaned forward, anxious to hear Jane's words.

"Isabella knew Thom Boyle for most of her life. You see, I'd always imagined that I'd be the star. But everything went downhill when I met Isa's father and became pregnant. Around that time, I had an audition with Thom. I didn't get the part, but we struck up a friendship. It wasn't long after that, the no-good jerk abandoned me with an infant. It was tough trying to find work and take care of Isa. That's when Thom stepped in. We became close, lovers in fact. And he assumed the role of a surrogate father for my daughter. Thom adored her. Bought Isabella whatever her little heart desired."

Beth nodded, urging her on.

"Then I made one of the biggest mistakes of my life. I dropped Thom and entered a disaster of a marriage. Six months later, it was Thom's shoulder I was crying on. But he'd moved on and was involved with someone else."

Beth didn't understand why Jane Reid was pouring out her life story to her. But there was no way she was going to stop her.

"Even though our relationship had waned," Jane continued, "Thom hadn't forgotten about us. When I suggested Isa had talent," she paused.

Beth recognized a look of satisfaction or was it pride, she wondered, crossing Jane's face.

"You're probably aware that Isabella worked as an ad model since she was six months old. Well, anyway," Jane continued, not waiting for a response, "Thom took over. At that time, Isa, a precocious four-year-old, loved being the center of attention. The timing turned out to be spot on. Thom had been searching for a child actress and Isa turned out to be perfect for the part." A wistful smile lingered on her face. "That breakthrough role paved Isabella's way to the starring role as Amelia, the youngest of the three kids in the hit sitcom, *Mother Knows Best*. You know, she won a Young Artist Award the first season the show aired. She was only six years old. And her career has only taken off from there. Thanks to Thom."

The dreamy look vanished from Jane's face. She frowned and shot Beth a menacing look. "I'll never forgive Skye Andrews for what she's done."

"But—but—"

"I understand why Isabella's anger escalated over the years since I left Thom, the only man she considered a dad. She pretended to be in love with him to get even with me. But since his murder, the two of us have worked out our differences. At Thom's funeral, we sat with the family, well, what's left of it. Cody, beside himself with grief, wouldn't let go of Thom's eighty-four-year-old mother's hand. Everyone—"

"Mother," Isabella said, approaching the table with Fox at her side. "Jeremy's going to be my guest at the studio. Isn't that wonderful?" She shot a brilliant smile at the bewildered Fox. "Isn't he adorable?" Isabella didn't wait for an answer. "Come on. I want to introduce you to Hugo. Hugo Daines. He's our new director."

Fox glanced at Beth with a tiny nod.

Isabella grabbed Fox's hand and nudged him toward the outskirts of the eating area where Daines conversed with a petite woman. A cameraman trained his lens on them.

"Who's that with Hugo Daines?" Beth asked.

Jane turned her head. "Mindy Marks. She's probably interviewing Hugo for *Celebrity Files*. She interviewed Isa a couple of days ago. She's planning to air the interviews during the premiere week of *Dark Grace*."

Beth squinted. "So that's Mindy Marks." She glanced at Jane. "We have a scheduled interview tomorrow. I'd like to introduce myself." Beth stood and grabbed her water bottle. "It's been lovely chatting with you."

Jane nodded as her gaze shifted away from Beth.

Beth glanced in the direction that captured Jane's attention and spied Isabella with a death grip on Fox's arm. Goodness, Beth thought, Isa's all business when it comes to riling her ma. *One way, I suppose, to retaliate against Jane for her overbearing and controlling ways. Isa might be a coddled young woman, and her ma a control freak, but I truly doubt they had anything to do with Thom's murder.*

It seemed the interview ended. Beth didn't want to miss the opportunity to deliver a message. Any questions regarding Skye Andrews were incontrovertibly off the table.

Chapter Forty-Five

Beth slowed her steps as Daines approached. Intent on reaching Mindy Marks, she nodded at the director and continued walking.

"Hey, Beth," Daines said.

She paused and glanced at him over her shoulder.

"Have you seen Toni?"

"Not since breakfast. Sorry." Beth half-turned toward the director.

"She's in the next scene, and I want to go over some tiny changes in the script. Probably holed up in her dressing room." Daines nodded as if proud of himself for solving the mystery of the missing actress. "You think we can try again? Tonight at my place for drinks, a light repast, and then, well . . ." He stepped next to her and tucked his arm around her waist. "I promise. You won't be disappointed."

She'd had plenty of experience with creepy guys making advances when she modeled and learned a thing or two about how to deflect their unwanted attention. "Tonight?" she asked, looking into his eyes shielded by the ever-present sunglasses. "Ah, sorry to disappoint you. I have a special dinner date planned with my husband." She slipped free from his grasp.

He took off his baseball cap with the movie's title stitched on its panel and combed his fingers through his hair. "I still have a hard time visualizing you being married to—to—that big, hulking guy."

She held back the laugh wanting to surface, recalling the shocked look on his face when "her husband" interrupted their dinner date. "You know the saying, 'opposites attract,' which in our case is God's honest truth."

"Well, whatever. Look, I've gotta find Toni," he said under his breath as he strode off.

Beth feared the unwanted conversation with Daines stole her chance to connect with Mindy Marks. She sighed with relief, catching sight of the reporter chatting with Isabella Reid. Jeremy stood silent. But from the solemn look on his face, she imagined he scrutinized every word passing between the two women.

She joined the little group. Deep in conversation, it took Isabella a few seconds to realize that Beth was standing next to her.

"Mindy, you know Sibèal, don't you?" Isabella asked.

Mindy Marks pulled her eyes away from the young actress and targeted Beth. A frown wrinkled her forehead, but a second later, it smoothed out. "Why didn't I know you had a role in the movie?"

"Only a bit part," Beth said, sizing up the woman. Petite with shiny long blonde hair and aqua blue eyes. *A pretty little package.* "If you blink, you'll miss me."

Mindy smiled a perfect smile.

"Mindy," said Isabella. "We have to get back to the set." She grabbed Fox's hand.

"Nice meeting you, Detective." Mindy nodded at Fox. "Always a pleasure, Isa."

The two of them took off, and Mindy faced Beth. Her eyes seemed to sparkle with excitement. "I'm interviewing the cast members for my show. *Celebrity Files.* And since we have an appointment for tomorrow." She glanced at the cellphone screen she'd fished from the pocket of her begonia-colored ankle pants. "Here it is. We're scheduled for two-thirty. But it'd be wonderful if we could do it now."

"Now?" Beth took a deep breath as an icy chill crept along her back. *My fey.*

She wanted to block Mindy Marks' voice, edged with an unpleasant shrillness that clashed with her flawless looks. Beth needed to concentrate and discern the forewarning offered by her sixth sense. She closed her eyes, cleared her mind, and hoped against hope that an image, word, or phrase would surface.

"Are you okay?" Mindy's voice broke her concentration.

"Ah, sure," Beth said, swallowing her disappointment.

"The more I think about it, an interview now would be perfect. With you dressed in your costume and all. What is that—a nurse outfit?"

"'Tis." Beth glanced at the inexpensive Timex that the wardrober had attached to her wrist.

"Oh, no. Don't tell me. You have to get back to the set?"

Beth noticed the glimmer in Mindy's eyes dim with displeasure.

"I won't be going to the set. My bit is finished, it is. So, if you like—"

"Fantastic." Mindy gestured to the cameraman, who'd made himself comfortable at a nearby table. "Bring over a couple chairs." She pointed toward the hedge a few feet away.

With his handheld camera seated on the table, he followed Mindy's instructions. She shot off a couple more orders regarding how she wanted him to handle the shoot.

Beth stopped listening and sat on the edge of one of the chairs. While Mindy remained occupied, she'd hoped to decipher the message from her *fey*. She couldn't hold back her excitement, believing her sixth sense wanted to reveal the truth regarding Thom Boyle's murder. *I need to relax. Clear my mind.*

All too soon, Mindy dropped into the chair opposite her.

"With me doing the interview now, my schedule for tomorrow will open up," Mindy said. "You have no idea how much prep work this job entails. But I can't complain. I love it. This show is heads and shoulders better than that silly lingerie program I hosted. I imagine all of us have to suffer some in this business to achieve the success we truly deserve. Like I was saying to my fiancé, you know, David Regan, he's the director of my old gig, *Lingerie Exposed* and . . ."

Beth willed for Mindy to stop prattling on. When the reporter finally took a breath, Beth said, "Before we start, I want you to understand. If you bring up any inquiries about Skye Andrews' troubles, the interview ends."

Mindy pressed her lips into a tight line. "Oh, yeah. Your agent mentioned something about that. But are you sure? Getting a perspective from one of Skye's closest friends could bolster sympathy for her. Have you read what people are posting on social media about Skye? Scathing stuff."

Beth shook her head. "Not a word about Skye."

"Oh, okay," she said after what seemed to Beth like ten minutes. After a deep exhale, Mindy looked at the cameraman, with the camera perched on his shoulder. A wide smile crossed her face. "The last few days, I've been on the set of the upcoming—sure to be a blockbuster—movie, *Dark Grace*. I'm pleased to have with me supermodel and actress Sibèal."

"It's grand altogether to be with you, Mindy."

"Let's talk a little about your role in *Dark Grace*."

"As you see from my costume, I play a nurse. It's a small role but a pivotal part in the movie."

"Interesting. But now, you've piqued my curiosity. Share a tidbit about the character you portray. Earlier, Antonia Wright talked about her role as a recovering alcoholic who is the supervisor of the homicide department investigating a very intriguing murder."

Another chill ran through Beth as an image of Zach's mansion filled her mind. She jumped away from the chair. "I'm sorry, but I have to go."

"What do you mean," Mindy raised her voice, "you have to go? We've only started—"

"I have to get to Zach's—something's not right. And Toni." She raced past the cameraman and broke out into a full-fledged run, unaware of the camera trained on her. And that Mindy Marks trailed on her heels.

Chapter Forty-Six

Shane fingered his cleft chin, wondering what to do next.

"Don't be disappointed," Esma Flores said, looking at him over the top of her laptop. "Sometimes, it takes years to recover lost art. And unfortunately . . ." She shook her head.

"I was sure Renaldo Jones was guilty of stealing Greyson's paintings." He lifted a pen and rolled it between his palms. "After Jones balked for an hour about his innocence, my gut told me he was lying. But then, with a smirk, he finally agreed to a polygraph. I felt it in my bones, once confronted with the results, the guy would fall like a house of cards. But after waiting two hours while four tests were administered, I still can't believe the charts revealed Jones' answers were non-deceptive." Shane dropped the pen and grabbed his coffee mug. He swallowed a mouthful of the tepid liquid. "Either Jones is innocent, or he's an expert at beating a lie detector test."

"Wasn't Chaz Reynolds the polygraph examiner?"

Shane pressed his lips together and nodded. "I know. There's no way Jones could've conned him. Reynolds is one of the best. Dammit." Shane slammed the mug down.

"Has Greyson offered a reward?"

"He hasn't, no. The missing artwork seems to have taken a backseat to his wife's problems. Greyson posted two million for his wife's bail. But I'll contact him about it." Shane scribbled a note on a pad and slipped the jotter into his shirt pocket.

271

"Do that. Also, make sure the media doesn't let the story go cold. Once Greyson offers a reward, alert the television stations and provide them with photos of the stolen art."

"Will do."

"Remember, the point of a heist isn't about stealing the art, it's about the selling. And it's damn hard to unload hot artwork."

Shane leaned forward in his chair, considering her words.

"There's always the possibility that Greyson's stolen items have wound up in a private collection," Flores said. "After all, he didn't keep it to himself that he'd amassed a showroom of priceless art. That big spread in the *American Art Connoisseur* magazine advertised that Zach Greyson has one of the most impressive private galleries in southern California. For all we know, his Picasso could be hanging in someone's bedroom as we speak."

"If that's the case, we can kiss goodbye the possibility of ever recovering them."

"True. Because it'd be easy enough for a hired hand skilled in electronics to break into the Greyson mansion, nab the paintings, and deliver them to an art collector in exchange for a hefty commission."

Shane resumed fingering his dimpled chin, not liking the sound of Flores' words.

"But if Greyson's reward is tempting enough, the thief might decide to double-cross the guy who hired him," Flores said. "Offer up a name for the cash."

"Yeah, but the thief would be just as guilty. They'd both wind up in the slammer."

"You'd think. But sometimes, we have to hold our noses and make a deal."

"Like hell, if I'd do that," Shane muttered. "Look, I'm gonna touch base with a couple of the major auction houses. See if they've heard anything."

"Go right ahead. But don't hold your breath. Greyson's pieces have been listed on the Art Loss Register and with the FBI and Interpol. It would take all of two minutes for Sotheby's, Christie's, or any auction house to discover the Greyson items were stolen. Since we haven't heard from any of those houses, it's plain to see the paintings haven't surfaced yet."

Shane ranked his fingers through his sun-streaked blond hair. "Is it always this discouraging? Because at this point, I'm thinking it's easier to identify a homicide suspect than locate a stolen work of art."

"You haven't heard the worst scenario. If Greyson's artworks have found their way to the criminal underworld, they've taken on a whole new currency. Collateral."

Shane blew a stream of air through his lips. He'd never even suspected there'd be a black market for artistic masterpieces.

"For example," Flores said, "drug traffickers use stolen artwork for loan security. And artwork can be traded for weapons. The scary thing is that criminals have no idea how to care for frangible art pieces. Like Greyson's stolen *Madonna and Child,* which is over five hundred years old. Moisture is the main enemy. Not many thieves know to wrap paintings in tissue paper, breathable sheets, or foam to protect the fragile painted surfaces and store them in a temperature-controlled environment."

"What you're saying is that Greyson's paintings could already be damaged beyond repair."

"A possibility. However, if recovered, a skilled art conservator would have the expertise to restore the damage. That, of course, would depend on the amount of deterioration."

Shane's office phone rang. He held up his hand, urging Flores to hold her thoughts as he answered the call.

"Shane. This is Trey. You gotta get over here right away."

"Whoa, slow down." Shane sensed the urgency filling the young man's voice. "What's the trouble?" Trey's deep breaths filled his ears as if he'd sprinted a 100-meter dash in record time. "Look, relax. Take some deep breaths and tell me what's going on. Start at the beginning."

"Okay." Trey paused for a couple of seconds. "Zach and Bruno left like two hours ago for Miss Andrews' place in Malibu to meet with detectives regarding the home invasion. After they took off, I drove to the Fowler museum to—well, that doesn't matter. I got home about ten minutes ago. The gate was open. At first, I wasn't concerned because Sofia usually forgets to close it. But her car is gone, so she's not home. Plus, it's the regular staffs' day off, so no one should be inside the main house. I walked to the front entrance, and I couldn't believe it, the door was wide open. I went inside and checked the alarm. It's been tampered with again. I bet the security system is down too. The main house has been broken into."

Shane wanted to say, "Are you kidding me?" Instead, he mumbled, "Okay."

"I can't wrap my brain around what's been going on. Now another robbery?"

"Where are you?"

"Out back. Between the cabana and the tennis court."

"If the perp is still in the house, you might've already been spotted. Get in your truck and take off. We don't want a replay of what happened a few months ago when you faced a deranged killer."

"You think the intruder is armed?"

"Can't say. But we don't want to take any chances. Right?"

"Yeah, sure. Right."

"I'm leaving my office now. I should get to Zach's," Shane said, checking his watch, "in under twenty minutes." Lights and siren on, I should cut the travel time more than half, he calculated. With another strict warning to leave Zach's property, Shane ended the call and slammed the receiver on its base.

"A lead?" Flores asked, wide-eyed.

"Not sure. But I'm heading over to Greyson's. Something fishy is going on."

• • •

Beth's *fey* couldn't have been clearer. Something's terribly wrong at Zach's house, and Shane's in trouble.

She ran blindly, relying on instinct to lead the way. Beth's heart pounded and lungs burned as her feet hit the road's unforgiving surface. After about a half-mile, she slowed her pace. The buildings looked alike except for the gold letters marking each soundstage. A maddening thought invaded her brain.

Could I have taken off in the wrong direction?

Beth turned in a tight circle gasping for breath. Not knowing in which direction to continue, she took a few tentative steps but stopped hearing her name. She looked over her shoulder and spied Jeremy Fox. He tossed the cigarette from his lips and jogged toward her.

"You okay?" Fox said.

"I have to get to Zach Greyson's house," Beth puffed out the words. She grabbed his arm. "Come with me. I may need your help. My Shane's in trouble."

She started to move, but he held his ground.

"Trouble?"

"I'll explain on the way."

She tugged him forward, and he took a few steps. "Parking Lot A is . . ." Beth stopped, and her brow wrinkled, taking in his perplexed expression.

"You're turned around. It's this way." Fox pointed in the opposite direction. "Come on." He started jogging, and Beth matched his pace.

Settled in her SUV, Beth pulled out of the lot and headed toward Motor Avenue. "It shouldn't take longer than fifteen minutes to get to Zach's." She freed a pair of sunglasses from a storage case. She slipped them on and slowed down, nearing a traffic light.

"Care to enlighten me?" Fox asked, glancing at her.

"It's my *fey*. Shot me an image of my Shane that made me tremble."

"Have you considered you might be overreacting?"

"What? Wait. You believe. You said so yourself, you did."

"In psychic ability?"

"Because if you don't believe in my gift, get out right now. It's an easy walk back to the studio."

"We've hired people who claim to have extrasensory perception as a tool of last resort. With some startling results."

"Then you shouldn't be doubting me." Beth tapped the steering wheel, waiting for the turn signal to change. The instant the green arrow flashed, she swung left, a bit too fast, onto Avenue of the Stars.

"So what has your, um, *fey* shared with you?"

She raised the sunglasses on top of her head and glanced at him. "No specifics. But my sixth sense is telling me trouble is brewing, and Shane's in the thick of it."

Chapter Forty-Seven

Shane tapped the brake, turning into Greyson's long driveway. "Really?" he muttered, noticing Trey's pickup in the parking circle. An initial spark of anger turned to concern, hoping to God nothing had happened to the young man. He pulled his unmarked police sedan next to Trey's truck and hopped out.

He jerked around, hearing his name. Shane sighed in relief, spotting Trey, who seemed to have appeared from nowhere.

"Why the hell are you still here?" Shane asked, brushing back a lock of hair the breeze had blown onto his forehead.

"Had to pack some art supplies. Decided to head over to Point Dume to paint *en plein air*. The rocks, mountains, and surf are always a good subject. Being close to nature helps me deal with the emptiness of losing Lexi."

Shane placed a hand on Trey's shoulder. "Sounds like a plan. You need help loading your truck?"

Instead of answering, a quizzical look crossed Trey's face.

"Something wrong?"

"Look," Trey said, pointing at the upper corner of the house. "Someone's opening a window. If I'm not mistaken, that's Zach's hobby room."

Shane faced the house, shielding his eyes, and saw two double-pane windows opened at the top and the bottom. Questions flew through his mind. He didn't know the answers, but his gut told him whatever the hell was going on, wasn't good.

Shane ran to the front entrance, crossed the lavish foyer, and pressed the up button next to the elevator. He spun around, hearing footsteps slapping the marble floor, and faced Trey. The elevator door slid open, and Trey jumped inside. Not wanting to waste time arguing, Shane entered the lift.

"Zach will be devastated if his hobby room is trashed again," Trey said.

During the short ride, Shane relived the last time he'd raced to Zach's hobby room. The sight confronting him could've been taken out of a horror movie. Aquariums overturned, lizards scurrying under tables, and snakes wriggling across the floor except for the python threatening Emma's life. Greyson had jumped into action and grabbed a fire extinguisher.

The elevator door opened, and they burst out.

"Stay here," Shane ordered.

"I have the key." Trey pulled out a yellow coiled ring from his back pocket. He walked past Shane, and the wooden floor creaked under his heavy footfalls. He paused at a closed door.

Shane caught up, and Trey handed him the keys. "It's the large brass one."

He grabbed the doorknob. It felt warm. "You smell something?" Shane stuck the key into the lock and cracked the door open.

Coils of black smoke greeted them.

Inside the room, glowing orange flames wavered from a mass of bedcovers set beneath a wooden table. The fiery tongues skipped, pecking the wooden surface. Trey raced to the windows and slammed them shut.

Shane's eyes jumped, scanning the room for the fire extinguisher. The canister stood in the spot he'd remembered. He sped to the counter, lifted the extinguisher, and pulled the pin. Moving closer to the blaze, he aimed low, pointing the nozzle at the base of the fire. He squeezed the handle and swept the burst of white spray from side to side.

"Looks like it's out," Trey said through his t-shirt pulled over his mouth.

"Yeah," Shane said as the pounding of his heart slowed.

"If the fire took hold, this part of the house would've gone up like a tinderbox," Trey said. "Zach's never upgraded this part of the house. It's all 1920s wood."

"You would think," Shane said, placing the spent fire extinguisher on the floor. "But newer construction materials burn quicker than these older structures. And fabrics used for our modern furniture don't help any." He turned and faced Trey. "Whoever tried to torch this," he said, yanking his thumb over his shoulder toward the interior of the room, "could still be somewhere in the house."

"Right," Trey said, freeing his cellphone from the back pocket of his jeans. "I better call Zach. He's gonna be pissed. Some of the critters," he said, waving his arm, "are dead. Asphyxiated."

"Just what he needs. More bad news." Shane shook his head. "Greyson can wait. You need to pick up with your original plan and head out to Point Dume."

"I think I'll stay closer to home. Like the guesthouse."

"I don't recommend that. No. This situation could turn out to be more dangerous than a small fire."

"Well, okay. If you think that's best."

Shane draped his arm across Trey's shoulder. "I'll walk you out."

Once outside, Shane watched as Trey took off in his ratty old pickup and disappeared through the main gate.

"Whoever set the fire has access to the house," Shane muttered. *Knows how to disarm alarm systems. And has keys. The same person who stole Greyson's artwork?*

· · ·

Beth pressed hard on the accelerator as she negotiated Tower Road's narrow twisty path, not unlike other residential roads in Beverly Hills.

"Slow down," Fox said, gripping the grab handle above the passenger door. "You're gonna have an accident."

Instead of slowing down, she pressed harder on the pedal. "How can I? The image my *fey* gave is smoke. Smoke and flames. I think Zach's house is on fire. With my Shane inside."

"It won't do any good if you crash into a tree."

The panic coursing through Beth made her head pound and her vision blurry. Fox was right, even if it was the last thing she wanted. She tapped the brake, and the arrow on the speedometer inched downward.

She willed her heart to stop pounding. But it refused. Her breath emerged in ragged bursts as she took the curves with sensible caution. Nearing Zach's house, Beth slowed even more as a pickup truck lumbered down the ribbon-like road. She leaned on the horn, catching a glimpse of the driver. *Trey.*

The truck stopped. Beth shifted in reverse and backed up.

"What are you doing?" Fox asked.

Not answering, she rolled the window down.

Trey lowered his half-opened window. "Hey, Beth, did Shane tell you what's going on?"

"He's alright, isn't he?" Beth tried to keep her voice steady, but despite the effort, her inflection wavered.

"Yeah, sure. He's fine. But someone broke into Zach's place. Started a fire in his hobby room."

"In the hobby room? Please, no. Have all the creatures perished because—"

"Not all of them. It wasn't much of a fire. Shane shut it down with an extinguisher.

But—"

"But what?"

"Whoever tried to torch Zach's house might still be inside. Shane is doing a search."

The dread that propelled her to Zach's estate intensified. "Do you know who might've set the fire?"

"Not a clue."

"Is Zach with Shane?"

Trey shook his head. "That reminds me, I gotta call Zach. Give him a heads-up."

The blare of a horn caused Beth to jump. She glanced in the rearview mirror and spied a delivery truck. "Thanks," she said.

"Don't go to Zach's," Trey called as Beth lifted her foot off the brake. "Shane wouldn't want you . . ."

Trey's voice faded as she picked up speed.

"He's right, you know," Fox said.

"Right?"

"If there's a perp inside the house, that's no place for you."

She flicked the turn signal and pulled through the open gate leading to the Greyson estate. "You do have a gun?"

"No."

"Don't police detectives always carry their guns?"

"Not if they're twenty-five hundred miles from home and on vacation."

"Makes sense. But." Beth chewed her lip, driving around the circle. She parked next to Shane's cruiser. A cold chill ran along her spine. *My fey wouldn't have brought me here unless Shane needed me.* She flung open the car door. "Come on."

"If you think there's trouble," he said, handing Beth his cellphone, "call the police."

"Not yet. Shane will be *effin'* and *blindin'* if the police barge in, and there's no one to be found."

"Better safe than sorry."

Another surge of icy chillness engulfed her. Gooseflesh sprouted on her arms. "We're wasting time. Please, God, we're not too late."

Beth jumped out of the SUV and ran toward the main entrance. She sensed Fox on her heels but didn't waste a second to glance over her shoulder and check. Shane needed her.

• • •

Shane returned to the third floor, deciding to work downward, from the top of the structure to the bottom. After emerging from the elevator, he glanced into one of the rooms. Nothing much to see except plastic packing boxes filled with holiday decorations. Christmas. Thanksgiving. Fourth of July. The other two rooms stood vacant. At one time, he guessed, these large rooms must've been servants' quarters.

He hurried down the scuffed wooden staircase, opened a door, and stepped into what seemed like another world. The second floor housed eight bedrooms and as many baths, opulent with rich fabrics and furnishings. He glanced into a bedroom. The king-sized bed stood stripped bare to the mattress. *Probably the bedding used to start the fire upstairs.* Beside the bedrooms, he discovered the floor accommodated Greyson's bowling alley, billiard room, lounge, and trophy room.

"The trophy room," he muttered. Beth described it as a shrine dedicated to the actor. He stepped inside, shaking his head. *Beth nailed it.* Displayed on the mantel stood Greyson's Oscar, Golden Globes, and various other awards. The lavender walls held framed magazine covers, film stills, and movie posters featuring the not-so-modest performer. The room looked pristine like all the others he'd checked.

Shane moved from the room toward the east wing and the gallery. He touched his hip and felt his empty paddle holster. Driving to the estate, Shane realized he'd left his gun behind, locked inside his office desk. Not wanting to lose precious time, he'd opted to continue driving. Now Shane wished that he'd returned to the office and retrieved his Glock. Deciding not to beat himself up over a stupid mistake, he picked up speed and raced down the wide carpeted corridor. I should've checked the gallery first, he chided himself, recognizing he'd made another foolish mistake.

The hall's massive French doors stood wide open. It took a second to process the sight before him. A woman dressed in a silky blouse, form-fitting slacks, and a mass of red-blond hair tied in a knot on top of her head poured liquid from a five-gallon plastic gas container onto a pile of paintings heaped on the floor. For an instant, he thought it was Skye. Until she paused and lifted her head. Their eyes met. He hadn't the slightest idea of her identity, but her intent loomed without a doubt.

"Who the hell are you?" She barked out the words as if the gasoline fumes chafed her throat.

"I was gonna ask you the same question."

She placed the red container on the floor next to her high-heeled feet and screwed up her face. It took on the likeness of a horrifying mask straight out of a nightmare. Her eyes, like flinty sapphires, flashed with anger.

"I'm a cop." Shane lifted the badge that hung from a lanyard around his neck. "And you're under arrest."

"Ha. Like hell." She whipped a firelighter stick from her back pocket and pulled the trigger, and a yellow flame shot out from the end of the metal rod. She waved it in front of his face.

Shane lunged toward her. She swung the lighter away, and the flame went out. He reached for her arm but missed as she pivoted away, landing next to the gasoline can. She lifted the plastic container and pitched it at Shane. A stream of liquid sloshed onto his shirt, soaking his tie and trousers.

The stink of gasoline filled his nostrils. A spark of anger flashed through him, but his fury quickly ebbed, replaced with a cold finger of dread. His only option—hightail it out of the gallery. Quick. Before the lunatic with the lighter turned him into a human torch.

"Well, Mr. Policeman, who's gonna be fingered for this bonfire of the vanities?" She pointed at the pile of soggy canvases. "When your charred body is discovered in this burnt-out ruin of a showroom, it won't give up a single clue," she said with a curled lip. "Except that you never learned not to play with fire." She lit the lighter, and Shane jumped backward. He scrambled into the widened corridor and stopped a dozen feet away from the flame.

A shadow caught his eye. Beth touched his arm before moving toward the gallery. Shane reached for her, but she slipped from his grasp.

"Stop." Beth's voice rang out. "You'll do more than burn paintings. You'll set yourself on fire."

"Beth?" The woman lowered her arm, and the flame died.

Shane moved closer to Beth and he pulled out his cellphone. Drenched in gasoline, he pegged it useless, imagining the phone bursting into flames. Fox came up behind him. "Get Beth the hell outta here," he instructed the detective.

Fox raised his hand, urging Shane to hold up. To allow Beth to interfere.

"Zach wounded you," Beth said, taking a step closer to the madwoman. "Zach took your love, and when he finished, he ripped your heart out of your chest and tossed it aside like a piece of rubbish."

The woman nodded.

"You've no choice but to destroy the things he loves. His snakes. His art collection. His wife. Revenge for his betrayal. The only option to restore your scarred soul."

"Yes. Yes." The woman's eyes brightened. "You understand."

Beth took slow, quiet steps as if approaching a wounded animal.

"I have to destroy Zach," the woman said with a downward glance at the paintings. "He's the one who twisted razor wire around my heart, piercing it, shredding it to pieces."

Shane glanced at Fox. Their eyes met, as if giving each other a telegraphic message.

"You stole Zach's favorite paintings." Beth's soft, calm voice sounded like velvet.

"A taste of what was to come." Her eyes took on a crazed look as she shook the lighter.

"And trashed Skye's house."

"Skye." The woman's face went cold. "That silly prima donna. Tell me. God tell me, how could Zach cast me away, Antonia Wright, for *her*? An uneducated, whiney, spoiled brat. Where I've taken the art form to its highest pinnacle, she's lowered acting to a mere imitation without heart or soul. Oh, but she's an expert at flaunting her body because her mind is vaporous. Empty as a drum."

"You found a new love," Beth said. "But, I suspect Zach wasn't the only one who betrayed you." Beth extended her hand toward Toni, but she raised her palm, urging Beth to back off.

"Thom." A high-pitched cackle flew through Toni's lips. "Generous, faithful, devoted Thom."

Shane took a step closer to Beth, and Fox followed his lead.

"He bent over backward to help that washed-up crackhead. Pleaded with Skye to play nice—a total waste of breath. And then offered me a marriage proposal. With a caveat. Cody, the dimwit, was part of the package. Thom imagined us as a blissfully happy threesome. Hell would freeze over before that perversion would ever happen."

Could it be? Shane squinted, his eyes burning from the fumes clinging to him. *This woman is Boyle's killer?*

"That would never do, no, it wouldn't," Beth said. "You poor lamb. Suffering at the hands of callous, ungrateful men."

Toni dropped the lighter and flung open her arms. "How dare they," she hissed.

Color crept up her neck and flamed across her cheeks. "Those sniveling jerks think they can toy with my emotions. Treat me like a plaything. Well, they have another thing coming. I vowed to God I would show them up, make them suffer, and get my justified revenge."

"That's why you killed Thom," Beth said.

Shane leaped and grabbed one of Toni's outstretched arms while Fox nabbed the other one.

"I'm arresting you for breaking and entering, theft, arson, attempted murder, and suspicion of Thom Boyle's murder," Shane said.

"Murder?" Toni snapped. "I didn't kill him. But kudos to whoever did."

Chapter Forty-Eight

Beth stood beneath the entrance portico leading into Zach's mansion, where she had a clear view of the parking circle, and watched Shane clasp handcuffs onto Toni's slim wrists. The actress stood silent, having assumed a stoic mien as Shane recited her rights. *Perhaps Toni realizes that earlier, she'd said too much. Her hatred stemming from Zach's abandonment must've been building for years. And, I imagine, working alongside Skye had been the tipping point.* Even though Toni had a motive for killing Thom, Beth believed the actress. After all, a broken engagement would've sufficed, that's if she'd accepted Thom's proposal.

Beth moved to the porch's edge, hoping to hear their conversation but still staying out of the detectives' way. But then, she abruptly changed her mind. *I should be standing next to Shane. Because if it wasn't for me fey.* The thought made her shudder. With deliberate steps, she crossed the portico but stopped mid-step as a police cruiser with lights flashing sped into the parking circle. Two uniformed officers alighted from the patrol car and joined the detectives.

Shane pointed to himself. Beth caught a couple of words, as he unfolded the facts as to why a pungent, almost sweet, chemical odor exuded from him. Toni stood erect, her chin high, and lips pressed, forming a thin line. Beth felt a twinge of compassion for the woman, sadly realizing that the award-winning actress had thrown away her life over a bout of overblown, all-consuming jealousy. *Blinded by betrayal, Toni attempted to kill my lovin' man.*

Beth heard a swishing noise. She tilted her head and closed her eyes, straining to pinpoint the sound. After a couple of seconds, she dismissed her concern, owing it to the breeze whisking through the tree branches. She refocused on the group of officers. Determined to close the gap between them, she moved away from the portico. After a few steps, she froze. The sound behind her wasn't a switching noise any longer but whispering. She abandoned the portico and crept around an arrangement of shrubs. Beth set her fists against her hips, finding Mindy Marks and her cameraman crouched behind the greenery.

"Did you get it? The cop handcuffing Toni? And them putting her into the squad car?" Mindy whispered to the guy with the camera. "This is gonna be phenomenal."

"Excuse me," Beth said.

Mindy twisted and faced Beth with the look of a deer in headlights.

"What the *feck* is going on here?" Beth glared at Mindy.

"Just doing my job, Beth. And I have you to thank. You led us here."

"I led you?"

"When you ran away from our interview, we followed." She pointed from herself to the cameraman. "Oh. My. God. What a story this is gonna make." A radiant smile broke across the reporter's face. "I have a few questions. We got you on tape, so I know you were inside with Toni and the cops. What are they? Undercover detectives?"

"Hold it right there. I have nothing to say. I won't be part of some mad frenzy to air this tragedy on the *telly*."

"OMG." Mindy's voice jumped an octave. "Toni Wright killed the movie director. Thom Boyle."

"It's nothing like that. No."

Mindy's face fell for a split second before it lit up again. "Then it had something to do with Zach Greyson. Toni and Zach had been an item like—like forever."

All three of them jerked their heads at the sound of a car racing down the driveway. The man raised his camera, rested it on his shoulder, and aimed the lens at the vehicle.

Beth spied Bruno behind the Bentley's wheel. Even before the sedan came to a stop, Zach jumped out.

"Are you getting it?" A new level of excitement filled Mindy's voice.

"Enough of this," Beth said. She ran out from behind the shrubs. "Bruno," she called, pointing over her shoulder. "Reporters."

Not even taking time to close the driver's side door, the bodyguard bounded to her side.

"It's Mindy Marks."

Without a word, Bruno strode to the spot Beth indicated. She trailed behind Bruno, unable to match his long strides.

"You're trespassing on private property," Bruno said, his voice like thunder. "If you don't leave, there's more than enough cops here to haul your butts into a jail cell."

"It's my right as a news reporter to be here," Mindy said. "Freedom of the press."

The man lowered his camera and moved away. "C'mon, Mindy. Let's get outta here." He crossed the lawn to the driveway and kept walking.

"Okay. Okay," Mindy said, turning her face away from Bruno but settling on Beth. "Please, just a morsel. That's all I'm asking for."

Bruno stepped next to Mindy and towered over the diminutive reporter. "I asked you nicely, lady. But now, you leave me no alternative."

"Alright. I'm leaving," Mindy huffed. Holding her head high, she stomped toward the driveway.

Bruno followed a few feet behind the reporter, assuring Mindy's departure from the Greyson estate.

Emerging from behind the bushes, Beth spied Shane and Zach with their heads together. *Jeremy must've left with Toni and the uniformed officers.* She raced toward them, as a surge of relief rushed through her. *The mystery of Zach's stolen artworks has been solved.* Even so, a twinge of regret touched her, since, at the expense of uncovering the theft, there'd been casualties. Some of Zach's priceless paintings. Soaked with petro, she imagined they'd be beyond repair.

It took a couple of seconds for the men to realize Beth stood next to them.

"Beth," Shane said, "you were amazing. The way you talked that Toni Wright down so we could nab her."

"Thank you," Zach said. "If it wasn't for you, my gallery—hell, the entire house would be engulfed in flames."

Though Zach smiled, Beth perceived a trace of sorrow clouding his eyes. Or was it regret? Remorse taking hold of his heart, revealing that he'd treated a lover shamefully, causing her to seek revenge in the most cutting way.

"My Shane was so brave," Beth said, beaming. "Doused in petro, he didn't flinch as Toni waved a lighter in front of his face. Speaking of which," she said, eyeing Shane, "you reek."

"The crime scene investigation team is on the way," Shane said. "So, I'm gonna wash up here," he said, gesturing toward the mansion. "And give them these." Shane motioned to his soiled clothing. "Evidence that Wright attempted to murder me."

Beth inhaled sharply as a wave of dizziness made her head spin.

"You okay?" Shane grabbed her shoulders.

"I'm fine. Must be the petro fumes." She couldn't tell Shane the thought of losing him was too much to bear. If she spoke the words, she'd break down. He'd been an unbreakable support from the moment they met. Time after time, he'd buoyed her up with his loving concern. A pillar of strength that made her stronger too.

"You think Toni's responsible for Boyle's death?" Zach asked.

Shane half-shrugged. "Wright denied it. But I think she's capable after the way she flicked that lighter under my nose hell-bent on torching me. So, I wouldn't be a damn bit surprised."

"Wouldn't that be great?" Zach said. "Skye would be exonerated and our lives would finally snap back to normal." He pulled a pack of cigarettes from his shirt pocket. "Except, I can't wrap my head around all of this. Toni trying to set my house on fire and framing Skye for Thom's murder."

"Toni may not be responsible for the murder," Beth said.

"But. But, didn't she admit to killing Boyle?" Zach frowned.

"Not yet," Shane said. "But if she did it, we'll get a confession."

"Okay." Zach looked at Beth as if he'd just remembered something. "Detective Fox mentioned your sixth sense fired a message. An alert. That something terrible was happening here."

"So it did," Beth said. "An image of smoke and flames. And that my Shane was in trouble. I'm only sorry it hadn't forewarned me that your precious paintings were in jeopardy."

A couple of cars pulled up beside them.

"The CSI team," Shane said. "Look, I need to clean up." He turned to Beth. "I don't know when I'll get home. Probably be a long night questioning Wright. So don't stay up." He paused for a second. "Why are you dressed like a nurse?"

"We'll talk about that later after we've both had a good night's sleep." But sleep was the last thing on Beth's mind. The little voice in her head told her there was something she needed to do before heading home. And it had to do with the murder of Thom Boyle.

Chapter Forty-Nine

Intent on dropping by the Sunset Tower Hotel to check on Willie, Beth first stopped by Summit Studio to return her costume. Not sure if the news about Toni's arrest had been made public, Beth kept her fingers crossed she wouldn't run into anyone from the *Dark Grace* set. She breathed relief when the only person she met was the costumer. And the woman seemed more interested in looking at her cellphone screen than holding a conversation.

A bit more confident walking the grounds, holding a studio map, she found the way back to the car park. Beth plugged the hotel address into her dashboard GPS and drove away, hoping never to see the likes of Antonia Wright and Hugo Daines again.

She put the fifty-two-dollar charge to park in the hotel lot on her credit card and entered the lobby. Tossing her auburn hair behind her shoulders, Beth made a beeline for the front desk. Bathed in the soft light cast from three small brass lamps, the wood paneled wall glowed with warmth. A young woman looked away from the computer and offered Beth a smile.

"May I help you?"

Beth glanced at the name badge pinned to the receptionist's uniform. "Hello, Rachael. I'm here to see one of your guests. Louise Wilson."

The woman lifted a nearby telephone. "One moment. Who may I say is calling?"

"Beth Getty."

Rachael widened her eyes and tilted her head as a confused look filled her face. "I could've sworn you were the model, Sibèal. Guess you get that a lot." Not waiting for an answer, she tapped the phone's keypad.

Beth traced the scar crossing her cheek as she waited. A vision of Willie popped into her mind. It'd been happening ever since Toni's arrest at Zach's house. The message from her *fey* wasn't clear, but Beth suspected it meant something important. Since Thom and Willie shared a lot of history, she put two and two together and figured Willie knew something about Thom's murder.

Even if it's only a kernel of a clue. It just might be the missing piece needed to solve the case.

"Ms. Getty."

The receptionist's voice started her.

"Room 214."

Beth dropped her hand.

"The elevator," Rachael said, pointing, "is around the corner."

"Thank you," Beth said with a hint of a smile.

Beth tapped her foot for the entire elevator ride. "She must know something," Beth whispered as she stepped into the corridor. *Or my fey wouldn't have directed me here.*

She followed the room number sign, turned right, walked halfway down the hallway, and stopped in front of door 214. A streak of uncertainty raced through Beth as she shifted from foot to foot. She shut her eyes, took several deep breaths, and cleared her mind. An image of Willie with her short pigtails and soulful eyes surfaced. *That does it. Willie must hold the key to solving Thom's death.*

Beth blew out a puff of air and knocked.

The door opened a few inches. Willie peered around the door's edge. "I have a migraine. And really Beth, there's no reason for you to check up on me. Did Daines send you here?"

"Daines?"

"Oh, it must've been Sam. Does he think I'm faking to get out of work?"

"Nothing, like that, no. I wanted to make sure you're okay."

"Except for the searing pain in my head, I'm fine." The door started to close.

"Wait. Can I come in? I'm worried about you."

After what seemed like forever, the door opened. "Well, okay. But only for a couple of minutes."

Beth stepped inside the room, surprised that Willie was dressed in a pair of faded jeans and a sweatshirt with *Dark Grace* emblazoned across its forest green yoke. Not in the dressing gown Beth had expected. Taking a closer look, Beth found it hard to believe this was the same girl she'd breakfasted with that morning. Willie's flawless complexion had taken on a splotchy appearance. Puffy red eyes told Beth she'd been crying and her golden-brown hair, pulled to the crown of her head, stuck straight up in a short ponytail. *Must be a killer headache. The poor girl.*

The room looked much smaller than Beth imagined, with the queen-sized bed taking up most of the space. Beige curtains with black trim blocked the light from the floor-to-ceiling window, and dusky shadows filled the room. Beth frowned, noticing an opened suitcase on the bedspread that matched the curtain design. "What's this about?" She pointed to the valise.

"That's none of your damn business."

Willie's words felt like a slap across Beth's face.

She's always been friendly, energetic, and upbeat. Her migraine seems to have altered her personality.

"I—I didn't mean to pry. I hope you feel better soon." Beth stepped backward toward the door.

"Don't go."

Beth stopped.

"I guess I'm actually relieved you showed up." Willie sighed. "I was about to booty bump. You know, plug some cocaine."

Beth swallowed the words of reproof that itched to emerge as she freed the chair from the corner desk and sat. "I thought using drugs was in your past."

Willie chewed her bottom lip and shrugged.

"So," Beth said, "You're going somewhere."

"There's no use hanging around here. I'm going home. I miss Darnell, my fiancé."

"What about your job?"

"The film is about finished. The props department will get along fine without me."

"So you've given up on your dream."

"Dream? You mean wishful thinking. I blew that a long time ago."

"Thom believed in you. And Sam thinks you're a crackerjack assistant. Could be that your days on the screen are behind you, but your talents could lie in production. I'm sure Sam could—"

"Why was that cop on the set today?"

"Detective Fox?"

"He's a Baltimore cop, isn't he?"

"Right. He's doing a little digging around. He's not completely sold on the idea that Skye committed murder."

"Who does he think did it?" Willie grabbed a sweater lying on a creamy leather bench that hugged the wall, folded it, and placed it in the suitcase.

"Toni Wright."

Willie's eyes shot open. "Toni?" She chewed a thumbnail already worn to the quick. "I kinda believed it was Toni all along. Her motive seemed stronger than Skye's."

"How's that?"

"Thom cared about his friends. A lot." Willie removed the sweater from the suitcase and refolded it. "I doubt he'd kick Cody to the curb because of Toni. Let's face it, Antonia Wright believes the world revolves around her. So sharing her boyfriend would've been out of the question.

Out of anger, and I've seen her temper, she could've done it." Willie began pacing along the tight space between the window and the bed. She started with slow, steady strides, but in a matter of seconds, they accelerated into swift, clipped steps like a contestant in a race-walking competition.

Beth stood, sensing Willie suffered from more than a headache. "Something's bothering you."

Willie trudged to a stop and began to shake.

Beth raced around the bed and touched her arm. "How can I help?"

"There's nothing you can do," Willie said, sinking onto the bed. She slammed the suitcase shut and began to rock, hugging herself. Tears streamed down her face.

Beth had never seen anyone have a complete meltdown. At least, that's what it looked like. "I'll find the hotel doctor," Beth said, not even sure if the hotel maintained a physician.

"No," Willie whispered between sobs. "I think . . . I think . . . I need to talk to Father Dan." She wiped the back of her hand across her eyes. "He's an exorcist."

Beth nodded.

"I-think-I'm-possessed-by-a-demon. A devil."

She spoke the words fast, tripping over each other, that Beth barely made sense of them.

"Satan himself. Father Dan will know what to do."

She must've taken some drug that's addled her mind. Beth noticed a tumbler on the nightstand. It held a finger of amber liquid. *Did she mix cocaine with alcohol?*

"Listen to me. I'm going to get help." Beth grabbed the cellphone from her tote bag.

"No. NoNoNoNoNo."

"Have you been drinking and taking drugs?"

Willie pulled a bottle from her sweatshirt's kangaroo pocket. She flashed the aspirin container at Beth. "This with a little bit of whiskey. It's safe." She touched her stomach.

Beth wasn't certain if what she said was true or not. "Tell me what's going on."

"Just tired. Forget about what I said about being possessed. That must've sounded crazy." Willie stood, moved to the nightstand, and downed the remainder of the drink. "All that talk about the occult and devil worship on the set must have gotten to me. A couple of guys from the crew brought in an Ouija board to conjure up some spirits. Evil spirits."

"That could be dangerous," Beth said.

"They were just kidding around. But the guys scared me when they said Beelzebub was in the room. That's one of the demon names used in the film. Anyway, they said the devil spirit jumped inside of me. I didn't sleep, like, for two days. That's when I really started using coke again. And then the murder happened." She scrubbed her face.

A burst of coldness prickled Beth's spine. She narrowed her eyes, struggling to zero in on her *fey. Could Willie be involved with Thom's murder?* She shook the outrageous idea from her mind. But then an icy chill engulfed Beth that took her breath away.

Willie closed the suitcase. "I can't stay here any longer. I need Darnell. He'll be able to make things better." She pressed her lips together.

I can't let Willie slip through my fingers, Beth thought, until I know the connection between her and the murder. "How would you like to fly to Baltimore in style?"

Willie cocked her head in Beth's direction.

"I'm overdue for a visit with Skye. A friend of mine owns a jet. Cancel your flight and come with me. I'll swing by and pick you up. Say, tomorrow around noon?"

"Really?" A glint of light brightened Willie's dark eyes.

"I'm the only passenger, and there's plenty of room. I'd love the company, and that way, you'll save the airfare." Beth sent up a quick prayer, hoping Willie would accept the offer.

"Okay. Sounds good."

"Lovely." *Now, all I have to do is convince Zach that a trip to Baltimore is in order.*

Chapter Fifty

On the terrace near the pool, Beth sat across from Fox, where they ate the leftovers meant for her romantic dinner with Shane. He'd arrived a half-hour earlier with an update that Shane would be detained at the office for at least a couple more hours. Antonia Wright requested a lawyer so the interrogation succumbed to a swift end. Except that she'd agreed to a polygraph to clear herself as a suspect in the Thom Boyle murder case.

"I don't know how Toni thinks she can whittle her way out of the theft charges," Beth said. "Not to mention arson and the attempted murder of my Shane."

"Doesn't look good for her," Fox said, lifting his wine glass and taking a sip. "Did you know that Wright has a Ph.D. in electrical engineering?"

"I didn't, no." Beth handed him the basket filled with warm bread. "That certainly explains how she disarmed Zach's security system."

Fox took a slice of focaccia, broke off a bite-size piece, and dipped it into a bowl of spiced olive oil.

"I think Toni is telling the truth about one thing. She didn't murder Thom," Beth said.

"Your sixth sense showed you something?"

"Nothing concrete. Only a strong sensation, leading me in a direction that doesn't make much sense. Not yet, anyway."

"Your insight was spot on today. Chances are, you're onto something. Is your intuition confirming that Andrews killed the director?"

"Skye? No." Beth pressed her fork through the salmon filet on her plate. Instead of taking a bite, she laid the utensil down. "Louise Wilson."

"Louise Wilson?"

"I'm not saying she's responsible. But." She pressed her lips together, debating whether to share the connection she'd drawn between the 1922 murder case and that of Thom Boyle. "Are you familiar with the case of William Desmond Taylor?"

He shook his head.

"He was a Hollywood director murdered in 1922." Beth shared the details she'd gleaned from the pages of *Jazz Age Deception*. Including the startling fact that all the leading suspects from the hundred-year-old crime lined up with people of interest in Thom's murder.

With his eyes fixed on her, Fox listened without interruption.

"I was adamant about coming to my own conclusion regarding the 1922 murder. But earlier, when I arrived home, I pulled out the book and read the final chapter. Of course, the author's hypothesis has never been confirmed as fact, and the case is still open. But to prove my hunch, I need to go to Baltimore. And," she paused for a second, "I'll need your help."

• • •

Beth sat up in bed, resting against a pile of pillows. She'd read the conclusion of *Jazz Age Deception* twice more and hoped she was on the right track. "There's only one way to find out," she murmured. She closed the book, glanced at the nightstand clock, and decided not to wait up for Shane. A thought of Jeremy flicked through her mind. It hadn't taken much effort to persuade him to catch the first available flight back to Baltimore now that he believed in her *fey*.

She wasn't betting on getting much sleep. Beth couldn't squash flickers of anxiety, causing her to waver over tomorrow's plan. "No need to be worried, at all," she told herself. "Especially since the arrangements fell into place."

After Jeremy departed for his hotel, she'd rung Zach. He'd thanked her again for saving most of his beloved art collection. It didn't take long for the conversation to switch to Skye. He'd disclosed the details of the catastrophic assault on her Malibu beach house. Skye hadn't taken the news well. With a promise to keep Skye's mind off her troubles, it took little persuasion to coax Zach into agreeing to fly Willie and her to Baltimore. Before ringing off, Zach revealed that he, too, had become a believer in the veracity of her *fey*. As a result, his confidence soared that Beth's sixth sense would lead the police to the actual person who'd pulled the trigger—and pinned the murder on Skye.

About to click off the bedside lamp, her mobile pinged. Beth grabbed the phone next to her. A text from Zach. She read the message with a smile. *Take-off 2moro @ 1.*

"Perfect."

"What's perfect?"

Beth glanced from the mobile to Shane, standing in the bedroom's doorway. "Zach's going to fly me to Baltimore along with Willie. Louise Wilson."

His forehead wrinkled.

"Skye's devastated about the house and needs comfort. Since Zach can't be with her—"

"Why am I not surprised? You can't help being a loving and caring friend. My true *a thaisce*."

"Ah, my darlin' Shane. You're my treasure too." She reached out to him, and he sat on the bed's edge.

"Who is this Willie person?"

"Like me, she had a bit part in *Dark Grace,* and we became friendly. She planned to fly to her home in Baltimore. And once I decided to visit Skye, it made sense for Willie to hitch a ride with me." She hated lying to Shane once again, but she didn't want him to worry. "I'm going to surprise Skye. The only problem," she said, shaking her head, "I promised the wee one I'd bring the rest of Cloud's litter with me. I hate to disappoint her."

Shane squeezed her hand. "You'll find a way to soothe Emma's disappointment."

"I have the photo books I had made for her—one about each kitten. It was to be a Christmas gift . . ."

Shane kissed her cheek. "No doubt, Skye's *effin' and blindin'* to high heaven about her house," he said, using his best Irish accent. "Greyson texted Skye photos of Wright's handiwork."

"Ah, now. Maybe that wasn't such a good idea, so."

"Probably not. But the good news is Charlie Newell, the caretaker attacked in Skye's media room, has been transferred from the ICU to the step-down unit."

"Meaning he'll make a full recovery?"

"Fingers crossed."

"I'll say a decade for his recovery." Beth reached for the rosary on her nightstand. "It's been quite a day. Truly, I'm *knackered.*"

"Beth." He crossed his arms. "Are you keeping something from me?"

"Whatever do you mean?"

"I might not possess a psychic ability like your *fey,* but I can detect when you're concealing something from me."

Beth yanked off the spread and slipped out of bed. "You believe in my *fey?*"

"After what happened today, how can I not? You saved me from that crazy lady who wanted to turn me into a human flambeau." He gathered Beth into his arms.

"I've waited so long to hear those words."

"You know, I'm all about the facts, my dear Betty Getty. And seeing is believing." He took a backward step holding her at arm's length. "There's no way, in hell, you could've dreamed up that woman who planned to incinerate Greyson's art collection. And me along with it."

"Thank the Lord I got there in time."

"I hate to think what could've happened. Anyway, thank God for your *fey.* But the way you talked her down can't be chalked up to a sixth sense." He shook his head. "Your de-escalation skills rival those of the most talented cops I know. You were amazing."

Heat touched her cheeks, and Beth imagined she was blushing. "I've only wanted you to believe in my special gift."

Shane pulled her close and kissed her hard on the lips. He took her hand and led Beth to their bed.

Beth didn't want to hamper his intent for lovemaking. She wanted nothing more than to revel in their intimacy but decided to share her latest hunch. *Now that he believes in my gift, he'll take my intuitions seriously. Not attribute them to coincidences or plain dumb luck.*

Beth released his hand, walked around the bed, and lifted a book and notepad from the end table. "The real reason I'm heading to Baltimore is because of this."

"My book about the William Desmond Taylor case?"

She flipped through the pages of notes and handed him the pad. "A list of suspect names I compiled from both murders."

Shane perused the page. "Suspects in both cases match? That's weird." He moved to the chaise lounge and sat on its satiny edge. "I don't remember all the specifics of the Taylor case, but consensus points to the stage mother, Charlotte Shelby, as responsible for Taylor's death. But really, Beth, this might be a coincidence that the cases appear similar."

"I've interviewed the possible suspects who might've wanted Thom dead."

Shane raised his eyebrows, but she didn't stop to explain.

"The only person of interest left to consider is Louise Wilson, who matches Margaret Gibson. In the book, the author concludes that Taylor's attempts to squelch the 1922 drug trade in Hollywood caused his death. And that Gibson was the one who pulled the trigger."

"I've heard that theory before." he said, swiping a lock of hair off his forehead, "but it didn't hold water."

"What do you mean? It makes perfect sense. And if history is repeating itself, Willie has to be considered a suspect. Her promising acting career tanked because of drug addiction. And she admitted to using drugs again after Thom Boyle's murder. Perhaps because she couldn't deal with the guilt. The only problem is why. Why would a Baltimore barmaid want to kill a Hollywood director?"

"Most likely, she wouldn't."

"Logically, yes. But murder deals with emotions. Envy, greed, hatred."

"So this Willie person hated Boyle?"

"Not in the least. Thom did everything possible to help jumpstart her defunct career."

"If that's the case, it looks like you're off-base."

"You could be right. But my *fey* sent me a warning. The meaning hasn't surfaced yet, except that it has something to do with Willie. I need to find out. It's my last hope to exonerate Skye."

"What does Fox make of all this?"

"Fox?"

"Come on, Beth. You've had to discuss this with him."

"I didn't offer Jeremy any specifics. Only that I have a hunch."

"I see." He glanced at the list again. "What's your plan?"

"I don't know. I'm trusting my *fey* will enlighten me."

"I don't want you accusing Louise Wilson of murder when you're alone with her. Like when you two are in Greyson's jet."

"I wouldn't do anything like that, I wouldn't. Now, if she admits to the murder, I'll text Jeremy. So he can meet us at the airport with an arrest warrant."

"I almost forgot," he said, touching the dimple in his chin. "Antonia Wright's polygraph chart came back non-deceptive. Seems she didn't murder Boyle. So, you were right on that score." He dropped the notebook onto the lounge and walked to her. With one swift motion, he picked Beth up, laid her on the bed, kissed her forehead, the tip of her nose, and her mouth. "I never would've believed in a million years, I'd marry a true blue one-hundred percent psychic," he whispered in her ear.

"Ah, my darlin' Shane. I won't be needing the help of *me fey* to know what's on your mind." She giggled.

"I hope not," he said and covered her mouth with his, silencing the tinkling of her laughter.

Chapter Fifty-One

Beth swiveled in the jet's leather club seat toward the aisle and faced Willie sprawled on the divan. Her deep, even breaths told Beth the woman was still asleep as she'd been for the past four hours. Quite a different sight from yesterday when an agitated Willie paced in the tiny hotel room overwhelmed with emotion. She honestly didn't know what to make of the actress-turned-property assistant and *freastalaí beáir*—bartender. She shook her head and turned toward the window. There was nothing to see but silvery clouds stretched beneath them like a soft blanket.

Beth pressed a button on the inside of the chair to recline back and grabbed a couple of pretzels that Willie brought along as a snack. She studied the photograph of Shane's greatpa on the back cover of *The Complete Works of Shane T. O'Neill.*

Uncanny, she thought, how closely Shane resembles his greatpa. A smile tucked in the corners of her mouth. *'Tis ironic that with Shane's aversion toward "Hollywood types," his great grandfather aspired to become a leading man. Until, of course, he took up the pen.* She opened the book to the final short story. *Greatpa's Irish roots come shining through with his gift for words. A fine writer, if I say so meself.* She glanced at the story's title, "A Mysterious Murderer Comes to Hollywood," and recalled that Shane had mentioned the collection held a story based on the murder of William Desmond Taylor. *I wonder who Greatpa thought killed the director.* She tilted her head toward the window. *Surely, there are as many theories as there are suspects.*

"Hey, Beth."

"Ah, you're awake." Beth placed a laminated bookmark against the page and closed the book. "A good nap?"

Willie took a deep breath and raised her arms, stretching. "Wonderful. I feel so much better now that I'm on my way home. I kinda missed the regulars at the Firebird Tavern and Grill—that's where I work." She slid her legs over the edge of the couch and sat straight, rolling her shoulders. "Hungry?" Willie reached for the backpack at her feet and pulled out a couple of protein bars. "Want one?"

"Thanks, but no. I could go for a *cuppa*. Can I get you a cup of tea? Coffee?" Beth adjusted the seat upright and locked its position, set down the book, and stood.

"Coffee would be good," Willie said. "Black."

It took Beth only a couple of minutes to pour two mugs full to the brim. Before moving back to the passenger cabin, Beth stepped into the cockpit. "Would you lads like a *cuppa* or a cup of coffee?"

The co-pilot looked away from his instruments, smiled at her, and shook his head.

The captain glanced in her direction and offered a wink. "That's darlin' of you," he said, "but I'm grand." He lifted a water bottle.

Beth cringed at his fake Irish accent. She overlooked it, knowing he must be an excellent pilot since Zach hires only the best.

She moved through the galley kitchen with its gleaming mahogany cabinets and granite countertop. Taking careful steps as a touch of turbulence hit the plane, she reached Willie and handed her the mug.

Willie took a sip. "Mm," She held the mug between her hands as if warming them. "Go back to your reading. No need to entertain me. I'll . . ." She jutted her chin toward the large screen above the fireplace.

"Speaking of reading—"

"I'm not a big reader, but I like to crochet. I make Afghans and scarfs, those kinds of things."

"Lovely." Beth reclaimed her seat and took a sip of tea. "My ma was teaching me how to knit before she died. I never did get the hang of it."

Willie raised her mug but kept her eyes focused on Beth.

"I was wondering, during your time working in movies, did you ever hear about the 1922 murder of a Hollywood director?"

"Can't say that I have." Willie scooted toward the edge of the soft leather divan.

"I read a detailed account of the murder, which has never been solved. The curious thing is that the death of William Desmond Taylor mimics Thom's murder. Some experts believe Taylor was killed because he tried to clean Hollywood of drugs. Mainly cocaine."

Willie chewed her lip. "That's good."

"Good? That he wanted to clean up Hollywood?"

"Well, sure." Willie shrugged. "But really, that happened a hundred years ago. It doesn't matter now."

"Perhaps." Beth took a sip of tea and placed the mug on a table opened from its position against the wall. "We should be arriving at the airport-," she said, checking her Cartier rose gold and diamond watch, "-in about fifty minutes." She touched the watch's tan leather strap before dropping her hand.

"That's gorgeous," Willie said, gesturing toward Beth's wrist.

"A birthday gift from Skye."

"You two must be super close friends. I bet that watch cost a mint."

"It's funny how two people can be so different but become truly close friends. That's how Skye and I are—different goals, hopes, and dreams." Beth paused for a second. "Truth be, though, both of us are crazy about cats."

"Cats, really? I'd never imagined she'd be one of those crazy cat ladies but, I could see her admiring one of the big cats like a . . ." Willie squinted as if considering her choices. "A panther. Sleek, lithe, beautiful, but with a menacing growl." She placed the sea-green mug in a built-in cup holder, pulled a couple rubber bands from a back pocket, and pulled her hair into her usual pigtails. "She was always friendly to me. Too bad Skye's locked up for a murder she didn't commit." Willie grabbed the mug, took a gulp, and lowered the ceramic cup keeping her eyes focused on it. "I guess that happens sometimes."

Willie let something slip, Beth thought. *After all, how does she know Skye's innocent?* "What makes you say that?"

Willie shrugged, tore open the protein bar wrapper, and took a bite.

"Do you know who is responsible for the murder?" Beth asked, leaning forward.

"Nah, nothing like that. It's just hard to believe that Skye would—you know."

Beth didn't want to let the thread drop. After yesterday's warning, she still believed Willie held the missing piece needed to solve the murder.

"I can wait to see my fiancé." Willie's face brightened. "He's gonna pick me up at the airport. He has something for me," she said, looking at her hand.

"An engagement ring?"

Her head bobbed up and down.

"Tell me about him."

"He's great." Willie popped the last morsel of the bar into her mouth and raised the mug. She took a long draught of coffee. "This is some plane. Looks like it seats ten passengers."

Willie wanted to change the subject. *Why?* The last thing Beth wished to discuss was Zach's jet. Even so, she'd take the lead and circle back to the most pressing issue on her mind—the missing piece that ties Willie to Thom's death. "This beautiful plane belongs to my friend, Zach Greyson. Skye's husband."

"Oh?" Willie's eyebrows shot up.

"Zach bought the jet a couple of years ago. He's not the original owner but benefitted from the stunning upgraded interior." Beth ran her fingertips along the club chair's creamy leather armrest. "Skye swears he purchased the jet due to a mid-life crisis." She took a quick sip from her cup, pleased at how smoothly she'd brought the conversation back to Skye. "But, it's been a godsend these last few weeks, allowing us quick passage to visit

Skye while she awaits her murder trial." She pursed her lips as Willie chewed a worn-down fingernail. "I have a feeling it won't reach the point of a trial. My gut's telling me the true killer will soon be revealed."

Willie shifted her sight away from Beth and focused on the carpet's floral design.

"Surely, I've told you I have a sixth sense."

"Sixth sense?" Willie tentatively raised her eyes.

"The Irish term being *fey*. It's an intuitive ability. A gift I possess that gives me insight beyond normal perception. Some people call it a second sight into a person's soul."

"What? You mean . . . You can read people's minds?" The color drained from Willie's face.

"It's a bit more complicated. But yes, something like that." With a smooth turn of the chair, she faced Willie and stood.

"Don't. Don't come near me." Willie raised her hand, warning Beth to keep her distance.

"What's wrong?"

"You know, don't you?"

Beth took a step closer.

Willie flung the near-empty coffee cup. Droplets of hot liquid stung, dotting Beth's Milano silk blouse. The mug crashed against a window. Beth slammed her eyes shut, willing her *fey* to intervene. Nothing surfaced. She decided to go along with Willie's assumption. *Pretend I know everything.*

"That's why you brought that cop to the set." Willie's voice took on a shrill, piercing sound. "And last night, you acted concerned. Like you cared. But all you wanted was to get me to Baltimore, to have me arrested. Is that cop gonna be at the tarmac waiting with handcuffs?"

"I do care." Beth moved closer.

Willie drew up her legs and clasped them next to her chest. Her eyes took on a crazed look like that of a wild animal being prodded into a cage.

I talked down Toni Wright. I can do the same with Willie. At least, God, I hope so, Beth prayed, swallowing a mouthful of air. Beth took a backward step and crouched down, becoming eye level with the panicked woman. "Please, believe me. I want to help you."

Willie stared right through her.

"I want Darnell," Willie whispered.

A biting chill ran through Beth. *Darnell? The boyfriend is involved in the murder?* A comforting warmth eradicated the icy bitterness lodged in Beth's chest and filled her with confidence.

"You were in Thom's trailer when he was murdered. You weren't alone. Darnell stood by your side."

Willie's head dipped. She clasped her folded arms against her chest and began rocking. "I didn't want to do it. But Darnell—Darnell said we didn't have a choice. Thom was gonna ruin everything."

"You shot Thom." Beth rose and towered over the cowering figure.

"Uh-huh." Willie looked up, her cheeks wet with tears. "I loved Thom. I really did. You believe me?"

"Yes. Of course, I believe you."

Willie sprung to her feet, grabbed Beth's arms, and looked into her eyes. She began to tremble, and Beth pulled her close, encircling Willie in her arms. Like the bursting of a dam, a torrent of pent-up emotions burbled, and Willie's sobs rose above the hum of the plane's engine. She croaked painful groans into Beth's ears that turned into raspy whimpers accompanying a cascade of tears. After what seemed like an eternity, Willie became silent, pulled away from Beth, and dropped onto the divan.

A word rang in Beth's ear.

Record.

Beth reached into her oversized tote bag, pulled out a pocket package of tissues, and handed the pack to Willie. Keeping her eyes trained on Willie as she blotted her eyes and blew her nose, Beth grasped her mobile. She held the phone inside the bag and swiped the screen. With a quick glance at the display, Beth chewed her lip as she located the voice app.

Her fingers flew over the screen tapping, menu, settings, and incoming call options.

When she looked up, Willie busied herself gathering the spent tissues. She squeezed the soggy Kleenexes into a wad and, dragging her feet, headed to the trash container tucked inside the galley.

Beth's mobile sounded. "A call from my Shane," she lied, pulling out the cellphone as Willie reclaimed her spot across from Beth. "I'll talk to him later," she said, tapping the activation number on the keypad. Satisfied that Willie's words would be recorded to voicemail, she laid the mobile on the table.

"I love Darnell more than my own life," Willie said in a shaky voice. "And I want to be his wife, have kids, the whole nine yards."

Beth kept her eyes riveted on Willie.

"He promised we'd get married. I only had to do one thing to prove how much I love him. Then he'd give me everything my heart desires. The world on a platter, he said. But I only wanted his unconditional love that would join us forever."

Beth nodded, urging her on.

"I kept wondering why I had to verify my love for him. I objected because what he wanted me to do seemed crazy. But I trusted him."

"Love makes us do foolish things."

"Exactly. But you gotta believe me, Beth. I didn't want to do it, but Darnell insisted." New tears filled her eyes, and Willie brushed them away. "Darnell is really smart and a successful businessman. He sells drugs." She pressed her lips together as if she'd said too much.

"Over-the-counter or prescription?"

"Illegal," she said with a sigh. "He has a bunch of clients. Sends the stuff through the US mail just like a legit outfit."

"He sends drugs through the post?"

"That's how it's usually done."

Beth glanced at her mobile, hoping the voice app picked up Willie's words. "Was Thom Boyle one of Darnell's associates?"

"Thom? Hell, no. He hated drugs. And honestly, I never could keep a secret from Thom. But, I guess me doing cocaine wasn't really a secret." Willie raised her face and targeted Beth with bloodshot eyes. "He couldn't leave it alone. Thom was determined to find out who supplied my cocaine. I couldn't tell him that it was Darnell, but Thom suspected as much."

"I'm thinking Thom only wanted to help you."

Willie nodded. "I promised Thom I'd quit. I meant it too. If only he'd leave Darnell alone." She squeezed her eyes shut for a second. "Thom agreed. So I thought everything was good." She stood and began pacing.

Her steps became quicker and quicker. Instead of working off steam, it seemed that with each step, Willie became more agitated. She abruptly pivoted and faced Beth.

"That wasn't good enough for Darnell," Willie said. "He pounded the idea into my head that Thom lied. That Thom had connections with the authorities because he was a crusader in the war on drugs." She dug her hands into the pockets of her faded jeans. "Darnell wouldn't let up. The only words, seeming to come out of his mouth—Thom lied." She stamped her foot.

"He planted a false narrative into your head?"

"Oh, no. Darnell was right. Cuz one day, Thom promised Darnell would be arrested for ruining so many lives—mine included. I tried to explain that Darnell provided a service. You know, supply and demand. And he was actually helping people."

Beth wanted to jump out of her seat and shake some sense into her. Thom had probably wanted to do the same thing.

"Darnell came up with the plan that we'd have to pin the murder on one of the actors. I didn't like that idea, but Skye was the only actor that handled the prop knife. We decided she'd be the perfect fall guy. After all, she and Thom always seemed to be at each other's throats. I had to agree with Darnell. Skye was the logical choice."

"You set Skye up."

Willie nodded.

"How?"

"You know this already, don't you?" A shade of suspicion touched Willie's words. "That second sight of yours showed you all this?"

"Truly, it has." Beth's heart raced. She couldn't allow Willie to put a lid on the confession. "But talking about it with a friend who cares about you might make you feel better."

Willie chewed on her thumb nail as Beth held her breath.

"You might be right. It's been bottled up inside me. It feels good to get it off my chest." Willie lifted her backpack and placed it next to her on the divan. "It was easy. Sam and I were preparing for a shoot, and I handed Skye a knife that resembled the prop. Of course, I was wearing gloves, but Skye wasn't."

Ah, sure, that answers the question of Skye's prints on the knife.

"You switched knives," Beth said.

Willie nodded. "I put the knife with Skye's prints into a baggie and slipped it into my backpack. Then . . ." She twisted and looked out the window. "This is so hard to say out loud."

"You're doing fine," Beth said, hoping to God she wouldn't clam up. Beth leaned forward and placed her hand on Willie's knee.

"We were running out of time. No amount of pleading changed Thom's mind. He swore he'd turn Darnell in. On the final day of shooting, I went to Thom's trailer pretending I wanted to watch the dallies. He hugged me; I kissed his cheek and slipped out the gun Darnell gave me. I whispered, I'm sorry, but I don't think Thom heard. I pulled the trigger."

Willie turned away from the window and folded her hands in her lap. "Darnell waited outside the trailer. He took the gun, slipped on latex gloves, and slit Thom's throat. Hardly any blood seeped from the cut, so it didn't look too bad. But when he turned Thom's body over, I saw a pool of blood." Her face remained expressionless as the words fell through her lips as if reading an article from a magazine.

"He dipped his finger into the blood and wrote a word on the floor."

"Cut."

Willie glanced at Beth with a tiny nod. "He repositioned the body and staged the scene—placed a pillow under Thom's head and stuck the knife underneath his body." She peered into the opened backpack then reached inside the canvas bag. "I've been doing coke ever since that day."

"Now that you've admitted—"

"I can't forget the shocked look on Thom's face."

"Perhaps it was a look of disbelief. You betrayed him with a kiss."

"Don't you think I regret it? That guilt isn't eating me up. My friend dead and an innocent person taking the rap."

"Then rectify the situation. Go to the police."

"Police? How the hell can I do that? Darnell is my everything. And for his sake and mine, I am gonna make things right." Willie pulled her hand out of the backpack, holding a double-barrel pistol. She aimed the compact gun at Beth.

"Whoa." Beth forced herself to remain calm as she looked into Willie's eyes. They looked hard and cold. "Put the gun down. We can talk this through."

"There's nothing left to talk about. My man's not going to jail because of my guilty conscience."

"Okay," Beth said, taking a backward step. "We'll come up with a plan."

"Plan? What kinda plan will keep me out of jail for the rest of my life? I'd rather be dead."

"Don't say that. You need to take a deep breath. Once you calm down—"

"I am calm. And my mind's made up. I refuse to allow Darnell to be locked up because he's helping people like me. It's not fair."

"Maybe it isn't. But taking someone's life is wrong. Confess. Repent. No sin is too big that it can't be forgiven."

"Tell that to a judge. To Cody. To Skye." Willie shook her head. "No. It ends here." She extended her arm, aiming the derringer at Beth. Her hand shook. "Sorry, Beth. There isn't any other way."

Searing heat like a lump of glowing coal ripped across Beth's right arm, shredding her sleeve. She fell to her knees and clasped her hand over the wound. She raised her head in time to see Willie press the gun against her temple.

"No," Beth screamed, but it was too late.

Chapter Fifty-Two

Beth dropped down next to Willie, crumpled in the aisle, and reached for her wrist, seeking a pulse. Unable to feel anything, Beth placed her ear close to the injured woman's lips. The lightest breath brushed Beth's cheek with a rapid succession of exhales. Then nothing. Beth's stomach tightened until a few more breaths flowed.

"What the hell is going on?" The co-pilot called, entering the passenger cabin. He paused a few feet away. "Are you okay," he said, gesturing to Beth's injured arm.

"I'm alright. But it's Willie. She shot herself." Beth gave him a quick glance then turned to the motionless figure on the cabin's floor. "Hold on, darlin' please, just a wee bit longer. We're going to get help. Don't give up. Keep breathing."

Willie's eyes opened, and stared at Beth.

Beth grabbed her hand. "I'll find Darnell and bring him to you."

Willie squeezed her hand. "Darnell . . . I had to . . . protect . . . him. Cop." A second later, her hand relaxed, and her jaw fell open.

"Willie. Willie," Beth said, not quite believing that, even now, the woman wanted to shield her boyfriend from the police.

"She could be already gone." The co-pilot said into the cellphone pressed against his ear.

The words rattled Beth.

"Okay. Will do." He handed the phone to Beth and crouched over Willie. He checked her neck for a pulse, tilted her head back, and tapped her chest. A moment later, he started compressions.

"Hello," Beth spoke into the mobile. "I witnessed the shooting."

The emergency dispatcher asked for details, which Beth readily offered.

"She fired at you?" The dispatcher asked.

"With a tiny handgun that looked more like a toy than a weapon. But the shot only grazed my arm. Then Willie turned the gun on herself, she did." Beth glanced at the bloody elliptical-shaped furrow slashed a few inches below her shoulder.

"Keep that arm elevated and apply pressure until a medic evaluates it. EMS and the police are on their way. They'll meet the plane when it lands."

The co-pilot stopped the compressions and threw his hand toward Beth, asking for the cellphone. She handed it to him. While he talked to the dispatcher, she gazed at Willie. The color had drained from her face, and her eyes held the stare of death. She said an Ave under her breath for the tortured soul and asked for God's mercy.

The co-pilot resumed CPR as the plane started to descend.

• • •

Beth's arm throbbed as the plane hit the tarmac with a butter-soft landing. She glanced out the window, and an array of patrol cars, two ambulances, and even a fire truck sat on the runway. The pilot ushered EMS and uniformed officers into the passenger cabin and a paramedic jumped into action. A middle-aged cop with a florid face and a uniform shirt stretched across his belly approached Beth, still seated near the cockpit.

"Who are you, and what happened here?" The cop demanded, fishing a pad and pen from his front shirt pocket.

After stating her name and relationship to Willie, she glanced from the shrouded body to the cellphone in her hand. She swiped the screen, found the recording, and prayed that the exchange taped. Even so, the idea of reliving the final moments of Willie's life made her stomach do somersaults. She unfastened the seatbelt and sighed in relief as Willie's voice sounded from the phone's speaker. The cop's stern look turned to astonishment. He pulled out a pair of latex gloves, squeezed his meaty hands into them, and took the phone from Beth, pocketing it into an evidence bag. He said something about her arm.

Numb, hurting, and mentally exhausted, she didn't have the strength to answer. She twisted in the swivel chair and spied Red at the cabin's entry. A trickle of relief eased her shot nerves as she stood and moved toward him. She collapsed inside the security of his arms.

"The Greyson plane is a crime scene?" Red asked. He stepped back, zeroing in on Beth's tattered and blood-soaked sleeve. "What in God's name happened?"

"A poor confused woman committed suicide and did this." Beth glanced at her arm.

Confusion shot across his face.

"I'm okay. You can see the bullet only grazed my arm. But it hurts like hell." She attempted a smile, but instead, a jolt of pain made her grimace. "I've got proof that Skye is innocent. The actual killer . . ." Everything around her began to spin. She reached for Red as a falling sensation seized her.

He grabbed her by the shoulders and slipped an arm around her waist. Ignoring the protests of a female cop, he guided Beth to the divan and laid her on the soft leather cushions. She blinked a couple of times to clear her vision, but then everything turned black.

When she came to, Beth couldn't move, strapped on a stretcher inside a medic unit. An EMT with a sprinkling of freckles on her nose offered Beth a smile.

"Hey." She squeezed Beth's hand. "You passed out. We're taking you to the hospital. A doc will look at your arm and patch you up."

Beth nodded, still a bit dazed.

"Your friend will meet you there."

"Friend?" Beth whispered. "Oh, Red."

"A detective will want to talk to you."

Beth closed her eyes, wishing Shane could be at her side. He'd be furious, as usual, that she'd once again put herself in harm's way. *That's not right*, she thought, since no one would ever have considered Willie a threat.

The siren stopped blaring for a second before the ambulance came to a standstill. The sound of squeaking wheels filled Beth's ears as the paramedics transferred her into the emergency room. The female EMT pulled back a curtain, revealing a small cubicle and helpful hands lifted Beth onto a hospital bed.

"I'm fine," Beth protested as a paramedic covered her with a blanket. "I'm taking a spot from someone who's really sick." He only nodded, grabbed the curtain, and pulled it closed behind him.

She wanted to ring Shane. But without her mobile, that wasn't possible. Sealed to her fate, she closed her eyes as a bout of exhaustion swept over her. Seeming as if only seconds had passed, loud voices startled her awake. A woman in a white coat with a name embroidered above the breast pocket faced her. Though she didn't introduce herself, Beth took her for a doctor. The woman asked a few questions about how she felt, shone a light into her eyes, and inspected Beth's injured arm. She left Beth's bedside with a nod.

A blood pressure cup squeezed her good arm while a machine stationed behind the bed hummed and occasionally beeped. *I must've been hooked up when I fell asleep.* She reached for the cuff, but her hand dropped when the curtain opened.

"Ms. Getty. I'm Detective Binard. How you doing?"

"I'll be better once I'm out of here."

"That's understandable. So what exactly happened in that private jet between you and the deceased Louise Wilson?"

She explained with as few words as possible why Willie had shot her and taken her own life. When he seemed satisfied, she asked for her mobile containing the much-needed evidence that would free Skye.

320

"We need to hold on to it for now," the detective said.

"But it has proof that will exonerate my friend. I need it. Now."

"Look, I'm sorry but . . ." He shrugged and left the room.

Pressure wrapped around Beth's head like a vise. She fumbled with the cuff, determined to catch up with the detective. A nurse wheeled a computer and entered the cubicle. Beth dropped her hand. After a cursory "How do you feel?", she took Beth's vital signs, cleaned the lesion, and covered it with a bandage. The nurse handed Beth a prescription for pain medication and instructions on wound care. After a brief explanation regarding the orders, she informed Beth that after completing paperwork, she'd be free to leave. The nurse helped Beth into a wheelchair and opened the curtain. Red stood there with obvious concern written across his face.

Before he could utter a word, Beth demanded his mobile. "I have to make an urgent call. To Detective Fox."

At two minutes past midnight, Beth contacted Fox. They set up a meeting for nine that morning after she breathlessly shared that the Frederick County police held the evidence needed to vindicate Skye.

Beth shifted from foot to foot on the sidewalk outside the emergency room while Red fetched the car, anxious to see Skye's face when she learned the truth.

• • •

Within an hour of Beth's call, Fox arrived at the Frederick Municipal Airport. He met with the crime scene investigators and discovered that the bullet's trajectory, the angle of the entrance wound, stippling on the skin, and the position of the fallen gun pointed to Louise Wilson as the shooter. An attempted murder-suicide.

All he needed now was the confession recorded on Beth's cellphone. Fox contacted the detective handling the case and met him at police headquarters. After listening to Willie's taped admission, Fox realized that Beth, without an iota of police training, had cracked the case of Thom

Boyle's murder. The voicemail, a piece of direct evidence, would clear Andrews of all charges.

But, he thought while pursing his lips, *we need to locate Wilson's accomplice.* Though his full identity remained unknown, Fox believed Wilson's cellphone records could offer the vital information. But obtaining a court order to access the data and then analyzing it would take time. He wanted to nail the guy now. The drug dealer who framed an innocent person for a murder he orchestrated and caused a confused, love-struck woman to off herself.

Knowing sleep wouldn't be an option, Fox opted to head to the office. He dreaded the long night ahead, searching the database for drug dealers named Darnell. He stifled a yawn as the little voice in his head told him it'd be a useless task, but he didn't really have any other choice.

· · ·

Though he'd been up all night, Fox beamed when Beth entered the Baltimore City Homicide Unit. The ashen circles under her eyes assured him that she hadn't slept much either, but sensed a spark of hope flickering there. "Have a seat," he said, gesturing to the guest chair opposite his desk. "How are you?"

"A bit worse for wear." She shrugged. "Any news?" Beth sat on the chair's edge, keeping her eyes targeted on the detective.

"I've contacted the DA's office with the evidence you provided us." He shot her a quick smile. "I tip my hat to you. First, you talk down an arsonist and then record a killer's confession. Can I interest you in applying for a job with us?"

Beth's cheeks warmed, taking on a pinkish glow.

"The good news is that the murder charge against Miss Andrews will more than likely be dropped."

Beth let out a deep sigh. "What a relief. Thank you, Jeremy."

"Don't be thanking me. You're the one who single-handedly cracked the case. You deserve some kind of citation."

"I've already received my reward seeing Skye's face when I told her Willie confessed. A quick look of shock and then radiant joy. I couldn't ask for more." The light faded from her eyes. "If only we could locate the mysterious Darnell, who is, in all likelihood, still pedaling that poison. And open to killing anyone who happens to get in the way of his business."

"My thoughts exactly. Were you able to gather any specifics about this Darnell person?"

"Not really. Willie was careful not to divulge much. Only that he's rich, handsome, and that the two of them were engaged. She protected him to the very end."

Fox tapped his fingers against the edge of his desk. "This may be far-fetched, but Wilson's final word was cop. Do you think this Darnell character could be a cop?"

Beth squished up her forehead.

"Just a hunch."

"I don't know," Beth said. "Truly, I thought Willie's words revealed her final wish to protect Darnell from the law." She touched her lip with her forefinger. "It's frustrating because my *fey* hasn't offered even the tiniest insight about the man who masterminded Thom's death."

"Morning, J." Tamera breezed into the office. "How was California? Not good, I guess, since you're back already. The beaches not . . ." She stopped, noticing Beth.

"Tamera Stevens, this is—"

"Sibèal?" A quizzical look crossed Tamera's face.

"Please, call me Beth," she said, extending her hand to the detective.

After a quick handshake, Tamera moved to her desk.

"Join us," Fox said. "I wanna run something by you."

Tamera wheeled her office chair next to Beth and sat. "What's up?"

"First, the good news. My suspicion that Skye Andrews didn't commit murder panned out. Thanks to Beth," said Fox. "She recorded the killer's confession on her cellphone."

"Wow. That's like—like something an undercover agent would do, not a celebrity model. It's hard to believe but really great. Wonderful."

"It is," Fox said, leaning back in his chair, "except the killer's partner is still at large. Seems that the movie director stuck his nose where it didn't belong. Boyle tried to shut down a pretty powerful drug dealer named Darnell. That triggered his murder."

"Darnell?" Tamera frowned.

"Uh-huh. Remember that discussion we had about your ex—"

"You're not suggesting that Darnell—"

"Not exactly," said Fox. "But you did hint that he was living a double life and could be involved in the drug trade."

Tamera shook her head. "He explained all that. Turns out," she said, taking a quick peek at Beth. "Darnell is renovating houses for resale. He's been quite successful." Her words, though confident, didn't stop the furrows arising on her brow. Her lips spread into a taut line that punctuated the inquiry.

"Right, maybe he is flipping houses," Fox said. "But the dealer's name *is* Darnell."

"Darnell." Tamera's voice jumped an octave. "This damn city is full of men named Darnell."

Fox picked up a pencil and tapped it a couple of times on the desk's metal surface. "Do you know the name of the woman Darnell is planning to marry?"

"Oh, that. Well, we talked last night, and he decided to call the wedding off. He decided that she's way too immature to be a stepmother to our kids. Still has a lot of party girl in her."

"You talked last night? How did he sound?" Fox dropped the pencil and rubbed his chin.

"Fine." Tamera crossed her arms against her chest. "He wanted to take the kids out for ice cream, but it was like ten p.m., past their bedtime. What does that have to do with anything?"

"Not much. But, Tammy, my gut's not usually wrong. It was on target about Andrews.

How 'bout if we do a little test. Have him come in for a Q and A. To rule him out and ease your mind. And for the sake of your kids' safety."

"You've got to be kidding," Tamera said, widening her eyes.

"It couldn't hurt, could it?" Beth asked.

"It'd be a damn waste of time," Tamera said. "You have zero proof that Darnell has anything to do with selling illegal drugs, let alone a murder."

"True." Fox nodded. "But I know you, Tam. You won't have a moment's peace if there's the slightest chance Darnell could somehow be involved."

"Whatever." Tamera threw up her hands. "But mark my words, this is gonna turn out to be a complete waste of time."

Fox picked up the desk phone and tapped the keypad. "Hey, Darnell. This is Fox. We've got a suspect here that we're interrogating and would like you to sit in on it." He paused. "Uh-huh. He's small potatoes, but we think he might be able to point the finger at a big-time dealer who's a homicide suspect." He looked at Tamera and nodded. "Yeah, okay, sounds good. Room six." He returned the phone to its base. "He's on his way."

• • •

Beth's heels clicked against the gray tile floor as she walked alongside Fox to the interview room. Tamera trailed behind them. Beth imagined that Tamera was still huffing with indignation that the whole interview thing had been set in motion. Shane shared numerous times how some of his interrogations had led to nothing but added frustration. Beth hoped for Tamera's sake that's the way this meeting would turn out. She chewed her lip, willing her *fey* to point her to the architect behind the director's murder. And that her first instinct had been correct—a drug dealer who'd persuaded Willie to commit murder. Not a cop.

"Darnell should be here any minute," Fox said, glancing at Beth. "Wait around the corner," he said, pointing down the corridor, "there's chairs and vending machines."

"Right," Beth said with a nod.

"I'll meet with you after the interview."

Tamera caught up with arms folded and faced them. "Really, J. This is a waste—"

"Hey, guys." Darnell's voice echoed in the deserted hallway.

Beth studied the approaching man. He could've stepped off the cover of GQ magazine impeccably dressed in a powder blue suit that set off his tawny, golden-brown skin. He pivoted his six-foot-five frame toward Beth and smiled. A smile that could melt even the stoniest of hearts.

"This is Beth Getty," Fox said, introducing her.

"You must be Darnell," Beth said, taking his outstretched hand. The minute she touched his skin, pictures flashed like the frames of a motion picture before her eyes. Thom Boyle welcoming Willie into his trailer . . . Willie kissing his cheek . . . Thom falling to the floor . . . and Darnell—the man now squeezing her hand—slashing the director's neck as his words filled Beth's ears, *"We've no worries, now that he's dead. My lucrative enterprise is safe."* And then one final frame. Darnell sliding the knife under Thom's lifeless body.

Beth swayed, and Darnell grabbed her by the shoulders.

"You okay?"

She searched his bright hazel eyes. Warm, concerned, friendly. Yet, he was the devil that drove Willie to murder and suicide.

"Detective Fox," Beth whispered. "I feel a wee bit dizzy. Do you mind helping me?"

Darnell released her, and Fox wrapped an arm around Beth's shoulders. Once out of earshot, he asked, "Your *fey?*"

They turned the corner, and Beth faced him. "I don't want to believe that a law officer—"

"You mean?"

"My *fey* showed me everything. Willie and Darnell worked as a team. He's just as responsible as Willie for the murder."

"You're sure."

"I've never been surer in my life."

"Okay, then. You stay here." With long strides, Fox retraced his steps leading back to the interrogation room.

Beth dropped into one of the white plastic chairs and considered the vending machines. Anything to take her mind off of the situation. *Tamera is going to be crushed—and the poor children.* She reached into her tan leather tote and searched for a couple of dollar bills. She'd thrown some loose chain into the bag, which now seemed empty without her mobile. Grabbing a bill and some coins, she tapped her foot as a surge of excitement bounded through her. *I can't sit here like a bump on a log sipping water. I've got to find out what's going on.*

She dumped the money back into her bag, jumped up from her seat, and hurried to room six. After looking up and down the corridor, making sure the coast was clear, she pressed her ear to the door. "Damnation," she swore under her breath, unable to hear a word. She stepped across from the interrogation room and waited.

• • •

"Have a seat," Fox said, ushering Darnell into the compact room. He pulled out the chair closest to the door while Fox sat across from him. Tamera settled at the short end.

Darnell leaned back and folded his arms behind his head. "So where's this small fry dope peddler you want me to question?"

"Actually," Fox said. "We want to ask you a few—"

"What J. wants to know," Tamera said, her voice on edge, "did you have something to do with the murder of that Hollywood director?"

"What? Hell, no." Darnell dropped his arms and landed his opened hands with fingers splayed on the table. "That actress, Skye Andrews, offed him."

Tamera eyed Fox. "I told you. A waste of time."

Fox raised his hand, motioning Tamera to chill. "We have it on good authority that you were in the director's trailer."

"You got that wrong, bro. I wasn't nowhere near any trailer.

"No," Darnell said.

Fox glanced at Tamera. She sat with her hands folded on the table and though quiet, her eyes flashed daggers.

"Do you know Louise Wilson?" Fox asked, refocusing on Darnell.

"Who?"

"A waitress at the Firebird over in Hampden. Occasionally works on movie sets. A bit player. Prop assistant. Known to her friends as Willie."

"Never heard of her."

Fox ran his thumb across his chin. "That's funny. I understand that she was your fiancé?"

"Listen, Fox. You got that wrong. I don't know any Willie whatever." He stood. "I gotta go."

"Not yet. No." Tamera broke her silence.

"What the hell? Come on, Tam. You know me. I could never do something like that."

"Let Jeremy finish," she said.

"Whatever," Darnell said, flopping back into the chair.

"The thing is, we found a fingerprint that didn't belong in that studio trailer," Fox lied.

"Your fingerprint."

Darnell shook his head as a smile broke across his face. "Man, this is too damn funny.

My fingerprint wasn't in that trailer cuz I was never there."

Fox withdrew Beth's cellphone from his inside jacket and slipped it out of the evidence bag. "This is Louise Wilson's phone," he said, hoping Darnell would believe him. "She shot herself. But before pulling the trigger, she made a confession." He tapped the phone's screen.

The cocky expression slipped from Darnell's face. His eyes narrowed, and his square chin jutted out. Cocking his head, he looked at Tamera. "Baby, you believe me. I didn't murder no one. I swear to God. Just because some woman, I don't even know, pointed a finger at me doesn't make it true." He balled his hand and slammed it against the table.

Tamera extended her hand and placed it on top of his fist. He relaxed his fingers under her touch. A second later, she removed it and cleared her throat. "Our kids met your girlfriend—fiancé."

Fox turned toward Tamera, not knowing if she was lying.

Darnell pressed his lips together.

"Would her picture with our kids be in there?" Tamera pointed to the cellphone. "Don't let the children be dragged into this."

"Tam, I swear I didn't do it. She shot him."

"With your pistol," she whispered.

He scrubbed a hand across his face.

"You know what comes next," Fox said. "Give me your gun. You have the right to remain silent. You have the right to an attorney. If—"

"Hold up." Darnell stood and pulled the pistol from the concealment holster clipped to his belt. Instead of placing it on the table, he pointed it at Fox. "There's no way I'm going to jail." He jerked the barrel away from Fox and pressed it under his chin.

"Darnell, no," Tamera said.

He backed away from the table and inched toward the door, not removing the gun from his throat. With his free hand, he reached behind, and flung the door open.

The loud bang of the door slamming against the wall made Beth jump backward. Darnell paused for a second as if surprised to see her. That moment of hesitation gave Fox enough time to free his gun and aim it at

Darnell. As if relying on instinct, Darnell grabbed Beth, pulled her next to him, and shoved the muzzle against her head. "Don't make me do this," he said through clenched teeth.

• • •

The force of the gun against Beth's temple caused the breath to die in her throat.

She wanted to demand that Darnell come to his senses and give himself up. But Beth knew that wouldn't work. *Stay calm,* she ordered herself though her heart pounded so hard its thumps sounded in her ears. *StaycalmStaycalmStaycalmStaycalm.* Beth closed her eyes, afraid she'd faint since the pressure of his body against her injured arm caused searing pain like bursts of fire to engulf her arm. *Fire.* An image of Toni waving a flickering lighter flew through her mind. *I talked Toni down. I can do the same with Darnell.* She blinked a few times, clearing her vision, and noticed Jeremy. He stood in the interview room's doorway with his gun drawn.

"Give it up," Fox said. "Shooting her will only make things worse. Two life sentences. No parole."

Darnell yanked Beth a few steps down the hallway as she swallowed the yelp that wanted to escape. *I can't let him blow me feckin' brains out.* Praying to God for the right words, she croaked, "Willie loved you."

He loosened his hold on her.

"She took her life to protect you. Don't throw it away."

Darnell moved the gun beneath his chin.

"Don't," Beth said. "That's the last thing Willie would've wanted. Respect her memory with owning up to the crime."

"I only did it for the money. To give my kids the stuff they want. To make them happy. A good life."

"Of course, you did," Beth cooed the words though she didn't believe him. *Darnell wanted the good life for himself.* "You mean more to your children than what you can give them. Nothing is too terrible that you can't be forgiven. Repent. Do your time. Show your little ones what it means to be a man of honor."

"Honor? You're kidding me. I can't."

Tamera sidled around Fox. She moved closer to Darnell. "For the love of God, don't do anything stupid. Beth is right. Think of what this will do to our children."

"I am thinking of them. Once the truth comes out, you won't be able to make it go away. What do you think their reaction will be? Finding out their dad's a dirty cop. I already know. They'll hate me."

Tamera stepped closer. She pressed her hand against his chest. "I know, and I don't hate you."

He blinked as if forbidding tears from forming. Beth took a few steps away, moving closer to Fox. It was then, she spotted police officers with guns drawn at each end of the corridor. Fox reached out, caught her arm, and shoved her into the interrogation room.

She peered over his shoulder. Tamera covered Darnell's hand with hers and gently removed the gun from his grasp.

Chapter Fifty-Three

Beth couldn't help but smile, taking in the group of friends helping themselves to warm pita bread and platefuls of horiatiki salad. In preparation for the dinner, she'd covered the patio table with a blue and white checkered cloth and stuck a couple miniature Greek flags into the centerpiece. Not that any of the guests hailed from Greek ancestry, but because tonight the menu centered on delicacies from the Grecian mainland. Roasted eggplant pastitso, salmon with lemon and dill, gigantes plaki, lemon rice, baby potatoes, and for dessert, traditional bougatsa.

Shane refilled their glasses with limniona, a deep purplish-red wine. As afternoon rays of sunlight fell on the glasses, the liquid sparkled like fine-cut rubies. Gavin Collins lifted his glass and took a sip. "I've never tasted such a fantastic wine before. It's rich and expressive. Punched with flavor without being too sweet. Delicious."

Shane eyed his former LASD partner.

Before he could comment, Beth said, "The owner of the restaurant, Taverna Aviti, orders the wine directly from Thessaly. It's almost impossible to find locally."

"I'll have to contact her and order a couple of bottles," Zach said, glancing at Skye as she dipped a morsel of pita into a dish of oil chocked-full with rich, earthy herbs. She popped the bread into her mouth and nodded.

"Speaking of wine, it's time for a toast," Beth said, "or two."

Gavin jumped up, raising his glass in front of him. "I propose a toast to Bonita, my future wife, who has made me the happiest of men by saying yes."

Beth and Bonita clinked glasses. She noticed the color rise, giving a glow to Bonita's tanned cheeks.

Zach stood. "To the amazing Beth Getty."

"Hear, hear," Shane said, beaming.

"She not only single-handedly saved my priceless collection of paintings but risked her own life to bring the true killers of our friend, Thom Boyle, to justice." Zach turned his sight to his wife. "Proving Skye's innocence and restoring her reputation."

After another round of clinking glasses, Beth stood. "Thank you, Zach. But truly, my *fey* directed my steps. Along with the guidance I found from a book that showed me history can indeed repeat itself." She took a sip of wine and set her glass on the table. "It's time for the main course." An inner warmth flowed with gratitude for her friends and especially for Shane.

Finally, he believes in my special gift, my sixth sense, my fey.

Beth entered the kitchen and pulled open a chestnut maple cabinet. She removed several serving dishes and set them on the center island. *You'd think, I'm planning to feed an army*, she thought, shaking her head. In the two weeks since the murder charges had been dropped against Skye, Beth had settled into a more normal routine. The youth shelter being her top priority. Even though the details of establishing a non-profit, from applying for tax exemptions to obtaining licenses and permits, filled her hours, she couldn't dispel the longing to visit her Irish homeland. She'd tried, though not always successful, to push those feelings aside, by busying herself with interviewing candidates for the director position of the newly christened shelter, Oasis House for Youth.

"You need help?" Skye said, walking into the kitchen by way of the breakfast room, carrying a stack of dirty plates.

"That'd be lovely."

Skye moved to the dishwasher, pulled it open, and placed the plates into the racks. "I'm relieved you had this little dinner party catered. According to Shane—"

"Now, don't be listening to my darlin' husband. He thinks it's funny to spread untruths about my cooking. I'm as fine as a cook as you—"

"Alma prepares our meals for a reason."

"That's beyond the point, it is. But for sure, I'm no expert when it comes to these Greek dishes. And since we're celebrating Gavin's engagement, I thought it'd be nice to have the meal delivered from one of their favorite restaurants."

A tiny smile tugged at Skye's lips. "Those two are crazy about each other. Just like you and Shane." She closed the dishwasher's door. "I want you to know how thankful I am. If it wasn't for you," she said with a slow shake of her head.

"Ah, come on with yourself. How many times are you planning to thank me? 'Tis *me fey* that led the way to the true culprits." Beth pulled open the top drawer of the warming oven. "But there is one way you can show your appreciation."

"Anything."

"Agree to sit on the board of directors for Oasis House."

"Your shelter for homeless kids?" Skye's eyes grew big. "You want me?"

"Of course." Beth slid a spatula under the salmon filet and placed it on a platter.

"What would I have to do?"

"Act as a member of the shelter's governing body. Assist in overseeing every aspect of Oasis House for Youth. It'd be a two-year term."

Skye pursed her lips as if weighing a decision.

"It'd warm my heart if you'd agree."

"But what can I offer?"

"It's true that attorneys and accountants, social workers, clergymen, and business leaders are the typical types selected to sit on the board of a homeless shelter." Beth lifted a tray of rice and scooped the grains into a serving dish. "You never lived on the street. But you know firsthand what it's like to be lonely, unloved, and misjudged. You experienced fear, uncertainty, and hopelessness as a child tossed from one foster home to another. Your insight would be invaluable."

Skye bit her lip, and her eyes welled. She moved next to Beth and hugged her.

"Hey, what's the holdup?" Shane entered the kitchen through the butler's pantry. "Where's the grub?"

Skye dropped her arms and faced Shane wiping the tears from her cheek.

"Is everything okay?" He asked, moving closer to them.

"Couldn't be better." Skye lifted the platter of fish. "I'll take this outside." She crossed the kitchen, heading for the French doors leading to the terrace.

Shane pulled Beth into his arms and kissed her. "After all the hell you've been through, you make me so proud, my darlin' Betty Getty. Entertaining our friends and celebrating their good fortune."

"'Tis nothing. Chalk it up to my *fey*—"

"I'll never doubt your gift again." He brushed the scar on her cheek and moved in for another kiss.

"I should have known." Collins stood hand in hand with Bonita. "Making out in the kitchen while the rest of us are starving."

Bonita shook her head and tossed her dark ponytail over her shoulder. "Skye sent us in to bring the food out."

Beth gestured to the line of dishes, pulled open another warmer drawer, and lifted out a container.

"Gigantes plaki. I'm not surprised," Collins said, pulling on a pair of oven mitts. He took the stainless-steel tray from Beth and placed it on the counter. "One of Shane's favorites." He began dishing the beans into a bowl.

"The rice smells heavenly," Bonita said. "Lemony." She lifted the dish and headed out through the French doors.

"How about after dinner we watch one of Skye's films? Afterward, we can take a midnight dip in the pool." Beth looked at Collins expectedly. "Did you two bring your bathing suits?"

"Swimming?" Zach stood in the pantry's threshold, his brow furrowing.

"Why shouldn't we make a night of it," Beth said. "We have so many blessings to celebrate."

"Can't argue with that," Zach said, eyeing Shane as he cut the Greek lasagna and placed the rectangular slices onto a platter.

"Is that roasted eggplant pastitso?" Zach asked. "My God, I haven't had that for years. Not since I made that period film in Greece."

"I've never had it," Bonita said, reentering the kitchen. "But it smells out of this world."

"This is about it." Beth handed her a bowl of baby potatoes with roasted peppers drizzled with olive oil and seasoned to perfection.

As Zach and Bonita carried the dishes out of the kitchen, Beth willed to block all sadness from her mind. But she failed. The loss, still too raw, filled her with a pang of sorrow. She sighed as a memory of her *ould flower,* Deirdre, who lost her life a couple of months ago crossed her mind.

"Beth?" Shane looked up from the platter of pastitso. "You okay?" He stepped closer and wrapped his arm around her.

"I was thinking about Deirdre. How much she would've loved being here with us."

"She would've been the life of the party."

"That she would have. I was thinking, once the shelter director is hired, I'd like to spend a week or so in Ireland. During the rare moment, I find myself missing my old home. And me da."

"Sounds grand altogether," Shane said with his best Irish accent. "I only wish I could tag along. But with my job—"

Beth stopped him with a kiss.

"Don't tell me you guys are at it again?" Collins said with a grin. "Which way to the wine cellar? We're out of limniona."

"Ah, pity, so am I. But there's a pinot noir and a chardonnay for the fish eaters in the fridge."

Collins moved toward the panel-covered refrigerator. "You guys haven't had many dinner parties lately. Too busy tracking down stolen art and murderers." He winked at Beth. "But, I hope this starts a new tradition."

"What a lovely suggestion. Especially since there aren't any better friends I'd want to spend time with," Beth said.

"I second that," Shane said, lifting the plate of pastitsio.

"Great. How about next Friday night?" Collin said, pulling the bottles out of the fridge.

"As my darlin' Shane is prone to say—sounds like a plan."

Thank you so much for reading *Death Cut*.
If you've enjoyed the book, we would be grateful if you would post a review on the bookseller's website where you purchased it.
Just a few words is all it takes!

Acknowledgements

Special thanks to Sheri Williams and the team at TouchPoint Press and to my editor Kimberly Carlisle Coghlan. Cheers to my critique group members, L.R. Trovillion, R. Lanier Clemons, Kim Hamilton, Mike Sage, P.J. O'Dwyer, and Missy Burke, for their inspiration and insight.

A very special thank-you to Candice Jarrett, Joan Long, and Margie Longano Miklas for their feedback and for writing wonderful testimonials for *Death Cut*.

For their unfailing support, I'd especially like to thank my siblings, Roy, Patricia, and Thomas. Heartfelt appreciation and thanks to Shirley Pratt, Wendy Happel, and Pegi Taylor. Above all, thanks to Chuck Smithson, my husband extraordinaire, for his unending belief in my talent, encouragement, and love.

Made in the USA
Middletown, DE
14 March 2024

51406654R00208